MW01134214

This book is dedicated to the memory of **Officer Rufus James Hardee,** and to all of the dedicated Miami Officers, both past and present, that have followed in his footsteps.

Officer R. Jim Hardee, as he was called, was one of the first four officers hired to **"Protect and Serve"** the citizens of Miami. He had the distinction of carrying badge # 1, and is pictured above wearing the first uniform issued by the Miami Police Department, circa 1906.

A special Thank You to his Granddaughter **Suzanne Hardee,** for providing us with the above photo, and some interesting family stories and history.

THE MIAMI POLICE WORKSHEET

CHIEF PHIL DOHERTY

A chronology of Miami's exciting events on the streets of the Magic City during the twentieth century from the eyes of the cops who were there.

Copyright © 2012 by Phil Doherty.

Library of Congress Control Number:		2012917811
ISBN:	Hardcover	978-1-4797-2278-5
	Softcover	978-1-4797-2277-8
	Ebook	978-1-4797-2279-2

All rights reserved. No part of this book may be reproduced or transmitted in any form or by any means, electronic or mechanical, including photocopying, recording, or by any information storage and retrieval system, without permission in writing from the copyright owner.

This book was printed in the United States of America.

To order additional copies of this book, contact:
Xlibris Corporation
1-888-795-4274
www.Xlibris.com
Orders@Xlibris.com
118191

CONTENTS

THE EARLY YEARS

ROARING TWENTIES

GREAT DEPRESSION ERA

AMERICA AT WAR ERA

BIG CITY MIAMI

HEADLEY'S REIGN

IN OUR LIFETIME

POST-TRAUMATIC STRESS

PREFACE

During the first half of the twentieth century, Miami transformed from a winter retreat for wealthy Americans to a midsized southern city, especially during the winter and spring months. After World War II, Miami morphed into an international, bilingual hub during the second half, at the same time struggling to accommodate the civil rights transition that affected many of the nations' population centers, as well as absorbing a significant portion of the population of Cuba, who fled the nearby island country to escape the Communist regime.

This *Miami Police WORKSHEET* highlights some of the public as well as the less-known law enforcement events that occurred in these decades through the eyes of some of Miami's street police officers. Come ride along with us during this *very* exciting time.

The author/compiler is Chief Phil Doherty, retired MPD, along with Lieutenant Harvey Bach, Ret., and other MPD guys and gals. This book would not be possible without access to the Internet sources, especially local newspaper files, as no living person could provide the early stories.

THE MIAMI POLICE WORKSHEET

The police WORKSHEET is a chronological log, prepared daily by each field officer and detective. The report documents in brief the calls for service handled, the traffic tickets issued, the cases handled during each day's work, and other citizen contacts. In the period of years covered in this book, it is estimated that ten million worksheets were prepared and submitted by Miami officers, documenting an average of ten contacts daily. The average citizen would not encounter during their lifetime the confrontations and tense situations that the average Miami officer encounters daily.

We have selected a tiny slice of these contacts for presentation to the reader. Space prevents many thousands of others, equally as interesting, to be printed. Many of our stories were from the pages of early newspapers, primarily the *Tropical Sun*, *Miami Metropolis*, *Miami News*, and *Miami Herald*. One must keep in mind that newspapers dwell on bad news such as crime and corruption (because it sells), and countless "good" stories of law officers just doing their duty go unreported. Nevertheless, these stories provide a glimpse back in time that we think you will enjoy.

Our society depends on the urban police officer to keep our citizens safe. These WORKSHEET logs are ample proof that most Miami PD officers did in fact accomplish that role, some of whom paid the ultimate sacrifice while doing so.

Our stories are tragic and/or funny; others are silly, chaotic, degrading, heroic, dramatic, or just plain interesting.

We hope you enjoy the product.

THE EARLY YEARS

A NEW CITY IS BORN

At the time of its municipal birth in 1896, Miami was just one of the small sparsely populated settlements of Dade County, with most of the city's inhabitants living in what is presently the downtown Miami business area, primarily on the north side of the Miami River. The FEC railroad line had just been extended to Miami from Palm Beach the previous April.

Law enforcement in Miami prior to the 1896 incorporation was provided by the Dade County sheriff, who was headquartered in the then county seat of Juno, many miles north of the city, headed up at that time by Sheriff R. J. Chillingsworth, assisted by his Miami deputy, S. S. Puckett. The county area then also covered what is now Palm Beach and Broward counties. The only local Miami protection was supplied by a night watchman—A. E. Froscher, in the business area, whose salary was paid for by the shop owners for keeping an eye on their property.

"Dade County Deputy Sheriff S. S. Puckett has been providing law enforcement services to Miami without pay except small items as may come to him for making arrests and serving papers. He announced he is willing to serve as Town Marshall until Miami is incorporated and a Marshall is elected, if the citizens compensate him for his time" (*Miami Metropolis*, 1/5/1896).

On July 28, 1896, 368 male voters incorporated the new City of Miami. The voters present included 206 white men and 162 black men. Women still had not gained the right to vote at that time.

Young F. Gray, a twenty-six-year-old man with no previous law enforcement or other recorded civic involvement, was an employed dynamite expert for Henry Flagler's projects. He became the first marshal of the young city, defeating S. S. Pukett by a vote of 247 to 97. Gray was immediately sworn in by new Mayor John Reilly the evening of the vote (*Miami Metropolis*, 7/28/1896).

After Gray's election and prior to the necessary ordinances being enacted for him to exercise his office, he replaced Puckett as the Dade deputy, when the former resigned and announced his intention to repair to Orange County (*Miami Metropolis*, 7/31/1896).

Marshal Gray made his first recorded arrest on October 14, 1896. Gray and Constable Frolhawk arrested Asbury Duckett for the knife murder of Ben Worthy at Wood's Saloon, north of town. The motive for the killing was a pool room bet. After a justice of the peace hearing, Duckett was ordered held for manslaughter. Marshal Gray took prisoner Duckett to the county jail in Juno to await grand jury action (*Miami Metropolis*, 10/14/1896).

In late October 1896, the commission voted a salary of $50 monthly for the city marshal position and noted that he would always be on duty. At that meeting, Marshal Gray appealed to the commission to provide him one other man to handle the city's sanitation duties.

In early December that year, a contract was awarded to D. Merrit to build a city jail at the cost of $771. The jail was completed by Christmas Day with the police on the first floor and city hall above it.

Gray was the only Miami policeman until 1898 pulling his goat-drawn wagon, collecting stray dogs and unwanted law breakers in the city of 1,500. He was also the building inspector, street superintendent, sanitary inspector, and tax collector

Marshal Gray, after a fairly uneventful first year, was reelected without opposition in October 1897. One of the few stories of that first year was that Wm. Lavender, a cook employed by Gray to prepare meals for prisoners, was arrested for stealing Marshal Gray's shoes, hat, and revolver, for which he was sentenced to a sixty-day confinement (*Miami Metropolis*, 5/14/1897).

Gray received 112 votes in his reelection bid, with barely only 115 voters participating out of the 451 voters registered. Gray served three one-year terms before moving back to becoming a farmer in the town of Union, Spaulding County, in west-central Georgia. Gray died in 1944 at the age of seventy-four (U.S. Census, City of Miami Publications, *Miami Metropolis*, 8/25/1905).

Gray was replaced as city marshal by the election of R. S. Flanagan.

Author's Note: Although the principal subject of this book revolves around the City of Miami Police Department, many incidents and events will also involve the Dade County Sheriff's Office, the Miami Fire Department, and the Coral Gables Police Department, due to the intermingling of personnel, responsibilities, and actions of these entities with the Miami police force, particularly in the formative years of the late 1800s and early 1900s.

FIRE DESTROYS MANY DOWNTOWN BUSINESS

Events during the first few years of its municipal existence include a fire on Christmas week in 1896 that destroyed three blocks of the Miami downtown area, starting with the Brady building and spreading to twenty-seven others. Two hundred citizens escaped the inferno. The mainly wooden buildings were soon replaced with brick structures, with the rebuilding commencing while the cinders were still warm (*Miami Metropolis*, 1/1/1897).

SPANISH-AMERICAN WAR AFFECTS MIAMI

The Spanish-American War, lasting from April to mid-August 1898, had a significant effect on Miami. U.S. troops were quickly mobilized and positioned in southern bases for possible deployment to Puerto Rico and Cuba. The U.S. Fourth Army deployed six regiments of the First Division to Miami on June 25. The force of 7,500 men in two battalions were the First and Second Texas Regiment, the First and Second Alabama, and the First and Second Louisiana. General W. W. Gordon and General William Oates were the battalion COs under the division commander, General Warren Keifer.

It is interesting to note that Oates, a former Alabama governor, had been a colonel in the Confederate Army and had fought at Gettysburg.

Placing so many troops in a small city of only two thousand inhabitants with meager medical facilities proved inadequate. Many of the troops came down with typhoid fever that killed six, and others contracted measles and other illness. The troops were ordered redeployed to Jacksonville on July 31.

Some sketchy reports indicated that so many troops interacting with the small population, all southern volunteers, caused friction and some bloodshed, particularly in the black Overtown area of Miami.

Most of the rowdyism was traced to Company L of Texas. One night in July, L Company marched into the black section and shot out every kerosene lamp burning.

On July 28, 1898, Virgil Duncan, a private in Company M, First Texas Regiment, shot and killed Sam Drummer, a black cook, after observing what the soldier thought was a vile act of bumping into a woman. Duncan fired four shots into Drummer and was immediately arrested by Army Lieutenant Smythe. A coroner jury exonerated Duncan. He was then given a general court martial by the army, charging him with first-degree murder. Duncan was found not guilty and released from confinement.

The official army version of why the regiments were transferred to Jacksonville after only six weeks in Miami was provided by General Gordon in his report.

"The fact that the number of troops were too great for the resources of a place where almost everything had to be created, Miami simply did not have the resources and facilities to accommodate 7,500 troops and 2,000 citizens."

After the departure of the troops, yellow fever spread throughout Miami, resulting in a quarantine that lasted up to the end of that year. Miami became a closed city during that time, and even the local newspapers suspended operation until January 1, 1899, which left a void in reporting the happenings in this new city.

In 1899, Miami's "COLORED TOWN" was created from land donated by Henry Flagler and Julia Tuttle, adjacent to the downtown Miami business area, within the confines of then Sixth Street to Twelfth Street, prior to the 1921 renumbering of the streets (U.S. Census, City of Miami Publications).

Author's Note: Before venturing into our Miami street stories, the author presumes that the images the reader possess of Florida law enforcement in the early days of Miami differs primarily from today only in the technological gadgets and modes of transportation that are now present. Wrong! To acquaint our readers with the law enforcement's state of the art and the criminal society then prevalent in Florida as the twentieth century emerged, the story of the infamous Davis murders, the Dora Suggs murder, and the notorious Ashley Gang are presented, as well as their effects on Miami.

FATHER AND DAUGHTER MURDERED

On June 30, 1905, the *Miami Metropolis* (forerunner of the *Miami News*) newspaper, reported that C. E. Davis, a farmer, and his daughter Elsie Davis were murdered in their home while they slept, four miles west of the city, the previous Saturday night.

The description of the crime and the crime scene, committed over a hundred years ago, was documented in exacting detail by the Metropolis newspaper reporter. The account, although lurid, explains the state of the art on the process of major crimes investigations during that period.

The following outstanding *Metropolis* account is copied *exactly* as it appeared on June 30, 1905.

Headline states, "Crime the Most Shocking of Any in the History of the County. Bodies Discovered Last Monday by Davis's Son." Further, "Believed the girl was criminally assaulted." "Dead Man's Pistol Used and Two Shots Fired into His Daughter's Body, While One Ended His Life."

One of the most shocking and brutal assassinations in the annuals of Dade County and the State of Florida was committed some time during Saturday night four miles west of the city, when C. E. Davis and his grown daughter, Elsie D. Davis, were murdered as they lay in their beds, by a person or persons unknown.

This was the information brought to the city Monday morning about 6 o'clock by Ed Davis, a son and brother of the murdered people. The news spread rapidly, and within a few minutes thereafter, Sheriff Frohock, representatives of the press and numerous citizens were en route to the scene of the crime. Indignation was freely expressed, and the same became more pronounced after the full facts and realization of the enormity of the butchery had been learned, the general expression being that lynch law should deal justice to the guilty person or persons, if captured.

Crime Beggar's Description

The crime beggar's description or realization, except to those who visit the Davis home and there saw for themselves the result of what culminated from an attempt, if not successful, in criminal assault upon the girl whose chastity is unquestioned. That assault upon the person of the young woman, was the cause of the crime, is the universal opinion of the public. Signs bear out this fact, but it is probable that it will never be established by medical examination as the body of the dead girl was in such a state of decomposition that the physicians, who made an examination previous to the removal of the bodies from the home, said that would be impossible for them to make a positive statement that criminal assault was made, though they expressed themselves that such was probable.

A Terrible Scene

A Metropolis reporter was at the scene of the crime shortly after the news was received in the city. Little groups of men, demoralized, but incensed, were gathered around and about the yard and on the porches of the house. A stillness pervaded the air, strong men talked in whispers, stood of amazed, or solicited information. From a little window on the back side of the second story of the east end of the house a bare foot and six inches or more of ankle could be seen, as the man victim lay diagonally across the bed in her chamber. Many eyes viewed it, many hearts beat with emotion and the fire of vengeance was increased until some had worked themselves in a frenzy. A few woman, neighbors and friends of the deceased, gathered at the house, but their voices were hushed and eyes dimmed with tears.

The four sons of deceased, Frank, Ed, Robert and Leo Davis, and H. Davis, a brother, mingled with the crowd but were so affected that they hardly realized the enormity of the crime or the great bereavement they had suffered.

Sheriff Frohock was early on the scene, and after summoning the coroner's jury there was considerable delay awaiting the arrival of Drs. Skaggs and Pugh who had been sent for to hold the post mortem examination before removing the bodies. Later they arrived and, assisted by Dr. Vanlandingham and with the jury and representatives of the press, repaired to the two upper chambers of the home in which lay the bodies of the victims.

Girl's Body Examined

The body of the girl was first examined. It lay with the head towards the foot and diagonally across the bed. A sheet and her night dress were wrapped about the head and shoulders in a tangled mass. Her flowing black hair, blood soaked and matted, covered the face and stuck in the clotted blood which saturated the bed and dripped through to the floor. In the breast were found two gaping wounds, one near each nipple. Both went through the body and one of the bullets through the mattress to the floor where it was found by Juryman Belcher. Both shots were fired at close range and apparently while the assassin was over his victim. The night dress was powder burned and blackened on the left side showing that the weapon was within a few inches of her when fired. The other wound, the one in the right breast, came out underneath the arm, or through the ribs, and would not have caused instant death, though the other went through and near the heart.

Fought For Her Life

There are only two wounds on the body through the condition of the bed and the room indicated that the dead woman fought for her life and chastity. One of the knuckles on her right hand had a large piece of skin knocked off while her wrists bore evidence of having been held in a tight grasp and bruised. On the floor near a table lay an overturned box of face powder with the contents scattered. A large rug that covered the floor was also turned up and disarranged, indicating that the murderer had stood with his feet on the floor while combating with the woman. Under the bed were her shoes and stockings, while her clothing, those she probably wore last, lay on a chair, showing that the girl had retired for the night and was probably asleep when disturbed by the intruder.

A Bird Witness

In the east window, and within a few feet of the head of the bed, stood a canary bird and cage, and it is probable that the little pet was the only living witness to the assault and murder of its mistress. No song pealed from its throat and it hopped excitedly from one perch to another as the dozen or more men filed into and occupied the room. "If it could only talk and tell what it saw," remarked a juryman.

In Davis Rom

Leaving the room of Miss Davis, that of her father, opposite and separated only by a few feet, at the top landing of the stairs, was visited. The body lay flat on the back, lengthwise, and in the middle of the bed with the head upon two pillows. Decomposition had set in and reached a stage where the skin and flesh were peeling off the breast. It, like that of the girl, was saturated with blood, through but one wound, a shot in the right side of the neck, ranging downward and coming out the shoulder, was found. This shot was fired at a greater distance than those that killed the young woman as the clothing was not powder-burned, and according to the opinion of the examining physicians, based upon the condition of the head and throat, the was wound was not sufficient to cause instant death and that, after being shot, the victim was choked and strangled to death. This, however, is not a certainty as the general condition of the body was such that the swollen and congealed condition of the head and neck might have been caused by decay, through, hardly probable.

38-Caliber Weapon Used

The weapon used was one carrying a 38-calibre ball and the probability is that the murders were committed by an Iver Johnson pistol, which Mr. Davis is known to have owned and which a thorough search of the house failed to reveal. That the same weapon killed both parties is evidenced by the finding of a second bullet buried in the pillow under Mr. Davis' head and which is the same size as the one found under his daughter's bed.

This ended the physicians' examination and the bodies were ordered delivered to Undertaker King for burial.

No Motive Established

What could be the motive of the crime? If Mr. Davis had an enemy it was not known. He moved to the county fourteen years ago and settled, coming from Delaware county, Ohio, and engaged in truck farming and fruit culture. Besides his sons, and brother mentioned above, he leaves a bereaved mother, Mrs. Barbara Davis, of this city.

Saturday, he, with his daughter, visited the city, and having an engagement to go to Fulford yesterday morning with M. E. Burbanks, for some citrus fruit trees. Miss Davis promised to spend the day in Miami with Mrs. V. A. Rutherford, but her failure to come caused no alarm as it was supposed that her father had deferred his trip or that some other event of ordinary occurrence had detained them at home.

Called at House Yesterday

Yesterday morning Mr. Burbanks, who resides a half mile or so from the Davis home, went over to tell Mr. Davis that he would be unable to go to Fulford with him. He was not found at home and Mr. Burbanks, without going to the upper story of the house and believing that his friend and daughter had gone visiting, returned home. He went again to the Davis home in the afternoon and found him still absent. He still thought nothing was wrong, and this morning went to the Davis home for the third time, and after finding things as he had yesterday went to the home of Ed Davis, one of the sons of deceased, living near his home and told him of his father and sister being away all of yesterday and last night.

The Bodies Found

This was strange and together they returned to the Davis house and Ed Davis went to the two chambers above. He first entered his father's room and found him in bed. He was lying on his right side. Bathed in blood and cold in death. He turned him on his back and then rushed to his sister's room. There a still more gruesome and heartrending sight met his eyes and almost caused his heart to stop beating. With this information he came into the city and spread the news and alarm.

When Was Crime Committed

At or about what hour was the crime committed? This, like all connections with the tragedy, is a mystery, though it evidently occurred Sunday morning. Dr Skaggs says that it was at least twenty-four hours before the bodies were found. H. Davis, brother of the deceased, says that about midnight Saturday night he heard one shot and a scream, but paid little attention to it as his brother frequently shot owls at night and his daughter, being of a lively and happy nature, sometimes gave a scream that could be heard to his house, about a quarter of a mile away. This is the only clew so far gained, as to the probable hour of the assignation.

Various Opinions Expressed

Various opinions are expressed, as to the cause of the killing, and the general ideal is that more than one person as connected with it, that it was for the purpose of committing an assault upon the young lady and that the person or persons were familiar with the house knew where both Mr. Davis and his daughter slept. It is also a question of surmise which was killed first through it would seem that Mr. Davis was first attacked so as to get him out of the way of interference with the dastardly assault upon his daughter. These and kindred other opinions prevailed, but the above would seem to correctly cover the situation.

No Clue Left

No clue was left by the murderers as to their identity, though it is apparent that they went out the back way and through a barrel gate leading to the stable as blood spots were found on the top bar, which was down. The prints of a large shoe, square toed, were also tracked several hundred feet toward the nursery and this may furnish a slight clue. Otherwise the crime is shrouded in mystery.

Reports In Circulation

Several reports of threats were in circulation. One that Mr. Davis has been threatened by a negro whom he had had in his employ, while another was that he had difficulty with negroes over some watermelons. These were dispelled by statements from his sons who say they know of no such threats or difficulty, though they state that some few weeks ago some person or persons unknown, visited the field and destroyed a quarter of an acre or more of young melon plants. Their father never knew who did it or had any difficulty with any one over the offense.

The Davis Home

The Davis home is situated about four miles to the west of the city and about a half mile down the road leading east from the little school house along the main road. It sits about forty or fifty feet inside a front wall or fence of native stone and is built of logs one story and a half high. Through the center of it there runs from front to back a wide hallway or opening, with the stairway leading up from the back part of the hall and landing at the entrance to the room occupied by Miss Davis. On the ground floor and under Miss Davis room is a bed chamber furnished, but unoccupied. Opposite and under the room where Mr. Davis slept is the parlor, while in the rear of this room is the kitchen.

Under the stairway is a closet and against this stood a double-barreled shotgun loaded with No. 1 shot, and alongside of it a small .22-caliber rifle, also loaded. Inside the vacant or extra bed chamber, down stairs, hung another gun in a case, and under this on a nail Mr. Davis always kept his pistol hanging in a holster or a breast strap, such as are used sometimes by sheriffs and police for carry their pistols of in the pocket or around the waist. This pistol is supposed to have been taken by the assassins and used in murdering the defenseless man and woman.

The House Never Locked

Mr. Frank Davis, one of the sons of the deceased and an employee of the local post office, said that his father never locked up the house at night, that they were not afraid of molestation and feared no harm. Sometimes his sister would take the pistol upstairs but that it usually hung on the peg in the room below. My father generally retired early in the evening, but my sister did not. She was very fond of reading and frequently set up until midnight, enjoying books and novels. I don't think my father or sister either, had an enemy in the world. "Their murder is a mystery I can not fathom."

Posses Organized

Believing as they do that the crime was committed for the purposes of criminally assaulting Miss Davis, many of those present at the Davis home this morning expressed themselves that it was the work of negroes and declared that if the negro quarters at Lummus' mill, half a mile away, were searched thoroughly that a clue and possibly the guilty parties would be found there, and immediately after the adjourning of the coroner's jury, consisting of J. B. McKenzie, T. E. Cheatham, J. G. Crosland, E. C. Grant, S. A. Beicher and F. B. Stoneman, to meet tomorrow at 9 o'clock, Sheriff Frohock began organizing a posse, and this afternoon at 2 o'clock a score of determined men armed with guns took to the woods and will scour every section thoroughly in their effort to capture the fiend or fiends, is where acts have startled and shocked the community, and worked the people into a frenzy that will defy the law if the murderers are caught.

The outrage is one of the most atrocious ever committed in the State and it is one that calls for the most determined efforts and full justice in the apprehending and punishing of the guilty, and on every hand there is universal condemnation. Private rewards have been offered for the capture of the murderers, and it is expected that both the county and State will add other amounts as incentives in ferreting out and capturing the fiends. One of the private rewards offered is $100 by W. W. Prost, who is doing so appends this statement

The newspaper article went on to discuss the rewards over $2,000 offered, including $250 from Governor Broward, as well as the community reaction to the crime and the reporting on the funerals. The investigation of the crime continued on for months and years under the direction of Sheriff Frolock and his deputy, A. P. Gore. The reward money was eventually returned to the donors when no arrest was made.

The anxiety created in the minds of Miami residents no doubt caused them to be more than ever in favor of having an efficient police department in the city (*Miami Metropolis*/News, 6/30/1905).

Author's Note: Outstanding reporting by Metropolis reporter in describing this case.

DORA SUGGS MURDER

Governor Broward signed the death warrant for Edward (Cady) Brown to be hanged on June 5 for the December 1905 murder of Mrs. Dora Suggs. When read the death warrant by Sheriff Frohock, Brown said, "I don't know how they can hang a man for something he knows nothing about." The execution will take place in the jail yard of the county jail, with the gallows enclosed by a high board fence.

The crime took place when Mrs. Dora Suggs, a farmer's wife, was returning to her home near Coconut Grove on the evening of December 14. She was dragged from her wagon and chased into a wooded area and brutally beaten in a fierce struggle. Her death was caused by being struck by rocks that caused her skull to be crushed. Her body was in a horribly mutilated condition when found.

Edmond Brown, a Negro male, was arrested the following day. He was indicted by the grand jury on first-degree murder charges and was tried and convicted in Dade County Circuit Court. His appeals were denied, and he was sentenced to die by hanging for his crime.

The execution was set for June 1906 after the appeals were settled.

On the day of the execution, it was reported that Brown slept well, ate a hearty breakfast, and displayed a remarkable coolness and nerve during the trying time previous to leaving his cell. He sang audibly as he marched to the gallows and spoke a prayer, ending with a thank you to Sheriff Frolock for treating him so well.

A crowd of several hundred gathered in the jail area to watch, getting only a partial view due to the temporary fence. Just before pulling the rope, Sheriff Frohock told Brown that this was his last chance to confess before dying. Brown reportedly replied, "You tell them."

"Tell them what," asked the sheriff, "that you are guilty?"

"Yes," came Brown's answer, audible to those standing closest to the gallows.

Sheriff Frohock was assisted at the gallows by Deputy Gore, the jailor Charles Mann, and the ex-city marshal Robert S. Flanagan. A committee of twelve town leaders and elected officials were the official witness, including Chief Frank Hardee of the police department (*Miami Metropolis*/News, 6/8/1906).

CHIEF HARDEE—MIAMI'S FIRST CHIEF

Elected in 1906, Chief Frank B. Hardee, b. 1871, is listed on the 1910 U.S. Census with his spouse, Geneva, and two children, was born in Georgia, and married to Geneva H. Hardee (forty-nine years old in the U.S. Census report of 1920). Hardee listed his father's birthplace as Virginia and his mother's in Georgia. The following others were listed at his home in this report:

Frankie l. Hardee, 17
Nedra M. Hardee, 14
Mirian J. Hardee, 11
James Willis, 25
Fernance P. Willis, 25
James L. Willis, 7 mos.

Another son, Minor Lyn Jones Hardee, born February 17, 1907, two years after his father became chief, later worked at a bank for years until World War II, then becoming a crew chief on B-17 and B-24 bombers, flying more than forty combat missions over Germany. Minor died in 1991 in Miami at age eighty-three.

Chief Hardee served three terms, ending in 1911, when he chose not to run for reelection. He then entered into the booming Miami construction business (U.S. Census Reports, City of Miami Publications).

MIAMI POLICE BADGE NO. 1

It was reported at a Jan 6, 1905, city council meeting that Mayor Sewell appointed Rufus James Hardee, twenty-nine (born December 12, 1876), as a temporary policeman. R. C. Flanagan was city marshal at this time, having succeeded the first marshal, Young F. Gray. Rufus J. Hardee, brother of the first chief of police, Frank B. Hardee, had the distinction of being assigned to wear Miami PD badge no. 1 after the issuance a year later of police uniforms by his brother, the chief.

Rufus Hardee (who went by his middle name of James) was listed with his first spouse, Mary B. Hardee, born 1886. In the 1920 U.S. Census, Rufus was listed as a contractor with Carl Fisher's company, living at 31 Eighteenth Street, Miami, with spouse, Nola Hardee (Miami changed the street numbering system in about 1921). In the 1945 Census for Miami, Rufus was listed as a guard, living at 3135 NW Thirdy-third Street. According to that report, Rufus Hardee was married to Nola Hardee and had three sons—Carl, Herbert, and Walter. Rufus Hardee was listed at the time as having eight years of schooling. Son Walter was in the U.S. Army, and the other two boys were students in school. Rufus Hardee died in Dade County in November 1969. Suzanne Hardee, granddaughter, recalls the large funeral procession for Rufus, with numerous police motorcycles driving down NW Seventh Avenue. Suzanne also advised that she was in possession of a photo of Rufus Hardee in police uniform with badge no. 1 displayed. A similar photo is in possession of her elderly uncle Herbert Hardee (Rufus's son), who resides in Homosassa, Florida. An attempt will be made to copy the photos for display in the police department.

The *Miami Metropolis* newspaper ran an article in March 1905 detailing the history of the young city from the first origination to the present day. Their accomplishments in this short time were considerable and boasting was most appropriate. The full report may be viewed on a University of Florida newspaper archive website (Personal note—MPD relative, *Miami Metropolis*/News, Miami police reports).

ORGANIZING THE FORCE

In 1905, Miami opted for a new political scheme that established a chief of police position, replacing the "town marshal" as the city's law enforcer. The October 6, 1905, *Metropolis* newspaper reported the election results. Only 299 votes were cast. John Sewell was elected mayor, and the man selected in the primary for chief of police was Frank B. Hardee, defeating the incumbent city marshal, Robert S. Flanagan.

One of the first acts of Mayor Sewell was to order that the Miami Police Department be increased in number and be uniformed. The news story that day reported the following:

> The MPD to be increased and uniformed. Four new men to be added and made to wear uniforms thus increasing the efficiency and improving the appearance of the men.
>
> The MPD is to be increased and uniformed, this was the statement made this morning by Mayor John Sewell who said that he would appoint four new policemen at an early date and see that the whole force is uniformed. Marshall Hardee and the members of the force have uniforms en route and will don them the first of the month. They are of modern metropolitan style and cloth pad and will make an improvement in the appearance of the men besides giving them a power that is more respected by offenders and criminals than is the law.
>
> Mayor Sewell entertains the opinion which would prevail throughout the world, that a uniform not only adds to the appearance of an officer, but that it increased his efficiency; many a man will respect a uniform and not resist arrest, who would not hesitate to assault an officer in civilian clothes. This fact has been proven by experience. Then too, a uniform gives prestige to the wearer; it shows an up-to-dateness and force recognition from a stranger and causes the realization that the city is policed and protected in an efficient manner.
>
> All of these facts the Mayor has considered and there is little doubt but that the public will concur with him in his desire

and intentions to increase and uniform the police department. (*Miami Metropolis*, 10/6/1905)

The new city charter in 1905 called for the marshal's term to be increased to two years. Frank B. Hardee was elected as the first chief of police with the city council voting to pay him $65 a month. At the city council meeting of November 3, 1905, Chief Hardee was presented with a "very attractive and expensive gold badge on behalf of council member Hahn and certain admiring friends."

At the next two council meetings, Mayor Sewell and Chief Hardee recommended the following permanent police officers to be hired. The council agreed and the officers were sworn in: Rufus James Hardee, John Frank Coleman, J. R. O'Neal, and Joseph M. English. These four, along with Marshal (now Chief) Frank B. Hardee, were the first five uniformed police officers in Miami police history.

J. D. Godman and J. W. Grant were also sworn in as special police officers without salary.

The November 10 *Metropolis* edition also contained a story about the reward for the killers of C. E. Davis and his daughter Elsie in June 1905 in Miami and the disposition of same if no arrest is made.

Just as the police department was getting organized, another violent crime occurred in the outlying district. The *Miami Metropolis* reported that on the previous Monday, November 18, 1905, Dora Suggs, twenty-nine, was savagely murdered en route to her home west of Coconut Grove. She had been in a mule-pulled wagon but was beaten and killed in an open field nearby. At the time, the locale of this murder was actually outside of the then city limits of Miami; therefore, the crime was investigated by Dade County Sheriff Frohlock, but the crime had a significant effect on the young city of Miami.

In December 1905, Mayor Sewell and Chief Hardee appointed Charles H. Smith as a police officer for the holidays. He also appointed unpaid policemen L. A. Cooley, L. L. McNeill, Albert Carroll, and R. C. McGriff, and a month later, appointed Alvas A. Bunnell and C. C. Pierson as regular police officers and J. W. Rogers as a special policeman for the Royal Palms Property, whose salary was paid for by the hotel.

In April 1906, a V. J. Flury was appointed as a special police officer at the dock without pay, taking the place of C. Beidler, who resigned, as well as appointing L. W. Umstead a city police officer, replacing John F. Coleman who resigned.

It was also reported that Chief Hardee announced that 256 arrests had been made in March 1906. Chief Hardee also made a request to the city council for funds to buy a patrol wagon (horse-drawn). His request was referred to a committee (*Miami Metropolis*/News, 10/6/1905 and 11/18/1905).

OFFICER QUALIFICATIONS—1906

At the city council meeting of June 29, 1906, Councilman Crosland asked Mayor Sewell what the qualifications for police officer were due to a complaint a citizen had made. Mayor Sewell replied:

> "The Mayor makes the appointments which are confirmed by the Council. Candidates must have been in the state [Florida] for one year, Dade County for six months and the City of Miami for ninety days." It was pointed out that one police officer did not meet that qualification but Chief Hardee advised that the man was a temporary replacement for a regular that was off due to illness, and that the replacement was the only man Hardee could find to serve. (City of Miami Publication)

VAGRANTS

An interesting story ran in the January 4, 1907, edition of the *Miami Metropolis* concerning vagrants in Miami. The headline read, "The Vagrant Must Go—Decision of the Sheriff." "Eight 'Gents of Leisure' Taken on Raid in North Miami and Colored Town Last Night—Information Filed Against All of Them."

> Sheriff Frohock has gotten tired of the large number of habitually idle negro and white men, who frequent North Miami and Colored Town (both areas just outside the city limits and under the jurisdiction of the Sheriff), some of them having been hanging around these parts for months and even years without working or having any visible means of support, and last night, accompanied by two or three of his deputies, made a raid on these gents of leisure.

North Miami and Colored Town were given a through scouring and when the job had been finished, seven Negroes and one white man were in the toils and escorted to the jail where they were locked up on the charge of vagrancy. A number of others getting wind of the presence of the officers proceeded to make themselves scarce and in that way evaded arrest, though Sheriff Frohock states they will be taken into custody as soon as located.

This morning, County Prosecuting Attorney R. R. Taylor filed information direct against the eight prisoners, charging them with vagrancy and they will be taken into the County Court which convenes next Monday for trial. It is probable the majority or all of them will plead guilty to the charge. (*Miami Metropolis*/News, 1/4/1907)

MORE MPD CHANGES

On January 18, 1907, W. G. DeBerry was appointed as a police officer in place of Rufus J. Hardee, who is now detailed at the Royal Palm Hotel. DeBerry will serve until Hardee is relieved from further detail at the hotel. The giant Royal Palm Hotel pays the salary of the officer assigned at the hotel during the season (MPD records).

At the city council meeting of April 26, 1907, Marshal (Chief) Hardee was instructed to reduce the police force one or two men after May 1. At that time, many of Miami winter residents headed back up north about the first of May. (It should also be noted that the country was in an economic depression in 1907.) (MPD records)

On May 3, 1907, Chief Hardee announced a change in the watches (assignments) for his officers. The story:

The Police Dept Changes Watches

Where the Men Will Be Assigned Until Further Changes Are Decided Upon—Limits of Each Beat Defined.

The police department changed watches this morning and from now on the watches and beats will be covered as follows:

South Beat: Officer Hardee on duty from 4 AM to 12 noon, Officer Stephens from 12 noon to 8 PM, Officer Freeman from 8 PM to 4 AM.

North Beat: Officer Griffing from 4 AM to 12 noon, Officer DeBerry from 12 noon to 8 PM, Officer Sistrunk from 8 PM to 4 AM.

South Beat runs from 10th Street to 20th Street, and from the east to west boundaries of the city, and North Beat from 10th Street to 1st Street, with the same territory east and west.

The officer heretofore patrolling the south side has been laid off for the summer; the policeman on south beat now covering that territory. (*Miami Metropolis*, 5/3/1907)

Also in the spring of 1907, R. S. Flanagan announced his candidacy for the position of chief of police for a two-year term. Flanagan previously was the town marshal for several years. There were then four announced candidates: incumbent Frank B. Hardee, J. D. Godman, and A. P. Gore, a Dade Co. Sheriff's deputy (*Miami Metropolis*).

In September 1907, the city council set the salaries of the chief of police position to $1,200 annually. Police officers with less than six months, $540 annually, more than six months of service, $720 annually (*Miami Metropolis*, 9/1907).

As noted previously, the 1905 election results placed its first chief of police, Frank B. Hardee, thirty-eight, in office. For the past two years, Frank Hardee has been serving as the town marshal. Despite the announcements of three other candidates for the job, Hardee ended up alone on the ballot for chief. There were only 155 votes cast in the city election.

According to his granddaughter Suzanne Hardee, Chief Hardee appointed his younger brother to the Miami Police Department—Rufus James Hardee, DOB: June 8, 1876—and was issued badge no. 1. Rufus was assigned to a walking beat. Both Hardee brothers served the Miami Police Department until October 26, 1911, at which time C. R. Ferguson was elected chief of police. Frank Hardee was not a candidate for reelection, although Rufus Hardee, a current patrol officer and the chief's brother, was listed on the ballot for the job of chief, but was unsuccessful (Personal Note: MPD relative, City Publication).

BEAT ASSIGNMENTS CHANGE

On November 8, 1907, Chief Hardee announced a change in police beats for the city. These were seven-day-a-week assignments. No days off.

North Beat: Officer W. G. DeBerry from 12 noon to 8 PM, William B. Curry from 8 PM to 4 AM, and J. C. Tucker from 4 AM to noon.

South Beat: Officer R. J. Hardee from 12 noon to 8 PM, W. J. Whitman from 8 PM to 4 AM, and E. V. Stevens (Stephens) from 4 AM to 12 noon (MPD records and *Miami Metropolis*, 11/8/1907).

SECOND TEN YEARS

In December 1907, a citizen charged Chief Hardee with a violation of his duties for releasing information to a suspect. A hearing was held by the city council and Hardee explained the situation. The council agreed with him and the complaint was ruled not valid (MPD records and *Miami Metropolis*, 12/1907).

In January 1908, one of the city council members recommended that the police force be reduced to four members from the present six plus the chief. A hearing was set for the following month. This action was due to the economic depression of 1907, which affected the entire country. The following meeting (January 10, 1908), Mayor Wharton appointed three men as special police officers for the holidays: F. H. Pfender, H. H. Marsh, and J. J. Hardee (MPD records and *Miami Metropolis*, 7/1/1908).

A review of the 1910 U.S. Census Reports also showed several others persons listed as city policemen that year:

Frazier J. Bates, 42, born Florida, with spouse, Josephine, living at 336 Ninth Street

William B. Curry, 30, born the Bahamas, with spouse, Gertrude

Charles Sheppard, 34, born Florida, single

Thomas Caswell, 38

Elmer Hodge, 25, single

Dan Hardie, who had been the fire chief of Miami since its formation, was elected sheriff of Dade County in January 1909. Hardie built the fire department from scratch and was very well regarded for his energy and efficiency. Henry Chase, twenty-four, was elected fire chief the same year, replacing Dan Hardie. Both men, obviously very friendly with each other, conducted a side business that they created, operating the C&H line of ten buses, until selling out in 1914.

Hardie work was lessoned a bit by the fact that Palm Beach County was formed from a portion of Dade County in 1909. The former sheriff John Frohock became a Miami businessman and a bondsman after his term of office, continuing his energies to Miami (Miami PD records and *Miami Metropolis*/News).

In 1910, the population of the City of Miami was 5,000 (a 400% increase in one decade). In the same year, the original city hall was built at Flagler Street and SW First Avenue. During this era, Charles Robert Ferguson became the second chief of police. Under his leadership, the position of desk sergeant and the ranks of captain and lieutenant were created. The police department hired the city's first traffic officer and motorman. The motorcycle policeman had instructions to arrest anyone who exceeded the new 12 mph speed limit (City of Miami Publications, *Miami Metropolis*/News).

On January 15, 1911, the city council voted to increase the pay of each city police officer, $5 a month (*Miami Metropolis*/News, 1/15/1911).

After six years, and with a population of over 5,400, the City of Miami elected their second chief of police, Charles R. Ferguson, thirty-three years old. In November 1911, Chief Hardee did not seek reelection, but his brother, Rufus Hardee, did, but was not elected. The vote was Ferguson, 316 votes; Thomas R. Caswsell, 172; and Rufus Hardee, 139.

Chief Hardee addressed the city council and stated that he had been the police chief for six years and made 188 arrests. New Chief Ferguson, who had been a deputy sheriff under Sheriff Hardie for several years, appointed the following as police officers.

William J. Whitman, Gordon R. McDade, Edwin V. Stevens (Stephens), J. C. Richardson, Edward D. Russell, Frank Hoff, Lewis Gingras, Frazier J. Bates, William F. Freeman, and E. H. McDade (Miami PD records, *Miami Metropolis*/News, 7/11/1911).

The following May, an Alex Gingras was appointed as a police officer (MPD records).

When the new form of city government went into effect, an MPD officer, "Chief" Paul G. Phillips, was elected as the police judge (municipal judge).

The *Miami News* reported on June 5, 1911, that a citizen named Schmid criticized Officer Thomas Caswell and was struck with a billy club. Schmid had gone to Chief Hardee's office to provide bond for a young employee who had been arrested by Caswell for vagrancy. When Schmid berated Caswell, he was struck in the head with a night stick and slightly injured. Jim Hardee, the brother of the chief and an MPD officer, stepped in between the men.

The young man who had been arrested stated in court that he worked for Sheriff Hardie and was a witness in two local controversial cases. The judge dismissed the vagrancy charge and issued a warrant for Officer Caswell's arrest for assault (*Miami Metropolis*/News, 6/5/1911).

Various minor arrests were noted in the local newspapers. On July 21, 1911, Officers McDade, Hodge and Hardee made some gambling arrests. Chief Hardee and brother Rufus Hardee each made an arrest on October 6, 1911, and Chief Hardee made an arrest, showing they were active in their jobs right to the end of their tenure. Officers Curry, Hodge, Caswell, and Phillips also made arrests that day (*Miami Metropolis*/News, 7/21/1911).

Chief Hardee's term ended October 26, 1911, with Charles R. Ferguson taking over as chief, besting two others who sought the position, including Chief Hardee's brother, Rufus Hardee. Ferguson would remain in this position until William Whitman became chief two years later. Following Ferguson's term as Miami chief, he returned to the Dade sheriff's department as a deputy under Sheriff Dan Hardie (MPD records, *Miami Metropolis*/News, 6/5/1911 and 7/21/1911).

On January 12, 1912, the *Metropolis* had a story on the murder of Tom Tiger by John Ashley in Palm Beach County. On February 12, 1912, it was reported that escaped criminal Ashley was possibly spotted in Fort Myers. No further sightings were made and it was probable that the witness was in error, according to the published report. All police agencies were advised to be on the lookout for Ashley, a criminal who was quite feared (*Miami Metropolis*/News, 1/12/1912 and 2/12/1912).

PARCEL MURDER—MORE TROUBLE

A Mr. Cox, one of the suspects in the Parcel murder case in April 1911, had his case finally adjudicated after several trials on accessory to murder for helping the Parcel girl's father to dispose of the body in the Miami River. Just after being cleared, Mr. Cox was himself shot outside the courtroom by a Mrs. Howell who stated Cox was threatening her for testifying against him. She was acquitted of the charges of attempting to murder Cox the following April (*Miami Metropolis*/News, 4/1911).

PROMOTIONS

It was noted in the press that in April 1912, Edwin V. Stephens was serving as the desk sergeant. A 1912 photograph of the department's staff showed two sergeants. It is believed that the second sergeant was Gordon R. McDade.

The first female deputy sheriff in Florida was appointed by Sheriff Dan Hardie. She was Belle Hodge, the younger sister of Elmer Hodge, an MPD officer and later a constable (Personal knowledge—author, U.S. Census Reports, *Miami Metropolis*/News, 4/1912).

A photo published in the local paper in 1912 pictured the following MPD officers: A. B. Smith, William Meredith, Edwin V. Stephens, Gordon McDade, Harry Doane, J. B. Watkins, Harry Lee, L. M. Stevens, William Chandler, Ned Russell, J. D. Dorman, Edward McDade, Harry Starling, Harry Morris, J. Robertson, and two unidentified officers. Some of these officers were reserves (*Miami Herald* photo—1912).

In January 1913, there were nine full-time police officers working under Chief Ferguson. Three officers were assigned to the downtown business area, three others stationed in the colored area, and two were desk sergeants and one a motor officer (MPD records, *Miami Metropolis*/News, 1/1913).

PADDED CELL

In February 1913, the *Miami Metropolis* newspaper reported on the installation of a padded cell for insane prisoners.

> Pursuant to the recommendation of the Grand Jury, a padded cell will be provided in the county jail for insane prisoners. The matter having been brought to attention of the commissioners in session this week by Sheriff Hardie. The need for a padded cell was apparent to every member of the Board, and the Sheriff was instructed to see the improvement at once, the commissioners telling that official to use his own discretion as to what is best to be done.

> It is the Sheriff's idea to partition off one end of the hall on the second floor and to thickly pad this with canvas covered mattresses.
>
> Heretofore, when insane prisoners come under the care of the Sheriff he has either placed them in the hospital or detailed a deputy to keep in close watch that no harm would come to the unfortunates placed in the iron-barred cells of the county jail. (*Miami Metropolis*, 2/1913)

August 1913 brought a third chief of police to Miami. William J. Whitman, a current police officer, was elected to the position, besting A. R. McAdam. At the same time, the geographical limits of colored town were expanded after much discussion as to whether to do this "by custom" or by law. Some voices at the council meeting stated that it would be not legal to codify these parameters, but others said it was lawful.

The area was then expanded to the west, close to what is now NW Seventh Avenue (U.S. Census Reports, *Miami Metropolis*/News, 8/1913).

ELECTION RESULTS

The results of the city election in July 1913 were reported in the local newspaper. Whitman was elected as chief of police, with 425 votes, with A. R. McAdam runner-up with 136; W. W. Hendrickson, 124; Frank Hardee, former chief, 116; C. R. Ferguson, the current chief, 97; L. E. Gingras, 17; and Charles Shepard, 12, the latter two being current police officers with MPD (*Miami Metropolis*/News, 7/23/1913).

Also on that date, Chief C. R. Ferguson was fined $5 in court for actions stemming from a public dispute with Officers Mattison P. Merritt and Wm. M. Meredith, whom the chief had disciplined for fighting (*Miami Metropolis*/News, 7/1913).

LAYING DOWN RULES

The city council in August 1913 lay out for the first time a set of rules for the conduct of Miami police officers. The press headlined the story by stating,

Divorce Police from Booze & Cards Is Planned

The Chief of Police W. Whitman issued an order that:

    (1) Not to enter a saloon except as duty calls

    (2) No card playing in the police station.

    (3) Officers must wear the uniform while on duty.

Officers were also advised not to carry on long conversations with loiterers but to walk their beat.

The council also wanted the chief to add a "roundsman" (a patrol supervisor). At this time, the department's force consists of fourteen police officers, two sergeants, and the chief of police (*Miami Metropolis/News*, 8/1913).

In November 1913, it was reported that Chief Whitman replaced three officers. Out were G. W. Robertson, R. H. Smith, and M. T. Cann. The replacements were M. M. Richards, R. H. Starling, and G. L. Chandler.

Chandler had recently been the town marshal in North Miami (*Metropolis*/News, 7/8/1913).

MOTORCYCLE TRAFFIC ENFORCEMENT

The first motorcycle squad for Miami PD began to train on September 12, 1913, with three or four officers trained to ride a speedometer-equipped motorcycle that the city had just purchased. There were numerous complaints of vehicles speeding on Biscayne Drive, causing accidents and problems. The motorcycle officer was to issue tickets to anyone exceeding the twelve-mile-per-hour limit, the law at the time. This was one of Chief Whitman's then-progressive steps to improve the department (MPD reports, *Miami Metropolis*/News, 9/12/1913).

ANNEXATION

In November 1913, Miami annexed some of their nearby neighborhoods, increasing the size of the city to fourteen square miles with a population of about fifteen thousand residents. Additional annexation will come about in 1925.

Also this month, a twenty-one-year-old volunteer city firefighter, John Thompson, was killed when his fire truck flipped over en route to a call just north of town. Seven other firefighters were injured, one seriously. In other news, the mayor ordered the police chief to dispatch a police officer to each fire to handle the traffic and crowds at the scenes.

It was also announced that three new officers were hired for the force: G. W. Roberts, M. T. McCann, and R. Stalling.

A report on the MPD budget shows that the chief was receiving $100 a month, two sergeants budgeted for $75 monthly, and nine officers receiving a total of $675 a month. Uniforms were allocated $254 monthly while bicycle supplies totaled $25.50 monthly (*Miami Metropolis*, 1/17/1913).

One of the movements connected to the push for alcohol prohibition was the establishment of the Law Enforcement Movement of Dade County. This citizen's group announced a set of rewards to assist in curbing illegal alcohol establishments in the area.

The group would pay whistle-blowers a reward of $25 to any police, sheriff, marshal, or constable for the arrest and conviction of any violators of the liquor laws. Fifty dollars would be paid for the second conviction.

A reward of $500 would be paid for the arrest of any law officer who accepts graft for allowing the illegal booze outlets to operate.

One thousand dollars would be the reward for providing information on any chief of police or sheriff for accepting graft, and $1,500 for the arrest of any judge who would accept illegal payments for protecting these establishments.

The movement had a budget of $10,000 in contributions for paying these rewards (*Miami Metropolis*/News, 11/25/1913).

HANGED FOR RAPE

In April 1914, Clarence Daly was hanged for the rape of an elderly woman that occurred in June 1913. The execution took place in the courtyard of the county jail in downtown Miami. Daly was the first white man to be hanged in Dade County. A stockade fence was erected to shield the gallows from the street (*Miami Metropolis*/News, 4/1914).

TEN COMMANDMENTS

Chief Whitman posted "Ten Commandments" of parking in the newspaper in an attempt to achieve some sense of order out of the chaos of parking autos in the downtown area. The recent influx of autos, combined with the numerous bicycles, horse-drawn wagons, and pedestrians, were causing "gridlock" in the business area (*Miami Metropolis*/News, 9/4/1914).

INDISCRETIONS

Chief of Police William J. Whitman was accused of entering a woman resident's home while drunk in June 1914. A city council hearing was held and Whitman admitted his guilt. The council voted 4-3 to remove him, but a unanimous vote was required, so he remained on the job. He was ordered by the commission to never drink again.

Whitman was later charged and tried in the court for this offense and was obviously absolved as he was reelected for another term the following year.

One the same date, Officer Frank McDade, Gordon McDade, and Harry Lee were allegedly drunk on duty and the council asked for a hearing (*Miami Metropolis*/News, 4/23/1915).

In 1914, an MPD officer named W. H. Morris was arrested for unnecessary force during an arrest of a black male. He was said to have hit the citizen in the head with his pistol while trying to collect some overdue sanitary violation fine (*Miami News*, 7/1914).

In June 1915, William J. Whitman was reelected chief of police, fending off Raymond Dillon, Elmer Hodge, J. I. Wilson, and Ewd R. Lowe (*Miami News*, 6/1915).

In April 1915, Mayor Watson reinstated three police officers who had been suspended for being drunk on duty. He was quoted in the *Miami Metropolis* of April 23, 1915, "that they were good, hardworking officers who only were drunk" (*Miami Metropolis*/News, 4/1915).

It was in this same month that Broward County was created from portions of Palm Beach and Dade counties.

The local paper (the *Metropolis*) reported in May 1915 "that the police officer directing traffic in the middle of Miami's busiest intersection, Avenue D and 12th Street [now named Flagler Street and Miami Avenue] was provided with a huge umbrella to shade himself from the sun while managing the traffic during the hot daylight hours. He was also supplied with ample amounts of iced lemonade to help him keep his cool while handling this vexing assignment" (*Miami Metropolis*/News, 5/1915).

A fact published in the *Miami Metropolis* newspaper on February 19, 1915, concerns the process of appointing the chief of police and stating the number of members of the force at that time. The story is quoted exactly:

> The Chief of Police is elected by the people, while members of the force are appointed by the Mayor with the consent of the City Council or by the City Council. At present, the force includes a captain, two sergeants and fourteen policemen, two of whom are plain clothes men. (*Miami Metropolis*/News, 2/19/1915)

It was noted earlier in Chief Whitman's term that Gordon R. McDade was a lieutenant on the force.

In June 1915, Lieutenant McDade was forced to resign by Mayor Watson for conduct unbecoming an officer as a result of displaying his weapon while drunk and disorderly on a train in Key West while off-duty. His position was filled by new Lieutenant J. H. Nepper (*Miami Metropolis*/News, 6/5/1914).

MPD NEWS BLOGS—1915

From Miami newspapers:

Chief Whitman and Mayor Watson meet to plan adding patrol boats to MPD (*Miami Herald*, 2/2/1915).

It was noted that the eighteen officers on MPD are now on an eight-hour day—seven days a week (*Miami Herald*, 4/15/1915).

Ashley trial moved to Miami after hung jury in Palm Beach (*Miami News*, 4/9/15).

Chief Whitman has an officer meeting each arriving train from up north to pick up "suspicious" persons (City of Miami publications).

J. D. Dorman was also moved up to the lieutenant ranking (*Miami Metropolis*/News, 12/1915).

Broward County was established from parts of Palm Beach and Dade counties (*Miami Metropolis*/News, 4/30/1915).

FIRST MIAMI OFFICER SLAIN

June 2, 1915, became a sad day for the Miami Police Department. The first City of Miami policeman was killed in the line of duty. Officer John R. Riblet, thirty-one, a native of Paulding Village, Ohio, died in a shootout with Bob Ashley, a member of the notorious Ashley Gang who were trying to free his brother, John Ashley, from jail. Riblet was the first of many Miami officers who have been killed in the *line of duty* (MPD records).

THE ASHLEY GANG

In 1904, Julius (Joe), and his wife, Dudis (Ma) Ashley, moved their brood of children from Fort Myers to the Stuart area to work on the building of the Florida East Coast railroad. The father settled the family into a home in a rural area called Gomez, near Hobe Sound, in what was then Palm Beach County. The children were boys named Bill, Ed, Frank, Bob, John, and daughters Daisy, Mary Mobley, and one other. Son John Ashley's mistress was Laura Upthegrove, the so-called Queen of the Everglades, a very large woman who usually carried a .38 pistol on her hip.

The family's criminal activities first came to public light in 1911. John Ashley, then twenty-three, known as "The Swamp Bandit," embarked on a hunt for otter hides in the wild swamps of the area together with his trapping partner, Desoto Tiger, son of Tom Tiger, a prominent leader of the Seminole Nation. When John returned from the swamps with a large load of otter skins, there was no sign of Desoto Tiger. John then took the eighty-four hides to Miami and sold them for $1,200 at Girtman Bros. store, operated by the Girtman family who had been doing business with the Ashleys for several years. A few days later on December 29, 1911, a dredging machine, digging a canal from Lake Okeechobee to the Atlantic, unearthed the body of Desoto Tiger. Another Seminole,

Jimmy Gopher, advised Palm Beach Sheriff George Baker that John Ashley was the last man seen with Desoto Tiger.

John Ashley was arrested for Tiger's murder, and his first trial in Palm Beach County resulted in a hung jury. When Ashley heard that the Palm Beach state attorney was changing the trial venue to Dade County, a less-friendly jurisdiction, John broke free over a chain-link fence while being transferred from the city to the county jail and became a fugitive. He traveled across the country to Seattle, Washington, and was not heard from for two years, until, homesick, he turned himself in to Sheriff George Baker in Palm Beach in 1914, but soon escaped again.

On February 1, 1915, five of the gang was suspected of robbing the Palm Beach Limited, a Florida East Coast train, in the Fort Piece area. The gang robbed the male passengers, but an alert porter quickly shut a train car door that prevented the gang from gaining the baggage car's stash of cash and valuables. This crime, and the following Stuart robbery, was highlighted in the *New York Times*, causing quite a stir.

On February 23, 1915, the gang robbed the First Bank of Stuart. During the Stuart bank robbery, which netted them $4,300, they again missed a larger amount of money when they could not open a locked cash box. During the bank robbery escape, John Ashley was accidentally shot in the cheek by an accomplice, Kid Lowe, causing John to lose his sight in one eye. His eye was later replaced with a glass one, requiring him to wear a black eye patch the remainder of his short life.

He was soon apprehended while seeking treatment for his wound and was transferred to the custody of Dade sheriff Hardie in Miami to stand trial on the Tiger murder. His first trial in Miami resulted in a conviction and a death sentence. This case was quickly reversed, and a second trial was planned.

The Ashley Gang began planning to spring John from the Dade County jail. His impatient brother Robert went to Miami on the night of June 2, 1915, along with two confederates. The following morning, Robert Ashley killed Dade County Deputy Wilbur Hendrickson and Miami Officer John R. Riblet and was himself fatally shot by Officer Riblet before the officer died. Specific details of this tragic event will be presented in Riblet's story that will follow.

In November 1915, John Ashley went on trial in Miami, represented by the famous Florida jurist Alto Adams (who later headed up Florida's supreme court). The murder charge in the Tiger case was dropped amid claims that the Ashley Gang had threatened to "shoot up the town" if he was convicted. Adams proposed a guilty plea in the bank robbery case in exchange for dropping the murder charge. Ashley was then transferred back to Palm Beach County and pled guilty to the Stuart bank robbery. He was sentenced to seventeen years in Raiford State Prison.

In February 1918, Ashley escaped from a prison road chain gang and resumed his life of crime. The advent of prohibition provided another source of revenue to the gang who set up a prohibited liquor importation scheme between the West End in Bimini and the Palm Beach area. They also engaged in piracy, hijacking the shipments of other bootleggers on the high seas or when the illegal goods landed in Florida. In between, they continued their bank robbery activities. It has been said that as they robbed banks in Fort Meade, Avon Park, Boynton Beach, and other small Florida towns, they would simply state on entering the banks, "Ashley's here," and the tellers would quickly fill up their bags even without the need of showing the gang's weapons. In 1920, Sheriff George Baker of Palm Beach County was replaced as sheriff by his son, Bob Baker, who continued the pursuit.

In June 1921, John was arrested in Wachula, Florida, while delivering a load of liquor and was sent back to Raiford prison. In addition, he was also held on federal charges of AWOL from the U.S. Navy, where he briefly served on the USS *Maryland* while on the lam from Florida authorities. In October 1921, Ashley brothers Ed and Frank disappeared, presumably at sea, while on a rum-running enterprise to the Bahamas in rough weather. John Ashley believed the deaths were the work of three rival gangsters, who themselves disappeared mysteriously at sea shortly after the brothers' disappearance. It was rumored that the Ashleys were responsible. With John Ashley absent, and the brothers missing, the gang was taken over by Hanford Mobley, John's young nephew, son of Ashley daughter Mary.

In September 1923, the gang, with John Ashley back in charge after again escaping, robbed the same Stuart bank, gathering a large haul of cash and securities, with Mobley dressing as a woman. Sheriff Bob Baker of Palm Beach County tracked them to Plant City and arrested Mobley and Clarence Middletown. He jailed them in Fort Lauderdale this time to prevent another escape from the friendly atmosphere that prevailed in Palm Beach. This tactic proved of no avail as Mobley and Middletown escaped with the assistance of an inept jailor. Another gang member also escaped from a road gang along with Ray (Shorty) Lynn, who then joined up with the Ashley gang.

On September 12, 1924, a blustery day, the gang robbed the Bank of Pompano at NE First Street and First Avenue, driving away with a haul of $23,000. Just before closing, Cashier C. H. Cates and teller T. H. Myers were on duty in the bank. Earlier in the day, John Ashley and his gang hired a taxicab, tied up Wesley Powell, the black cab driver, to a tree in Deerfield, took his cab, and told him they were on the way to Pompano to rob the bank. They told Powell to take a good look at them so he could tell Sheriff Bob Baker who they were and dare him to come after them. During this robbery, Shorty Lynn and Clearance Middleton were armed with pistols while John Ashley stood in the doorway with a rifle. John left a bullet with the tellers advising them to give it to Sheriff Bob Baker as it will be similar to the one they will pump into the sheriff if he tries to apprehend them. When leaving in the stolen taxi, Ashley leaned out the car window while holding up a sheet with the loot and shouted to E. E. "Gene" Hardy, who owned a garage on the corner of South Dixie Highway and knew the Ashleys, "We got it all this time, Gene."

An irate Sheriff Bob Baker sent a posse, led by his cousin Deputy Fred Baker, to a camp, still two miles south of the Ashley homestead. A barking dog alerted the gang to the posse's arrival and a shootout followed. Joe (Pa) Ashley was immediately shot dead in a tent on the premises. Gang member Albert Miller was shot but escaped and was recaptured the following day. Laura Upthegrove, John's mistress, was wounded and captured. John hid in the woods armed with a rifle. When he heard a noise near him, he shot into the trees and Deputy Fred Baker fell dead. The posse continued the hunt for many days and ended up burning down both the Ashley home and the adjoining home of Mobley Hanford as well as a grocery store owned by gang member Miller.

On November 1, 1924, John Ashley, seeking revenge for his father's death, gathered his gang lieutenants with the intention of heading for Jacksonville to sister Daisy Ashley's house to plan a "hit" on Sheriff Baker on the upcoming night of Baker's reelection as sheriff. The sheriff received a tip from one familiar with the gang, believed to be George Meriot (according to O. B. Padgett), that the gang was heading north to Jacksonville to Ashley sister Daisy's home.

Sheriff Baker dispatched three of his deputies—Elmer Padgett, Henry Stubbs, and L. B. Thomas—to meet up with the sheriff of St. Lucie County, J. R. Merritt, and two of his deputies, O. E. (Three Finger) Wiggins and Chief Deputy Smith, at the Sebastian Inlet bridge on Dixie

Highway in St. Lucie County, sixty miles north of Stuart. The group of law officers placed a chain across the bridge with a lantern and soon a car containing two innocent bystanders came upon the chain and stopped. While questioning the two men, the black Ford touring car carrying the gang came along. The deputies hid while the car came to a stop at the chain and then surrounded the car, ordering the four bandits to get out. The four were then handcuffed, three together and John separately. Sheriff Merritt then asked the two bystanders to drive him across the bridge so he could reach his hidden police car that he could use to transport the prisoners to jail. While momentarily gone, John Ashley supposedly made a move to retrieve a gun. He was shot dead, most likely by the big six-foot-four-inch Chief Deputy Padgett. The other gang members, Mobley, Middletown, and Ray (Shorty) Lynn, were then shot dead by the other deputies, all with twelve-gauge shotguns.

Sheriff Merritt recovered a Winchester rifle that Ashley was carrying in the car to keep as a souvenir. One of the Palm Beach deputies plucked the glass eye out of John Ashley and turned it over to Sheriff Bob Baker of Palm Beach. Baker kept the eye for a period of time, intending to wear it as a watch charm, but Laura Upthegrove threatened Baker with death, so Baker returned it before the funeral. The sheriff said he knew he would have to kill her over the eye and it wasn't worth it.

It has long been discussed that the gang was killed while handcuffed. The deputies disputed this and a coroner's jury ruled that the marks on their wrists were caused by the medical examiner rather than handcuffs. The innocent bystanders, T. R. Miller and S. O. Davis, stated that when they drove across the bridge to return Sheriff Merritt to his car, the four men were handcuffed. However, the coroner's jury verdict a few days later was that these killings were cases of justifiable homicide.

Years later, one of the deputies who was at the bridge, Three Finger Wiggins, confessed to Ada Coats Williams, a teacher and author, the identity of the deputy who actually fired the shot that killed John Ashley. Williams had promised not to tell the story until the last deputy on the scene was dead. That same year (1936), Wiggins died in a Bartow rest home and Williams went on to write a book, *Florida's Ashley Gang*. The best guess is that Deputy Elmer Padgett fired the shot that killed John Ashley, although Padgett has denied that he fired a shotgun, stating that he was armed only with his Colt revolver. Padgett was also on the raid that killed Pa Ashley, and John Ashley had sworn to visit the Palm Beach courthouse with the intention of killing Padgett and another deputy.

Ironically, Padgett, a year later, became the chief of police of Stuart for two years but was arrested, tried, and convicted of murder in an unrelated case and served almost a decade behind bars in the Florida's prison system.

That bloody event at the bridge just about concluded the criminal activities of the Ashley Gang. The only surviving brother, Billy, went on to live a fairly quiet life although he was caught in later years operating a moonshine still, but did not resist arrest. Laura Upthegrove, John's mistress, committed suicide by drinking a glass of Lysol two years later. Sister Daisy also died at her own hand. Ashley descendents to this day claim that John Ashley and his gang were murdered by the deputies on the Sebastian bridge that night in November 1924. Frontier justice, some call it. The bridge has since been replaced by a concrete structure in a different location. In the Mariner Sands Country Club in Stuart, in the Ashley Family Cemetery, one can still observe the grave markers of John Ashley, Ray Lynn, and Hanford Mobley. The body of Middletown, described as a product of the Chicago underworld, was claimed by relatives.

The citizens of Palm Beach county and surrounding areas breathed a sigh of relief. This reign of terror by the Ashley gang prompted numerous articles and discussions over the years, particularly in the Stuart area. A restaurant in Stuart, said to be the site of the First Bank of Stuart (some said it was across the street), was sort of a shrine to the gang for many years but recently closed its doors (November 2009) for lack of customers. It also has been said that the Ashleys hid stashes of money in the wilds around Stuart, but to this day, none of the money has surfaced. (The area of Stuart that the Ashleys roamed became Martin County in 1925.) (*Miami News* and *Herald*—several articles, *Palm Beach Post*, *Evening Independent*—St. Petersburg, *St. Petersburg Times*, *Sarasota Herald Tribune*, *Lakeland Ledger*, *Milwaukee Journal*, and *Florida's Ashley Gang*, Ada Williams, 1936.)

OFFICER JOHN R. RIBLET KILLED—LINE OF DUTY

The infamous Ashley Gang from the Stuart area plan to free their gang leader John Ashley from the Dade County jail where he was being held for the Tiger murder charge earlier was leaked to authorities. The Dade County lawmen had received word and prepared with extra guards and double locks. On June 2, 1915, John Ashley's brother Bob Ashley, then twenty-three, traveled to Miami, allegedly with two confederates, and knocked on the door of Dade County jailer Wilbur Hendrickson, who lived with his young wife and nine-year-old son, in a home adjacent to the county jail on what is now known as Flagler Street. When Deputy Hendrickson opened the door, Bob Ashley shot and killed him and took the jail keys. Hendrickson's wife, Marion, attempted to shoot back at Bob Ashley but her gun jammed. In the ensuing confusion, Bob Ashley dropped the jail keys and ran to a nearby garage but was unable to locate his getaway car. He then ran out onto the road and hijacked a ride with a truck driver, T. H. Duckett, and headed down the street. Duckett intentionally stalled the truck, which allowed an on-duty Miami police officer, John R. Riblet, who had been sitting in front of the city hall near the jail with Desk Sergeant Edwin V. Stephens, time to commandeer a passing auto driven by Will Flowers and catch up with the hijacked truck on Avenue L and Eighth Street (which is near the current intersection of NW Fifth Street and Seventh Avenue). Both Bob Ashley and Officer Riblet emerged from their vehicles and exchanged shots at close range. Riblet was stuck in the head with a bullet but was still able to fire off two rounds that struck Ashley. Sergeant Stephens did not fire any shots. Sheriff Hardie, who lived around the corner on D Avenue (later changed to Miami Avenue) and others, rushed the three wounded men to Jackson Memorial Hospital, but all three soon died. The deaths of Officer John Riblet and Deputy Wilbur Hendrickson during this attempted jail break were the first Miami PD officer and the third Dade County sheriff's officer to die in the line of duty.

Interesting facts of Officer John R. Riblet's life have recently been located, including that his grandfather also died violently in another combat. At the time of his death in 1915, Officer John Riblet, thirty-one, a slim five-foot-eight-inch native of Paulding Village, Ohio, was married to Madge Riblet. He was also survived by his son, Merrell; his parents, David and Maggie A. Riblet; a younger brother, Ralph; and two sisters, Ida Mae and Nettie V. The date that John Riblet joined the Miami Police Department is not exactly known, but presumed to be in 1914. Riblet and family were listed as living on Seventh Street in 1913. His pay while an MPD officer was $25 monthly.

As a young man, Riblet joined the army in 1902 for a brief stay, but was discharged after he left his post in Texas for some unexplained reason. His family believes he transferred to the navy for a tour of duty at that time. John Riblet and wife, Madge (Bell) Riblet, a Ft. Pierce native, had only that one child, Merrell Edward. John's younger brother Ralph never strayed from Ohio nor ever married. One of his sisters, Ida Mae, married a Perry Castleman of Ohio and had a son by the same name, both of them dying in a boat accident. The other sister, Nettie Viola (Riblet) Perl, had three sons, Richard, Willard, and Robert, as well as one daughter, Margaret. No further family records were located.

The child, Merrell Edward Riblet, was born in Miami, Florida, about 1912, to John and Madge Riblet (b. 1884) according to the 1920 U.S. Census, with the father listed as being from Ohio. Merrell died in 1928 of blood poisoning after accidentally shooting himself in the foot while hunting. Also listed in the 1920 census, at the home of Madge Riblet, 99 Northport Drive, Miami, were three boarders (the Stanton family). The street address on the census form was prior to Miami changing the street names in 1921. Madge Riblet, then thirty-six, was listed as being born in Florida, the head of the household, occupation <u>widow</u>, and her father being from Illinois. In the local Miami census of 1935, Madge was listed as living at 5129 NW Seventeenth Avenue, Miami, with a William and Clare Tubbs, her sister.

A city census in 1945 showed Madge, listed as a housewife, as living at 3430 NW Twenty-second Avenue (Allapattah section), Miami, with her sister Clare (or Clara) and husband, William Tubbs. Clara died in Miami in 1963. Clara's daughter, Mae (Tubbs) Heirs, lived in Miami until her death in the last decade.

As locating John Riblet data was quite difficult, the authors will present the source for historical purposes. There was scant information written about this hero police officer over the years, but thanks to the computer age, some information has now been located. The 1920 U.S. Census search located Merrell Riblet as the only Riblet born in Miami prior to 1920. That info led to Madge and her sister, Clara, and Clara's spouse, William S. Tubbs, b. about 1883 (from Connecticut), listed as living in Fort Pierce with Clara, thirty-three years old (b. 1887). A 1900 Census first-name search of Madge in Fort Pierce found Madge and Clara in the same family group. A Madge E. Bell, eighteen, was listed, as well as a Clara, fourteen. James E. Bell, forty-six, his wife, Emily A., thirty-eight, and four younger children—Harry, eleven; Frank, nine; Annie, five; and Harriet, one.

The 1910 U.S. Census listed Clara with William in Fort Pierce and Madge, unmarried, still with the James E. Bell family in Fort Pierce.

A Florida Death Index listed Madge Emily Riblet as passing away in Miami in 1949.

John Riblet was the son of David M. Riblet, (1861-1934), a lifelong Ohioan married to Maggie A. David, who was only one year old when his father (John's grandfather) joined the Union Army during the civil war in 1862. Two years later, David was orphaned as John Riblet (1836-1864) was killed in action with Company I, 100th Infantry, in the battle of Utoy Creek near Atlantic during Sherman's march to the sea. Daniel's mother remarried an A. L. Hussey, who raised young David in Hanover, Ohio. The ancestors of John Riblet, Miami officer, were as follows:

Father:	David Riblet, 1861-1934
Grandfather:	John Riblet, 1836-1864
Great-Grand Fth	Henry Riblet, 1792-1868
Great-Great	Abraham Riblet, 1771-1812
Great-Gt-Gt	John Bartholomew Riblet, 1731-1795 (emigrated from Germany in 1737)

Dade County sheriff's deputy, Wilbur W. Hendrickson, forty-five, was the other lawman killed by Bob Ashley that night in the attempt to facilitate the escape. Hendrickson lived next to the jail, on what was then known as Twelfth Street. His wife, Marion Ona (Platt) Hendrickson, thirty-two, survived him, as well as a son, Wilbur W. Jr., nine.

Deputy Hendrickson, an Ohio native, was the son of Simeon and Clara Hendrickson of Fairport, Ohio. Mrs. Marion Hendrickson passed away near Bullard, Georgia, in 1953. (3, 13, 21, and 7, 6/3/1915) (#2, #3, #5, #7, #8, #14, 15, 16, 18, 21, 6/1915) (MPD records, Ancestry.com, U.S. Census Reports, *Miami News* and *Miami Herald*—several articles, *Palm Beach Post*, St. Petersburg's *Evening Independent, Sarasota Herald Tribune, Desoto County (Fl) News,* all in 6/1915)

On the same day that Riblet's murder was published, in Miami, another story in the *Metropolis* documented the sensational Boggs case murder that took place in November 1914. Two burglars were tried and convicted of the horrible crime (*Miami Metropolis*/News, 6/3/1915).

Chief Whitman asked for the resignation of Officer D. Q. Willis for tampering with a crime witness. It was noted that there were 572 applications on file to fill this position.

A young resident of Miami since 1901, Leslie Quigg announced his candidacy for sheriff of Dade County. He was defeated in the 1917 election. He later served three times as Miami PD chief of police (*Miami Metropolis*, 3/22/1916).

Four men announced their intention to run for the job of chief of police (*Miami Metropolis*/News, 4/20/1917).

THE EDDIE KINSEY MURDER

In 1917, Lieutenant William C. Shields, a seven-year veteran of MPD and the second in command, was arrested in connection with the homicide of Eddie Kinsey, a young informer for the department. Kinsey had been providing information to officers on locations where illegal liquor was being sold. It was alleged that Shields and two others beat Kinsey, shot him, and tossed his body into the river on October 1916.

The case was investigated by Officer W. B. Jones on special assignment and the County Attorney's Office. Lieutenant Shields resigned prior to the trial. The case was dismissed at an initial hearing due to Shields having an alibi backed up by several others. Officer Jones returned to his downtown beat after the investigation.

Shields had resigned prior to the Kinsey trial because of his involvement in a fight with other Miami officers over an unrelated incident.

MPD officers mentioned as witnesses in this case were F. M. McDade, M. C. Hart, Lieutenant H. B. Doane, Otis Bunnell, John Campbell, William B. Curry, H. L. Pinder, E. J. Starling, and Edward McDade (MPD records, *Miami Metropolis*/News, 2/19, 2/20, and 4/20, 1917).

LIFE SAVED BY A TOBACCO CAN

A gunfight in downtown Miami between Officer Edward Rowe and an offender on May 4, 1917, resulted in the death of the bad guy. Rowe was struck in the chest by a bullet, but a can of tobacco in his shirt pocket deflected the slug and saved his life. The offender was not as lucky.

Officer Rowe left the department shortly after that close call and became a real estate broker (*Miami Metropolis*/News, 5/4/1917).

ODD FELLOWS HALL TORCHED

The hall utilized by the black residents of Miami for many social and community events was bombed at 2:00 AM, on a Sunday morning in July 1917. The police stated that the crime was precipitated by the issue of blacks driving autos in the Miami, an act fought fiercely by white chauffeur (taxi) drivers. Miami Police Lieutenant William Curry had passed by the building just prior to the explosion that caused considerable damage. The black community demanded action from the authorities.

The white drivers had the practice of stopping cars driven by blacks (most of them chauffeuring rich northern visitors), demanding that the owners hire a (white) driver while in Miami.

Finally, the police and community leaders put a halt to this discriminating practice after a local black dentist, Dr. William Scott, and a local funeral director purchased their own car and were constantly harassed by the white drivers. In early July, Lieutenant Curry of MPD arrested five white men for harassing Dr. Scott. They were jailed, later fined, and sentenced to suspended jail sentences, which brought these unlawful actions to a halt (*Miami Metropolis*/News, 7/7, 7/8, and 7/17, 1917).

DEVELOPING A POLICING SYSTEM

In 1917, the department numbered twenty officers and a new chief, Raymond F. Dillon, thirty-four, was elected and served from November 1917 to August 1921. His predecessor, Chief Whitman, did not run for reelection. Dillon was the last elected chief of police in Miami. Chief Dillon oversaw the establishment of eighteen police call boxes and the hiring of the first policewoman, Mrs. Ida Fisher, who was hired to work with delinquent young girls.

The Miami PD also instituted the Bertillon system of fingerprinting and added a new Ford, the department's first automobile, to their list of "modern" equipment (MPD records, City of Miami publications, *Miami Metropolis*/News, 7/1917).

Archduke Ferdinand of Austria was shot dead on June 28, 1914, in Sarajevo. The assassination set off World War I, the war to end all wars.

1917-18 ACTIONS

Chief Whitman resigned three months prior to his elected term expiration. A temporary replacement was Lieutenant William B. Curry, a twelve-year MPD veteran, appointed by Mayor Parker Henderson to fill the remainder of Whitman's term. Ray Dillon, recently elected in June, will assume the chief's job on November 1 (*Miami Metropolis/* News, 7/25/1917).

Whitman had been under much criticism due to the inability to solve the Kinsey murder and the bombing of the Odd Fellows Hall.

"Lieutenant William B. Curry assumes the office and duties of the chief of police this morning, succeeding William J. Whitman, who resigned last week after having been subjected to a long period of public criticism because of the lack of efficiency in the police department under his direction" (*Miami Metropolis/*News, 8/1/1917).

Officer C. E. Brogdon of the Miami Beach police department paid a $10 fine in city court for speeding. The ticket was issued by a City of Miami officer. The Miami Beach officer warned the judge in court that he better watch his speedometer while riding in the vicinity of Miami Beach (*Miami Metropolis/*News, 8/21/1917).

Chief Curry furloughed three police officers to reduce expenses. Night beatman Singleterry and Williams were let go as was Officer James W. Northrup, who worked the Avenue D bridge. Curry said that Northrup has not made one arrest during the several months he was assigned at the bridge post and that paying him $90 a month were a needless expense (*Miami Metropolis/*News, 8/31/1917).

Chief Ray Dillon became chief on the first of November. He immediately assigned one police officer to each school in the city. Two days later, Chief Dillon fired Lieutenant Curry who had been acting chief for three months. He also fired Desk Sergeant C. A. Lindstrom, replacing him with Lieutenant H. L. Pinder, and Sergeant George T. Warner replaced Lindstrom. The chief also promoted F. A. Roberts to motor sergeant. The following regular police officers were retained: Night Sergeant Harley (Harlan) B. Doane, plainclothes officer J. W. Bishop, Motor Officer Roberts, and patrolmen R. H. Starling, J. S. Phillips, Finch Cochran, Alex Gingras, D. A. Shields, E. J. Starling, W. B. Waters, William Meredith, Arnold Albury, W. B. Jones, Leon Sawyer,

D. L. King, W. H. Noris, and J. W. Northrup (*Miami Metropolis*/News, 11/2/1917).

A wag reported in a *Miami News* column that "a title for an official song for the police department has been suggested; You may be deaf tonight but you will get your hearing in the morning" (*Miami News*, 4/30/1917).

Chief Whitman took a several-month leave of absence in late 1917, resulting in the appointment of Lieutenant Curry as acting chief of police. A local news editorial remarked on what action Curry was taking.

> Several improvements have been made in the Miami Police Department since Chief Curry took office a few weeks ago. One of these has been the renovating of the headquarters office in the city hall. New furniture and fixtures have been installed, making it much more business like appearing place.
>
> The Chief is working steadily on the establishment here of the fingerprint system of cataloging criminals. Sergeant Lindstrom has been studying the plan assiduously and has now qualified as a first class finger print man. (*Miami Metropolis*/ News, 8/25/1917)

Officer Singleterry was walking his beat in the back alleys of downtown when he heard what appeared to be a gambling game coming from the rear of Davis' Café. He climbed to the roof and observed through a ransom a dice game in progress. He summoned help from Officer Starling and Pinder, and the three officers arrested six patrons for gambling. All were fined in city court the following morning (*Miami Metropolis*/News, 1/1/1918).

A subject was arrested when his fingerprints matched a wanted person from another state. The subject's prints were sent to New York City where Gotham cops matched the prints to a wanted felon who had a long record in their jurisdiction (*Miami News*, 1/14/1920).

Miami motorcycle officer George Miller was hospitalized as a result of a crash on Twelfth Street when his motor skidded on the street car tracks. Miller was severely cut on the face and head (*Miami News*, 1/15/1920).

Sergeant John S. Phillips shot himself in the foot while cleaning his .25-caliber automatic. The bullet passed through his foot and shoe but did not strike a bone. He is expected to recover quickly.

Last summer, Phillips was accidentally hit on the head by a baseball bat while watching a game at Royal Palm Park. Prior to that incident, Phillips, while fighting a fire at the Florida Conservatory of Music, a ladder fell and struck him on the thumb (*Miami Metropolis*/News, 1/17/1920).

ROLL CALL—EARLY OFFICERS

A review of the old newspapers and other sources mentioned the following men who served as Miami police officers from 1896 to 1921. Others also served.

Bates, Frazier J. b. 1858, Southern Carolina
Bunnell, Alvus A., permanent officer in December 1905
Carroll, Albert, appointed December 1905 as unpaid special
Caswell, Thomas, 1910 census and on-the-job in July 1911
Coleman, John F., November 1905-May 1906
Cooley, L. A., appointed December 1905 as unpaid special
Curry, William B., on-the-job, November 1907; acting chief, 1917
DeBarry, W., appointed in January 1907
English, Joseph M., late 1905 to 1911
Flanagan, Robert, marshal, November 1900-October 1905
Ferguson, Charles Robert, elected chief in 1911-13
Flury, V., April 1906 as an unpaid officer at the docks
Freeman, W. R., on-the-job in 1907, reappointed in 1911
Frohock, John, marshal, October 1899-November 1900
Gringas, Alex, on-the-job in May 1912
Gingras, Lewis, appointed as an MPD officer in 1911
Girtman, John, acting marshal, June-October 1899
Gray, Young G., first marshal of Miami in 1896
Griffing, Arthur, on-the-job in November 1907
Godman, J. D., appointed as a special officer in 1905
Grant, J. W., appointed special officer in 1905
Hardee, J. J., appointed in January 1908 for the holidays
Hardee, Rufus James, 1876-1969, appointed 1905-1911
Hardee, Frank B., elected chief, July1905 to 1911
Hodge, Elmer, on-the-job in 1915
Hoff, Frank, appointed as an MPD officer in 1911
Marsh, H. H., appointed in January 1908 for the holidays

McCann, M. T., appointed November 1913 to 1915

McDade, E. H., appointed as an MPD officer in 1911

McDade, Gordon R., 1911-1917 as lieutenant

McGriff, R. C., appointed December 1905 as unpaid special

McNeil, L. L., appointed December 1905 as unpaid special

Morris, W. H., on-the-job in 1914

O'Neal, J. R., appointed in 1905-1911

Pfender, F. H., appointed in January 1908 for the holidays

Phillips, Paul G., on-the-job, 1911; later elected police judge

Pierson, C. C., appointed in December 1905

Riblet, John R., on-the-job, 1914, killed in June 1915

Richardson, J. C., appointed in 1911

Roberts, G. W., appointed November 1913

Rogers, J. W., appointed in December 1905, Royal Palm Hotel

Russell, Edward D., appointed May 1911

Sheppard, Charles, on-the-job 1910

Sistrunk, Earnest, Sr. (Ed), on "beat" schedule May 1907

Smith, Charles H., appointed December 1905

Stalling, R., appointed November 1913

Stevens, E. V., on-the-job May 1907; first desk sergeant, 1915

Tucker, J. C., on-the-job November 1907

Umstead, L. W., appointed May 1906

Whitman, William J., appointed in 1911; chief, 1913-1917

ROARING TWENTIES

BIG CHANGES IN CITY GOVERNMENT

In mid-1921, Miami's city government switched to a commissioner-manager form of government, bringing sweeping changes to the police department. The chief and the new public safety director would be appointed by the city manager, and police officers would fall under civil service guidelines. Miami's first city manager was Col. Charles Coe, an outsider with military experience. Coe appointed a local leader as public safety director. On August 15, Coe appointed another local man, Howard Leslie Quigg, thirty-three, known as H. Leslie Quigg, as the new chief of police despite the fact that Quigg did not apply for the position.

Chief Quigg was extremely popular, having had a reputation as an athlete, but had absolutely no police experience. Quigg ran unsuccessfully for Dade County sheriff in 1917. He had been a grocer and a farmer. However, before his first tenure as chief ended, Miami's modern police force grew from forty to over two hundred members in only five years.

Quigg was born in Orange County, Florida, moved to Miami in 1901, and died at the age of ninety-two in Taylor County, Florida. He became a legend in the Miami during his long association with local law enforcement as well as his service as a city commissioner in the 1940s and as dock master at Miami's Dinner Key yacht basin in the 1950s and '60s. Quigg was a boxer and marathon runner in his youth and a ventriloquist and a renowned hypnotist in later years. He was at one time the lightweight boxing champ of Florida.

Beginning December 13, 1921, long-awaited civil service guidelines were enforced, which required all policemen to be between the ages of twenty-five and forty-five, pass a physical and written exam, be at least 5'9" tall, and serve three months' probation. The department was then reorganized into four divisions: traffic, detectives, vice squad, and motorcycle corps.

Chief Quigg (1889-1980) mastered the art of public relations. He created a special force of school policemen to protect the city's children and spoke out forcefully for gun control. He also created a courtesy campaign that improved relationships between the police and the public. During this same period, Miami annexed the sections of Coconut Grove, Lemon City, Buena Vista, Allapattah, Little River, and Silver Bluff, increasing the city from thirteen to fifty square miles. In a statistical report at that time, it was noted that MPD had escorted one hundred undesirables out of town.

Quigg ran into extreme legal difficulties in later years, was arrested, cleared, fired, and later rehired. He served as chief of police during three separate periods, extending into the 1940s, then served as a city commissioner and later as dock master. Additional stories on Quigg are posted in further stories in this book.

New rules for the department were issued by the city manager and Chief Quigg shortly after the new regime took office.

Strict military order will be observed hereafter according to the new orders issued. The orders include instructions to obey commanders without question, be courteous to the citizens, and to make arrests in an unobtrusive manner as possible.

The desk sergeant will inspect the officers daily to see that they are neat and clean and that their firearms are in working order. Officers are to carry themselves in a military manner with their hat in proper position. Use of tobacco or alcohol while on duty shall not be permitted and that excessive use of alcohol, on or off duty, will result in termination. Each officer will be held accountable for the good order of their beat or district. Loud and profane talking by police officers will not be tolerated.

These constitute the first ten of the regulations issued for the conduct of the police department (MPD records, *Miami News* and *Miami Herald*, 1921).

It was noted that Detective Sergeant Hardy Bryan was promoted to lieutenant by Chief Quigg, replacing F. A. Roberts who was requested to resign for the good of the services. Bryan, from Suwannee County, Florida, came to Miami ten years ago and joined the MPD two years ago. He was promoted to sergeant ten months ago.

Lieutenant Hardy served many years with the Miami police and was later joined by his son by the same name, providing a Hardy Bryan on the force for over fifty years (Personal knowledge—author and *Miami News*, 10/5/1921).

HOBO EXPRESS

For many years, both Miami and Fort Lauderdale justice authorities maintained a practice of running drunks and vagrants out of town as to not "spoil" the cities for the tourists. The paddy wagons would load up at the station after morning court with whatever "bums" received a suspended sentence from the city judges. The first leg of the run would be to the Broward County line where the "bums" would be transferred to Broward vans and shuttled all the way up to the Martin County line where they would be instructed to head north. This practice continued for years even as the Martin County sheriff complained to his southern neighbors and the governor of Florida.

As a rookie, the author would occasionally ride with a much-older officer in the paddy wagon and heard many stories of how the downtown merchants would complain about the bums on the street, causing the duty captain to instruct the paddy wagon crew to sweep through downtown picking up down-and-outs on Flagler Street. The wagon, once it was filled with ten or twelve derelicts, would then be driven up to the Broward County line in Ojis where their cargo was dumped out.

In later years when the hobo express of early days was now frowned upon, the wagon would make their collection and take the unfortunate group over the Rickenbacker Causeway to the Miami Beach city limits and dropped off. Miami Beach PD caught on to this practice and would make reverse runs back over the causeway to drop off the same men at the NE Fourteenth Street exit. It would not be unusual for some of the bums to experience several rides across the bay during the same day (Personal knowledge—author).

OFFICER CROFF RUN OVER

Officer Frank Angelo Croff, a twenty-eight-year-old rookie motorcycle officer, was struck and killed by a drunk driver on May 22, 1921. Croff, riding alongside Officer Mel Tibbitts, was riding south on NE Second Avenue and Twenty-second Street just after a rainstorm when a speeding Cadillac struck Croff from behind, dragging him for two blocks.

Tibbitts swerved away and struck a telephone pole but was uninjured. The Cadillac then struck a Nash auto head on and came to a stop in front of MPD Officer Joe Byrd's home. Tibbitts, Byrd, and several bystanders lifted the car off Croff, who died as the men pulled him out. The driver, William McCarthy, was charged with second-degree murder, later reduced to manslaughter. There was no record found of the disposition of the case.

Croff, born in Italy in 1893, had immigrated to America in 1904 and joined the MPD in 1920. Croff also served in the U.S. Army and was a member of the National Guard at the time of his death. Croff left a wife and one daughter and was buried in the Miami City Cemetery alongside Officer Richard Marler who was killed in the line of duty later in 1921.

Foster Sloan, a former MPD officer, admitted that he was in the car as a passenger that struck Croff. He was initially charged as an accessory before the fact, later changed to a manslaughter charge. McCarthy and Sloan went on trial in August for manslaughter, but the trial outcome could not be located.

The chief of police in this period was Raymond Dillon, who commanded the force of forty officers (Wilbanks, *Forgotten Heroes*, 1996, and *Miami News*, 5/23/21).

Author's Note: Retired MPD Vet Ginger Jones is the granddaughter of Officer Croff.

BATTLING THE BOTTLE

Throughout its history, MPD has devoted a significant portion of their resources to handling the problems associated with alcohol. Initially, the City of Miami resolved, and inserted a clause into the deeds, that there would be no liquor establishments within the city limits, with the exception of the Royal Palm Hotel. The original city limits only encompassed what is now the downtown business area. The Central Negro District was not within the original city area, so many liquor establishments opened in that area less than twenty feet outside Miami. The sheriff had the jurisdiction at that time. As the city expanded, the bars and liquor stores then were the city's responsibility. Arrests by the local force were predominantly alcohol related. In 1913, the legal sale of alcohol was prohibited in Dade County and then nationally (1920-1933).

The problem then became the "blind tigers," illegal liquor bars and sales outlets, as well as bootleg rum running from the Bahamas.

The gangster element that was drawn to the city by the prospect of great fortunes through the illicit traffic in liquor remained after the repeal of prohibition, shifting to gambling and prostitution and to legitimate enterprises such as real estate and the hotel industry. Not surprisingly, Miami acquired a reputation as a "wide open" city, an image far removed from the visions of its founders, but obviously approved by the "power people."

The years did not change the situation much as drunken arrests and related alcohol crimes continued to this day. The city built a stockade on the banks of the Miami River and the "convict" labor was used to build roads and other municipal projects under a system of "renting" out the convict laborers to private operators.

In later years, the city built a large prison/stockade on Milam Dairy Road, which could house several hundred prisoners, mostly incarcerated for alcohol-related offenses. The result was that numerous habitual offenders were serving life in prison on the installment plan, thirty days in, thirty days out. In the 1970s, this facility was turned over to the Dade County authorities.

The state of Florida later instituted the Myers Act, which decriminalized the offense of being plain drunk. Prior to that act, down-and-out drunks needing medical care and protection would "dry" out at the stockade, performing various municipal tasks or picking vegetables for the stockade at south Dade fields. They would also receive needed medical care that would often restore their health prior to being released from custody. When the act became law, the needed social services of the community were not ready to supplant the stockade services. The result was that the homeless drunks then resorted to living in the streets, with virtually no medical availability, often being the target of criminal youths who would rob and assault them for their meager possessions (Personal knowledge—author).

Author's Note: Another law with unintended consequences.

FRIENDLY FIRE DEATH

Rookie MPD officer Richard Roy Marler, thirty-four, was shot and killed accidentally by a Dade County deputy sheriff on November

28, 1921, during a manhunt for an armed robber and suspected killer who was "running amuck" with a shotgun. There was information that the suspect intended to barricade himself in the Deering estate in the south Coconut Grove area of Miami. Sheriff's deputies James Flood and Detective Jack Adams came upon MPD Officer Marler and a black civilian guard, Clarence Porter, and mistook Porter for the dangerous offender. In a "friendly fire" error, Adams fired at Porter and hit Officer Marler. Witnesses later testified that the two sheriff deputies had been drinking and that Marler was standing up in uniform with the spotlight on him when Adams fired.

The case went to the grand jury, but no outcome has been located. Deputy Adams was anguished after the shooting when he realized he has shot Marler, whom he knew from Marler's directing of traffic downtown. Adams left the sheriff's department and became a bondsman. Fifteen years later, Adams committed suicide by shooting himself in the head.

Richard Roy Marler, born January 7, 1887, in Missouri, died November 28, 1921, in Miami, Florida. Richard Marler was the son of Sion and Eliza Jane (Whaley). His siblings were brother, William Marler, born 1882 in Tennessee; sisters Jennie (Marler) Waters, born 1889 in Missouri, Julia, born 1890, and Florenie, born 1898.

The Marler family was from Union, Tennessee (Wilson County), moving to Missouri in the mid-1980s. Father Sion Marler was a salesman. The family later moved back to Wilson County, Tennessee, after all the children were born.

Richard was a locomotive engineer living in Creek County, Oklahoma. He married a Minnie Cruger Jacobs, born in 1889 in Waco, Texas, and had two children, one of whom was Dorothy Lorenza Marler, born November 29, 1908, in Brownsville, Texas. No record has been found of the other child but both were alive in 1917 when Richard stated to draft board that he was supporting a wife and two children under the age of twelve. Dorothy Marler, the daughter, never married.

The wife (first wife), Minnie (Jacobs) Marler, died in 1980 in Oklahoma City. In 1910, the daughter Dorothy, then two years old, was listed as living with her maternal grandparents, the Jacobs, in Brownsville, Texas. Neither the wife, Minnie, nor the other child was listed with Dorothy.

In 1917, Richard was living in Sapulpa, Oklahoma, while working for the railroad as an engineer. Sapulpa is slightly west of Tulsa. There was no record of which spouse he was living with at that time.

In 1920, Richard was listed as living in Missouri City, Texas (Fort Bend County), which is between Houston and Brownsville, Texas. He was listed with his second wife, Clara L. Marler, age twenty. In August 1921, three months before he was shot to death in Miami, he joined the Miami Police Department.

After his death, Clara returned to Oklahoma and was listed as marrying Ernest Handcock in 1934 (U.S. Census reports; Ancestry.com; *Miami News*, 11/1921; Wilbanks, *Forgotten Heroes*, 1996).

By the end of 1925, the MPD had grown to 312 members, a 400 percent increase in one year, to handle the land rush in the South Florida area (MPD records).

CHIEF DENIES MIAMI PD STILL HAS ELECTRIC CHAIR

A grand jury report declared recently (1923) that the MPD was using an electric chair to obtain confessions from criminal suspects. Chief Quigg responded publicly, stating that the department denies that they still have an electric chair in the station for that purpose. Quigg said that "we had a chair quite a while ago, which had some secondhand batteries taken out of Ford cars, but upon the recommendation of City Manager Wharton, we tore it up, and that was over sixty days ago."

The chief said that a thin wire was laid along the seat portion of an ordinary chair with the wire connected to the car batteries. He said it wasn't used to extract confessions but that it was used at one time and investigators were able to recover $1,600 worth of stolen goods (*Miami News*, 1/6/1923).

Other news stories from the *Miami News* newspaper during the next two years included the following:

> Despite the country being dry (Prohibition), there still seemed to be plenty of alcohol flowing in Miami. It was reported today that liquor raids were conducted last night by Chief Quigg, Det. Sgt. Forrest Nelson, Detectives Leon Sawyer and G. S. Wilkinson at 66 NW 5th Street and 389 SW 15th Road. (*Miami News*, 1/4/1923)

> Downtown beat men, Officers Poston and Robertson, arrested Horace Albury for carrying a concealed weapon. (*Miami News*, 3/13/1923)

A taxi driver named R. D. Niles was arrested for the murder of fellow cabbie, W. R. Asher, after MPD motor officer P. C. Lathan reported that he observed the two men together in a car heading over the causeway toward the beach and that Asher appeared to be either drunk or doped up. After an investigation by Chief Quigg, Dets. Morris, Rose, and Mitchell, it was determined that Niles planned to take over all the assets of Asher after his death, and an order issued to pick up Niles.

Downtown Miami Officer Crown located the offender and arrested him. At a subsequent trial, Niles was convicted of first degree murder which then carried an automatic sentence of execution in Florida's new electric chair. (*Miami News*, 4/23/1923, MPD records)

The Miami Police had a superior Rifle team during this period. A news story reported that the team was practicing for an upcoming match against other departments and army groups. Members of the MPD team noted were: Edward C. Allen, Harry Morris, J. A. McLendon, D. E. Rose, Marshall Campbell, and Forest Nelson. (*Miami News*, 5/1/1923)

Officer Walter J. Carr, a motor officer, is in Terrace Hospital on NE 17th Street, recovering from being shot in the head by L. L. Copeland last Sunday. Carr continues to recover and expects to be out of the hospital soon. He was wounded last Sunday. (*Miami News*, 1923)

Sgt. Wever (latter killed in line of duty), the motorcycle supervisor, located a cat burglar in a Northeast apartment house. A squad from the station was summoned to surround the house, then breaking down the door to arrest the suspect. The raiding party consisted of Lt. Bryan, Dets. Sawyer, Wilkinson, Rose, and Morris; assisted by uniform officers Haddock and Joe Jenkin. (*Miami News*, 7/17/1923)

Motor Officer L. P. Brantley attempted to pull over a speedster he was chasing. The offender, Edward Litchfield, swerved into Brantley catching his motor on the car and dragging the officer down the road. Brantley, still on his machine, pulled out his revolver and shot the driver. Litchfield in now in the hospital and is not expected to live. (*Miami News*, 7/23/1923)

Former MPD Chief of Police Frank B. Hardee is now a Deputy Sheriff for Dade County, under Sheriff Lewis Allen, former MPD officer. (*Miami News*, 4/23/1923)

Three big-time safe crackers (they called them "Yeggs" back then) were arrested yesterday by Chief Quigg, Detective Rose, Sgt. Keys, and Officer Roscoe Dunn. The trio was picked up on information provided from Tampa police. (*Miami News*, 12/4/1923)

Ned Allen, a former MPD officer who had been recently fired by Chief Quigg for conduct unbecoming an officer, was arrested in Fort Pierce for passing bad checks. (*Miami News*, 5/9/1924)

BARBERSHOP SHOOTOUT

Miami officer Charles W. Potterton was shot through the lung, within two inches of his heart, Thursday night. An exchange of bullets with Marion Blocker, a 6'4", 200 lb. ex-convict and another assailant took place at an Overtown barbershop, NW Sixteenth Street and Third Avenue. Officer Potterton and his partner, C. A. Biggers, were surprised as they entered the barbershop to make a comparatively minor arrest on a traffic warrant.

Potterton's coat showed that a bullet entered at the left lapel area and exited through the back. Two bystanders were also wounded.

After the shooting, Officer Biggers telephoned headquarters for help. Chief Quigg, Lieutenant Bryan, Officers E. J. Starling, Harry Morris, and sheriff's deputy M. H. Rolfe, a brother-in-law of Potterton, responded. The wounded Potterton was rushed to Jackson Hospital.

Portions of Officer Biggers's statement follows:

I was driving the police machine and Potterton got out ahead of me (at the barbershop). He had just put one foot on

the step at the entrance and I was standing on the curb when
suspect Blocker began to shoot at him from within the shop.
Then another Negro began to fire in my direction. Potterton
was only a few feet away from Blocker when I saw a flash
from the Negro's gun. Potterton quickly drew his gun and
began to shoot back at the Negro, while I got mine out and
fired four shots at the other man as I saw him still firing at the
officer. I was shooting to save Potterton. After emptying his
gun, Potterton stepped back to the Essex auto, reloaded his
gun, and fired one more shot before he fell from the effects
of his wound.

Blocker and the other assailant fled on foot, but Deputy Rolfe found
Blocker lying dead a block away with five bullet wounds. The other
assailant escaped. Potterton had been a witness against Blocker in a
previous case at which Blocker had been sentenced to two years in state
prison.

Officer Potterton recovered and continued on to a long career in the
Miami department. Later news articles indicated that he was still on the
job in 1949 as a detective captain (*Miami News*, 10/3/1924).

MOTOR OFFICER SHOT

On March 15, 1925, Sergeant Laurie Lafayette Wever, thirty-four,
a four-year veteran of the MPD, was shot and killed while chasing two
armed robbers in Miami. Sergeant Wever, the commanding officer of
the twenty-man motor squad, was a four-year veteran of the MPD. He
was born in Bartow, Florida, in July 4, 1891, enlisted in the U.S. Army
in 1909 and joined the MPD in 1920 (or '21). In 1920, according to the
U.S. Census, he was living in Bridgeport, Connecticut, working at the
AT&S Co. He was survived by his wife, Theresa, and two daughters,
Doris and Lois.

The offenders were two Ohio white men, Walter C.

Valiton, alias William H. Fox, born 1907, and John Naugle, born
1902, of Columbus and Toledo, Ohio. They had been on a Florida crime
spree when the encounter with Sergeant Wever occurred. Sergeant
Wever spotted their auto while responding to a burglary at NW Seventh
Avenue and Eighth Street. He stopped the auto, searched it, and found
burglary tools in the trunk. He demanded the two follow him to the

police station, but they fled in their stolen Essex auto. Wever chased them on his motorcycle, catching up with them in front of the Savoy Hotel on NW Second Street. Valiton leaned out the car window and fired four shots at Wever, who was rushed to the hospital, dying an hour or so later just as his wife came to his bedside.

Valiton later admitted shooting Sergeant Wever five times with a revolver. After the shooting, the two suspects fled the Miami area in an auto, heading north through the Everglades. They were apprehended the day of Wever's funeral in a shack/camp while sleeping later that night in the town of Fulford, Florida (now North Miami Beach). Fourteen heavily armed officers, led by Chief Quigg, raided the hideout and arrested them without a struggle. The shack also contained the fruits of their crime spree. The suspects were immediately transferred to a jail in Jacksonville as it was feared that a crowd of citizens gathered at the Miami jail would lynch them. No record of the trail could be found.

Two photographs were found of Wever's funeral in Miami. The funeral procession of Miami police cars were headed up by two hooded KKK men driving small motorcycles. Sergeant Wever was buried on March 18, 1925, in one of the most spectacular processions and funerals ever seen in Miami. The service was held in the First Baptist Church at NE First Ave and Fifth Street, with five thousand people attending. The story of the funeral and the KKK's participation was detailed in Dr. William Wilbanks's book, *Forgotten Heroes, Police Officers Killed in Dade County*. It was said by Wever's family that he was a member of that group, but at that time in the early 1920s of Miami's history, the group was generally thought of by the Miami residents as a sort of "community group" and not of the virulent hate group it became to be in America.

Sergeant Wever was buried in Miami's Woodlawn Cemetery. The community paid off the mortgage on the Wever home and set up a fund for his widow.

Walter Combs, longtime Miami funeral director, said in 1965 that Wever's funeral was the "most lavish funeral" he ever conducted in Miami. "The MPD escorted the cortège with motorcycles and marching men. A flat bed truck was turned into a float. It carried a floral tribute shaped like a motorcycle" (Wilbanks, *Forgotten Heroes*, 1996, and City of Miami publications).

News Item:

A proposal by Chief Quigg to raise the salaries of MPD officers $5 a month on July 1st was forwarded to the city commission. The news story detailed the current salaries.

Police Officer—$125 monthly, $140 after one year

Motor Officer—$150, Desk Sgts—$155,

Detectives—$160,

Lieutenants, Detective Sgts, and

Booking Sgts—$175

Chief of Police—$275

All personnel were on a seven-day week, with two weeks' vacation in summer. (*Miami News*, 5/7/1924)

DO NOT JAYWALK

A Miami PD officer, L. M. Johnson, working the traffic detail downtown, fired four shots from his pistol at two jaywalkers on Flagler Street today. One shot hit bystander Mrs. Myers in the neck, seriously wounding her. She was rushed to Jackson Hospital for treatment.

A crowd of witnesses immediately converged on the police station protesting the officer's action.

Chief Quigg suspended the officer immediately and later fired him after an investigation (*Miami News*, 7/10/1925).

During mid-1925, Miami city administrators brought in police experts from New Orleans to assist in overhauling the organizational structure of the Miami police. Following meetings with Stanley Ray, a public safety commissioner of New Orleans and Chief Quigg, the following promotions were announced:

—Chief of Detectives Forrest Nelson was promoted to assistant chief of police

—Homer S. Redman, from assistant traffic director to captain of Uniform Division

—Guy Reeves, special agent of the U.S. Justice Department to chief of detectives

—P. B. Gibson to inspector of police

—J. W. McCarthy to traffic lieutenant

—M. A. Tibbets to lieutenant of motorcycles

—J. J. Connelly to assistant traffic director

—G. S. Wilkerson to sergeant of detectives
—W. C. Thurman to secretary to chief
—L. P. Bradley to sergeant of motorcycles
(MPD records and *Miami News*, 9/12/1925)

In September, Officer Alex Gingras, fifty-five, a police officer for eight years, retired on one-half pay, $75 a month for life, for disability due to an on-the-job injury.

Chief Quigg hired Roy S. Parker to be a traffic officer at E Flagler Street and NE First Avenue. Parker should easily be visible to both motorists and pedestrians as he was six foot, ten and a half inches tall, and weighed 210 lbs. (*Miami News*, 11/24/1925).

Parker joined with another huge MPD officer handling traffic in the downtown area, Frank Leavitt.

Leavitt was one of our most famous Miami PD guys, known all over the world as "Man Mountain Dean," real name Frank Leavitt, "Soldier Leavitt." He was a Miami PD officer in the mid-'20s until 1930. He was later a famous national wrestler and promoter in the 1930s and 1940s.

Chief Quigg hired Leavitt, a 340-pound Georgia hillbilly, to be a traffic officer on Flagler Street. Leavitt joined the army in World War I at age fourteen and also served in World War II. His wife was his manager and together they banked most of his earnings during his wrestling career, accumulating a million dollars over the years (a huge sum back then). Leavitt died in 1953.

No records are available but it can be assumed that very few offenders (if any) resisted arrest when Parker and Leavitt were on duty (MPD records).

TRAFFIC COP KILLED

A sixty-six-year-old officer, John D. Marchbanks, directing traffic downtown was struck and killed at Flagler Street and Bayshore Drive on February 16, 1926, by an auto driver, J. L. Smith, twenty-seven.

MPD Detectives E. W. Pearce and L. H. Haddock arrested Smith for reckless driving and manslaughter. No record could be located on the disposition of the case.

Marchbanks, a native of Hall County, Georgia, was an eight-year veteran of the department, joining the MPD in January 1918 at age fifty-six. He was survived by his wife, Elizabeth. A friend, Sergeant J. J. Brown, was reported to recall that he and Marchbanks had joined the MPD the same day, and Marchbanks, the senior man in traffic, had been assigned to foot traffic duty downtown his entire career.

In 1925, Miami had twenty-five thousand autos and traffic was choking the downtown streets, which required the department to assign 75% of the force to handle the downtown traffic mess (*Miami News* and *Miami Herald*, 2/16/1926; Wilbanks, *Forgotten Heroes*, 1996).

Norman Franks, MPD motor officer, chased a bandit car containing a gang of robbers. Franks leaped from his motor and singlehandedly arrested the entire carload. He was highly praised by his bosses.

Fame is fleeting though, as a few years later, he was beaten and tossed out of the police station by Detective Mitchell. Franks had quit and was attempting to rejoin the department (*Miami News*, 4/15/1926).

HOMICIDE UNIT FORMED

The Miami Police Department organized a Homicide Unit in July 1926, according to a story in the *Miami Herald*, July 23, 1926, and *Miami News*, 7/16/1926.

"Miami is to have a police homicide squad to do nothing except combat the 'murder' wave now sweeping the city." That announcement was made Friday by Police Chief H. Leslie Quigg at the Dade County Law Enforcement meeting in the courthouse. Chief Quigg did not give details of the organization, saying that details were being worked out rapidly and that the best experts obtainable would be placed in the squad. He said that the great number of murders in Miami has made the formation of a homicide squad a necessity. He mentioned as proof of the "murder wave" the fact that six Negroes were slain in one night recently. (*Miami Herald*, 7/23/1926, and *Miami News*, 7/16/1926)

HURRICANE OF 1926

When news from Cuba warned that an impending storm was heading north, Miami Police Chief Quigg released all local prisoners from the jail so that they could assist their families in storm preparation with instructions to report back to jail after the storm had passed.

In the aftermath of that great hurricane of 1926 that ravaged the south Florida area, the sheriff of Dade County, Dan Hardie, and Chief Leslie Quigg announced "that all able-bodied men who did not assist in the cleanup of the area would be arrested."

Some good came out of the hurricane. The Ku Klux Klan's $150,000 building at SW Fourth Street and Eighth Avenue was destroyed by the storm (*Miami News*, 7/4/1926).

An armed robber swore that he would not be taken alive. Detective W. J. Driggers confronted the violent criminal at NW Sixth Avenue and Thirtieth Street and seen to it that the bad guy got his wish. Detective Driggers shot and killed the suspect during the confrontation. Driggers was not hurt (*Miami News*, 9/13/1926).

BEAT MAN KILLED BY AUTO

At West Flagler and Twelfth Avenue, Officer Samuel J. Callaway, fifty, was directing traffic when an auto ran the red light. Callaway jumped on the running board of a passing auto, which then was involved in a crash at NW Fourth Street and Fourth Avenue. Callaway was thrown to the ground and sustained injuries that caused his death three days later, January 10, 1927.

The identity of the driver of the car that ran the red light was never identified and the death was ruled unavoidable.

Callaway was buried in his native Maryland (*Miami Herald* and *Miami News*, 1/11/1927; Wilbanks, *Forgotten Heroes*, 1996).

KLAN ESCORT HURT

A Miami police motor officer was hurt when his police motorcycle went into a ditch while he was escorting a Ku Klux Klan motorcade today. MPD Sergeant W. B. Poe was thrown from the motor as he escorted a 100-car motorcade of Klansmen from Miami to Homestead. Sergeant Poe was wearing a white Klan hood over his uniform as he was working the escort. Poe stated that he was wearing the hood to cover the MPD markings on the motorcycle.

Chief Quigg, when queried, stated "that he had given permission for the escort, but was under the impression that the motorcade was to be confined to the City of Miami only" (*Miami News*, 5/20/1927).

OVERTOWN SHOOTOUT

A young officer, Jesse Morris, twenty-four, was killed in the line of duty during a shootout on July 8, 1927. Morris, Officer John Holland, and Detective Leon Sawyer were in the area of NW Second Avenue and Eleventh Street just before their 10:30 PM quitting time. A man had shot six other persons that evening, including his own father. The last shooting was heard by the officers. They encountered Charles Lee, twenty-nine, and exchanged shots with him. Officer Morris was hit in the side by Lee's shotgun slugs as he fired five shots at Lee. Officer Holland fired six more at Lee, wounding him. Morris was rushed to Jackson Hospital but died minutes later. Lee died two days later at the hospital.

Morris had joined MPD two years previously, joining his brother-in-law, Marvin Faircloth, on the force. Morris had been born and raised in Oklahoma but headed for Miami for work easier than at Oklahoma's lime quarries, where he previously toiled.

Officer Morris was a traffic officer that was working extra duty in the central Negro district on the orders of Chief Quigg, who had been assigning four extra officers each evening to combat the crime in the colored area. Morris was buried in a family plot out in Lawrence, Oklahoma, after services in Miami led by Lieutenant W. J. McCarthy. Morris's widow was awarded half of her husband's salary for one year. She later remarried and died in 1934 during childbirth (Wilbanks, *Forgotten Heroes*, 1996, and MPD records).

JOHNSON ACCIDENTALLY KILLED

On Sunday afternoon, September 25, 1927, forty-year-old MPD Officer Albert Johnson was accidentally shot and killed while on duty at NW Twenty-second Avenue and Twenty-third Street by a close friend as the two were in the process of shooting the friend's sick dog. The killing was ruled accidental and no charges were filed. Johnson, a Georgia native, died instantly from a shot by his friend that missed the dog.

Johnson had joined the MPD in December 1925. He was survived by his wife, Vera, and was buried in his hometown of Carrolton, Georgia (Wilbanks, *Forgotten Heroes*, 1996).

Babe Ruth hit his sixtieth home run on September 30, 1927, off Washington Senator lefty pitcher, Tom Zachray.

MOTHER OF ALL POLICE CHASES

Prison terms totaling forty-two years were meted out Friday (November 5, 1927) to four bandits who arrived in Miami Thursday morning and before night had robbed a store, attempted another robbery, and surrendered after one of the most thrilling chases in Miami police history. Two were caught by a lone motorcycle officer, and their confessions led to the capture of the others. (No police units at that time were equipped with a police radio.)

The men pleaded guilty when arraigned before Judge Tom Norfleet in criminal court at 1:00 PM Friday. Within thirty-six hours of their arrival in the city, they will be on their way to Raiford to begin their long prison terms.

James H. Travis, alias Charles Dries, was sentenced to twelve years for armed robbery and attempt to kill when he admitted that he was the one who shot at the pursing policemen. Louise William DeMotte, alias William C. Garbett, was sentenced to twelve years for armed robbery. Edward Hawkins and Randolph Golden received nine years each as accessories to the crime.

Dries and Garbett were captured by L. G. Crews of the motorcycle squad after other policemen had been outdistanced, thrown from his motorcycle when the bandits attempted to run him down. After he had caught up with them, traveling seventy miles an hour, Crews fired from the ground where he fell, regained his machine, and sped on finally taking them singlehanded.

The men robbed the A & P grocery on 756 NW Fifth Avenue about 3:00 PM and, shortly afterward, attempted to hold up the Gateway Garage on NE Second Avenue and Thirtieth Street.

"I had a tough hour and half ride following them," Crews said in describing the furious chase over more than thirty miles of Miami and Hialeah streets. "They led me a merry chase over Twentieth Street to NW Twenty-second Avenue, and then to NW Fifty-fourth Street, where they swerved off into the woods and open lots.

"It was all I could do to follow them through the woods to Thirty-sixth Street. They then struck out for Hialeah. At Palm Avenue, they tried to run me down by cutting the corner short, as I was on the inside of the road. I whipped my motorcycle off the road and their car barely struck my rear fender, throwing my machine to the ground.

"Lying on my stomach, I fired three shots. This was the first time I shot at the bandits. Two of my shots struck the steering wheel and one hit the steering post, I believe. Seeing the bullets didn't stop them, I regained my motorcycle and resumed the pursuit down Fifty-fourth Street to NW Second Avenue, then north to Fifty-ninth terrace and the railway, where they were cornered and forced to surrender."

The two men captured by Crews gave their names as L. E. DeMotte, thirty-one, Richmond, Virginia, and James Henry Travis, thirty-two, Jacksonville. DeMotte later said his real name was Charles Dries. In their confession, they implicated two others. Acting on this information, Detective Frank Mitchell and Detective Ralph Kymer arrested two men at 324 NW Thirty-sixth Street about 10:00 PM Thursday. They gave their names as Randolph Golden, twenty-three, and Edward Hawkins, twenty-two.

Garbett, in his confession, said the car used by the bandits was stolen in Detroit and that he, with Hawkins and Golden, had started south in it. Brush, he said, was picked up at Delray. The four arrived in Miami Thursday morning. All had been drinking, he asserted, and as they were out of money, they decided to rob the grocery store to get money with which to buy more liquor.

The robbers obtained only $60 at the grocery and then fled, stopping at the filling station on NE Second Avenue. There they went inside, then came out wearing smoked glasses and attempted to hold up Charles A. Needham and R. A. Crawford, attendants. Failing to obtain money, they left hurriedly, driving west. As they started, one of the men shot at J. J. Nation, city park department employee, who was directing Negroes at work in the street.

When the report of the second robbery attempt reached headquarters, all reserves were called out. Crews, with Detectives Robert L. Wood and Cecil Knight, in an automobile, picked up the trail of the bandits soon after they turned south off NE Thirtieth Street, into Biscayne Boulevard. Crews said he recognized the car by the license number, although the color was dark and not red, and the top was up and not down, as given in the first descriptions. The chase came near enough to the bandits to shoot for the first time. Their fire was returned, Brush doing the shooting, according to other bandits who had only one gun among them.

A random shot from the bandit car struck Charles Smith, Negro, in the wrist as he stood on his porch at NW Third Avenue and Eighth Street.

Rounding a curve north, the cars passed NW Eleventh Street, or Allapattah Drive, at sixty miles an hour and continued on NW Eighth Street road toward Jackson Memorial Hospital. By this time, the bandits had exhausted their ammunition and there was no more shooting until Crews fired at them in Hialeah.

The windshield and spotlight of the car in which Detectives Wood and Knight were riding were broken by bullets. In rounding a curve on NW Eighth Street road, Crews's motorcycle turned on its side, but he succeeded in righting it.

The police automobile was forced to abandon the chase when it "froze," officers said, and Crews was alone in the pursuit after that.

In commenting on the capture, Police Chief Quigg remarked that this police car bore the number 13 and certainly proved unlucky for Wood and Knight, who might have been with Crews at the finish except for mechanical trouble. He said that as a reward for their good work, Crews, Wood, and Knight each would receive five days' vacation, to be taken whenever the policemen desire it.

Carl Tuten, a Hialeah motorcycle policeman, later was reported to have aided Crews in the roundup of the bandits. Tuten said he saw Crews was in trouble and that he made ninety-two miles an hour at one time in overtaking the Miami policeman and the bandits.

City Manager W. A. Snow and City Commissioner Harry E. Platt personally congratulated Crews on his work. Crews, with his hand still shaking from gripping the bars of his motorcycle during the chase, said he was glad of the opportunity.

On November 10, 1927, the city commission wanted Chief Quigg to present Crews with a gold medal for bravery. Chief Quigg did not think he should and explained the reasons in a letter to the *Miami News* on November 27, 1927. Chief Quigg explained that giving Officer Crews a gold medal would not be wise as an award for his accomplishment, saying, "I know he is as brave as they make them," as he explained his reasons that a gold medal, as voted by the city commission, would not be wise. Quigg said, "Personally, I think Officer Crews did a remarkable piece of work in this particular and want to give him every credit for his part in it, as well as the work done by Officer Knight and Wood, who also were in this chase, as well as Officer Tuten of the Hialeah police department." Quigg continued, "What I wish to do is to maintain harmony in the police department and not cause friction among the men, which might be done in the awarding of a gold medal to Mr. Crews, and when it considered that we have had between twenty and twenty-five acts of bravery in the past two years, which possibly were acts fully as brave as that one on the part of Officer Crews."

Quigg went on to say that he knows personally of the courage Crews has displayed, not only on this occasion, but on others. "However, we have discontinued, as the line is too hard to draw [on the awarding of medals] and it is bound to lend to petty jealousy and work against the moral of any department, and that is the way I feel about the awarding of gold medals for acts of bravery, but I want it understood that under no circumstances am I discrediting the work of Officer Crews and the others in this instance."

Author's Note: Officer L. G. (Leston G. Crews) continued his successful MPD career. In February 1933, Crews was one of the Miami officers who arrested Guisippi Zangara for the murder of Chicago Mayor Cermack during the attempted assignation of President-elect Franklin Roosevelt in Miami's Bay Front Park. Crews was honored again in 1938 for being the top pistol shooter during a national pistol match. (Miami had top national honors for two years running in pistol matches.) Crews later retired and died in Marathon, Florida, in 1974, at age seventy-four.

Officer Wood was indicted by the grand jury in 1928 for the murder of a prisoner, Victor Parnell. The same grand jury indicted Chief Quigg and several other officers and detectives for the murder of Harry Kiel in 1925. Wood was later acquitted as were several of the others mentioned. These stories appear elsewhere in this publication.

Cecil Knight, Wood's partner in the chase, was Captain Cecil (Hamp) Knight, who was one of the most famous Auto Theft detectives in the nation for many, many years. "Hamp" retired after a great career that covered over forty years in the MPD and later passed on. He was also the father of now-deceased MPD Vets Major Bob Knight and Captain Jimmy Knight, and the grandfather of our own MPD Vet Lyriss Underwood, VP of the Miami Police Veterans Association (*Sarasota Herald Tribune, Miami News, Miami Herald*, all 11/4/1927).

DETECTIVE SLAIN

Auto Theft Detective James Frank Beckham, twenty-nine, was shot and killed by a bootlegger about 11:00 PM on February 3, 1928. The fatal event began when Detective Beckham and Detective J. A. McLendon received a report that there was a shooting near NW Sixth Court and Fifty-fourth Street. McLendon had emerged from the police car to question one suspect when a truck with another subject sped off then stopped at 5451 NW Sixth Court. The driver ran into the home, and before Beckham could emerge from his unit, four shots ranged out. Buckshots came through the windshield and the detective was killed instantly. The shots were fired by bootlegger Charles Haynes, twenty-seven, who claimed he thought he was being robbed by bandits in a quest to carry away the load of illegal liquor in Haynes's truck. After shooting Beckham, Haynes moved the body out of the truck and placed Beckham's revolver in his hand to help justify the claim of self-defense. Earlier in the evening, three men had shot up Haynes's home in an attempt to hijack his liquor.

Haynes was arrested and severely beaten by three MPD detectives, one of whom was Detective Tom Nazworth, and placed under the care of a doctor at the jail. Chief Quigg, after an investigation, suspended two of the detectives indefinitely and a third received a fifteen-day suspension.

A charge of first-degree murder was made against Haynes, but he was found guilty only of manslaughter and the judge only sentenced him to "time served," which was the ninety days he was in jail awaiting trial. Judge Rose advised that his light sentence of Hayes was due to the heavy beating that was administered by the detectives.

Several months after his release from jail, Haynes was killed in an airplane crash in Canada.

Beckham, a Georgia native and an army veteran, left a wife, Allie, and three daughters. He was buried in Cairo, Georgia (MPD records and publications; Wilbanks, *Forgotten Heroes*, 1996).

CHIEF ARRESTED

In March 1928, a Dade County grand jury indicated seven Miami police officers in three separate cases. Included in the indictments was

Miami Police Chief H. Leslie Quigg, who was arrested along with Lieutenant Mel Tibbits and Detectives John Caudell and Tom Nazworth in connection with the murder of a thirty-year-old Negro room clerk, Harry H. Kier. Three of Quigg's officers, intending to run the subject out of town on July 15, 1925, on Quigg's orders, took Kier to the then rural area at NW Seventh Avenue and Eightieth Street, on the north side of Miami, where he was shot dead by Detective Nazworth. Kier, a room clerk at the Hotel El Commodoro, a downtown Miami hotel, allegedly had attempted to act a liaison between a seventeen-year-old female hotel guest and a male unknown to her. Kier was taken from the jail by four officers who were running him out of town. The officer who shot Kier and the two others were arrested. A fourth officer (Officer William M. Beechy) tipped off the authorities two years later, and Chief Quigg and two supervisors were also indicted by the grand jury for covering up the crime and suspended from the force. After a trial in late April 1928, at which Beechy and former Detective E. W. Pearce testified against Quigg, and former officer C. O. Huttoe, now a Seaboard Air Line special officer (Huttoe later rejoined the MPD), testified for him. Pearce, a former Broward County deputy and currently a Dade sheriff's candidate, had been fired for drinking on duty by Quigg. Beechy had been fired by Quigg for accepting graft from bootleggers.

The jury found Quigg and the others not guilty and they were released from jail. Quigg had been incarcerated in the county stockade for three months awaiting trial. The court's charge to the jury was to either convict for first-degree murder or acquit as the statute of limitations have expired on lesser charges. The officer who committed the shooting, Detective Tom Nazworth, claimed self-defense in the case, stating Kier went for his gun. During the shooting, Lieutenant Tibbetts (off-duty motorcycle supervisor) was mistakenly shot by Detective Nazworth.

After the murder charge was dismissed, Chief

Quigg was then charged with assault and battery and he was again acquitted when the victim/witness refused to return to Miami for the trial. Quigg was fired as chief a few weeks later for neglect of duties. Quigg was reinstated sometime in the early 1930s by the courts, serving until 1944, when he was again dismissed. After his retirement from the police department with a pension of $85 a month, Chief Quigg was elected to the city commission for several terms and was employed as the city's dock master at Coconut Grove's Dinner Key yacht basin in Miami.

It was interesting to note that the hotel manager who originally brought Kier to Quigg's attention was S. D. McCreary, later a police chief and Miami City manager and Quigg's boss. (More about McCreary later.)

The same 1928 grand jury indicted Detective R. L. Wood for the murder of carpenter Victor Parnell, a white prisoner. In addition, Officers Nelson E. Ward and Officer R. L. Glisson were charged with killing John Mabry, a black male prisoner. Officer Ward and Glisson had been shot and wounded during a prior gambling raid in which Mabry, the alleged shooter, was arrested, tried, and found not guilty. Mabry was later arrested for stealing a photograph record by the same two officers and was fatally shot by them while allegedly resisting arrest while en route to the police station.

On July 16, 1928, Detective Nazworth was found guilty of assault and battery on prisoner Charles Haynes, a suspect in the earlier murder of MPD officer Beckham and fined $250. Nazworth left the Miami department but remained in law enforcement as a Georgia prison guard. The 1930 U.S. Census indicated that, at that time, he was a Gadsen County deputy sheriff in upstate Florida. Nazworth died in Dade County, Florida, in 1944.

Guy C. Reeve, chief of detectives, was appointed acting chief of police while Quigg was under indictment and suspension. Reeve was sworn in as permanent chief on June 1, 1928, and H. H. Arnold appointed as public safety director (Helena (MT) *Daily Independent*, Chillicothe (OH) *Constitution—Tribune*, Kingsport (TN) *Times*, Dunkirk (NY) *Observer*, Dade County Grand Jury Report, *Miami News*, and *Miami Herald*, both 8/28/1928).

AFTER THE TURMOIL

As a result of the uproar caused by the arrest and later acquittal of Chief Quigg for murder, the city appointed a new public safety director and a new chief of police. Some of the results of these actions can be seen from news articles that appeared in the *Miami Daily News* during that period.

The reader should keep in mind that bad news sells more papers than good news and that during this period, thousands of incidents of good work was performed by members of the MPD.

On May 24, 1928, Chief Quigg was dismissed by City Manager Snow for neglect of duty and for the good of the services. The action was based on the grand jury report. The manager read to the commission one line of the report: "Quigg is wholly unfit for the office, under him the Police Department has become cruel and because a 'militant, tyrannical group that follows standards foreign.'"

June 1—Guy Reeve was promoted to chief from detective chief. Quigg says he will no longer fight for the position. Reeve had been hired in 1925 as the chief of detectives after serving nine years with the U.S. Justice Department. After Reeve's MPD service, he was the chief deputy in the Dade County sheriff's department (1933) and was appointed as the U.S. marshal for the South Florida district in 1935.

Lonnie Scarboro will take over the job of chief of detectives that Reeve was holding prior to Quigg's dismissal. H. H. Arnold, former MPD officer, takes over as the public safety director.

June 4—Public Safety Director Arnold advises publicly that all "bookies" either quit their activities or will be jailed.

June 6—Chief Guy Reeve established the first MPD police school (Picture shows about thirty MPD guys in a classroom).

June 5—Lieutenant Wm. J. McCarthy and Detective Roy Norcross make gambling arrests and confiscate slot machines. Also, the budget for the PD for next year was announced to be $461,000.

June 10—Four MPD officers to stand trial for the beating of C. E. Haynes. It was charged that Detective Tom Nazworth, R. L. Wood, Ralph C. Rymer, and Isey Bandrimer savagely beat Hayes the night that Officer Frank Beckham was killed by Hayes. Tom Nazworth is now working as a prison guard in Climax, Georgia. Wood and Rhymer were acquitted but Nazworth was convicted and fined $250. No mention was made of Bandrimer's disposition.

June 17—Chief Reeve orders crackdown on bookies. Detectives C. W. Hodges, J. A. McLendon, Officers G. S. Wilkerson and John Driggers made several arrests. Even Detective Chief Scarboro himself arrested a bookmaker.

June 18—Detective Frank Mitchell was fined $250 for hitting a former decorated officer, Norman Franks, breaking his jaw. Mitchell claimed that Franks was continually hanging around the station trying to get his job back (he was suspended in 1927 because of domestic problems). Detective Harry Bouterse, Officer H. S. Frye, and T. L. Bishop testified for Mitchell, saying Franks was a troublemaker.

June 19—Charles Haynes, the slayer of Detective Frank Beckham in February, was freed by the judge after being convicted of manslaughter. He had been in jail awaiting trial since the killing. The judge gave Hayes "time served" (three months), saying his decision was predicated on the savage beating by the detectives.

June 20—The *Miami News* ran a photo of thirty-plus police officers in a classroom getting schooled on correct police procedures. No story accompanied the picture.

Also on this date, Detective R. L. Wood was acquitted of the murder of Victor Parnell. The victim was shot by Wood while in the process of running him out of town. Wood, accompanied then by now-deceased Detective Frank Beckham, claimed in court that Parnell attempted to stab him.

Sergeant Frank Mitchell was suspended fifteen days for assaulting former MPD Motor Officer Norman Franks in the police station (#7, 6/22/1928).

June 23—Desk Sergeant John Phillips was demoted for failure to take action on a report that a citizen was contemplating suicide. Phillips took no action on the information nor did he make a report. The citizen did in fact commit suicide that evening.

It was also noted in the *Miami News* that Chief Reeve started a police training school, compiled a police regulation booklet, and inaugurated a merit system (All items from #7).

Author's Note: The police rules and regulations booklet, the first-ever issued to MPD officers, was quite comprehensive, detailing the duties of each rank as well as providing much fingertip information for each officer. The editor has obtained an original issue of this booklet from the granddaughter of deceased police Captain Barrick. The booklet will be turned over to the current chief of police for display in the Police Academy.

July 5—Officer Jesse W. Campbell got his jaw broken by an irate husband when the husband located Campbell in a movie house with his wife. Officer Pat Cannon, called to the scene, was disciplined for failing to make a report of the incident.

July 6—Officer Harry Bouterse was fired by Chief Reeve for an alleged extortion attempt. No details offered.

July 12—City Manager Arnold announced that a police gym is being established in the city hall annex. Also, a former officer named

Stenhouse, who had served as Chief Quigg's secretary, was killed by a female acquaintance. (She later was sentenced to five years in prison.)

July 17—The paper noted that Sergeant W. M. Glisson won the "donut and sinker" contest at the station house by consuming forty-eight donuts and two quarts of coffee, defeating Lieutenant McCarthy and G. S. Wilkerson by many donuts.

July 19—The new Seventy-ninth Street causeway opened for traffic.

August 7—A conference on MPD police pensions was held. Attending was City Manager Snow, Captain Forrest Nelson, Ed Melchen, Lieutenant Finch Cochran, and Lieutenant McCarthy.

August 24—New uniforms were issued to all uniformed MPD officers. The uniforms were grayish brown gabardine in tailored style. Motor officers were provided with chin straps, Sam Browne belts, and puttees.

August 25—The public safety director and the chief ordered a roundup of all "rowdies" as a result of a downtown shootout in front of the Mutt & Jeff poolroom. During that shootout, officers responded and Officer "Pistol Pete" Logan, on duty in the railroad tower, sounded the alarm while climbing down and chasing the bad guys. He was aided by Officers E. R. Milstead and Henry Owens, as well as Detectives William Driggers and Bob Johns. Officer D. D. Carver and C. G. Riley arrived and arrested some of the culprits. The city manager later orders the poolroom to be closed.

August 28—The city and county police departments announced a drive to arrest DUI drivers due to the high number of recent DUI fatalities.

August 29—The chief continues instilling discipline in the force. Officer H. Floyd was fired for drunkenness, Officer A. T. Richards was suspended five days for sleeping on duty, and Officer Frank Gerke and E. A. Herrick were disciplined for failing to check doors during their rounds. Officer G. J. David was fired for a law violation, and Officer Wesley Gardner was suspended for five days for sleeping on the job. Also, a twenty-three-year-old William Williams was fined $10 for pointing a gun at motor Officer L. G. Crews.

August 30—MPD Officer Earl Hudson, an amateur boxer, was knocked out in the second round at a boxing match in Atlanta, Georgia.

August 31—Six bootleggers beat up two MPD officers, Officers R. N. Harwood and A. V. Garbett, taking their weapons after a car chase in the northwest section. The gang, thought to be from Hollywood, escaped.

September 1—Officers T. E. Hart and Ben Frye arrested a city fireman for DUI.

September 6—The new Dade County courthouse opened. Headquarters for the MPD was supposed to be on one of the upper floors but the city manager advised that the police department needed to be on the street level.

Also that day, it was reported that Officer W. F. Gardner was fired for sleeping on duty and intoxication. Gardner missed his hourly call in and was found by Captain V. H. Mathis sleeping and drunk on his beat, with a pint bottle in his pocket. This was Gardner's second (and last) offense.

September 12—The paper noted that General Electric put on a demonstration of a television. It was a one-act play, showed on a screen only a few inches square, featuring only head shots of the two actors.

September 15—All MPD officers were required to take a job knowledge exam that covered subjects taught to them at the recent police school program.

CHASE KILLS MCCANN

Forty-five-year-old Officer Augustus McCann was killed when his police car crashed and overturned while chasing a speeding truck on September 28, 1928, at SW Twenty-seventh Avenue and Fourteenth Street. The truck was never found. With McCann during that morning was Officer W. G. Wilson who escaped with only bruises. McCann, the driver, had swerved to avoid a pedestrian that had emerged from a bus. The woman was injured as the car swept by.

McCann, a Georgia native and a three-year veteran of the MPD, having joined in October 1925, died shortly after midnight in Jackson Memorial Hospital. He was survived by his wife and two daughters. His remains were buried in Boston, Georgia (Wilbanks, *Forgotten Heroes*, 1996; *Miami Herald* and *Miami News*, both 9/29/1928).

OFFICER KILLED IN JAILHOUSE

Officer Sidney Crews, a patrol wagon driver, was shot in the city jail by a deranged prisoner, Doe Wilson, on April 24, 1929, and died of his wounds the next day. Crews and his partner, Lonnie Goodbee, were in the jail to kill rats with an air rifle. Crews took off his holster while shooting the rats with a BB gun. Prisoner Wilson grabbed Crews's gun and fired three rounds. One shot just missed jailor C. H. Belcher, and the other two shots hit Officer Crews. Detective John Driggers, nearby in the jail, shot the prisoner as he (Wilson) was standing over Crews with the gun in his hand. Wilson died at the hospital.

Wilson was being held at the jail pending the preparation of insanity papers after his arrest the previous day.

Crews, a native of Baker County, Florida, left a wife and seven children. He joined the MPD in 1921 after being urged to do so by his brother Walt, who had been a MPD officer. Crews was also related to MPD Captain Hardy Bryan.

Chief of Police Guy Reeve led more than fifty officers at the funeral service. After the service, the night shift marched the casket to the railroad station for transport up to Baker County (MPD records; Wilbanks, *Forgotten Heroes*, 1996; *Miami Herald*, 4/25/1929).

INSPECTOR FORREST NELSON

Forest Nelson, born 1892, joined the Miami force in November 1921. A year later, he was serving as a detective sergeant. In 1925, he was the chief of detectives and was promoted to assistant chief. In 1928, he was rolled back to the captain rank when Chief Reeves took over the department.

In June 1929, Nelson was suspended, then reduced to police officer rank. He was fired in 1930 by Safety Director McCreary. Nelson refused to turn in his badge and demanded a hearing. No grounds were presented and the court awarded him his job and rank back in May 1930.

Nelson later served as a police inspector and as assistant police chief during the 1930s and mid-1940s.

In the early 1940s, he was again demoted, and an attempt was made to discharge him due to the fact that he originally joined the department under a name other than his birth name. Nelson had changed his name from Epps shortly after 1910 when he entered into an acting career. The court again restored his job and rank. His name will appear many times in these MPD stories (MPD records, Personal note—MPD relative).

GREAT DEPRESSION ERA

LAYOFFS

The Great Depression took a toll on the MPD, forcing the layoffs of twelve officers in 1929 for budgetary reasons. The following is a list of officers furloughed by Chief Guy Reeve: O. C. Plummer, C. C. Papy, B. B. White, J. H. Mitchell, A. J. Butterworth, Richard Madison, J. C. Crawlelly, W. E. Groover, E. C. Moran, A. L. Dorr, and Fitzhugh Lee, the riot truck driver. Dorr had been on the MPD since February 1924, but the remainder had served just several months on the job (MPD records).

KU KLUX KLAN LEADER NOW BOSS OF POLICE AND FIRE DEPARTMENTS

Sam D. McCreary was appointed as public safety director of Miami, heading up both the police and fire departments in January 1930. McCreary had been the vice president of El Commodore Hotel in Miami for at least five years and was a member of the City Publicity Bureau. McCreary was the person who called Chief Quigg about the alleged pimping by H. Kier in 1925, which resulted in Kier being shot and killed by MPD detectives while they were running Kier out of town.

McCreary, a hotel manager, had no police or fire experience. However, in 1933, he was appointed as the chief of police in addition to his public safety director duties.

McCreary claimed in a 1935 newspaper interview that he had been head of the Miami Ku Klux Klan from 1924 to 1930. This information became public during a story on police brutality in 1935, which is described later in this book (*Miami News*, 1/31/1930).

NEWS BRIEFS—1930-32

1/13/30—Officer J. W. Grant arrested two suspects for attempted murder in the downtown area.

1/19/30—Detectives Holland and Brubaker arrested two thieves in connection with a Burglary ring.

7/22/1931—Chief Hardy Bryan promotes three officers to the position of traffic sergeant. They were J. H. Mansfield, E. L. Barrick, and Neal M. Coston.

8/5/1931—Guy Reeve regains the chief's job in court, replacing Hardy Bryan who has served since July 13, 1931, while Reeve was in court attempting to regain his position.

1/1/1932—*Miami News* story about a robbery homicide. Detective Chief Lonnie Scarboro, Chief Guy C. Reeves, and Safety Director S. D. McCreary were mentioned in the investigation.

1/3/1932—A gambling raid story mentioned Detective Chief Scarboro, Sergeant Ed Melchen, Detectives John W. Driggers, H. G. Howard, and Charles Potterton.

1/4/1932—Chief Reeve ordered Captains Bryan, Nelson, and Mathis to have their lieutenants and men arrest gamblers. Sheriff Lehman backed up the chief's order. No comment was made by Safety Director S. D. McCreary.

1/5/1932—Hardy Bryan sued Chief Reeve for the return of the chief's job.

1/18/1932—The city manager ordered Reeve removed and replaced by Bryan on July 18, 1931. Reeve was later reinstated by the court yet again.

6/4/1932—An MPD police pistol range opened at warehouse 8 of the municipal docks. Detective D. M. Kendall was chosen as range captain and Red Crews the instructor. All officers are to undergo range training in the next three months.

(All items from *Miami News*, 1932, dates indicated).

A FATAL DINNER DATE

On October 3, 1931, Officer Robert (Bob) L. McCormack, twenty-nine, was visiting Miss Dorothy Lager and her family in Miami and had gone out on the porch to rest before dinner. Later, Miss Lager went out to the porch and, on glancing down to the pavement, saw the policeman lying there face downward. He was rushed to a Miami hospital, but never regained consciousness and died on October 15, 1931.

McCormack, born in St. Louis, Missouri, on September 8, 1902, became an MPD officer on September 23, 1925 and was assigned to the motorcycle squad at the time of his death. He was living at 1252 SW Sixth with a roommate, William Oakford, who was also an MPD motor officer.

Officer McCormack's body was sent back to Missouri for burial by Philbrick Funeral Home. He was survived by his mother, Mrs. R. L. (Anne) McCormack, of Licking, Missouri, and a brother, John McCormack, of Miami.

An inquest was held on October 17, 1931, by Justice of Peace R. R. Williams and ruled the death accidental (*Miami News*, 10/15/1931).

ATTEMPT ON ROOSEVELT

In February 1933, President-elect Franklin Roosevelt, quite popular with the voters during the depression era, stopped in Miami at the end of his postelection vacation and became a target of an assassination attempt. He had been sailing on the yacht *Vincent Astor* for eleven days and now was to return by train back to Washington, D.C., to prepare for the upcoming inauguration. At 9:45 PM in the evening, Roosevelt arrived at pier no. 1 near downtown Miami, greeted by a crowd of dignitaries, and driven to a well-lit Bay Front Park along Miami's Biscayne Boulevard. Roosevelt had been expected to make a twenty-minute speech to a crowd, estimated at twenty-five thousand, interested in seeing the new president up close. Roosevelt was escorted by the Secret Service and Miami officers. His limo halted in front of the band shell. Efforts were made to mask the fact that Roosevelt was partially crippled by polio. For this event, to make his public remarks, he merely pushed himself to the top of the backseat of the open limo. Miami Mayor Gautier and Mayor Anton Cermack of Chicago welcomed him.

Roosevelt spoke for a few brief minutes and prepared to leave for the train depot. As the speech concluded, a short, stocky man climbed atop a cheap metal seat several rows from the front of the open band shell, pulled out a .32-caliber pistol, and fired five rounds from twenty-five feet away in the direction of President-elect Roosevelt. The crowd shouted, "Kill that man." The would-be assassin was identified as Guisicppi Zangara, a thirty-three-year-old Italian who had emigrated from Italy in 1923, a bricklayer by trade, who had spent most of his time in America in the area of Patterson, New Jersey, working odd jobs.

As Zangara, an uneducated veteran of the Italian army, fired, a brave Miami doctor's wife, Mrs. W. F. Cross, spoiled Zangara's aim as she threw herself in front of him clutching his arm. Six persons were hit by the gunshots. The two most seriously wounded were Mayor Anton Cermack, standing on the running board of Roosevelt's car, and Mrs. Joe Gill, wife of the president of Florida Power & Light Company, hit with a bullet to the stomach. Others hit were William Sinnott, a New York City police officer accompanying Roosevelt; Margaret Kruise, a New Jersey visitor; Russ Caldwell, Miami; and Miami Mayor R. G. Gautier, all with minor injuries. Zangara was immediately pounced on by citizens in the crowd in addition to Miami police officers Arthur Clark, Ray Jackson, Red Crews, and Fitzhugh Lee, all on duty in the park under the command of Captain Nelson. Roosevelt's car, driven by Miami officer Fitzhugh Lee (who was Chief Quigg's brother-in-law), started forward at the command of the Secret Service agent accompanying the president-elect, but soon stopped on Roosevelt's order to check on his friend Cermack.

Zangara was immediately whisked away by police to the seventeenth floor of the Dade County Courthouse on Flagler Street. He was questioned for two hours by Dade County Sheriff Dan Hardie, Secret Service agents Brodnax and Murphy, and Dade County Chief of Detectives Guy Reeve. Miami District Justice of the Peace Ferguson arranged quickly for a court stenographer and Zangara freely spoke about the crime, albeit in broken English, admitting that he had intended to shoot Roosevelt but the woman next to him pulled on his arm, diverting his aim of the gun that he had paid eight dollars for in a North Miami Avenue gun shop three days prior. Zangara, who claimed that his stomach was hurting for years causing him great pain, wanted to kill "rich" people who were hurting the "poor" people. He claimed that he wanted to kill President Hoover in Washington, but that he stayed in the warm Miami weather hoping to cure his stomach ills. Zangara further advised his questioners, "When I read in the Miami newspapers that the president-elect was coming to Miami by boat, I determined to kill him." Zangara had previously lived at 138 Jersey Street in Patterson, and in Hackensack, New Jersey, until he moved to Miami months ago. In April 1932, he resided at 20 NE Seventeenth Street in Miami and, by December 1932, had moved to a rooming house at 126 NE Fifth Street (Ma Green's place?).

Zangara was initially charged with four counts of attempted murder and was tried and convicted on these charges on February 20, 1933, less than a hundred hours after the crime. He entered the courtroom escorted by Dade Detective Chief Reeve and a giant deputy named Aughenbaugh and pled guilty. Judge E. C. Collins, despite the pleas of court-appointed attorneys, including Lewis Twyman, president of the Dade County Bar Association, James M. McCaskill, and the Italian-speaking Albert Raia, that their client was mentally unstable, sentenced Zangara to eighty years total. Zangara cried out to the judge, "You are stingy, why don't you make it one hundred?" The judge replied, knowing that the condition of Cermack and Mrs. Gill was critical, stated, "Perhaps you will get more."

The FBI's J. Edgar Hoover and the U.S. Secret Service looked into possible motives of Zangara for the shooting spree. The conclusion of both agencies was similar; that Zangara, an uneducated proponent of anarchy, operated alone in this crime. His prior movements were traced without discovering hard information of any conspiracy in the New Jersey area. Zangara had accumulated $2,500 in savings and had been withdrawing it to live on during the last year of his life in Miami. It had been said that he lost much of his savings at the Miami horse and dog tracks. He had only $43 on his person when arrested and $200 in a New Jersey postal account.

Mayor Cermack, meanwhile, was being treated for stomach wounds by doctors at Jackson Memorial Hospital, including Dr. G. Rapp, attending physician, and Dr. Frederick, renowned surgeon. Cermack was able to speak immediately after his admittance to the hospital, as Roosevelt visited him before the president-elect left the city for

Washington. Despite the care provided by the doctors, Cermack died on March 6, 1933, of peritonitis.

Zangara was returned to the court, pled guilty, and sentenced to die in Florida's electric chair. Zangara said he was happy with the verdict and sentencing. On March 20, 1933, fourteen days after Mayor Cermack died of his wound, Giuseppe Zangara was executed in Raiford State Prison. His last words were, "Good-bye to all poor people everywhere, PUSH THE BUTTON." Dade County Sheriff Dan Hardie accommodated Zangara's last request and the button was pushed.

It is interesting to note the comment Mayor Cermack made while hospitalized on hearing of the speed of Zangara's first trail. He was reported to have said, "If other states followed Florida's example of speedy trials, crime would certainly drop quickly all over our country" (*Fresno Bee*, 2/17/1933; *Nevada Journal*, 2/18/1933).

AL CAPONE

Al Capone, notorious Chicago gangster, would frequently winter in Miami's warm sun. He purchased, under the name of his wife, Rose, a home on a small island between Miami and Miami Beach and would spend many of the winter months partying and relaxing in the sun. Capone told Chief Quigg that "he had no intention of breaking the law in Miami." The locale of his home was actually within the city limits of Miami Beach. However, the Miami police in 1930 decided to copy the Chicago police's habit of jailing Capone for any possible violation they could think of.

In May 1930, Capone was arrested three times for "investigation" or vagrancy. One arrest on May 28 was made by Chief of Police Guy Reeve and Detective Chief Scarboro for vagrancy as Capone was attending a boxing match at the local American Legion hall.

Capone's attorneys responded by appealing to the federal judge Ritter for a restraining order against the department to prevent MPD for arresting Capone without a warrant. The same judge has previously issued an order preventing twenty Florida sheriffs from arresting Capone "without due process of law." The attorneys appeared before a Miami Justice of the Peace to charge Miami Public Safety Director Sam McCready and Mayor Ritter for the false arrest of Capone. The shoe was then put on the other foot as Capone was then charged with perjury for lying about the circumstances of the above arrest.

These cases all became moot in 1931 when Capone was convicted on income tax violation charges and sentenced to eleven years in jail, which he served seven and one half. After his release, he returned to his Miami Beach mansion in ill health and died in 1947 without suffering any additional arrests by the MPD (*Miami News*, various stories in May 1930).

CRASH KILLS MOTOR OFFICER

John Brubaker, thirty, died in a motorcycle crash on March 31, 1933, as he and Officer C. E. Campbell sped toward a burglary call. At West Flagler and Sixteenth Avenue, a twenty-year driver turned in front of Brubaker, resulting in a crash that injured the officer, who died of a fractured skull two days later. The girl advised that she had seen Campbell go by but claimed she had never seen Brubaker's motorcycle coming.

Brubaker, a Pennsylvania native and an army veteran, joined the MPD in 1928. He left a wife, Mattie, and two children at the time. His wife was pregnant at the time of John's death. The child, Roy Brubaker, later became an MPD police officer in 1956 and retired in 1979 after serving twenty-three years, many of them as a mounted unit officer. Officer Brubaker is buried in Miami's Woodlawn Cemetery (MPD records; Wilbanks, *Forgotten Heroes*, 1996).

*   *   *

The Pistol Teams fielded by MPD in the 1930s included the following officers: Sergeant L. G. Crews, E. H. Hanlin, Pat Baldwin, Charles Stanton, Lieutenant J. O. Barker, Lieutenant J. H. Collins, Gerald Baldwin, S. A. Tanner, Hubert Coleman, Cal Davis, and R. G. Stiles.

The team won many trophies in matches with other departments and army teams.

Longtime MPD Sergeant Mansfield was buried today in honor. His pallbearers were Captain Hardy Bryan, Captain Virgil Mathis, Captain Forrest Nelson, Captain Wm. McCarthy, Lieutenant Finch Cochran, Sergeant Ed Barrick, and Sergeant RoyPottroff (*Miami News*, 11/13/1933).

In December 1933, Constable John Dickson was killed by an offender. The suspect was arrested by MPD Chief S. D. McCreary and Detective E. W. Melchen (Wilbanks, *Forgotten Heroes*, 1996).

OLD-TYME CRIME PREVENTION

Leslie Quigg, longtime MPD chief of police, related this story to MPD vet Joe—, husband of Quigg's granddaughter. "Chief Leslie Quigg and I were talking one day at his house in Shenandoah and he related this story to me. He said that back when he was chief, the city and downtown merchants were having a real bad problem with pickpockets down on Flagler Street, and I think it was around Christmastime. He called in two of his detectives and told them to arrest a pickpocket and beat him up real good and bring him to his office. In the meantime, he called the newspaper and told them to send him a reporter and camera man. Well, several hours passed and the two detectives showed up at the chief's office with a pickpocket they had arrested and beat up. The newspaper reporter and cameraman took a photo of the beaten-up pickpocket and put it on the front page of the next day's newspaper. The headline read, "This is what happens to pickpockets in Miami." The pickpocket problem was solved in downtown. Times change.

GUNFIGHT KILLS DETECTIVE

Forty-year-old Detective Robert Lee Jester, a ten-year veteran of MPD, was shot and killed in downtown Miami on Saturday afternoon, November 18, 1933, in a shootout between two MPD detectives and two bank robbers. Jester, a World War I vet, joined the MPD in 1923 and was promoted to detective in 1925.

The department had received a tip that two armed robbers from Pennsylvania would attempt to pick up a money order at the Postal Telegraph Office, 45 E. Flagler Street, and assigned two detectives, Detective Jester and partner Detective Roy A. Hancock, to stake out the location. At 4:00 PM, one of the robbers, Leo Zalutsky, twenty-one, entered the store. Detective Hancock had left the postal office through the rear door to circle around through a drugstore and block the front entrance of the postal office. Detective Jester followed Zalutsky out the door where the bandit was joined by his partner, Anthony Hanson, also twenty-one. Jester grabbed Hanson at the entrance of the Seybold building and they struggled. Zalutsky ran up the stairs exchanging shots with Detective Hancock. Zalutsky slumped down when hit by Hancock's slugs so Detective Hancock turned back down the stairs to assist his partner just as bandit Hanson shot Detective Jester three times. The detective slumped to the ground and Hanson ran up the stairs toward Detective Hancock. Almost out of ammo, Hancock placed a well-aimed shot at Hanson's head that felled the bandit. Both Detective Jester and robber Hanson died en route to Jackson Hospital.

Zalutsky, wounded, but still able to run, continued up the stairs, climbed out a window, and slid down a utility pole and escaped. Zautsky later hired a cab to take him to his apartment at Thirteenth Street and Biscayne where the bandit instructed the hack driver to come back and pick him up later. A massive police manhunt was undertaken in the downtown area on this busy Saturday afternoon to no avail until the cabbie called in the info on the wounded killer's location. The still-armed Zalutsky was apprehended as he emerged from the apartment.

Zalutsky was sentenced to life imprisonment but escaped a total of five times over the years, and was a fugitive for as long as six years, one of the escapees. He was paroled in 1958, twenty-five years after killing Detective Jester.

Jester was survived by his wife, Elsie, and was buried in Woodlawn Cemetery in Miami after a funeral that every off-duty Miami police officer attended (*Miami News*, 7-11/19/1933; Wilbanks, *Forgotten Heroes*, 1996).

ONE TOUGH COP

Jim Maloney was a heavyweight boxer who won forty-nine of his fights, twenty-one by a knockout, in bouts with the biggest and the best boxers in America during the late '20s and early '30s. He defeated Primo Carnera, among other big names in the sport. In March 1934, Jim joined the Miami Police Department and was assigned to traffic duty. In 1935, while still on the Miami PD, he fought Max Baer on Miami Beach, losing the decision.

Jim was attending law school at the University of Miami while still on the department and later was the university's boxing coach. It is not known how long Maloney was on the department, but we will wager that he did not have any difficulty with the tough guys down on Flagler Street while directing traffic (MPD records, *Miami News*, 6/1924).

Several detectives were congratulated for making a difficult arrest in a complex extortion case. They were Detective Louis Allen, G. J. Davis, H. G. Howard, W. W. Potterton, H. Handford, Wesley Shannahan, B. M. Howard, and Sergeant Eddie Melchen (*Miami News*, 6/3/1934).

MIAMI PBA

The Police Benevolent Association was born in the midst of all the instability in the department. In 1935, a group of policemen organized the PBA, the first in Florida, to present a unified forum in civil service and employment matters.

LIST OF PBA PRESIDENTS

Fred Manning	1935-36
Edwin L. Barrick	1936-41
Melville A. Tibbitts	1941-42
Edwin L. Barrick	1942-43
Dalton D. Carver	1943-44
Walter E. Headley	1944-45
Charles C. Papy	1945-48
Forrest E. Nelson	1948-49
Thomas T. Sherman	1949-50
Harold B. Goodman	1950-51
Estol W. Hall	1951-53
Newell A. Horne	1953-55
Charles T. Renegar	1955-56
Leon S. Hall	1956-58
L. Ray Larsen	1958-59
Estol W. Hall	1959-61
Chadwick H. Kaye	1961-63
Alexander S. Gurdak	1963-65
Donald L. Printz	1965-75
James A. Cox	1975-77
Donald L. Printz	1977-78
James A. Cox	1978-86
William Glaister	1986-90
Jerry Kaline	1990-94
Steve Smigelski	1994-96

Thomas J. Roell   1996-2000
Robert A. Fielder Jr.   2002-02
James R. Billberry   2002-04
Walter A. Rodak   2004-07
William H. Farrington   2007-08
Gerald Green   2008-12
Joseph Longueria   2012-
(Miami Police Benevolent Association records)

BUSY SEASON—1935

Did you know that Charlie Chan was a member of the Miami police? He was Officer No. 237 by special order of Acting Chief William McCarthy. The sage Oriental criminologist, Worner Oland, known to all as Charlie Chan, received a special badge recently. His new movie opened in Miami, and all Miami police officers were invited to view the flick (*Miami News*, 1935).

The Federal Communication Commission issued a permit to Miami for a two-way police/fire radio system. Also, the radio system went from 100 watts to 500 watts according to MPD Chief Radio Operator Ben Denby (*Miami News*, 4/1/1935).

The radio system was initially installed on November 15, 1933, according to the MPD annual report.

Working detectives listed in February 1935 included G. J. Davis, J. L. Dees, W. S. Shanahan, Gwen Howard, Roy Hancock, Bruce Howard, John M. Driggers, and his brother William Driggers (MPD records).

"I RAN THE KLAN," SAYS POLICE CHIEF

The arrest of a seventeen-year-old youth for drunk and disorderly conduct at the Olympia Theater on March 9, 1935, set off a furor in Miami that lasted several weeks. George Kirkland, son of a prominent citizen, claimed to have been beaten at the police station following his arrest, causing serious injuries. The arresting officer, G. A. Denny, slapped Kirkland in the face several times and punched him in the stomach when the youth allegedly attempted to pull Denny's gun from under the officer's coat while the youth was being placed in a holding cell together with six Negro prisoners.

The youth's father bailed his son out of jail and took him to the home of Acting Police Chief Lonnie Scarboro, a personal friend, to display the injuries.

Scarboro immediately suspended all the officers that were present during the altercation, including Captain Virgil Mathis, Sergeant Eddie Barrick, and Officers Denny, S. D. Griffin, Curtis Lynch, L. L. (Mickey) Cochran, and A. D. Mikell.

A raucous three-day hearing was held by the Civil Service Board on the charges against the officers. Despite conflicting testimony, the board cleared all the officers, ruling that the force used by the officers was necessary for their safety.

Dade County Attorney Pine stated that he would file criminal charges against Officer Denny regardless of the outcome of the Civil Service Board hearing.

Acting Chief Scarboro immediately demoted Captain Mathis to lieutenant and ordered an investigation of the other officers. Captain Mathis was the on-duty commander at the time of the incident and was present during the alleged beating of Kirkland.

On March 27, the city commission conducted a hearing and recommended that City Manager Lee conduct an investigation and take whatever action is necessary to resolve the case. One point raised in the civil service hearing was the police department policy of placing whites or women into holding cells that contained Negro prisoners.

The chief of police, Sam McCreary (who was also the public safety director), had been absent from the city at the time of the incident. He now, under questioning, stated to the city commission his position on placing women and youths into holding cells with black prisoners.

"As head of the Ku Klux Klan from 1924 to 1930, I would be the last person to allow this condition," he said. "If a police captain even allowed it, he must have been a fool."

It should be noted that McCreary was appointed public safety director in charge of Miami's police and fire departments in January 1930, the same year he completed, according to his own words, his leadership of Miami's Klan (*Miami News*, 3/27/1935, p. 11).

The following month, a new city commission fired McCreary from the public safety job and, a month later, fired him as police chief.

Former Rochester, New York, Police Chief Andrew Kavanaugh was named safety director of Miami in charge of both fire and police departments. He was hired by City Manager L. L. Lee to replace S. D. McCreary (*Miami News*, 2/24/1935).

ACTING CHIEF McCARTHY

Suspended Chief S. D. McCreary will face the city commission tomorrow to contest his firing as chief of police, based on charges by City Manager L. L. Lee for incompetence and other charges. McCreary was indicted for bribery and conspiracy to protect gamblers (*Pittsburg Press*, 2/9/1935).

Captain William J. McCarthy, commander of the traffic division, was named acting chief. McCarthy outlined his plans for the supervision of the department, stating "There has been too much tendency for police officers and personnel to take up so much time with politics and not enough with their own duties. I will insist that the department be run with the sole aim of protection of life and property" (*Miami News*, 5/23/1935).

McCarthy was acting chief of police during the fall of 1935 when the terrible hurricane wiped out the Keys and took a good swipe at south Florida. McCarthy warned citizens to get their cars off the streets before the storm based on teletypes from Cuba on the ferocity of the winds.

A month later, McCarthy issued an order to round up all known criminals and bring them into the police station for questioning (We could do that then). Rumors were circulating that the big crooks from up north were going to make a move on the hotels and clubs in Miami, forcing the owners to "hire" them to protect the clubs, a scheme to take over the profits of the establishments during the upcoming busy tourist season. McCarthy was a tough cop but well respected by his officers and the local citizens (General knowledge and MPD records).

FREE RIDE FOR TIPSY DRIVERS

Miami had a new public safety director (who also headed the police department), Andrew Kavanaugh, in 1936, who implemented a plan to decrease auto fatalities caused by drunk drivers. Kavanaugh issued an order that allowed drunks to call the police for a free ride home if they thought they were too tipsy to drive. No fine, no arrest, no charges, no strings of any kind—just so you keep away from the wheel of the car until you become sober. He was motivated by six recent deaths caused by drunk drivers, including one of his own police officers, Officer Samuel Hicks.

"Let the other fellow drive," he urged. "If there is no other fellow, call a cab, and if you find yourself financially embarrassed, and still conscious enough to be safety-minded, call the police headquarters and we will see that you will be taken home in safety—only don't do it too often."

He said several men had availed themselves of the service. The policemen just drove their charge to the front door and helped them up the stairs—no extra frills, like circumventing irate wives or delivering the automobile too (MPD records).

McCARTHY MADE PERMANENT

William McCarthy, forty, who has been serving as acting chief since May 23, 1935, was appointed permanent chief of police last night by City Manager L. L. Lee. The former marine, wounded in France in World War I, has been an MPD officer since 1921 when he joined after a short stint as a Washington, D.C., officer. McCarthy was a traffic division lieutenant in 1925, having a detail of 250 men under him, more than there are now (1935) on the force. McCarthy became a captain of the traffic division in 1932.

McCarthy's tenure did not last long. In the spring of 1936, he announced that he was vacating the chief's position and wished to be assigned back to the rank of captain in charge of the traffic divison (*Miami News*, 12/28/1935).

OUTSIDER TAKES OVER CHIEF JOB

John B. Rowland, thirty-six, a Dade County States' attorney investigator, will become chief of police on May 18, 1936. He was appointed by City Manager L. L. Lee, replacing Chief McCarthy, who requested that he be returned to the rank of captain. A special civil service ruling was passed to protect the pension and seniority rights of retiring Chief McCarthy when he reverts back to his civil service rank of captain. "Smiling Mac" McCarthy was appointed acting chief on May 23, 1935, and permanent chief on December 28, 1935, succeeding S. D. McCreary, who had been both chief and safety director (*Miami News*, 5/3/1936).

Author's Note: No reason was stated in the news reports on why McCarthy stepped down. However, in a following story on the trial of Detective Chief Scarboro, possible reason(s) surfaced.

DUI KILLS OFFICER HICKS

Officer Samuel D. Hicks, a forty-eight-year-old MPD veteran, an Alabama native, was killed by a drunk driver on Sunday, August 9, 1936, at NW Fifth Avenue and Seventeenth Street. The driver, Heanon Arnold, twenty-five, was arrested for manslaughter, but no case resolution was located in the records.

Hicks, an MPD officer for eleven years, joining in 1925, and his partner Officer Raleigh Page, were in the process of arresting four suspects and searching their car relating to an earlier auto theft case when Arnold, driving a truck, ran down Hicks, who died shortly after arriving at Jackson Memorial Hospital.

Hick was survived by two sons, one of whom became an MPD officer in the 1940s (Louis Hicks). Officer Hicks's wife had died just a month before Hicks was killed. Hicks was buried in Graceland Memorial Park on SW Eighth Street.

The investigating officer was Homicide Detective A. N. Clark and the police chief at the time was John B. Rowland (Wilbanks, *Forgotten Heroes*, 1996; MPD records).

Chief Rowland announced the promotion of Lieutenant Redman to captain, and Dick Lemon and Ben Denby to lieutenant (MPD records).

THE AXE FALLS

New Chief of Police J. B. Rowland suspended the chief of detectives, Lonnie O. Scarboro, and three other detectives on two-score charges of brutality, incompetence, and neglect of duty today. This is one of the most sweeping changes the Miami department has known in years. The three other detectives suspended have been identified as Roy A.

Hancock, J. H. Williams, and W. C. Crawford, all ten-year-plus veteran officers.

Frank Mitchell, an MPD vet since 1921, was appointed as temporary chief of detectives. The suspended officers will be defended on the charges by attorneys from the Miami Police Benevolent Association. These attorneys quickly obtained an injunction to halt the upcoming hearings before Safety Director Kavenaugh.

The hearing went ahead and offered testimony by many witnesses, including Captain William McCarthy and Sergeant Louis Allen, both of whom occupied offices adjoining the scene of the beatings of the prisoners, the office of detective boss Scarboro.

The victim of one of the beatings, Mack Williams, a black male charged with burglary, testified that two additional detectives, Charles C. Papy and G. W. Wilkerson, also beat him, causing his eyes to close shut.

The hearings continued daily through the month of October and were highlighted by charges and testimony that Scarboro and the three detectives beat two prisoners with fists, sticks, and a hose. One of the detectives, Crawford, was also charged with visiting a Broward gambling hall while on duty.

The fourteen-day hearings were concluded in late October, but the safety director studied the transcripts for a month before handing down his verdict. In mid-December, Kavanaugh fired Chief Scarboro and Detective Williams, demoted Detective Hancock to patrolman, and fined Detective Crawford $75, before returning him to duty (*Miami News*, 10/4/1936).

After the above hearings were concluded and prior to the verdicts, Chief Rowland and Safety Director Kavanaugh promoted the following officers during the continuing shake-up of the command staff.

Forest Nelson was promoted to inspector in charge of uniform, Frank Mitchell was made inspector of the detective force, and William McCarthy was promoted to inspector of traffic. Chief Rowland also promoted Sergeant Roy Pottorf to lieutenant of the uniform division (*Miami News*, 11/10/1936).

Author's Note: Testimony during the Scarboro hearing brought forward the notion that Chief McCarthy had stepped down from the chief's job because of too much politics on the job and he wanted to return to his traffic command in order to "do well" for the citizens of Miami. It was also suggested in the above hearing that McCarthy refused to demote or suspend the three detectives as demanded by the public safety director (Miami Civil Service records).

State law enforcement officers arrested four persons in connection with the shooting of Curtis Ellis, a moonshine informant. Ellis, himself a big-time moonshiner, was to testify against gang members who had planned to kill witnesses in an upcoming trial. One of the intended victims was Miami Police Sergeant Cecil (Hamp) Knight (St. Petersburg (FL) *Evening Independent*, 12/9/1936).

OFFICER CHARLES PARKER

Officer Charles Parker,Sr., born July 7, 1899, in Shawnee, Oklahoma, left school early and put in two enlistments with the U.S. Marines, being honorably discharged in 1925. In 1930, the U.S. Census showed Parker as a Union County, Florida, police officer. Parker was married to Ollie Mae Parker (née Parker), of Raiford, Florida, for forty-two years. He joined the Miami Police Department in 1937 and retired in 1964. Parker resided at 3620 SW Third Street in Miami, Florida.

Parker's two sons, C. C. Parker Jr. and Raymond Parker, were also members of the Miami police force. The senior Parker died on October 31, 1968. An article appeared in the Miami newspaper when he passed away.

> Charles C. Parker, Sr., who during his 27 years as a MPD officer, had been the official driver for 12 City of Miami Mayors, died Thursday. He was 68. Mr. Parker, of 11425 SW 50th Terr, retired from the force in 1957. He first drove for Mayor E. G. Sewell in the 1930's.

> In 1954, he was dubbed the "Lost" chauffeur by Mayor Abe Abronwitz, when he disappeared for four weeks. In jest, Mayor Abronwitz offered a $50 reward for locating Officer Parker, who was found in a local hospital, waiting for his wife to recover from minor surgery.

> An October, 1941 story described a driver's license check where Parker had to show his license to a Highway Patrol officer while driving the mayor. (He had one.)

Upon passing, the elder Parker was survived by his wife, Edna, two sons, Charles Jr. and Raymond A., a daughter, Della Pearce of Palm Springs, FL, eight grandchildren and five great grandchildren.

His son Raymond Parker, also a Miami police officer, is the subject of a later story in this book (U.S. Census Reports, MPD records, *Miami News*).

MISCELLANEOUS ITEMS

A news photo showed motor officer Sergeant L. G. Crews sitting on an MPD motorcycle. His uniform had the triangle patch just above the sergeant stripes. This is the first photo of that patch (worn until 1964) that was found. Other photos of officers in the next few years did not show the patch, suggesting that initially only the motor squad was issued the triangle patch (*Miami News*, 1/10/1937).

A photo of the Miami PD Pistol Team appeared in the local paper on March 6, 1937. Members of the team were Sergeant L. G. Crews, E. H. Hamlin, Patrick H. Baldwin, C. O. Stanton, Lieutenant J. O. Barker, and Lieutenant J. H. Collin (*Miami News*, 3/6/1937).

During May 1937, the new mayor Williams was elected. He then led a majority on the commission to immediately fire Safety Director Kavenaugh. Chief of Police John Rowland quit the department the following day and Leslie Quigg was again appointed to the chief's position. Quigg let it be known that the policy of "liberality" would return to the gambling scene in Miami.

Chief Quigg quickly reinstated fired Detective Chief Scarboro and Detective Williams, who was fired by Safety Director Kavenaugh last year (*Miami News*, 8/1937).

Miami police were ordered to confiscate scooters and roller skates being operated in the streets as a safety measure (*Miami News*, 8/2/1937).

Captain Fred Manning, traffic commander, was sent to a police traffic school in Washington, D.C. (*Miami News*, 9/6/1937).

Also on this date, Detectives Henry G. Howard, E. S. Chambers, Charles Schwelm, and Nolan were mentioned in article about utilizing pawnshops to locate stolen items. Detective Sergeant Eddie Melchen and C. C. Papy were the subject of a story about other arrests.

The contract for MPD uniforms was awarded to Willis and Fink Tailors, on a bid of $3,265, plus $600 for hats (*Miami News*, 9/16/1937).

Coral Way was opened from Five Points to Douglas Road today (*Miami News*, 9/18/1937).

Officer Jesse James Clinton was dismissed by the city manager because he ran for a seat on the city commission. (The case dragged out in the courts for years.) (*Miami News*, 9/19/1937)

Radio Patrolman R. L. Gillette and R. Ryder mentioned in news story. Also, Officer Carl Spence and Raleigh Hill (*Miami News*, 10/4/1937).

Burglars stole MPD Officer Joe Mullis's revolver from his home while he was out (*Miami News*, 10/8/1937).

Inspector William McCarthy, Lieutenant D. G. Reynolds, and Lieutenant W. Lemmon were reported in the paper discussing auto inspections requirements in the city (*Miami News*, 10/12/1937).

PBA Attorney Pruitt filed notice of "unfair promotions," suits that were later dropped.
Another story discussed Fred J. Manning, the traffic inspector (*Miami News*, 10/14/1937).

Enoch Powell, special Negro police agent for MPD, was arrested for carrying a concealed weapon. The city attorney asked that charges be dropped.

Author's Note: This is the first mention I have found in which a black officer had been employed in an enforcement capacity in MPD history (*Miami News*, 10/20/1937).

NEWS BRIEFS—1938-39

News stories in the archives of the *Miami News* during 1938 mentioned numerous Miami officers, including George Campbell, Jesse Campbell, James A. Brown, Garbett A. Vander, William Carlson, and Harry Fouts. Worthy E. Farr Sr., Neal Coston, Kenneth M. Fether, J. D. Chesser, Edward D. Daly, Henry M. Cole, Barney Bryan, Captain Hardy Bryan, Hardy Bryan Jr., Earl Christianson, Walter E. Headley, Cecil (Hamp) Knight, C. O. Huttoe, and Pat Baldwin.

The date following the item indicates when the article appeared.

City police arrested two white men and a Negro, destroyed a 1,000-gallon-capacity moonshine still, and confiscated 18 jugs of whiskey in what Assistant Chief Forrest Nelson described as the biggest police still raid since prohibition.

Led by Nelson, Lieutenant Melvin Tibbets and Detective M. C. Tucker entered a garage in the rear of a house at 1175 NW Fifty-sixth Street. Arrested were James Sewell, twenty; John Kelly, twenty-two; and Abe Singleton, thirty-three, Negro.

The police destroyed the still. (1/3/1938)

Detectives Jerry Baldwin and Joe McLendon were pictured in the newspaper while investigating a 50K robbery. (2/9/1938)

Officer J. G. Schauers was fired for being involved in politics. He was an MPD officer from 1929 to 1937. (2/10/1938)

Eight police officers finished their one-year probation and became permanent officers. They were Charles Price, C. B. Newton, W. S. Scott, W. D. Wright, William C. Chalk, A. M. Carrier, George Hayden, and J. M. McDougall. Their pay was raised from $100 a month to $135 a month. Motor officers went from $130 a month to $140 a month. (2/11/1938)

Two youths, charged with disorderly conduct in connection with a "punchboard" racket, pled guilty before Judge Curry and fined $100. The boys were duplicating winning punch card numbers, collecting cash rewards. The two, Robert DuPree, nineteen, and Henry Smith, eighteen, were arrested by Detective Joe McNeill. Both were recently ordered out of West Palm Beach for similar offenses. (2/15/1938)

Sim Dawson, former secretary of the previous safety director Kavenaugh, has been brought up on charges of insubordination and disloyalty by Chief Quigg.

Dawson claims the charges are politically inspired. The city manager, A. E. Fuller, sitting in his capacity of safety director, took the charges under advisement. Lieutenant James Barker and Officers M. C. Tucker and C. B. Foss testified in substantiation of Chief Quigg's charges. (2/16/1938)

Traffic Inspector Wm. McCarthy set up a citizen "Secret Observers" program for traffic infraction reporting. (2/1938)

An escape of prisoner Paul Cooper from Jackson Hospital caused a downtown manhunt today. Cooper, a robbery suspect, was recaptured at Flagler Street and NW Second Avenue by Detectives J. A. McLendon and Sid Broom. (2/19/1938)

A suspect in the kidnapping of a fifteen-year-old girl was arrested by MPD officers A. W. Fairbrother and Raleigh Hill. Richard Darby, eighteen, admitted he took the girl Sunday night when questioned by Detective Lieutenant E. W. Melchen, saying, "I was crazy to do it, but I loved her so much." The girl was rescued by six dairy farmers after chasing Darby's car at high speeds on Milam Dairy Road. (2/23/1938)

Officer Joe Jenkins was suspended for sleeping on duty while on the Coconut Grove beat. (3/1/1938)

Officer Harold Nolle received a commendation from Gesu school students. Nolle had directed traffic in front of the Gesu school for the previous ten years. (3/2/1938)

The MPD Pistol Team is participating in the "Flamingo Open" pistol match. A news photo shows Sergeant L. G. Crews and Officer Pat Baldwin.

The pistol match team from MPD had the reputation during this era of being one of the finest in the country. Some of their regular members at that time were Cal Davis, Mel A. Tibbets, V. D. Rowe, Gerald E. Baldwin, and R. G. Stiles in addition to Crews and Pat Baldwin. (3/6/1938)

John Hepburn, thirty-five, opened fire with a .45-caliber automatic toward MPD officers R. B. Simpson and J. D. Chesser, who had attempted to question Hepburn about a package he was carrying. Hepburn then ran eastward on NW Fourteenth Street and confronted Fireman J. T. Clay, who was standing in front of the fire station. Hepburn shoved the gun into Clay's stomach and fired, but the weapon failed to fire.

Two snake hunters driving by in an auto, Jack

Shumaker and Wilbur Simmons, observed Hepburn's assault of Clay and joined the chase. Seventeen-year-old Shumaker fired two shots at Hepburn with a .22-caliber rifle and killed Hepburn instantly.

The "package" Hepburn was carrying was an old copy of *Our World Today*, belonging to the Florida library. (*Miami News*, 3/7/1938)

Miami passed an ordinance requiring boats to lower outrigger fishing poles while passing through bridges, thereby eliminating the necessity raising the bridges. Officer Bob Yancey, the lone harbor patrol officer, and Traffic Inspector Fred Manning were pictured in today's story relating to the court battle over the issue. (3/19/1938)

Edward White, fifty-four, of 2044 SW Second Street, was very happy to be arrested last night on bad check charges. When Dectives E. S. Chambers and Henry G. Howard arrived at White's home, they observed smoke pouring from a bedroom window. As the detectives battered on the door, White leaped from his bed, which was ablaze from the lighted cigarette he had dropped as he went to sleep.

Detectives Chambers and Howard beat out the flames without the aid of firemen. (3/21/1938)

Motor Officer John Thomas was injured while chasing a stolen car. His partner, J. W. Campbell, escaped injury. (3/24/1938)

A new "single fingerprint" system has recently been installed in the Miami police identification unit. Previously, all ten fingerprints were required for identification. Under the new system, a thief need leave only a single telltale print at the scene of a "job." Armed with one fingerprint, experts can turn to their files and identify the thief if he has a prior record. (3/24/1938)

A photo in today's paper shows police officer Bob Yancey, Harbor Patrol officer, showing off new equipment—a dive helmet—to perform underwater rescue work. (3/25/1938)

Officer Albert G. Hinson, fifty, who has served on the MPD since 1925 until injured on the job in 1935, has been awarded a retirement plan that provides him with two-thirds of his base pay. (4/7/1938)

Detectives Sid C. Broome and J. A. McLendon arrested an entire busload of Negroes because one of them yelled an insulting remark at the officers from the bus window. (4/8/1938)

Detective Chief Scarboro and Detective F. A. Jollay had a confrontation with an armed nut in the police station. No injuries. The subject was hospitalized. (4/10/1938)

Inspector McCarthy, traffic boss, and Captain S. W. Lemmon, the school officer, were featured in a local paper regarding their accident prevention plans. (5/24/1938)

The Miami PBA hosted a party for 1,600 schoolchildren at their third annual picnic at the Biscayne Kennel Club. The picnic was financed from proceeds of the annual dance, sponsored by the association.
The president of the PBA then was Lieutenant Edwin L. Barrick. A photo accompanied the story. (5/29/1938)

Miami Police Dispatcher Margaret Dow (or DOE) was mentioned in an article as being the first female police dispatcher in the United States. She made her first radio broadcast in 1937, the same day she received her radio license. From 1934 to 1937, only male Miami police officers were assigned as radio dispatchers. (6/17/1938)

Officers Harry Fouts and Carl Spense made a quick arrest via a radio BOLO, one of the first using the new two-way radio setup that MPD installed. They stopped the stolen car within a minute of the broadcast. (6/21/1938)

C. O. Huttoe was removed from Vice Squad as a result of pressure from Mayor Williams. Detective Fred Rowland was placed in temporary charge of squad.

News reports rumors that Sergeant Sid Broome will have the job soon. Huttoe remained at the same rank and will continue to earn $180 a month. (6/26/1938)

Detective Sergeant Sid C. Broome was fined $1 for improper parking of a detective car which was involved in a traffic accident downtown. Detective J. H. Williams was injured in that accident when a motorist struck the open door of the squad car parked on the wrong side of the street. (6/30/1938)

Officer Charles R. Reynolds has been assigned to the waterfront beat for years and states he *never* has made an arrest. (7/3/1938)

Officer Karl Lieb, thirty-eight, collapsed during the Fourth of July celebration. He was later reported in nonserious condition. (7/5/1938)

The MPD Pistol Team took first and third place in the Florida East Coast championship today at the Coral
Gables pistol range.

Team #1 (and their scores) consisted of Pat Baldwin (274), Gerald Baldwin (276), J. H. Collins (276), and Charles Stanton (263). Team #2 members were E. Hamlin, Cal Davis, Mel Tibbets, and J. Howard. Team #3 did well also. They were J. Youell, E. W. Hall, D. Reynolds, and Raymond Brock.

Miami Sergeant L. Crews hosted a post-match BBQ for all participants. (7/4/1938)

Meanwhile, at the MPD practice range in Opa Locka, things got exciting. Matt Vollmner, sixty-eight, the caretaker at the range, was shot in the leg when an unexploded pistol bullet caught in the cutters of the power lawnmower he was operating and exploded.

On the same day, MPD officer Ray Brock suffered a sprained angle at the range when he stepped into a hole while target practicing. (7/9/1938)

Detective M. C. Tucker arrested five men last night in a bar at NW Fifth Street and Fourth Avenue following speeches allegedly violently Nazi in character. The five will be tried in city court on Monday. Main figure arrested was Raymond Healy, twenty-six, termed by police a self-styled Hitler who came here recently from New York. Police took a briefcase from Healy containing a supply of anti-Jewish windshield stickers and a pamphlet in German.

A *Miami News* editorial blasted Chief Quigg for crossing over the line, ignoring First Amendment protections. They stated Quigg did the same earlier when Communists were making the same type pitch.

Detective Chief Scarboro assigns four detectives to investigate labor vandalism at new homes. The officers were Joe McNeill, Bryan Howard, J. L. Wilkerson, and Joe Jenkins. (7/18/1938)

Coral Gables Officer Homer Barton was shot in May 1938 by a crazy drunk with a shotgun while trying to serve a warrant. Miami officers W. S. Scott and Harry Bushman arrived at scene on Oak Avenue just inside of Miami City limits and were jumped by the offender. Sergeant Louis Allen came on scene as well as Detectives Charles C. Papy and Wesley Shananhan. They combined to overcome the offender. Chief Quigg took the offender to Jackson Hospital. The offender later recovered and was executed in 1941. (Wilbanks, *Forgotten Heroes*, 1996)

Patrolman Arthur Fairbrother, thirty-one, was in Jackson Hospital today suffering from bullet wounds when he was shot by Patrolman Gillette. Officer Gillette was called to Fairbrother's home to handle a domestic disturbance at which the drunken Fairbrother beat his wife and destroyed household furniture.

Upon Gillette's arrival at the home, Fairbrother threatened the on-duty officer with a knife and Gillette fired twice to stop the attack.

Fairbrother, who had recently been suspended for firing his revolver through the floor of a nightclub, was again suspended by Assistant Chief Nelson and will be booked into the city jail as soon as he is dismissed from the hospital. (St. Petersburg (FL) *Times*, 2/28/1939)

Mayor Williams was recalled in the city election along with two other commissioners. Their administration had been labeled the "termite administration." The recall election was prompted by many oddball moves by the recalled commissioners. (*Miami News*, 3/1/1939)

Lieutenant Roy A. Pottorf was suspended after being arrested for DUI by MPD officers Bob Bullock and D. B. Foss. It was not the end of his career as he was still on the force ten years later. (*Miami News*, 7/8/1939)

In 1939, Chief Quigg issued a permit for the KKK to conduct an auto parade down Flagler Street, which resulted in the heightening of tensions between the races in the city. (MPD records)

Officer Wesley Thompson (later killed in line of duty), of 644 NW Sixty-fourth Street, Miami, a motor officer, was reported in fair condition at JMH where he is suffering from severe bruises and lacerations received yesterday when his motorcycle collided head-on into an auto. George LeRay, fifty-four, driver of the auto into which the officer crashed, was not arrested. Investigators said Thompson turned into NW First Street from NW North River Drive, giving LaRay no opportunity to avoid the crash. (*Miami News*, 1934, date not recorded)

An inquiry on the operation of the department was blocked by the PBA by obtaining a court injunction. Slated to be called to the inquiry were Chief Quigg, Inspector Forest Nelson, Captain Mathis, Lieutenant J. H. Collins, Lieutenant Roy Pottorf, Detective Roy Hancock, and Detective John McLendon. (*Miami News*, 1939)

PAT BALDWIN DIES IN AUTO CRASH

Officer Patrick Howell Baldwin was killed in an auto accident yesterday. He was born in 1906 in Laurens, South Carolina. Pat joined the MPD on December 4, 1925, so was obviously only nineteen years of age when he started his police service with MPD. Patrick spent most of his fifteen years as a motorcycle officer. He was also a nationally known champion pistol shooter.

In early 1940, he purchased the old Silver Slipper nightclub (now the Miami PBA property on NW Fourteenth Street) with the intention of converting it into his family home with an adjacent pistol range.

On a rainy night in March 1940, Pat Baldwin was assigned to a police car rather than his motor due to the rain. His partner normally was John Thomas, but Thomas took the night off, so Baldwin was riding solo.

At 5:15 AM, Pat Baldwin fell asleep at the wheel on NW Thirty-sixth Street at NW Sixth Avenue and received injuries that caused his immediate death. He is now listed on our Line of Duty Death List (see MPDVETS website Memorial List).

Pat was one of the three brothers who served on the MPD. The others were Gerald Baldwin who retired in 1952 as a detective captain and Judson Baldwin.

The Baldwin family, originally from South Carolina, moved to Macon, Georgia, early in the twentieth century, where the third son was then born. The family moved to Miami in 1925 and two of the sons joined the MPD that year.

Gerald Baldwin, 1901-1972, who joined in 1925, was a desk sergeant in 1935, a patrol lieutenant in 1945, and retired as a captain in 1952. His last assignment was working in Chief of Police Walter Headley's office.

The third brother was Judson (Jud) Baldwin, 1916-1972, who joined the MPD in 1939, a year before his brother got killed. In 1945, Judson was a detective sergeant and he left (retired) in 1955. Judson passed away in 1988 at the age of seventy-two.

Patrick Baldwin's son, Patrick Baldwin, served in the MPD from 1950-1953 (MPD records and Wilbanks, *Forgotten Heroes*, 1996).

VICE SQUABBLES

Things got hot in both the city government and the police department immediately preceding World War II. The principal issue was vice enforcement. Chief Quigg publicly stated that the city wanted a "liberal" atmosphere in vice enforcement. C. O. Huttoe, who was Vice Squad commander during most of 1940 and '41, seemed bent on embarrassing Chief Quigg. On each occasion that Quigg announced that Miami was "closed" to gambling, Huttoe went out and made some raids. Some of the headlines in the *Miami News* during that period highlight the fights between the city manager, the safety director, the chief of police, and the Vice Squad.

The city manager announced a suspension for the second-in-command, Inspector Forrest Nelson, for taking a city car on vacation to Ohio for a month. The detention of the juvenile sons of a prominent resident over the alleged scalping of tickets at the Orange Bowl caused quite a commotion, and the reduction in the police officers' work week from a seven-day week to a six-day week occurred in this period (*Miami News*, various dates, 1940-41).

Detective Chief Scarboro was reprimanded by Chief Quigg for not allowing two juvenile sons of an attorney to call home after being detained at the Orange Bowl for alleged scalping of tickets. Scarboro himself denied the boys the use of the phone, and he and Captain Mathis, the duty captain at the station, were both reprimanded by Chief Quigg, but City Manager Lee upped the penalty to ten-day suspensions for both (*Miami News*, 1/11/1940).

Former officer Jesse (Jack) J. Clinton was suspended but then sued to regain his job.

Clinton had run for city commissioner in 1937 and was fired for becoming involved in politics (*Miami News*, 1/14/1940).

Captain Homer Redman was appointed acting chief by the city manager, while Chief Quigg was on vacation for five days, bypassing the department's number two leader, Inspector Forest Nelson (*Miami News*, 1/20/1940).

A federal grand jury called Vice Squad boss, C. O. Huttoe, and others concerning vice conditions in Miami (*Miami News*, 1/24/1940).

The same day, Public Safety Director Reynolds ordered Chief Quigg to clean up Miami's gambling problem. Quigg passed the order to Huttoe. The Vice Squad was comprised of Huttoe, Sergeants S. C. Broome, Jesse W. Campbell, and Francis Lee Napier.

City Manager Lee calls for Chief Quigg to "clip the wings" of ambitious vice detectives who were making raids obsessively to gain clout in obtaining promotions. C. O. Huttoe was promoted to lieutenant (*Miami News*, 11/3/1940).

It was reported in a column that Detective Fred Rowland was on the verge of a nervous breakdown but Chief Quigg was leery of removing him from the Vice Squad as it might look like Quigg's real motive was to slow down vice enforcement (*Miami News*, 11/12/1940).

Chief Quigg asked the safety director for a probe of Detective Rowland's mental state (*Miami News*, 2/24/1941).

Chief Quigg appointed Grace Tamasy to the position of policewoman in the MPD (*Miami News*, 3/18/1941).

Author's Note: Tamasy was assigned to the new MPD Juvenile Unit shortly after her hiring.

Detectives C. C. Papy and Roy A. Hancock were bypassed for promotion (*Miami News*, 3/25/1940).

The U.S. issues a 653-page report on corruption and brutality in the department. Some of the examples they cited were Detective C. C. Papy striking a prisoner with his fist, Officer John Suggs (now in the navy) for striking another prisoner, and Officer Nick Muslin for roughing up a prisoner and not acknowledging that it was an improper action (*Miami News*, 4/23/1940).

Author's Note: The author rode with Officer Muslin a couple of nights in the paddy wagon as a rookie in 1960. Officer Muslin appeared to be a laid-back nice guy who displayed no hint of being overly rough.

John Manny charged that Safety Director Reynolds had a secret contract with the city that he (Reynolds) would be put back into his old job as commander of the motor squad if he got bounced from the safety director's job. Manny also charged that Mayor Orr put pressure on the MPD to promote C. O. Huttoe to lieutenant. Huttoe had backed Abe Aronowitz's run for office while Chief Quigg backed another (*Miami News*, 6/2/1941).

Jesse Campbell, a probationary detective, replaced Huttoe as Vice Squad CO. Huttoe is assigned to the FBI to work on subversives. Detective Napier was also transferred out of Vice and reassigned to General Assignment (*Miami News*, 7/9/1941).

Safety Director Reynolds was ousted and Chief Quigg assumed full command of MPD (*Miami News*, 7/12/1941).

Feud between Huttoe and Quigg aired again in newspaper (*Miami News*, 7/13/1941).

Inspector Forest Nelson takes blame for taking a city car to Ohio on a month's vacation. He was suspended thirty days and forced to pay a $240 fine (*Miami News*, 7/23/1941).

Chief Quigg pledges to help FBI in subversive hunting (*Miami News*, 8/9/1941).

Lieutenant W. J. Hammer, commander of accident squad, proposed new effort on reducing accidents.

A news column reported that Lieutenant Huttoe was now back in the Vice Squad, raiding every gambling location after Chief Quigg stated (again) that the town was closed to gambling (*Miami News*, 10/27/1941).

The Miami City Commission ordered a shake-up of the police department. The city manager will be forced out for not pushing gambling enforcement. The commission also proposed that Chief Quigg be put on a paid leave of absence for sixteen months until he is eligible for retirement. City Manager Lee resigned the following day (St. Petersburg *Independent*, 11/13/1941).

The city commission granted police officers the six-day week, down from the previous seven-day week. They also proposed that during the winter season that the officers be assigned to seven-day weeks but will be able to add the extra days later in the year on their vacation period (*Miami News*, 12/3/1941).

On December 7, 1941, the Japanese bombed Pearl Harbor in a surprise attack. The U.S. was soon at war with Japan and Germany, lasting three and one-half years.

Also in 1941, Lieutenant Potterton's son was arrested for a string of armed robberies in the area. He had committed many of these crimes while wearing a stocking mask and was called by the press the "Stocking Bandit." The arrest was made by Miami detectives Bryan Howard and Joe McNeil.

Lieutenant Potterton's son had been raised by his ex-wife and had not lived with the police official for many years.

INSPECTOR BILL McCARTHY—RIP

William J. McCarthy, born in Waterfiet, New York, September 17, 1896, died at his desk in the police chief's office on September 10, 1941. His father was Peter McCarthy. He grew up in the Albany, New York, area, according to 1900 and 1910 the U.S. Census. McCarthy joined the

U.S. Marines on June 12, 1917, was wounded in action and mustered out in June 1919 at Quantico, Virginia. According to the U.S. Census in 1920, McCarthy was a twenty-four-year-old Washington, D.C., police officer.

McCarthy visited Miami area in January 1921 (family photos), later relocating to South Florida and joining the MPD.

The 1930 U.S. Census shows McCarthy as a lieutenant on MPD living at 2369 SW Sixth Street with spouse Beatrice, whom he married in 1926. In 1935, he was a captain on MPD working in the traffic section. In a 1937 newspaper photo, he was showed planning a presidential visit as the traffic inspector.

In 1940, McCarthy headed up the security detail for former King Edward, now Prince of Wales, on the visit of Edward to Miami.

In 1941, McCarthy, known as "Smiling Mac," was serving as the acting chief of police when he died.

McCarthy was pronounced dead at 4:50 PM, just nine minutes after the call for rescue squad went out over the police radio. At the time of his death, McCarthy was acting chief in the absence of Chief H. Leslie Quigg, who was on vacation.

McCarthy had complained of feeling ill during the lunch hour and was reported to have visited a doctor. He was told to take it easy, but he returned to his duties and attended a city commission meeting in the afternoon, which was hearing some traffic ordinances changes that McCarthy had requested.

After the meeting, McCarthy returned to his office. Traffic Captain Dick Lemmon walked in as McCarthy was hanging up the phone. Lemmon sat down and McCarthy said to him, "You know, Dick," then slumped in his chair, apparently fighting for breath. Other officers rushed in and the Miami Fire Rescue unit was called. Upon arrival, the three-man squad administered oxygen and Dr. George MacDonell, the city health director, in the building for the commission meeting, arrived and injected adrenalin directly into McCarthy's heart, but there was no response. The doctor then pronounced McCarthy dead but the rescue squad continued their efforts for another half hour, to no avail.

McCarthy, a New York state native, had been "gassed" in World War I action while serving in the Marines. "Smiling Mac," as he was known to thousands of Miamians, joined the Washington, D.C., police in 1920, remained there for one year, and joined the MPD on October 26, 1921, after spending a vacation in Miami.

His first assignment was as a traffic officer at Flagler Street and Miami Avenue where he remained for several years, getting known to thousands of Miami citizens. In 1928, he was promoted to lieutenant, and in July 1933, he was promoted to the position of traffic captain. In 1935, he was made acting chief of police and later chief of police. Less than one year later, he asked to go back to his first love, the traffic department where he was made a police inspector.

McCarthy left a wife, Beatrice, and two daughters, Barbara Jeanne, thirteen, and Yvonne Marie, nine, as well as brothers and sisters, most of whom lived in Miami.

McCarthy, a traffic expert, handled many special assignments such as the visits of the Duke of Windsor, President Roosevelt, and many other dignitaries.

A side story, also in the September 11 edition of the *Miami News*, was entitled "'SMILING MAC' McCarthy, Officer and Gentleman, Held Respect of All."

McCarthy's doctor, Dr. John Turk, revealed that McCarthy had four mild heart attacks during the previous week and had been urged to go home and go to bed. McCarthy said he had too much work to do.

McCarthy was buried at Miami's Woodlawn Cemetery after a huge funeral. The article went on to list about thirty honorary pallbearers.

The funeral director had to arrange a separate time for blacks to view McCarthy's body, as it seemed that he was very popular with all the people of Miami, rich and poor, cabdrivers and professionals, men and women, black and white (Miami PD records, *Miami News*, 9/11/1941).

THOMPSON KILLED DURING CHASE

On September 18, 1941, Motor Officer Wes Thompson, forty, was killed while chasing a speeding motorist at SW Third Avenue and Twenty-second Road. The power company was installing wires in the area and a wire was strung, ground level, on Third Avenue. The speeding auto followed by another vehicle, driven by a city construction foreman, R. H. Crandall, while the wire was being held on the ground by power company employees. As Crandall's car crossed over the wire, the muffler of his car caught the wire, forcing it up to eye level just as Officer Thompson's reach that point. The strung-out wire tore Thompson off the motor and he suffered fatal injuries.

Thompson, an Ohio native, joined the MPD in December 1935, and was assigned to Motors his entire career. He left a wife, Leona, and several children by her and his previous spouse. He was a veteran of the U.S. Coast Guard. Thompson was buried in Miami's Woodlawn Cemetery with a large contingent of MPD officers and American Legion in attendance.

The driver of the speeding car Thompson was chasing was never found and no charges were placed on the worker whose muffler caught hold of the wire and forced it upward into the motor officer's path (*Miami Herald*, 9/18/1941; Wilbanks, *Forgotten Heroes*, 1996).

It was reported in the daily newspapers that the eighteen-year-old son of the controversial Vice Squad head, Lieutenant C. O. Huttoe, had died in his home. No other details on the circumstances were furnished. The obit that day mentioned that the Huttoe family had come to Miami from Lawrenceville, Georgia, in the mid-1920s and that the elder Huttoe had joined the MPD in 1925 (*Miami News*, 5/11/1942).

Due to so many young men entering the military during World War II, the age hiring standards for the Miami PD was being temporarily relaxed in order to keep the force intact (1942).

The current standard of hiring only men of ages 21 to 28 for police duty was relaxed, and men of ages 40 to 55 (beyond draft age) would be hired on a case-by-case basis (*Miami News*, 5/12/1942).

A year-end report by Sergeant Mack Oakford, head of the Juvenile Bureau, reported a successful record after the first year of the new juvenile unit, established in mid-1941 (*Miami News*, 5/2/1942).

On the same day, a news story reported that Sergeant John Deas, Homicide Unit, CO, was making progress on recent homicide cases.

AMERICA AT WAR ERA

CAPTAIN ED BARRICK

Edwin Lawrence Barrick, born in Kansas City, Missouri, died on Monday evening, June 14, 1943, of a heart attack suffered at his home, 1921 SW Twenty-fourth Street, Miami, at the age of forty-eight. Barrick joined the MPD in November 1925, was promoted to sergeant in 1931, lieutenant in 1937, and captain in 1941.

He was the second Miami PBA president and was elected seven times to that position. Barrick was the PBA's leader from 1937 to 1941, skipped a year, and was then reelected in 1942 and again in 1943. The famous PBA Park was built during his tenure. He was sworn in for the seventh term as PBA president, five days before he died.

Barrick left a wife, Maude; a son, Russell Barrick; and two grandchildren. He was buried in Woodlawn Cemetery, Grave 2, Lot 222, Sec 15 on June 17, 1943.

The 6'4" tall Captain Barrick's last assignment was as the traffic captain. Clippings show that he was the graduate of a traffic institute for national high-ranking traffic officers that were conducted in Alabama in 1937. He was also involved in planning for visits by then President Roosevelt.

His granddaughter Nancy Peeples turned over to the author a copy of the first MPD Rules and Regulation, a very comprehensive booklet that each officer was issued in 1928, the first complete set of written rules the MPD issued. The booklet was still in Captain Barrick's possession when he died and will be turned over to the current chief of police for exhibition in the new police academy.

A picture has been located showing Barrick with a group of MPD brass, including Chief Quigg and Inspector McCarthy (MPD records, Personal note—Nancy Peeples, granddaughter of Captain Barrick).

Author's Note: At that time, Captain Barrick's death did not fit the criteria of a line-of-duty death.

U-BOATS IN SIGHT

One of the duties of the MPD (and Miami Beach PD) during the early days of World War II was to receive and pass on to the military, reports of German U-boats being spotted just off Miami's coastline. Over a six-month stretch in 1942, hundreds of American vessels were torpedoed by the Nazi's fleet of submarines just off the coast. Later in the war, the military devised a strategy to prevent most of these attacks, but Miami and Miami Beach was similar to an occupation zone with such a vast number of American GIs stationed in the area, especially at Miami Beach hotels. This encampment also brought on additional problems for the area police with a plethora of bars, prostitution houses, and the like sprouting up and requiring much police attention. The rare situation of a relatively small American city coping with war times was a primary factor in Miami becoming a vacation spot for all the ex-servicemen after the war who wanted to visit the warm climate and enjoy the "open" city that the era had spawned (General knowledge).

MIAMI POLICE JOIN THE WAR

During World War II (1941-45), a bulletin board was displayed in the chief of police's office listing of all the MPD guys who were then in the military. The following is a copy of that list, the exact date of which is unknown. Others may have entered the service previously or entered at a later time during the war. We consider these men double heroes.

ROY EDDY, USA
WM. J. McDOUGAL, USAC
A. H. RINGBLOM, USMAC
JACK J. HOWARD, USN
JOHN P. SUGGS, USN
WILLIAM W. HARRIES, USA

LAWRENCE G. NOLLE, USA
PERRY R. NICHOLS, USCG-S
PARK MORROW, USA
CHARLES W. PRICE, PAAF
NEWELL A. HORNE, USAC
PERCY WATSON, USN
WILLIAM L. O'CONNELL, USA-MP
FRED B. CLARK, PAAF
O. D. HENDERSON, USCG
JOHN R. RICE, USCG
A. M. CARRIER, USCG
PAUL M. TEDDER, FCC
NICK MUSLIN, USA
THOMAS A. SHEPARD, USCG
ALFRED BOLSTER, USMC
RAY H. KELLUM, USN
J. W. CAMPBELL, USMC
GUY C. HOWARD, USMC
C. B. (Buddy) KINDRED, USCG
ROY H. BASS JR., USA-MP
HARRY V. WILLIS, USN
C. E. BALDWIN, USN
C. ROY FORD, USCG
NELSON R. STEWART, USAC
ROBERT M. BULLOCK, USA-MP
WILLIAM J. GAINES, USCG
ROBERT E. EDMONDS, USN
J. LLOYD ANNIN, USAC
DONALD O. McDONALD, USMC
ROY CLARKE, USN-S
WILLIAM C. CHALK, USN-S
RHETTE S. CHALK, USN-S
FRANK GERLE, USN-CB
NEIL M. COLSON, USN-N
WILLIAM T. CLAY, USAC
JOEL McNEIL, USN-CB
A. Y. HALL, USCG
MARSHALL A. CAMPBELL, USN-S
FRED J. MANNING, USMC

O. W. FAIRCLOTH, USN-S
CAL L. DAVIS, USN-S
ROBERT C. YANCEY, USA-M
MACK OAKFORD, USA-M
G. D. ROGERS, USAC
BENJAMIN J. PALUMBO, USMC
R. A. McFARLAND, USMC
PAUL M. DENHAM, USN-CB
NORWOOD THOMSON, USA
HENRY A. SIMMONS, USA
HARVARD SWILLEY, USA-MP
JOHN F. THOMAS, USN
NEWTON A. CLARK, USN-S
JAMES H. BRIGMAN, USN-S
JIMMY ELLENBURG, USA
ROBERT L. MILLER, USA
RALPH L. MARTIN, USN

Source: List from Captain E. B. Hamm, Ret.

SIR HARRY OAKES MURDER

In 1943, England's rulers asked Miami police for assistance in investigating the murder of Sir Harry Oakes in the Bahamas. The chief sent Captain E. W. Melchen of the detective division and Captain James Otto Barker of the identification unit over to assist the crown in the prosecution of the crime. The sensational murder trial featured the testimony of these two Miami cops. The defense counsel loudly claimed that Barker had taken the suspect back to the murder scene and that was where the incriminating fingerprints came from. Charges were made against Barker at both the department and at the national identification officer's association but not proved. Captain Barker, after retirement, was slain by his own son during a drunken domestic argument (*Miami News*, 8/28/44, 11/12/43, and 7/9/43; *Pittsburg Press* 12/26/52; *Ottawa Citizen*, 5/20/59).

CHIEF QUIGG FORCED OUT AGAIN

Chief H. Leslie Quigg was suspended by City Manager Curry on nine charges of ineffective law enforcement and failure to obey orders. The action followed a "wildcat" strike by bus drivers who parked about one hundred buses around the courthouse area where one of the drivers was tried for a traffic offense. Quigg, with intentions of preventing a riotous situation, chose not to arrest the drivers involved in the blockade.

Quigg had been serving as chief of police since being appointed by the city manager in July 1937, replacing John Rowland, making this the third term of Quigg being chief in Miami. It was expected that Inspector Homer S. Redman would replace him. However, Detective Captain Frank Mitchell took over as acting chief of police, replacing Quigg, who was suspended by City Manager A. B. Curry. Mitchell, a detective back in 1924, had been a police inspector since 1933.

A few years later, Quigg was elected as a city commissioner. He served in that capacity from 1947 to 1949 and again in 1951-1955.

Quigg, born in 1887, was once the lightweight boxing champion of Florida (*Miami News*, 4/11/1944).

Lieutenant C. O. Huttoe was fired by Safety Director Rosenfelder after being suspended by Chief Nelson for participating in politics, which was prohibited at the time.

Huttoe, whose career has been extremely stormy, was originally hired on January 4, 1926, laid off in 1927 for economic reasons, later reinstated. He was promoted to detective in January 1930. Safety Director Kavanaugh sent him after moonshines as vice commander, and he was promoted to detective sergeant in 1936 and was promoted to detective lieutenant in August 1940. Huttoe was suspended by Chief Quigg in April 1941. Later, he was reinstated and assigned to the FBI for two years as a liaison in investigating subversive activities in the Miami area. He returned to the department in 1943 and served there until his latest termination (*Miami News*, 4/4/1944).

Judge Ross Williams declares that Quigg's dismissal was unlawful and he was reinstated on January 19, 1945.

Chief Quigg complained publicly that he was not consulted in the promotions of eleven police officers in the detective bureau who had been working as temporary investigators. The promotions had been made by the safety director. Quigg said that many good men were passed over in this promotional cycle and cited the cases of men he thought more deserving, including C. W. Potterton who had been an officer since 1921, Lieutenant R. J. Potorf, Acting Sergeant C. E. Rodgers, Sergeant H. B. Young, and Detective M. C. Tucker.

It was noted that J. T. Griffin was Quigg's secretary at this time. Griffin was later a patrol captain in the late '50s and early '60s, ending his career in the Property Bureau.

The Florida Supreme Court ruled against Quigg and he was out again. Charles O. Nelson, a sixty-eight-year-old former New York City police inspector, was sworn in. Nelson had earlier served as chief when Quigg was first fired in 1944. Quigg's petition to the U.S. Supreme Court was denied a hearing and he was retired on a city pension of $85 a month (MPD records and *Miami News*, 9/18/1945).

Author's Note: The tenure of men serving as chief of police over the years was very brief, with the exception of Quigg. Quigg was chief from 1921 to 1928, Guy Reeve from 1928 to 1931, Hardy Bryan for a few days in 1931, Reeve again to 1932, S. D. McCreary to 1935, Bill McCarthy to early 1936 (voluntarily stepped back to being the traffic inspector), J. B. Rowland to 1937, then Quigg again to 1944 (MPD records).

Safety Director Dan Rosenfelder met with MPD Chief Charles O. Nelson and Inspector Mel Tibbitts on a plan to buy three police accident prevention cars (and ten additional motorcycles) due to the incessantly high accident rate now that World War II was over. The car pictured was most likely a 1946 Plymouth, as passenger cars were not manufactured during the war (*Miami News*, 11/7/1945).

Author's Note: Prior to the war, in the years 1937-1939, several mentions were made of MPD accident prevention units. Perhaps that unit was suspended during the war due to fewer cars on the road and fewer officers on the force.

The MPD police radio system was split into two channels due to the heavy load of traffic on the sole one. Denby was then superintendent of city communications. Ben Denby, head of police and fire communications, stated, "Miami Police and Fire will be getting forty FM radios. Miami will be the first city in U.S. to put this new equipment into operation" (*Miami News*, 9/10/1945).

FALLEN HERO

On April 28, 1945, Chief Quigg announced that Marine Guy Cecil Howard was the first Miami PD officer casualty of World War II. Guy Howard, twenty-eight years old, was killed in action. He had been a detective in the Miami PD (MPD records and *Miami News*, 4/28/1945).

BLACK OFFICERS HIRED

Beginning as early as 1901, Miami's black community had asked for black policemen to be assigned to what was then known as "Colored Town." In 1944, during Charles Nelson's tenure as chief of police, Miami's black population was over forty thousand and the racial climate throughout the nation was very sensitive. To avoid public controversy, training sessions were held for black recruits in secret at the Liberty Square Housing project. Five brave black men completed the training and were sworn in as patrolmen on September 1, 1944. Those five men were Ralph White, Moody Hall, Clyde Lee, Edward Kimball, and John Milledge.

Patrolman Milledge would later become the first black patrolman to die in the line of duty on November 1, 1946. Ralph White remained on the force as a well-respected detective for almost four decades. On March 11, 1947, after another black officer was killed on duty, the Miami commission gave black patrolmen civil service status after one year of satisfactory service and, in 1963, fully integrated in the police department (Otis Davis, MPD Ret., Miami Community PBA president).

MIAMI'S BLACK POLICE PRECINCT

They Served—We Salute

In September 1944, the Miami Police Department began hiring black police officers. In May 1950, a police precinct was established at 480 NW Eleventh Street to provide a station house for black policemen and a courtroom for black judges in which to adjudicate black defendants. This building was unique as there was no other known structure in the nation that was designed, devoted to, and operated as a separate station house and municipal court for blacks.

The precinct closed in 1963 and the police department was integrated at the main MPD police station.

The precinct has now reopened as a museum, thanks to the efforts of some of these mentioned officers, led by the Retired Police Officers Community Police Benevolent Association.

The following is a list of the black police officers who served at the precinct, or earlier, during these years. Beginning in 1960, the black officers began attending the standard MPD Academy. We included these officers as they were assigned to the precinct and stood roll calls there until 1962. No complete records listing the names of the officers assigned to the precinct has been located. The below list has been compiled from the memory of the officers. We also honor the ones not listed.

Sgt. Lury Bowen
Sgt. Jesse Nash
Sgt. Clinton William
Victor Butler (LOD)
Edward Kimble**
Moody Hall**
James Albury
Cicero Anderson
James Bowe
Robert Boyd
Hernando Brown
Charles Bryant
Eugene Butler
William Carey
Patterson Clemons
Frank Cohen
Earl Cotton
Richard Davis
Clarence Dickson
Fred Ebron
James Farrington
Jerrel Ferguson (LOD)

Sgt. Louis Duty
Sgt. Leroy Smith
John Milledge (LOD)
Johnnie Young (LOD)
Clyde Lee**
Ralph White **
Cleophus Allgood
Willie Blount
M. C. Bowles
Amos Brooks
Rudolph Brown
Jerry Burrel
Willie Calhoun
Whitfield Carroll
Charlie Cohen
Buster Collie
Otis Davis
Joe Davis
Phillip Dixon
John English
Prince Farrington
Clyde Finch

Marion Finch
Jacob Frinks
Samuel Gerald
John Glass
Willie Gordon
Kenneth Hamilton
Orange Hayes
Harold Hill
Joe V. Hunt
William Jackson
Kenneth Jones
Earnest Kirkland
Archie McKay
Bennie Lewis
Nathaniel Mack
Calvin Mapp
Augustus Mathews
James McGruder
Edmond McKinney
Wilfred Miller
Harold Mitchell
Sammie Moore
Ledley Moss
Willie Nicholson
Clemons Patterson
Johnnie Pool
Freeman Pyles
Ben Riggins
Percy Rolle
Alexander Sampson
Reginald Sandland
Cecil Sims
John Smith
Rudolph Sweeting
James Thomas
Ruben Thompson
William Turner
James Washington
Earnest Washington

David Fincher
John Gay
William Gladden
Marcellius Goodman
Benjamin Guilford
Andrew Harris
Jesse Hill
Jimmy Hines
Robert Ingram
Willie Johnson
Earl Kirkland
Rumfle D. Kirkland
Clyde Lee
Howard Lewis
Nathaniel Maddox
Thomas Marshall
Alexander McDowell
Archie McKay
Moses M cMillan
Eddie Mitchell
Robert Monroe
Oscar Morley
Willard Myles
William Parks
Otis Pitts Sr.
Henry Puyol
Gaddy Rawls
Leroy Rogers
Amos Roundtree
Jerome Sanders
Monroe Shelman
Arnold Smith
James Stubbs
Robert Taylor
Charles Thomas
Roosevelt Tremble
Gary Ward
Dan Washington
John Westmoreland

William White   Jimmy Wilson
Leon Williams   Melvin Williams
Willie Williams

JAILORS
Earl Lightbourne   James Gunn
Emanuel Luckie   Stanley Sweeting
Richard Whitney

TYPIST CLERKS
Gwendolyn Thompson
Thelma Lewis   Orzella Ross
Mildred Smith   Veloa Williams

COMMANDERS (white) assigned to the precinct:
Captain Lawrence Nolle, Captain William O'Connell, Captain George Haller, Lieutenants James Ford, Kelly, Sherman Holland, Frank Morrow, Keith Wilson, Kelly, and Lieutenant Adair

> LOD = Officers Killed in the Line of Duty
> **= First Five Black Officers (1944)

Note: Each of these men listed have their own story. Many went on to be top MPD detectives and supervisors. Major Leroy Smith became the first black MPD staff officer, Chief Clarence Dickson the MPD chief of police (1980s), Calvin Mapp became a circuit court judge, and Lieutenant Robert Ingram went on to be chief of police and city manager in Opa Locka and then became a longtime member of the Dade County School Board.

They *all* served and we salute them.

A special thanks to Otis Davis, president of the Community PBA for his assistance.

Compiled by Phil Doherty, assistant chief (Ret.), Miami Police Department, Miami Police Veterans Association president, March 2010.

(Otis Davis, MPD Ret., Ancestry.com, and info from several of MPD's retired
  black officers, including Detective Archie McKay and Major Leroy
  Smith)

TRAFFIC COPS

By Old-Timer (MPD retiree—wishes not to be identified)

A telephone call came from a caller who was laughing so hard I could hardly understand him. He said that the officer at NE First Avenue and First Street was working traffic when a woman started to jaywalk. He responded by saying, "Lady, step back on the curb." She continued on. "Lady, step back on the curb," he repeated. She continued on. "Fatty, get back on the curb." The caller swore that she jumped back to the curb from the centerline. I called Norwood Thompson, who was assigned to the intersection, but he denied knowing about the incident.

I always tried to tell my wife of jokes I had heard, or pleasant people I had met during my tour of duty. Too many policemen bring their problems home with them. Times may have changed, but I still think policemen meet more nice people than unpleasant ones.

Author's Note: Many funny stories were submitted to the Miami Police
  Veterans Association website during the past twelve years by MPD retirees.
  Some of these tales have been included in this book, although some of
  the individual retirees requested we withhold their identity, and we have.
  Others are identified.
In order to retain the "flavor" of their stories, we have not edited their stories.
  Hope you enjoy their humor.

The website of the MPD VETS, a portion of which is open to the public, is www.mpdvets.org.

BIG CITY MIAMI

POLICE ACADEMY ESTABLISHED

In 1946, the Miami police opened their own recruit academy for training under the direction of Sergeant Walter Headley. Not only Miami officers but other Dade County police departments as well were trained. The department processed close to two thousand officers during the eighty-two recruit classes of twelve to sixteen weeks each, before consolidating the recruit training into a countywide program at the Miami-Dade CC in the early 1970s.

In 2009, Miami PD opened a new training center adjacent to their headquarters on NW Second Avenue and reinstituted their recruit training with Class No. 83. The department, in conjunction with the Dade County schools, also has opened the Miami Police High School with a curriculum focusing on law enforcement, CSI forensic training, and law, focusing on the youth of the inner-city population of Miami (MPD records).

Author's Note: In December 1946, it was reported that J. A. Youell was the lieutenant in charge of accident investigation. Youell continued his career into the 1960s and is regarded as one of the icons of the Miami Police Department. Youell, known as Jughead, served many years as Walter Headley's assistant chief of police.

He was one tough no-nonsense cop. Many of us still have scars from him (deservedly) chewing our butt. It was an honor working for him.

SNIPER KILLS MILLEDGE

John Milledge, forty-nine, one of Miami's first black officers, was shot and killed on November 1, 1946, by a single shot from a .22-caliber rifle slug while he stood near the entrance of Dorsey Park in Overtown. Milledge and two other officers were working a Friday night high school football game. Milledge had chased a group of youths who were attempting to scale the stadium wall to gain entrance to the park. One of the youths was Leroy Strachan, seventeen. Strachan, after being chased away by Milledge, went to a boy's house with some of the other youths and obtained a .22 rifle that he and another kid had used earlier in the day for target practice.

When the boys got within sight of the park entrance and saw Officer Milledge, Strachan told the other boys to get back and aimed the rifle at the officer and fired one shot while standing in the alley between two Overtown houses. The bullet struck Milledge square in the throat as he stood near the ticket booth at the entrance to the park. After seeing the officer fall to the ground as a result of the gunshot, Strachan and the other boys fled.

(Author's Note: The above account appeared in Professor William Wilbanks's book *Forgotten Heroes* (1995). Wilbanks's book contains a very detailed story of each of the Dade County officers who have been killed in the line of duty since the nineteenth century. Dr. Wilbanks has greatly contributed to the history of Miami area law enforcement.)

Back to the Milledge killing.

Officer James Washington was in the bleachers when he heard the shot and saw Milledge fall to the ground. Washington hailed a passing vehicle and transported the officer to Jackson Memorial Hospital where Milledge died twenty minutes later. All of the department's nineteen black officers on the force (at that time) were called into duty to help investigate this assassination. Sergeant Ray Tanner was then the precinct commander and overseen the arrest of numerous suspects on Friday and Saturday night, but all were later released. The investigation of the case went cold.

It was not until over forty years later that a witness, Mary White, phoned in a tip to Crimestoppers that she had seen Strachan, whom she knew, running from the crime scene carrying a rifle. MPD Cold Squad detectives, George Cadavid and Dave Bosworth, went to New York City, where Strachan had been living since the killing and interviewed him. Strachan finally admitted the shooting and the detectives came back to Miami and obtained an arrest warrant. Before Strachan could flee (with thousands of dollars and cash and checks on his person), he was arrested and booked into jail in New York City on February 15, 1990. He refused extradition, spending nineteen months in New York jails, until his attorney, William Kunstler, worked a deal with Dade prosecutors that Strachan would not have to serve "additional jail time." The deal was opposed by Chief Calvin Ross and Milledge's old coworkers, Ralph White and Edward Kimball, as well as Mayor Bob Ingram of Opa Locka, formerly a Miami police officer (and a godson). One great-great-niece approved of the sentence, but many other of Milledge's family opposed the light penalty for a cop-killing.

During Strachan's confession, he stated that he "told the crowd of ten to fifteen boys to stand back and then fired one shot from the rifle, striking Milledge in the neck." Not one of them ten to fifteen "boys" ever came forward with the information on the cop-killer. Strachan's family had sent him to New York immediately after the murder with the knowledge of his involvement as was also known to his neighbors. A real sad commentary on human values and responsibility.

In 1994, a new bronze marker was placed on Milledge's grave in Bamberg, South Carolina, his birthplace and final resting place. An MPD honor guard was present, led by Officer Robert Anderson (MPD records; Wilbanks, *Forgotten Heroes*, 1996).

In July 1947, the new chief of police, Frank Mitchell, placed the fifty-seven-man detective unit under Detective Chief L. O. Scarboro to increase efficiency. Lieutenant Huttoe was promoted to captain and made the assistant detective chief. Scarboro was reported to announce his retirement in a few months.

Chief Mitchell also abolished the Morals Squad (the Vice Squad), which was established in 1925 by Chief Quigg. Lieutenant H. G. Howard had been the CO of the Morals Squad.

The city manager, Danner, approved of the new alignment of the detectives.

Also, the Juvenile and Missing Persons Details were merged into one unit and placed under the command of Captain E. W. Melchen (*Miami News*, 1/1/1947).

It was also reported that Officer Eddie Motes lost a leg due to an off-duty motorcycle accident. Motes was one of the recent graduates of the thirty-man academy class in August 1946.

ANOTHER FRIENDLY FIRE DEATH

MPD Officer Johnnie Young was one of several officers who responded to a burglary-in-progress at 400 NW Fourth Avenue on March 7, 1947. Several patrol cars arrived simultaneously to the report that four youths were inside the store. Officer Bob McFarland, a white officer assigned to the precinct, went around the corner of the building and fired at a black male running. In the darkness, Officer McFarland did not notice that the man he shot at was his fellow officer, Johnnie Young. The wound proved fatal and Young became the second black officer killed that year.

McFarland was devastated at his mistake and later attempted suicide. Later, he left the MPD and joined the Dade County sheriff's department, rising to the rank of captain, and headed the Dade County stockade.

Four days after Officer Young was killed, the city commission voted to include all the black Miami police officers under civil service, which allowed some type of pension benefits for Young's widow. White officers had this civil service protection since 1921 (Wilbanks, *Forgotten Heroes*, 1996).

MUGGSY MULLIS

Known to all as "Muggsy," Melvin Mullis was laid to rest on September 7, 2010, with military honors at the Florida National Cemetery, in Bushnell, Florida. Melvin was born December 25, 1921, in Cochran, Georgia. Melvin is survived by his loving sister, Margaret Thomson; son, Steve Mullis; daughters, Sherry Ladue, Mary Ann Moss, Nina Jane Mullis; grandchildren, Amber, Michael, Cherie, Stevie, Ashley, Albert, and Lauren; and great-grandchildren, Raymond and Marquis.

Mullis joined the navy at the young age of sixteen. After serving in World War II, Melvin returned to Miami to join the Miami Police

Department. There Melvin was shot in the line of duty as a police officer and was near death. With the help of his mother, Evelyn Lucille Mullis, his sisters, and family, he made a full recovery. After receiving an honorable disability from the Miami Police Department, Muggsy did several security jobs, including security at the famous Dupont Plaza on Biscayne Boulevard and guarding the family of the shah of Iran in Nassau, Bahamas. Muggsy also worked for the United States Marshal's Service where he transported federal prisoners all over the U.S.

During his guardianship of peace at the Wounded Knee Uprising in South Dakota, his mother and father lost their first beloved son, Muggsy Jr., who served three tours in the Vietnam War. During his later years, Muggsy went to work as bailiff to Judge Joseph Gersten. Muggsy will always be remembered for his loyalty, lawmanship, love, wisdom, and his unique way of making people laugh (MPD records, *Miami Herald*, 9/12/ 2010).

Early Motor uniform and motorcycle

Miami Police Station 1145 NW 11 street

Patrol unit taking a break during 1989 Miami riots

1921 Miami motor squad

Dressed for the 1972 National Convention

An old "paddy wagon" and guests

The "new" Miami police station 400 NW 2nd Ave

A classic AIU unit—(Accident Investigation Unit), Kennedy and Berquist

Officer Dick Huss and Sgt. Moon (Miami unmarked police vehicle) circa 1949

Officer HS Bach in Overtown outside the legendary Reno Bar/Rockland
Palace circa 1968

Miami Police mounted detail riding in formation

Miami PD raiding a "moonshine" still circa 1919

Miami "bike patrol" photo courtesy of Rene Pimentel

Author Chief Phil Doherty in front of the Memorial wall

Miami Chief Walter Headley and Dick Cargill circa 1960

Miami City Hall circa 1910—population 5,000

Miami Chief Quigg at the wheel of a Miami PD cruiser

A Miami Police "Bomb Squad" member

A gathering of "classic" Miami Police units

Officer Zabinski, Refrigerator Perry, and Joe Longueira at the Orange Bowl

Officer Grambling getting some riding tips from a motor Sgt.

Chief H. Leslie Quigg inspects the motor squad—
Quigg became Chief in 1921

Officer Ken Underwood, Miami Honor Guard member

Miami PD also used 3-wheel Harleys—Officer G. Rasmussen pictured

A "classic" Miami PD Marine Patrol boat

Current Miami Police Marine Patrol boats

Major 20 ton drug bust

All Miami Police units together

HEADLEY'S REIGN

WALTER HEADLEY TAKES OVER

City Manager Danner announces the promotions of Detective Sergeant Walter Headley to assistant police chief and Lieutenant J. A. Youell to deputy chief. Other promotions noted were Forrest Nelson and M. E. (Mel) Tibbets to inspector, Captain Fred Bratt to traffic command, Lieutenant John Webber to captain of uniform section, and Detective Captain E. W. Melchen to chief of detectives (*Miami News*, 1/9/1948).

City Manager Danner was fired by the city commission. Chief of Police Mitchell immediately follows by announcing his retirement (*Miami News*, 6/2/1948).

Walter Headley is named as chief of police of Miami. Headley had been an MPD officer since joining in 1937. His first assignment was to the accident prevention unit. He later served in the detective unit and, during World War II, was on loan to the FBI (*Miami News*, 8/11/1948).

During his twenty-year reign, the Miami Police Department changed dramatically. In 1949, women became sworn members of the department with Officers Dorothy Asti Gramling and Lillian Gheer being the first two women trained in the police academy. Chief Headley built a separate new black precinct in 1950, which remained in existence until 1963 and obtained a new police HQ building at 1145 NW Eleventh Street. On November 10, 1956, more than one thousand police personnel moved into that new building, which would remain the MPD headquarters until 1976, when the department moved to the current station at NW Second Avenue and Fifth Street.

UTILITY POLE KILLS ROOKIE

A twenty-two-year-old MPD officer, Frampton Wichman Jr., was killed when struck by a falling utility pole on September 20, 1948, at Flagler Street and NE Second Avenue. A truck had backed into the rusted utility pole, which broke off, bounced off a taxi cab, and stuck Officer Wichman. The officer never regained consciousness and died four days later, on September 24, at Jackson Memorial Hospital.

Wichman, a Miami native and a graduate of Miami High in 1943, had served in the navy during World War II and seen action at Iwo Jima. Wichman joined the MPD in 1947 as a member of Academy Class No. 11, played on the MPD football team, and directed traffic on Flagler Street until his death. Sergeant Paul Denham (later Chief) was his supervisor and praised him as an outstanding officer.

Wichman was survived by his wife, Vivian. He was buried in Flagler Memorial Park, 5301 West Flagler Street (Wilbanks, *Forgotten Heroes*, 1996).

VIOLENCE AND INFIGHTING AT PD

Local stories in the *Miami News*, many of which involves infighting within the department over vice enforcement, made the news in the late 1940s. Sources of all these stories are from the *Miami News* on the dates indicated after each item.

In June 1947, C. O. Huttoe was demoted by City Manager Danner from probationary captain to lieutenant. (6/24/1947)

Officer Dallas L. Carroll, patrol section officer, was transferred from his patrol car duty to that of walking the Coconut Grove beat on midnight shift after raiding a Tamiami Trail bookie joint. This raid followed the city manager's directive that all police officers, not just the Vice Squad, should enforce the gambling laws.

Carroll was later jumped and beat up by several assailants while walking the midnight Grove beat, an obvious result of his earlier raid. (1/14/1949)

Clarence L. Holton, born 1908, an MPD officer from 1938 to 1949, was suspended by Chief Headley in 1949 from the guard force at the Twentieth Street stockade for fighting with another guard.

Holton came to work drunk. An on-duty guard relieved him of his weapon and told Holton to go home. Holton grabbed the on-duty officer's gun from the holster and attempted to shoot the other guard with his own gun. Fortunately for all, the other guard's gun was not loaded. Holton was fired and later passed on in 1983. (3/31/1949)

Author's Note: A photo of a police patrol wagon in the 1940s showed a photo of Guard George Holland and C. L. Holton standing alongside the paddy wagon. It was interesting to learn that Holland was born in India, immigrated to America, and lived in Montana prior to joining the MPD in 1935. He was still listed as a guard in 1945 Miami census.

Detective Lieutenant C. O. Huttoe was physically beaten by Detective Chief J. O. Barker and former MPD officer W. W. Davenport at the home of a woman Huttoe was visiting. Barker and Davenport broke down the door and attempted to take photos of Huttoe and the woman. Davenport had been recently fired from MPD and blamed Huttoe for his dismissal. Huttoe claimed that he was beaten because "he refused to go along with the graft setup in the department." Huttoe and Barker were both suspended by Chief Headley. The grand jury began looking into the altercation, calling in Headley, Detective Chief Mitchell, Lieutenant G. E. Baldwin of Internal Security, and the two patrol officers who responded to the fight call, Officers Adam Klimkowski and Joseph Mazloom. (*Miami News*, 4/28/1949)

Former Chief Quigg, now a city commissioner, stated that Huttoe has been at odds with his superiors for years, from Chief of Police Reeve, Chief Rowland, Chief Nelson, and Chief Mitchell, as well as Chief Quigg.

Detective Joe McNeil, Huttoe's assistant in Vice Squad, took over Huttoe's job while the investigation was being looked into.

City Manager O. P. Hart is considering abolishing the district system of the detective unit. (5/12/1949)

Asst. Chief Youell arrested two MPD officers for extorting a citizen, William Reddish, thirty, and Cullen J. Thompson, twenty-four. The pair had caught a Liberty City citizen in a compromising situation and attempted to extort money from him by threatening to tell his wife about his indiscretions. (5/14/1949)

Officer Dallas Carroll, previously moved to the Coconut Grove night beat for raiding a gambling joint, was jumped and beaten by three men while walking the Grove beat late one night. Coconut Grove merchants demanded that a police review committee of consisting of Asst. Chief Youell, Lieutenant Harold Goodman, and Sergeant Delton Dollar be assigned to look into this beating as it appeared to be in retaliation for Carroll's earlier raid on bookie joints. Some department insiders claimed that Carroll faked the injuries, but Lieutenant Goodman, Carroll's superior, reported that the evidence indicated that it was indeed an assault. (6/14/1949)

Detective Captain J. O. Barker became chief of detectives, replacing Asst. Chief Edward W. Melchen who died recently of a heart attack. Lieutenant H. Gwynn Howard will be the acting assistant detective chief. (7/5/1949)

Lieutenant C. O. Huttoe was reinstituted to his previous rank and position in July 1949. (7/12/1949)

Lieutenant Francis Lee Napier was reduced back to the rank of sergeant by Deputy Chief Youell. (7/23/1949)

HIGHLIGHTS OF 1950

Black MPD officer, Charlie Cohan, was killed by his own gun as he partied with his girlfriend in an off-duty incident. The gun discharged while the couple was playing with the firearm. (*Miami News*, 1/16/1950)

Two Miami officers, Cullen Thompson and William Reddish, were arrested by Asst. Chief J. A. Youell and Investigator J. W. (Jud) Baldwin when they arrived at a black citizen's home to collect extortion money. The officers had caught the citizen in a compromising situation with a young woman at a local lover's lane in Liberty City recently and forced the man to have sex with the woman. They then demanded money from the man in order to avoid arrest and for not telling the guy's wife of the situation. The citizen told his employer who called Baldwin.

Chief Youell and Baldwin set up inside the citizen's home and arrested the two officers when they accepted marked money from the extortion victim. The trial started today on the offense that occurred last May. (*Miami News*, 1/17/1950)

Negro officer John English was thrown through a plate glass window at a NW Second Avenue restaurant while investigating a bill-skip. After the offender tossed the officer through the glass window, he was shot twice by English's partner, Officer Cicero Anderson. The offender was taken to Jackson Hospital in critical condition. Officer English suffered only minor injuries. (*Miami News*, 1/16/1950)

A sensational million and a half Brink's robbery in Boston last week had a Miami connection today. New York police advised MPD that an Arthur Longaro was en route to Miami on the train and was allegedly involved in the huge robbery.

Miami detectives did not know the suspect's name but were advised what compartment he was riding in. The four detectives entered the train at NE Twenty-ninth Street prior to arriving at the Seaboard rail station.

Prior to confronting the suspect, who was allegedly armed, the four detectives planned their apprehension. Detective M. H. Wiggins said he would be the first to crash into the compartment, stating that he "was the oldest, with grown children while the other three had young 'kiddies' to worry about." The other three tossed a coin to see who would be Wiggins's backup. Detective Thomas Elder won the dubious prize while Detective A. B. Rossman and Jimmy King covered each end of the coach.

The arrest went off without violence and suspect Longaro was turned over to New York police after the MPD guys found $2,000 in new bills in the suspect's luggage. (*Miami News*, 1/19/1950)

Officers George Spell and Burt Langdale were injured in a head-on auto crash at SW Sixteenth Street and Twenty-seventh Avenue while running an emergency call behind an ambulance. Their vehicle went out of control and struck on oncoming auto head-on. Spell was in critical condition, but Langdale suffered only minor injuries. (*Miami News*, 1/12/1950)

Steve Brodie joined the MPD in 1925 served one year and then switched to the fire department where he served many years. Two of his sons were longtime members of the Dade County sheriff's office, where one, Tom, was an expert bomb disposal technician. (*Miami News*, 1/29/1950)

Officer James E. Hendrix was injured in an auto crash at NW Seventh Avenue and Fifty-second Street, investigated by Officer J. P. Adams and A. E. Wood. (*Miami News*, 1/30/1950)

The MPD police radio system was split into two channels on February 15, 1950, due to the heavy load of traffic on the sole one. Ben Denby was then superintendent of city communications.

Photo of an MPD officer directing traffic downtown wearing shorts was printed in the local newspaper. Some citizens liked the idea and others thought he looked "silly." (*Miami News*, 7/27/1950)

Safety Director Henderson calls the MPD brass into his office, one by one, to lay down the law to stop city gambling. Called in were Chief Headley, Detective Chief Howard, and detective district commanders J. C. Williams, Charles Schwelm, Ray Tanner, and Lieutenant J. D. Baldwin. (*Miami News*, 9/11/1950)

An investigation revealed that employees of the telephone company counting room have been stealing coins for quite some time. The local newspapers labeled the thefts the "Bra Conspiracy," as several female employees of Southern Bell was caught stuffing their bras full of coins at the end of each shift.

A Miami police officer and his wife, a Southern Bell employee, were among those arrested. Officer John Resick was immediately suspended by Chief Headley after his arrest. (*Miami News*, 10/3/1950)

A news story about Public Safety Director Henderson plans to roll back Asst. Chief J. A. (Jughead) Youell to the rank of lieutenant was in today's newspaper. Henderson was quoted as saying that Youell was running the department without utilizing his inspectors. (*Miami News*, 10/4/1950)

Officer J. C. (Jimmy) Borden and E. B. Hamm arrested a twenty-two-year-old thief after a hot chase through downtown streets. Arless Richart was booked for auto theft and burglary after the gun-drawn officers chased him on foot after the suspect crashed the stolen car. (*Miami News*, 10/7/1950)

Captain John Webber will be acting chief for two weeks while Chief Headley is in Denver attending the IACP convention and Asst. Chief Youell is in Los Angeles with the Miami PD motorcycle drill team. (*Miami News*, 10/8/1950)

Sheriff Jimmy Sullivan, a former MPD officer, was indicted by the grand jury in Dade for aiding racketeers from the S & G syndicate. Sullivan was immediately suspended by Governor Warren. Tom Kelly was appointed interim sheriff a month later.

Sullivan, who joined the MPD in 1934, served ten years downtown as a traffic officer at SE First Avenue and First Street. He ran for Dade County sheriff in 1944 and won by a landslide.

A recent investigation by Senator Kefavuer uncovered rampart corruption in both Dade and Broward counties. Sullivan was later reinstated but resigned when statewide prosecutors reopened criminal investigations.

A year later, Sullivan and his wife was indicated for income tax evasion. (*Miami News*, 10/16/1950)

Dismissed Miami officer Joseph Liquori, thirty-one, was found guilty this week in federal court for conspiracy to ship anti-Castro arms to the Dominican Republic. Liquori had been assigned as a liaison officer to the Dominican consulate in Miami and was a onetime aide to Dominican President Trujillo's son. The arrest was made in May 1959 as a huge C-74 Globemaster aircraft prepared to take off with the arms for Batista supporters in the Dominican Republic. (*Miami News*, 12/18/1950)

In November 1950, Chief Walter Headley proposes a statewide police officer certification program. (*Miami News*, 11/27/1950)

LaFLEUR GUNNED DOWN

Officer LaFleur was killed at 3:00 AM on February 16, 1951, during a gun battle with a man who was sleeping in a car at NW Third Avenue and Fourteenth Street. Officer LaFleur and his partner, E. B. Burrell, thirty-two, were riding the wagon. He was shot by two bullets in the chest and thigh and died shortly after at Jackson Memorial Hospital. Two of LaFleur's bullets misfired but it is possible he did hit his assailant. Lieutenant J. T. Griffin was the commander of the Negro precinct at that time.

The suspect was chased by Officers Ernest Hayes and Orange Hayes who were patrolling nearby. The suspect was chased to Fourteenth Street and the railroad tracks where Detective Neal Coston joined the pursuit. The suspect fired three shots at these officers, and Hayes shot back, possibly striking the suspect as a trainman advised the suspect ran past him bleeding from the neck and shoulder area (Wilbanks, *Forgotten Heroes*, 1996; *Miami News*, 2/16/1951 and 2/17/1951).

Author's Note: In 1992, MPD Detective Confessor Gonzalez reinterviewed an earlier suspect in LaFleur's murder who had unexplained gunshot wounds. Gonzalez was unable to make an arrest due to inadequate evidence. The case remains unsolved.

Officer LaFleur was a Booker T. Washington graduate and a World War II veteran who had joined the MPD on January 19, 1946 (MPD records).

MPD Officer William S. Scott was killed by Officer M. C. Bowles, who mistook Scott for a prowler. Officer Scott worked the train tower at Twentieth Street. Scott was in civilian clothes after going off duty at 10:45 PM and was headed for a restaurant. Officer Bowles observed him squatting in an alley at 1412 NW Third Avenue. Bowles fired when Scott picked up his revolver from the ground adjacent to where he was squatting.

Officer John Westmoreland was Bowles's partner. Lieutenant Brock was on the scene. No charges were filed (*Miami News,* 2/17/1951).

Author's Note: Many years later, in 1973, the author was promoted to captain and assigned to the patrol section day shift where Officer Bowles was a member. The heavy Bowles, hovering around 400 lbs, was consoled by me on his physical condition. I asked this veteran of many years of patrolling Miami's black area and who had survived several fatal gun battles how he could expect to run after the bad guys. His reply was a classic (and true): "Captain, *no one* runs from M. C."

LIFE AND TIMES AT MPD

By Wet No Name Officer

As many of you will remember the Orange Bowl parade extravaganza, there was none quite like this one ever! It was televised all over the world and was held each year on Biscayne Boulevard from SE Second Street north to NW Fifth Street and returning to Biscayne staging area. During this particular Orange Bowl parade, I believe was in 1950, as with the complete traffic shifts, I was assigned parade detail, and as planned, the procession was beautifully started and moved north on Biscayne Boulevard with light, music, bands, beautiful girls, and so on. Everything was going along quite smooth when it began to rain. I mean rain, rain, and more rain. The floats, marching bands began to unravel. The makeshift sets,(old wood crates) began to float down the street. The water came over the curbs eight to ten inches. More rain, torrential rain.

One of our fine traffic officers was assigned to intersection duty on Biscayne and Third Street, was being constantly harassed by a fall-down, mean drunk who wanted to go get into the middle of the street and join the bands. At this time, there was about six inches of water in the middle of the street. The floats were underwater, generators were wet, and chaos was setting in rapidly. Everyone was drowning. This drunk was warned again and again to stay out of the parade line, which he paid no attention. This particular traffic officer, who was having problems with this drunk, was a big man, and a quiet one, was known for his ability to handle any situation, but not take any crap from anyone. This confrontation between the officer and the drunk went on for thirty to forty minutes, and our officer could not take any more verbal abuse. He then proceeded to handcuff this drunk and place him under arrest. At that time, we did not have two-way radios at our disposal, and no station call box was handy, so our hero had a real problem on his hands. There is no way to transport the drunken citizen to jail. So our miserable, wet, tired officer handcuffed this drunk to a nearby steel light pole for further transfer to jail. The traffic officer continued his duties and assignments at his post, getting hundreds of people safely across the streets. It was now hailing. Golf ball-sized ice. Rising waters. The drunk was still handcuffed to the pole, sitting down in a foot of water, passed out. Finally, the sodden mess of a parade was over and we were relieved by the lieutenant and sergeant and told to go home. As you can expect and have experienced, seven to ten hours on your wet feet, you were ready.

We were relieved, and on the way home in my car, approximately 1:00 AM, my partner turned to me and said, "Oh, s—t, I forgot the drunk, he is still handcuffed to that pole." We went all the way back (we were almost home) and there was the drunk sitting down still passed out and the water was above his waist. We took the cuffs off of him, dragged him to higher ground, and left him. I am sure when he came to, he wondered how he swam that far. We finally slogged back to the car and went home, wet, tired, and oh ya, did I mention that it really rained that night?

Oscar L. Holbert, thirty-three, of 448 NW Eleventh Street, a former Negro policeman, was shot and killed earlier today in the central Negro district. Police found his body on the sidewalk near 349 NW Eighth Street. Police said Holbert had been shot three times by unknown persons. Homicide Detective B. J. (Bennie) Palmer is investigating (*Miami News*, 6/2/1951).

Patrol officers Joe Miguel and J. P. Bunch were arresting a masked Royal Castle robber downtown when the suspect pulled a gun on Officer Bunch. Officer Miguel then made a power tackle, downing the man and disarming him. Two additional officers, George Groner and Art Melonis, arrived, and all four police battled the offender to get him under control. The suspect was booked for armed robbery (MPD records).

CRASH KILLS BRIGMAN

On February 28, 1951, Officer James Brigman, twenty-nine, a South Carolina native, was killed in an auto crash at NW First Place and Thirteenth Street in Miami. An auto driven by Thomas McGill struck Brigman's marked police car, causing the auto to crash into a utility pole while the officer was hanging on to the open car door that had sprung as a result of the collision. His skull was crushed and died on the scene.

Mr. McGill was charged with reckless driving.

Brigman had joined the MPD in August 1941, later taking military leave from 1942 to 1946 to serve in the U.S. Navy. He rejoined the MPD in 1946, serving in the accident unit, often with partner Bill Pumphrey, until his death. Brigman was survived by his wife, Pearl, and was buried in Chesterfield, South Carolina, where he was raised.

His wife survived him by many years, recently passing away in Marathon, Florida, at an age of 101. At the time of her passing, she was the oldest pensioner in the Miami system (*Miami Herald* and *Miami News*, 3/1/1951; Wilbanks, *Forgotten Heroes*, 1996).

THE CASH GANG—BAD DUDES

Lee Cash, father (born 1901), and Robbie Cash, mother (born 1907), moved their family from Flintville, Georgia, to Miami in the early 1930s. They had four sons and one daughter and lived in the west end of Miami, near NW Thirty-seventh Avenue and Twenty-fifth Street. Three of the sons became the core of the infamous Cash Gang, a group of bandits who robbed and burglarized, not only in the Miami area but throughout the southeast. The son John Virgil Cash, called only Virgil, was the so-called leader of the gang. The gang had many run-ins with police agencies in the Miami area, often shooting at police when chased.

The Cash family comprised of the following:

Bobbie Lee Cash, daughter—Born 1925
            Lives in Florida
John Virgil Cash, son—Born 1927
            Died in 1975, Gwinnett County, Georgia
Fred James Cash, son—Born May 28, 1929
            Died August 29, 2003, Clarksville, Georgia
Frank T. Cash, son—Born 1932 (November 6, 1931)
            Died October 1976, Miami
Ray Cash, son—Born 1934 (March 26, 1934)
            Listed in Orange City, Florida

The wildest of their gang was a mean younger man, John Fulford. Born November 26, 1934, the son of a North Miami police officer, Sam

Fulford, living at 710 NW Sixty-third Avenue. Young Fulford, married Laure Daniels in 1953, divorced in 1958, and he then married Marilyn.

Fulford, who attended (or slept at) Kinloch Jr. High, went on to a criminal career at a very young age.

In 1947, Virgil Cash married Betty Elliott in Dade County and later divorced. Virgil's girlfriend during the 1953-54 crime sprees was an eighteen-year-old Billie Ann Bloom, who was reputed to be involved in the gang's heists.

Other persons considered as gang members included Blackie Bethel, Norman Stoddard, Lawrence Allen, Thomas Worsley (nineteen), Henry Artegus (twenty-five), Charles Gavin, Harvey Nall, and others. Specific mention is made of the gang's crime spree during the 1953-54 eras, although it began earlier and ended later.

April 24, 1953—Four armed, masked men forced a car off the road that was carrying a $4,000 payroll to the White Belt Daily from a Miami Springs bank. Fred Cash was quickly arrested at his home and Virgil Cash surrendered to his bondsman. Hialeah police put out a BOLO for Blackie Bethel. The robbers shot and wounded Dade County motor officer Mike Daugherty during the chase. The robbers were reported to have left the loot in the getaway car.

April 26, 1953—The Ft. Pierce *News Tribune* reported that MPD Detectives Johnnie Hammer and Herb Netsch were checking the backyard at John Fulford's house for stolen items and called Lieutenant Lochard F. Gracey by to check some items, when John Fulford came out of the house with a gun and took Detective Hammer hostage. Fulford held him for four hours until Hammer could talk him into releasing him.

September 1953—Virgil Cash and Fred Cash received a thirty-year sentence from Judge Ben Willard for the White Belt Daily payroll robbery. John Fulford was acquitted on a technicality but held on other charges.

November 4, 1953—Newspapers reported that Virgil Cash got a directed verdict, and Charles Gavin, former Sweetwater police officer, was acquitted. Fred Cash and Billie Ann Bloom, eighteen, got a mistrial due to a hung jury. (Newspaper did not say where the armed robbery was.)

March 26, 1954—A Tampa cigar factory was robbed of $36,000 by five Cash Gang members.

April 7, 1954—Ray Cash, twenty, and Lawrence Allen, twenty-five, were arrested in Gainesville, Florida, for a safe job at a grocery store. Shots were fired at the police chasing them.

April 24, 1954—The Statesville (NC) *Daily Record* reports that Virgil Cash and Fred Cash were arrested after a high-speed chase by NC Highway Patrol officers near Morgantown. A third man, Lawrence Allen, was arrested for unlawful flight to avoid prosecution on the earlier Gainesville, Florida, burglary. Fred Cash was wanted on robbery charges in Tampa. Several guns and burglary tools were found in the car.

April 29, 1954—Virgil and Fred Cash and John Fulford were arraigned in Tampa for the robbery of a cigar factory in March. Two other men were released from charges; Thomas Worsley, nineteen, and Henry Artegus, twenty-five.

August 10, 1954—The Florida supreme court refused to overturn Judge Ben Willard's decision to deny Virgil Cash appeal bond his conviction of robbery and shooting at police officers. His attorney was George Nichols.

Sources for this story were from interview and correspondence with retired MPD officer Ray Parker, plus *Miami News* articles on the dates indicated in the story.

GAMBLING MURDER

In August 1952, the lucrative bolita gambling scheme in Dade County was dominated by Howard Pinder. The dimes and dollars from the pockets of mostly poor folks in Dade County added up to big bucks. Pinder had suitcases full of cash in suitcases stored in the closest of his home at 20 NE Fifty-two Terr. One afternoon, several would-be robbers stormed the home that was then occupied only by Pinder's wife, Dora. She was in a back bedroom, ill with heart problems.

One of the robbers, a white male named Lewis, fired one shot at her, instantly killing the lady. When family members found her, they observed no gunshot wounds and immediately concluded that she died of a heart attack and summoned Dora's doctor. The doctor arrived before the homicide investigators (a Florida requirement in cases of unattended deaths) and ruled the death's cause a heart attack.

The detective from the MPD homicide squad, Bennie Palmer, then examined the body and detected powder burns around the dead woman's mouth. Further examination by Palmer found a tooth missing and a hole inside the room of her mouth where the bullet penetrated on its path to the brain. He summoned his boss, Lieutenant John Dees, and fellow investigators Charlie Sapp and Clarence Hall, and a full-scale homicide investigation began.

Weeks later, Detective Hall arrested suspect Lewis and jailed him in the Dade County jail after gaining an admission of guilt. The suspect was pulled out of jail at three the next morning by Dade County detectives and subjected to an allegedly rough interrogation that yielded the identification of accomplices. Miami PD screamed to high heavens at this interference with their case, causing Chief Headley to demand that Sheriff Tom Kelly to keep his hands off the politically charged investigation. Headley suggested that the state attorney's office take over the investigation. Later, the governor's office itself intervened and the case dragged out for years, causing much consternation at local, county, and statewide agencies.

Lewis was convicted of the crime, but the several other suspects gained a favorable verdict in the courts due to the screwed-up investigation.

Overshadowed by the infighting was the excellent work performed by MPD homicide investigators in a case that would have been just a routine heart attack death.

Howard Pinder continued on his career as a high roller in the bolita rackets, later being charged by federal authorities on income tax violations for the huge stash of unexplained cash. Sheriff Kelly was later voted out, the state attorney was replaced by Dick Gerstein, and the political push for city-county consolidation, pushed by Kelly, was shelved. All thanks to Detective Palmer's astute observations at the scene of the crime (*Miami Herald* and *Miami News*, 8/8/1952 and 5/12/1953).

Also, in August 1952, Detective Lieutenant C. O. Huttoe was given a five-demerit reprimand by Chief Headley by participating in a gambling raid conducted by Dade County detectives. Headley charged Huttoe for interfering in a case outside his own detective district. Huttoe's appeal of the penalty was denied by the police staff after a hearing. This event in Huttoe's career simply added to the many other gambling cases that brought him much attention during a thirty-year span at the Miami department (*Miami News*, 8/1952).

OFFICER DOWN

In the early morning hours of June 14, 1954, Miami PD officers Ray Parker and Tom O'Connell had a confrontation with Cash Gang members John Fulford and Harvey Nall. Other patrol officers, whom had a contact with Fulford the previous night, spotted Fulford's car and followed him, checking on the radio to determine if he was wanted, while Fulford sped away. At West Flagler Street and Thirty-fourth Avenue, the officers realized that another auto was trailing them. They stopped the second car, driven by Nall, as Fulford turned down Thirty-fifth Avenue. While talking to Nall in the street, out of their squad car, Fulford's car turned east on Flagler Street toward the officers. Fulford stopped, exited the car with a shotgun, yelling, "Now I have both of you @#$%^%$#@," and fired a shotgun at Parker who tried to shield himself behind the squad car door. Parker was hit on both legs with about twenty shotgun pellets as Officer O'Connell fired at Fulford, hitting him in the leg with one round. Fulford ran two blocks west and disappeared into a field. Parker called on the radio for assistance and about thirty Miami officers responded.

Officer O'Connell, together with Officers Edwin Sloan and M. C. (Max) Undorfer, entered the field searching for Fulford. O'Connell spotted him and fired twice before Fulford could raise the shotgun. Fulford was hit in the lungs and in the stomach. He was taken to Jackson Hospital in critical condition. Officer Parker was also treated by doctors, who removed twenty or so pellets from his legs. He later recovered. Additional weapons were found in both the autos of both Fulford and Nall.

Fulford was convicted and sent to prison for ten years by Judge Ben Willard. Following his release, he joined up with the Dixie Mafia gang based in Biloxi, Mississippi. This brutal gang, known throughout the

South, headed by Kirskey Nix, son of a high-ranking Texas judge. In June 1971, Nix, Fulford, and two others killed a New Orleans grocer during a home invasion robbery. Fulford was found guilty and sentenced to life in prison in Louisiana in 1972. He was beaten to death by another prisoner in Angola, Louisiana, prison in August 1993.

Virgil Cash was stabbed to death by another inmate in a Georgia prison on March 29, 1975. After his release from prison, Fred Cash became a car salesman in Gainesville, Georgia, and passed away in 2003.

Officer Tom O'Connell went on to be a Dade County judge and is now deceased. Officer Undorfer passed away a few years ago after becoming a very successful Miami business owner. Officer Sloan passed away in 1993. Officer Ray Parker, whose dad, C. C. Parker Sr., was also a Miami officer, passed away shortly after being interviewed for this story (*Miami News*, 8/8/1954).

The auto theft squad in 1954 was manned by Lieutenant Hamp Knight, Detectives L. F. Gracey, Ralph Esser, Charlie Johnston, Henry Simmons, Paul Nichols, and Ernie Bush (*Miami News*, 8/8/1954).

JUDITH ANN ROBERTS MURDER

On July 6, 1954, a six-year-old girl visiting her grandparents from Baltimore was abducted from her South Bayshore Drive home and killed. Her body was soon found just off the road. A long turbulent investigation resulted in the arrest and release of her grandfather and later her father as well as several other suspects. To this day, no one has been convicted of the tragic crime. The lead investigator was Detective Erv Whitman of the homicide unit, assisted by his partner, Detective Charles Sapp, under the supervision of Lieutenant Chester Eldredge and the detective chief.

The case was hampered by the change in state attorneys. Brautigan first was in charge, and later, a young Dick Gerstein took over. A Robert Franklin Jones was arrested in 1962 but later released.

Detective Whitman resigned in 1958 to begin a law practice and has followed the case to this day (he is now ninety-two), offering his assistance without compensation, in an effort to close out this terrible crime. Whitman is still a practicing attorney and was recently honored by France for his extraordinary valor during World War II (*Miami Herald*, 7/6/1954, MPD records, MPD Vets newsletter).

BURGLAR LEARNS A LESSON

The Hagerstown *Morning Herald* reported this funny story on July 10, 1954.

> It's getting so a guy can't even trust the police anymore. A burglar broke into the Miami Police Academy and got away with a number of bills ranging from $1.00 to $100. He was traced easily and arrested in Jacksonville. The money, used for instructing recruits, was counterfeit.

A LESSON IN LOVE

Many MPD vets love to tell the story about Sergeant Milt Olgle visiting a "friend." The friend's husband, a driver for a cement company, came home in his cement mixer vehicle one day and unloaded a couple of tons of wet cement into the open convertible of Olgle's new car. Sergeant Olgle had to run out quickly and purchase another car, exactly like the cemented one, in order to have to avoid explaining at home what had happened to his new car (Author's personal knowledge).

*   *   *

MPD vet Louis Grady Hammond, fifty-two, died of a heart attack at his home, 2901 SW Fifth Avenue. He retired in 1953. Hammond had a brother, Bill, a Dade County sheriff who was a fixture as a desk sergeant at the Jackson Hospital police ward for many years (*Miami News*, 1/14/1955).

In July 1955, Miami police patrol officers switched from two-man patrol cars to one-man cars, doubling the number of zone cars to handle calls for service. The number of paddy wagons was increased to pick up prisoners from these one-man cars. A local paper showed Officer E. W. (Gene) McCracken leaving the station in a one-man car (*Miami News*, 7/10/1955).

MOTORMAN LEAPS INTO MIAMI RIVER

The MPD motorcycle squad's office was located along the Miami River back in the 1950s. While waiting for roll call one day, one of the motor officers, Howard Shaw, egged on by Officers Danny Schooler and Eddie Edmonds, wagered Officer Bob Knight five bucks that he (Knight) didn't dare jump into the Miami River in full uniform. To the disbelief and laughter of the entire squad, Knight dove into the river and came out soaking wet, but five dollars richer.

Bob Knight, the son of MPD Captain Cecil (Hamp) Knight, later became CO of the motor squad and several other commands. Bob was appointed as a staff officer in the 1970s. Knight, a brilliant, hardworking officer, had a reputation of a stormy figure in the department, with occasional judgment problems. Knight retired as chief of detectives in 1978.

At least it was learned that Knight could swim (Several old motor officers, author's knowledge).

SNIFFING MOONSHINE

Sniffing moonshine whiskey in the line of duty gave Captain Raymond Brock, of the Miami Police Department, an early retirement and a pension of $339 a month back in 1955.

The officer headed a squad cracking down on illegal liquor in 1952. Brock's policemen brought him bottle after bottle of moonshine and Brock did a lot of sniffing. Finally, he was stricken with toxic neuritis, sent to the hospital, and told to take a long rest.

The Miami Retirement Board in December that year reported Brock suffered general muscular weakness, lack of coordination in walking, and neurological damage.

Captain Brock, an Ohio native, employed by the department for nineteen years, retired at age forty-seven. The usual retirement age then was fifty-five.

Brock was married to his wife, Helen, and lived at 159 SW Twenty-eighth Road, passing away twenty-six years later at age seventy-three, in Pinellas Park, Florida (*Syracuse Herald-Journal*, 12/1952, MPD records).

PROWL SQUAD GETS BUSTED

During the period of 1955-56, the MPD had a crime prevention patrol group called the Prowl Squad who were assigned to prevent burglaries. The selection of officers and the supervision of the group were evidently not of a high standard as several of the officers themselves were arrested for burglary and possession of stolen goods.

In January 1956, Officers Lewis L. Branning and Robert Burr were arrested for burglary and sentenced to a year in prison. Branning then provided information to investigators that others were involved. As a result, Sergeant Ray Kellum was tried for being an accessory to burglary and was convicted of larceny, which was overturned by the courts later with Kellum being reinstated. Robert Montana and Malcolm (Doc) Houston were charged with burglary, with Montana was found innocent but Houston was tried twice. The first jury was hung, and Houston was found not guilty at the second trial and later reinstated.

James Robertson, McAllister, Robert Fonner, and Howard Sonn were also charged, with Robertson pleading guilty and sentenced to jail. Fonner received six months, the disposition of the other two is unknown, but reports indicated that they were terminated. An Officer Dary White admitted committing burglaries with Robertson and was terminated.

The squad was disbanded and dispersed into the patrol section. One result of the group's disbandment was that one particular patrol shift was then labeled Ali Baba and His Forty Thieves. The shift commander at the time was Captain J. T. Griffin. We studiously avoided mentioning that label to him. The author was real happy to be assigned to super straight Captain Bill O'Connell's shift upon graduating from the academy.

The author joined MPD in 1960 and was assigned to a patrol shift with Kellum and Montana as sergeants and Houston as a patrol officer. Kellum was a rough-and-tough-type, hard-living guy and Montana a deeply religious individual who was as straight-laced as any I worked with. I rode with senior man Houston and found him to be a hardworking officer who taught me well. He never displayed any indication of being other than a good street cop. A few years later, I worked in the office of Patrol Major Bill Harries with Houston and observed, without question, that he was hardworking and knowledgeable, and displayed a professional approach to law enforcement. He remains a friend for over fifty years.

In the accounts researched, it was obvious that the "good" elements of the department took the swift and necessary actions to clean up the criminal group of officers resulting in the cleansing of the department (MPD records and author's personal knowledge).

CAPTAIN NOLLE SHOT AT HOME

Captain Bill Nolle, the commander of the black precinct, was shot at his home, 245 NW Forty-eighth Place, Miami, in late March 1957. Nolle, watching TV with his wife and niece, heard a noise at the front of the house and looked out the door. As he did, an assailant fired a shotgun into the jalousie door as Nolle ducked back. He was hit with two shotgun pellets, causing minor wounds. After treatment at Jackson Hospital, he was released the same evening.

Homicide detectives Ernie Bush and A. J. McLaughlin investigated and charged MPD Officer Harold Mitchell, thirty-three, for aggravated assault. Mitchell was a subordinate officer assigned under Nolle at the black precinct.

The investigation indicated that Nolle was wounded by shots from a twenty-gauge shotgun at 9:25 PM and his life was saved by ducking just in time, according to Detective Chief John Cannon. The shots were fired from less than twenty feet from the front door of the home.

Nolle had his unoccupied city car shot with rifle bullets the previous month, which were followed up with telephone calls to his wife stating that Nolle himself would be the target next time (*Miami News*, 3/1957, and MPD records).

COUNTY JAIL ESCAPE

By Officer X (Wishes not to be identified)

It was about 3:00 AM on a night in 1958, assigned to Unit 610. I was parked at a Royal Castle across the street from the courthouse and finishing an accident report when I felt a tap on my shoulder. Looking up, I saw a citizen pointing up to the east side of the courthouse. Climbing down, on white sheets were two men, climbing from the county jail on the top floor. I called the situation into the complaint room and heard the Ha-Ha's in the background when the dispatcher said, "WHAT." I repeated the situation and was told to QRX (stand by). The two men got to about twenty feet of the sixth floor and ran out of sheets. The fire department was called to provide a net for the men to fall into, but before they arrived, one of the men decided to try to jump down. He did and broke both of his legs and a hip. The other one started to climb back up and then decided it would be much smarter to wait for the firemen. They did arrive and the man fell into the net. Needless to say, he was put back into jail, but the other one got to go to Ward D at Jackson Hospital. It was funny.

DUI CRASH KILLS BURLINSON

Officer John Burlinson was driving east on SW Seventh Street at Sixteenth Avenue in his patrol car when he was struck by a drunk driver, William Jacobs, forty-four, who was initially charged with manslaughter. Jacobs was later convicted of reckless driving by running a stop sign and striking Burlinson's police unit. He refused the alcohol test and was not convicted of the DUI charge, which had been downgraded from manslaughter. The judge sentenced Jacobs to thirty days in jail.

Burlinson, twenty-six, a New Jersey native and a Korean War veteran, joined the MPD in 1954 with Academy Class No. 29, three years before he died in the crash on March 8, 1958. Detective Mike Gonzalez was the first police unit that arrived on the scene and attempted first aid. Burlinson had been ejected from his squad car, which then ran him over. There were no seat belts installed in the police units at that time. Inspector John Webber stated that the "idea of safety belts for Miami patrol cars had been considered and turned down" since policemen get in and out of their cars so often and would never wear them (Wilbanks, *Forgotten Heroes*, 1996).

Author's Note: In the early 1960s, lap belts were finally installed in all units. At present, full safety belts are part of the police car package when purchased.

Chief Youell was promoted to assistant chief in September 1948 by Chief Headley. Youell had been previously demoted by Safety Director O. D. Henderson, but that decision was reversed by the court (*Miami News*, 11/4/1959).

SAFE CRACKERS KILLED BY OFFICERS

The Dade County school administration building at 275 NW Second Street became a deadly scene during the early morning hours of December 14, 1959. Miami detectives had received a tip earlier in the week that safecrackers might soon target the credit union in this building. Periodic checks were made by members of the Safe and Holdup Squad. One spot check found a window open but no burglars, causing the detectives to commence a stakeout at the building. At 5:00 AM, four burglars arrived with three entering the building via the open window. The detectives moved in and the shooting started. Detective Paul Nichols, Detectives Eddie Edmonds, Burt Whittle, and W. E. (Jack) Farr Jr. killed two of the suspects and wounded a third. The fourth offender escaped.

Investigation revealed that two of the suspects came in from northern states and the third had recently been released from Florida's Raiford prison.

The safe contained only a few hundred dollars at the time of the attempted burglary (MPD records).

ETHEL LITTLE MURDER

A sensational crime during the late 1950s was the vicious murder of a lady, Ethel Little, at 1220 NW Thirty-first Street, on December 15, 1959. A suspect had confronted her in her own home and savagely attacked her, even cutting off one breast and sticking it onto a bedroom dresser mirror.

The response of the department was extremely strong due to the horrible crime. The investigation was led by Detective Bob Utes and his supervisor, Lieutenant Bill McClure. Many residents of the area were asked (and complied) to take a polygraph test. Many sex offenders were picked up and questioned. In an attempt to match a bloody palm print found on the mirror at the murder scene, the department requested voluntary palm prints from every male over fourteen years of age living within one mile of the crime location. Over four thousand residents visited Stanley's Market on NW Thirtieth Street to provide their palm print to a twelve-man police identification squad. No match was found and the Miami police were unable to solve the case.

Years later, Vernon Edwards, thirty-four, walked into a Georgia police station in Decatur and admitted he was the killer. He provided details to police that convinced them that he was being truthful and his palm print matched.

Edwards was transported back to Miami for prosecution. The author was present during his questioning by our top homicide unit investigator, Mike Gonzalez, now the lead officer. The author could hardly believe how normal and calm Edwards's demeanor was while discussing the horrible crime. The killer advised that his conscience had finally caused him to come forward with his confession to this murder as well as another Miami woman, Johanna Block, murdered a year after Ms. Little in the same general neighborhood.

The offender, then a teen, had been living in the neighborhood of the murder, but eluded the polygraph tests and palm print submissions his neighbors endured.

Edwards was married to a daughter of Captain Bratt, a former MPD commander, who urged him to come forward with the confession (*Miami News*, 11/20/76 and 12/15/59; *Sarasota Journal*, 7/24/72).

In June 1960, Class No. 44 graduated from the MPD police academy. Included in the class was Clarence Dickson, the first MPD academy-trained black officer, and later the chief of police. The author was among the twelve officers "badged" that day (Author's personal knowledge).

COME ON DOWN

Miami initiated an active advertising effort in the 1950s and '60s in an attempt to entice "snowbirds" to winter in the Miami area. Early television viewers in the Northeast were bombarded with TV ads and the Arthur Godfrey show to "come on down," and they did.

Miami became a "hot" city in more ways than weather. The rich came, the poor came, the Canadians came, and the crooks followed along to feed off all of them.

Many of the bars did not close until 5:00 AM and a few never closed (the Clover Club in Miami and the Johnson Club in Medley were a couple of the more notorious). The term B-Girls became known to all as they seemed to be in every bar, despite all kinds of ordinances being drawn up to combat them.

The grand jury made reports on the situation and the newspapers ran stories often. The MPD had a liquor squad back then and many wondered if they were assigned to stop the activity or promote it.

Just goes to show that advertising works (Author's general knowledge).

DO WHAT THE CAPTAIN SAYS

By Officer X (Wishes not to be identified)

All good books and stories begin with "Once upon a time," and this one sticks in my mind as being unusually funny.

The duty captain called in a radio car with two of our finest who were riding that zone, and he threw them a court order and told them to serve this legal document and take care of the matter. It is to be noted that the approximate time of this was 3:00 AM. Our two fine officers went to the address, knocked on the screen door, and hollered the usual, "Police." A man came to the door in his shorts and undershirt, said he did not call the police and what the hell did they want. They said they have a warrant for his arrest, and he replied, "What? And what is this all about?" One of the officers told him to come outside. The man refused, they opened the door slightly, and he was immediately pulled out of the house, on the ground, in a usual three-person tussle. The subject was finally handcuffed and thrown into the back of the police car, along with his pants and a pair of shoes, and was transported to the old PD. All the time the subject in the rear seat was hollering and cussing, keeping in mind that it was still around 3:00 AM. After arriving at the station, another scuffle to get him out of the car into the station, into the captain's office, and our two heroes were disheveled, shirts out, sweating, said to the captain, "We got him, sir." It was a tough battle. The captain said, "You got who?" The answer was the man that was on the arrest warrant. The captain said, "Hell, all I gave you was a witness subpoena, not an arrest warrant."

The subject then asked, "Will you take me home?" The captain told him we weren't running a taxi service.

For confidential reasons, I will not divulge the captain or the two fine officers involved.

SQUAD CAR COURT

The law in Florida previously charged the local Justice of Peace (five in Dade County) with holding preliminary hearings on all death investigations. It was not uncommon for the JP to come to the scene of the crime, especially in cases of an officer-involved killing, and hold an inquest in the rear seat of a police car. It has been told that JP Ralph Ferguson (and later a circuit court judge) would often be located at a card game in the PBA hall and driven to the crime scene to conduct the police car inquest (Author's personal knowledge).

"HOT" DOWNTOWN

During the late 1950s, Miami was experiencing a number of fires at businesses in the downtown area. Officer—, a beat officer assigned to this area, was suspected of igniting the fires himself so that he could observe the fires as well as the response by the fire guys.

He was fired of course, but did not go to jail. Our sources said he joined the army and later was convicted of assault when he was allegedly trying to put the move on another guy and ended up serving a term in prison. He passed away many years ago (MPD records).

UNGRATEFUL

By Point Control Guy (Not to be named)

One day a woman was walking next to the Dupont Building, known for its swirling winds. She was wearing a flared skirt, a blouse, and a hat. The wind loosened her hat and she bent over to grab it with both hands. The wind then blew her skirt over her head. This Good Samaritan police officer rushed to help her by pulling her dress down. He stood there while she adjusted her clothing as if expecting some reward. When it came, it was a slap heard halfway down the block.

DETECTIVE DISTRICTS—FIEFDOMS

In the 1950s on into the early '60s, the detective bureau had a separate homicide unit and auto theft unit. The remainder of the investigate units were placed into one of four geographical divisions, headed up by a detective captain. Three of the four districts were headed up at times by Captain Lee Napier, C. O. Huttoe, and Ray Tanner, all controversial during their career. They ruled their particular area like old-time sheiks engaged in a fierce rivalry with each other. A detective in one area would not venture into another's territory or case without being on the receiving end of unwanted grief. Numerous allegations of corruption surfaced during these times, many of which most likely originated in one of the other camp (districts). If it wasn't so serious, it would have been funny.

In October 1962, City Manager Mel Reese brought in a tough old marine colonel, Donald Pomerleau, as public safety director, the boss of the chief of police. Colonel Pomerleau cleaned house at MPD, reorganizing the detective division into Burglary, Robbery, Fraud, etc., units. This had the effect of breaking up this group of fiefdoms. During the same period, the ordinary patrol officer was released from official and unofficial restraints and began to stick their nose into areas of concern previously the sole responsibility of the detective districts. A new era began, led by the uniformed task force, a group of mostly young uniform officers who were allowed to enforce all laws in all areas. The department culture changed forever, not dramatically, but surely.

This forty-five-man group was also the first integrated unit in Miami police history, as several black officers (Pete Bryant, Jimmy McCray, Tom Marshall, and Sergeant Leroy Smith were among those assigned).

The author proudly looks back on his assignment to the task force, both as an officer and later a supervisor, as one of his finest of many tours of duty in various department assignments. Working with top cops was very satisfying and the CO's Captain Owsley, Lieutenant Ken Parker, and Lieutenant (later Chief) Garland Watkins.

ROOKIE STORIES

All of us cops have our rookie stories that we will never forget. The author, then new in town, came out of the service and joined the MPD at twenty-one in 1960. The recruit instructor was a sergeant named Zinkel, a Southern boy, who appeared to delight in creating discomfort among his recruits. He did not instruct any of the academic classes, so I was able to do very well. However, in the physical grind, he bore down on me, just maybe because he was not thrilled with my New England (Yankee boy) accent. Fortunately, due to my young age and recent military service, I was in good shape. Still, a daily routine for Zinkel would be for him to order me into extra laps or pushups or other torture not shared by the others under a grueling Miami sun. He would laugh when I would barf up my lunch on the exercise field every day until I started skipping lunch.

I wasn't particularly thrilled that I was becoming a police officer (I just needed a job), so I came close to quitting a few times until I would see that smirk on his face, which gave me that extra push to keep going. I made it through the academy's sixteen weeks in flying colors despite him.

A few years later, I was promoted from sergeant to lieutenant and guess who one of my assigned sergeants was?

Yup, you guessed it. I surprised him, for sure, by never mentioning his previous actions and treated him evenly. (But it was not easy to do that.)

SENIOR MAN/MENTOR

It was not unusual to assign one of the senior officers in the paddy wagon (we had three or four per shift) who had slacked off a bit on the work output or had got on the wrong side of the shift captain. The author was very fortunate to be paired with Bob Angelone, a heavyset, ten-year veteran. Bob taught me real police work in three months than the academy did. He also set me in the right direction on handling prisoners, talking to citizens, and steered me away from calls being handled by a few officers who had the idea that the job gave their property rights that no one else had (if you get my drift). Bob was tough or kind, depending on the nature of the call.

He later made sergeant and was an excellent, well-liked supervisor. We remained good friends for many years and I even bought two (junk) cars from him in the days of tiny paychecks.

Shortly after his retirement, he passed on. I still miss him.

COLD BEER, OFFICER?

On one of Angelone's days off, I was assigned to ride with a guy named J. P.—, a much-older officer. He was a pleasant fellow but did not provide me with a very good impression of what a cop should be. Our first stop on the afternoon shift was at Jeff's Bar, West Flagler Street and Twelfth Avenue. It was a very warm day and the wagons were not air-conditioned. J. P. led me into this bar where I thought he was going to check out the establishment's license or something.

Instead, he bellied up to the bar and ordered a cold beer *and* offered me one also. I said no way. After downing several quick ones, we headed back out to the wagon. I had to make a decision, even though I was still on probation. I grabbed the keys and advised that I will drive. He started to insist on driving but was already a DUI (probably also had a few on the way to work). I bluffed him by advising that I think we should go talk to the captain back at the station to resolve the dilemma.

Thankfully, he just said, "OK, kid, have it your way."

I sure was happy to see Angelone return.

TESTING THE ROOKIE

One midsummer afternoon shift, the author was assigned to walk the Seaboard Railroad beat. Nearby was Miami's railroad station, which had become a rundown area with s—kicker bars and crummy strip stores selling junk and miscellaneous equipment. Slim's drive-in, where the down and out hung around, was the center of activities along with a Royal Castle and the Shrimp Place, a famous seafood eating establishment that was just about the only upscale enterprise left in Seaboard.

A fellow officer, John Moriarty, had tipped me off that a couple of senior officers wanted to "test" me by egging some area toughs to "kick my ass a little" to see what I was made of. John's advice was for me to strike first before dark.

The senior's plan was for a couple of tough guys to confront me in an alley and give me a small whipping. I started with a hillbilly bar, pulling the plug on a loud jukebox that could be heard two blocks away, and snatched up a couple of tipsy bar customers before the remainder had got too liquored up to protest physically. The paddy wagon was called a few times, so by nightfall, the beat was "under control." By the time the setup was to begin in the back alley behind the stores, I was ready. Armed with a riot baton, I hid behind some boxes and jumped out at the two thugs following me and started swinging. One went down and the other ran. I had survived the evening.

During a later visit with the regular zone car officer, George Clark, I angrily accused him of the setup and was attempting to challenge him.

George just laughed and we later became lifelong friends. I guess I had passed the test—thanks to Moriarty.

NEED A WATCH, KID?

While riding the downtown wagon with Bob Angelone, the author was introduced to an old-time beat officer by the name of Russ—. During the conversation,—noticed that I was not wearing a watch (due to an allergy). He said, "Kid, you have to have a watch," as he rolled up his uniform shirt and displayed twenty or so watches on his arm. "I will sell you one for five bucks, take your pick."

I declined (probably would have got gangrene if one was worn) and then he started to explain what other wares he had for me to buy that was stored in his car down the street.

I often wondered just where he got all those cheap watches. Do you think he bought or bartered them from some of the winos and bums on his beat? Your guess.

Just part of my street education.

A 1960 BILINGUAL OFFICER

By Louis Cruz, MPD Ret.

The time was the early 1960s. There were very few Hispanic officers on the police department. I guess I qualified as Hispanic because of my Spanish surname. With "Cruz" as my last name, it followed that I must be fluent in Spanish. Marty Brown and his partner were dispatched to the old Greyhound bus station in downtown Miami reference a group of rowdy Mexican migrant workers. After futile attempts to communicate with the Mexicans, Marty got the bright idea to call for the only "Hispanic" that he knew was working that night—me. Upon arriving at the bus station, I approached Marty and asked what was happening. He told me that he was unable to get anyone in this group to identify themselves. He wanted me to get some names from them. "OK," says I. I grabbed one of the Mexicans by the lapel and gave it my best shot. In my best high school Castillian Spanish accent, and gesturing with my other hand, I asked him, "Whatsa-you-name?"

PS: My Spanish vocabulary was limited to a few cusswords at that time.

HOMEOWNER SHOOTS AT COP

When we hit the streets, we are somewhat aware that we will be dealing with dangerous people at times. The ordinary folks are considered "our friends" and supporters. We swore to serve and protect them. As a rookie back in 1961, the author experienced an incident that went against this theory, although the full circumstances show that the citizen made a somewhat "reasonable choice."

While riding zone 920 one summer evening, the station made us aware that remnants of the old Cash Gang had pulled some robberies and were being hunted. As the area I was assigned to was the "turf" for these thugs, I was alert and ready. A call went out to a residence west of SW Twenty-seventh Avenue, north of the trail, in reference to a possible burglar in a home that was temporally vacant due to the owner being out of town on vacation, according to the watch order on file. With the thought in mind that perhaps some of this gang was using this home as a safe house, I cautiously approached it without lights, coasting to a stop a half block away. My backup car, manned by Officer Gennette, did the same. He went toward the front as I maneuvered around to the backyard.

In order to get a better look, I snuck up to a rear bedroom window and peered inside the darkened room. In the next instance, a terrible explosion and a flash emanated from the window of this residential home that I was scoping out, and my uniform cap flew back. With my .38 revolver in my hand, I instinctively pushed the barrel through the window screen with the intent of firing back, but for some unconscious reason, did not discharge the gun in the direction of the flash. I then hit the ground and quickly crawled into some bushes and plants to obscure my presence. I could hear Gennette loudly inquiring if I was OK, but dared not to answer lest my location would be known by the shooter. Gennette went to his car radio and asked for assistance, stating my status was not known. As I lay in the evening dew of the bushes, the sounds of multiple sirens heading our way was clearly heard throughout the entire area.

As the cavalry arrived, I crawled back far enough to safety and shouted that I was OK. The home was then surrounded by uniformed officers and shouts by them were made to the occupants to come out with their hands our or else a tear gas barrage would soon begin. Finally, a veteran homicide detective arrived (I think it was Ernie Bush), and he went up to the front door and knocked loudly.

After a brief pause, an elderly gentleman opened the door with gun in hand and identified himself as the homeowner. The guy advised that he had come home early from vacation and forgot to cancel the standard police vacation watch order. He advised that he had seen a prowler wearing a white shirt looking in the window and fired his old gun at him. The detective took the old guy's gun as he appeared slightly foggy and the neighborhood quieted down, but not my heartbeat.

After the troops cleared, Gennette advised me that a civilian car had arrived earlier, before the first uniform car arrival, and Gennette had ordered him to "get the hell out of here, quick." We were later advised that the civilian car was driven by Chief Headley who was in the area to pick up a pizza and had responded to the call for help. The chief took it well, merely telephoning the complaint sergeant to get an explanation. Nothing further was said.

My sergeant, Carl Carter, then advised me, "Finish your report later, they are holding calls in this area." I guess he did not notice me still shaking as I donned my hat with the crease on top and went back to "serving and protecting."

LOUSY JUSTICE

Rebecca Nudel, a shop owner's wife, was brutally murdered at a SW Thirty-seventh Avenue store she operated with her husband one quiet midmorning day in June 1961. An employee of the pool supply shop, Daniel Grant, was later charged with the crime. As it was the author's first murder case, I was allowed to tag along with the detectives as they questioned the husband at the station. Officer Fitzpatrick and myself had picked up the employee at home in the Grove as a possible witness and transported him to the station. The author sat with Daniel Grant, while Detectives Bob Utes and Charlie Shepard ran a polygraph exam on the hubby of the murdered woman. While waiting, using his own funds, the author bought a burger and coffee for Grant and chatted with him while awaiting the detectives. The conversation convinced the author that the guy was very evasive and was extremely nervous.

When the detectives finally questioned Grant and ran a polygraph test, they too realized he was the offender and placed a murder charge on him. The author viewed the entire questioning through a two-way glass mirror in the homicide squad room. The detectives never raised their voice or physically struck Grant or even threatened him. They acted very professional, which greatly impressed the young rookie. The author then was instructed to book Grant into the jail that evening, making sure the jailers would provide him a late sandwich to supplement the earlier burger.

The following day, Grant took the detectives back to the scene and showed them where he hid the garrote that was used to strangle the victim and reenacted the crime, which was filmed by a mobile video machine that had recently been added to the MPD's identification unit. This was probably one of the first uses of this device for an on-scene investigation anywhere.

The jury found Grant guilty and sentenced him to die in the electric chair. The author appeared more nervous in court than the suspect. Grant later received a reprieve from the electric chair when the supreme court struck down capital punishment at that time in Florida.

Ten years later, Grant's attorneys filed a motion in court stating that Grant was tortured into making the confession to the detectives, a charge that was utterly untrue. The court sent the case back to the Dade County state attorney's office for a decision on a retrial while Grant stayed in jail.

The author, then a high-ranking MPD commander, communicated to Janet Reno, the prosecutor, that the original videotape of the confession was still in the property room and the detectives and the polygraph examiner were either still on the job or in retirement nearby as well as the identification officers who collected the evidence and filmed the reenactment. Reno, however, probably due to the anti-police attitude and racial turmoil prevalent during the late '60s and early '70s, declined to retry the case. So much for justice.

Grant was released from prison after ten years.

In an unusual twist on this case, Grant's son, with the exact same name, was later charged with murder. To this day, he sits in prison in upstate Florida.

COP ARRESTS SISTER FOR MURDER

MPD Officer Willie (Big Nick) Nicholson, thirty-five, working both on and off duty for three weeks, solved the murder of a bolita operator, Beatrice Dunaway, who was killed during a bolita counting house robbery. One of those arrested was his own sister, Eugenia Thomas, thirty-seven, the wife of black precinct judge L. E. Thomas. She was accused of plotting with two men to rob the counting house across from her NW Eleventh Street home on October 28, 1961.

Nicholson, working with Detective Bob Utes, spent many hours and days to solve the crime, finally arresting Aubrey Henry, twenty-seven, who implicated Clarence Simpson, twenty-eight. Simpson was arrested shortly after by Officer Amos Brooks and Roosevelt Trimble. Simpson implicated Mrs. Thomas as one who helped plot and allowed the two robbers to use her home to observe the counting house and was arrested. Nicholson, a highly regarded black detective, said, "Now I am sick," as he snared his sister. Equally shocked was his brother-in-law, Municipal Judge L. E. Thomas, when his thirty-seven-year-old wife was charged with a robbery that led to the killing. "It came out of a blue sky," said the judge to newsmen, "But I'll stand by her." Dunaway was killed when she resisted the robbers.

Mrs. Thomas was found not guilty at a later trial (*Miami News*, 12/21/1961; Lewiston (ME) *Tribune* and *Baltimore Sun*, 12/21/1961; *Palm Beach News*, 2/11/1967).

CHANGING UNIFORMS

The Cuban missile crisis in the fall of 1962 had an effect on the Miami PD. First of all, both New Orleans and Miami were two large cities lying within easy range of the Soviet missiles being stockpile by the communist regime of Fidel Castro, and second, many of the police officers on the force were activated by their military reserve units.

The largest contingent the Miami PD guys were in was the U.S. Air Force's 435th Troop Carrier Wing. They were immediately activated and sent to Barksdale AFB in Louisiana. This group included officers from many of the PD units that left the department to cover for the missing men who were ordered up for a period of eleven months. The reserve military officers in other branches were sent to scattered locations depending on the military job type they had.

When the author joined the police department upon receiving my military discharge, I remained in the Air Force Reserve for several years. Because most of the other MPD Air Force reservists were members of the 435th Wing, their officers asked me to join with them, but insisted that I change my military classification from communications supervisor to that of the air police. I declined the offer, despite a desire to serve with the same group that I was working with in the department.

When the call-up came, I was assigned to the Miami International Airport. My duties were primarily based at the main airport terminal. I only had to drive half the distance to work than I did normally heading for the police department. The only distraction was the numerous young ladies working the car rental agencies. After several weeks of arranging transportation and other support for CIA and military brass heading south to the Keys after landing in Miami, the crisis was grinding down.

My commanding officer at the airport was Charlie Price, a major at both my reserve unit as well as being the major of personnel at Miami PD (and a great guy). He gave me the option of hanging around the airport for several months or being released back to the department. He also converted my large bank of earned overtime (they didn't pay us for all overtime back then in the PD) to pay status, so I received pay from Miami PD as well as Uncle Sam. I also did not lose any seniority as the Barksdale guys did, and this action allowed me to be eligible earlier for PFC, and later eligibility for the sergeants' exam—and I saved on gas.

PROMISE NOT TO TELL A SOUL

By Cefalu's Sergeant

I was working the night shift with motormen Ross Cefalu and Bob Potter. It was just after dark, I was working channel 2 (central); Ross and Bob were on channel 1 (north end). I got a call to call the complaint sergeant. He was really excited, it seems that either Ross or Bob had taken off their helmet and put it over the speaker, which had keyed the mic, the speakers were mounted in the middle of the handlebars, on the motors. Ross was telling some very personal stories about him and a girlfriend, and in between, he kept saying, "Bob, you got to promise that you won't tell anyone about this."

Of course, Bob would say. Ross went into some very lurid descriptions and details of how big this girl was and so on, with Ross again asking Bob to promise not to tell anyone.

All this talk was coming over the police radio, so the whole world was hearing it firsthand. Of course they couldn't raise (contact) them, so that is why the complaint sergeant called me to find out if I had any idea where they were. I told him I would look for them on the Thirty-sixth

Street causeway (Tuttle) that was being built at that time, so I headed for there, as that was a favorite spot for the guys riding north and central to get away from it all. Before I could get out on the causeway, their mic cleared and right away, "801-804, call the complaint sergeant." They then found out how personal their conversion had been. And of course everyone else that was working that night promised Ross and Bob every time they saw them that they would not tell a soul either.

Ross Cefalu was one of the funniest guys in the world. Too bad he's not here to relate this story, as it would have been lot more entertaining coming from him.

Editor's Note: Ross Cefalu was not just a police officer. He was a pilot, a magician, a paid circus clown, and a storyteller extraordinaire. During World War II, army paratrooper Ross Cefalu went into France on D-Day, June 6, 1944, flying (aiming) a glider. An extraordinary human being.

DON'T TOUCH MY PRISONER

A perpetual problem in any department is that the conduct taught in the recruit academy is often at odds with the practices on the street. The author recounts one incident of where a senior officer used unnecessary force against a criminal despite any logical reason for doing so.

A call went out in reference to a burglary at the Red Rooster bar on North Miami Avenue and Twenty-third Street. The author, a rookie riding solo, received the backup call, but arrived several minutes prior to the senior officer who had been dispatched to the crime in progress. The rookie officer stealthily entered the broken front door and heard noises from the kitchen area. My shining light spotted the burglar, holding a kitchen knife, in the back area of the bar. With gun drawn, I ordered the man to drop the weapon and to go down. I handcuffed the offender, sat him down in a booth, and began to question him about a series of similar bar burglaries in the area. The burglar admitted to a couple of other cases just about the time of arrival of the primary senior officer.

Immediately upon entering the bar, the senior man struck the handcuffed offender in the face with his fist. Naturally, the confessions of the bad guy ended.

Incensed, I confronted the senior officer and threatened to beat *his* ass the next time the older cop struck my prisoner, a risky and defining moment in a young cop's career, as it did not take much for a superior to can a rookie on the word of one of his senior men.

In this case, the rookie lucked out as the offending senior guy, much smaller in statute, took the rookie at his word, backed off, and kept his mouth shut, probably realizing how difficult it might be to explain why it took him fifteen minutes to respond to an in-progress crime while riding a small zone that one could drive across in just a few minutes.

ROBBERS KILL OFFICER

Officer Jerrel Ferguson, a thirty-three-year-old black MPD officer, was patrolling alone the night of November 7, 1962. While en route to another call, Ferguson spotted two robbers he had arrested four years prior for robbery. They were driving without lights. Ferguson did not know that Gerald Fisherman and Willie Lawrence, both thirty, had committed two holdups this evening. As Ferguson was running a wants-check on the two men, his gun was snatched from his holster and he was shot five times at close range in the chest, instantly killing him. Driver's license and social security cards of the two men were found tucked over the sun visor of Ferguson's squad car. Both offenders were arrested later that evening by R. E. Dean and Sergeant Oliver of the Miami Shores PD and pled guilty in order to avoid the death penalty. The bandits admitted the slaying and the robbery of three insurance collectors in the Liberty Square project earlier. Both had recently been released from prison for 1958 postal robberies.

When arrested, the robbers had two loaded guns on the front seat in the car, but offered no resistance.

Fisherman escaped from prison in 1973 but was recaptured weeks later. Lawrence, permitted weekend furloughs from prison, was caught holding up a convenience store and charged with a series of crimes.

A 2010 check of the robbers showed that Lawrence had died and that Ferguson was living in West Palm Beach. The information in the statewide prison locator is a bit fuzzy, but it appears that Ferguson will complete his parole in November 2010.

The funeral services for Officer Ferguson were held at St. John's Church in Overtown where a large crowd of police colleagues and public attended. Both the chief of police and the sheriff attended, as well as a large number of police brass. Hundreds of uniform officers (including the author) from Miami and many other cities attended.

The *Miami Times* newspaper stated,

> The mammoth procession led by motorcycle escort, blinking bright red incandescents was immediately trailed by many squad cars that lighted up the highways (en route to the cemetery). They weaved in and out of the winding roads like a colossal dinosaur. There it was, Ferguson was once more left alone, to rest eternally among the departed. But, this time, all his buddies knew about it—because they had taken him there.

Officer Ferguson left six young children (Wilbanks, *Forgotten Heroes*, 1996; author's knowledge).

BAY OF PIGS RECRUITING STATION

During the Cuban exile CIA secret project to invade Cuba and dethrone the communist dictator Fidel Castro, the MPD got involved, whether they wanted to or not. Gun running, boat thefts, and extortion of merchants to supply cash to some of the "freedom" groups were common daily occurrences. One glaring example of the "secrecy" involved in the planned raid was the existence of an open Cuban exile recruiting station at West Flagler Street and Eleventh Avenue. One would think that it was a new Blockbuster store or the like, with a line stretching down Flagler Street every day. In the weeks after the opening of the recruiting office, practically each Cuban stopped and questioned by the author and other officers for any reason, would hear the halting English reply that "I am working with the CIA, so don't bother me."

The effort did bring some economic stimulus to the area as it seemed all of the persons questioned had brand-new cash in their pocket. But I often wondered if the real volunteers were outnumbered by Castro's agents.

Big secret, huh?

URBAN RENEWAL

By Unidentified Task Force Officer

Officer Steve Collins had developed a real good CI (confidential informer) and would pick him up in an unmarked task force car and drive him around Liberty City questioning him about illegal activities. Being the bookworm that Steve was, he remembered that the book said to switch to casual conversation after pumping a CI for information.

Therefore, Steve asked the young CI if he knew anything about Urban Renewal.

After a moment of silence, the young CI asked, "What his street name be?"

CULTURAL CHANGES AT MPD

In 1962, the city manager Mel Reese hired as public safety director a retired marine colonel, Donald Pomerleau. Pomerleau, in effect, took over the police department causing dramatic organizational changes, such as eliminating the detective districts, closing down the black precinct, and put the MPD on the road to utilizing computers for crime prevention and other law enforcement purposes.

Pomerleau's stormy term ended in February 1964 with his resignation. His advice after resigning, "Move out of the police station and don't let the city manager try to run it from city hall." Pomerleau said he tried to stay neutral in the cold war between the city manager and the chief of police but found the middle ground untenable. His parting words were, "It just was not worth it."

He did not last, but his changes did (Author's knowledge and undated *Miami News*, 2/1964).

ANOTHER NIGHT IN LIBERTY CITY

By Lou Kirchhoff, MPD Ret.

On a hot, muggy evening in Liberty City in 1963, Timothy Bell, described by fellow residents as sort of a wacko, went berserk up on the third floor of one of the green monster slums on NW Sixty-first Street, opening the gas valve and the water faucets in his apartment. Zone car officers were reluctant to approach due to the leaking gas. Dick Witt and Phil Doherty responded along with half the task force. They went up to the apartment with rookie Lou Kirchoff, who had the assigned call, confronted the crazed man who then began throwing knives at us. We used trash can covers to deflect them as mace or stun guns were not readily available then nor were vests worn by the officers. Finally, Bell retreated to the kitchen and threw what we considered his last knife. The knife whizzed over Doherty's head, deflected off Kirchoff's badge, tearing his shirt epaulet. Thinking that Bell was out of knives, Phil and Dick ran into the kitchen and jumped him, knocking him to the wet floor. To our surprise, he came up with a large butcher knife in his right hand. Phil held his wrist tight as the knife's point was aimed at Phil's chest and his hands were wet and slimy from the water on the floor and sweat dripping from his face. Dick pulled out a Kel light and pounded on Bell, hoping to dislodge the knife, but Bell, completely out of his head, seemingly ignored the blows from the light. I (Kirchhoff) was able to jump into the fray, kneeing the subject, and after what seemed like an eternity, Phil was able to grasp the blade and twist it from his hands, causing a flow of his precious A-Pos blood.

The firefighters arrived, shut off the gas (to our great relief), and Bell was strapped into a gurney for a trip to Jackson Hospital.

The squad bandaged us up and we all retreated to the station to pick up a spare shirt from Officer Washington's supply shop at the property room, and then checked back into service. It was later determined that Bell suffered an epileptic seizure and was completely unaware of his actions during the fit. All charges were later dropped for medical reasons and no residents sued up for denting their garbage can lids.

Just another night in Liberty City.

BOMBINGS OF MIAMI JEWISH LEADERS

A series of bombs targeted Jewish businesses and homes in Miami in 1961. Detectives Everett Kay, Eugene McCracken, and Lieutenant Sapp of the intelligence squad focused on a city employee as the suspect.

Rookie Miami officer Steve Plumacher was taken out of the police academy and placed into the city water department as an employee, working alongside the suspect, Donald Branch. After several weeks, Branch set up a bombing and Plumacher was supplied with fake dynamite sticks to place at a Jewish leader's home. Branch had previously set off bombs around the city, including one at the home of *Miami Herald* editor Don Shoemaker.

On February 19, 1962, Branch was arrested and sentenced to prison. Grateful members of the Jewish community in the Miami area, in appreciation for Plumacher's super work, paid for him to finish his college education. Steve later became a professor at a western North Carolina college. Steve is now deceased (Author's knowledge).

END OF A CAREER

MPD Officer Dirk Schel, thirty, was patrolling Zone 12, through the Farmer's Market area, NW Twelfth Avenue and Twenty-second Street, on September 27, 1962, searching for two B/M bandits who had just committed an armed robbery at Neville's Swap Shop, 2156 NW Seventh Avenue, Miami. Officer Schel, a three-year veteran, pulled up his zone car alongside a subject on foot when the man abruptly wheeled and shot Officer Schel through the right shoulder.

MPD zone cars and a Dade helicopter searched the area and soon arrested one man, James Ingram, in the market area. Ingram, twenty-four, was pointed out by citizens as a stranger to the market area. Ingram had removed his shirt in an attempt to evade detection. MPD advised that Ingram was a four-time loser with a criminal record.

About the same time, Officer Neil Garfield (I think Neil was on Motors then) found a snub-nosed revolver stashed between potato sacks in the market, near where Ingram was apprehended.

Another suspect, Earnest Washington Hudson, thirty, was arrested by MPD Officer Roosevelt Trimble at a gas station several blocks away. Hudson had recently been released from Raiford.

Officer Schel was transported to nearby Jackson Hospital by one of the arriving zone cars, Al Cinilia, and was later "up and around." Schel returned to duty several weeks later, but soon after, he left the department.

We did a quick street lineup, showing the employees of the shop the two had robbed to make an identification. Officer Schel later confirmed the ID, and the gun Garfield found did match up.

Dirk changed careers shortly after the shooting.

Records indicate that Dirk Schel is still alive up in the Palm City, Florida, area. He would be seventy-nine now (MPD records and author's knowledge).

GEORGE WASHINGTON SHOT ON CHRISTMAS

In the early morning hours before daylight on Christmas of 1962, the author was cruising without lights in his squad car and surprised two burglars breaking into the Dade Tire Co. on North Miami Avenue and Fourteenth Street. The author snuck up on them so quietly that he himself was startled and not quite prepared to handle two possibly armed bandits. The culprits jumped into their pickup truck and roared out of the yard. The author, fearing that they were armed (later found to be a crowbar in their hand, not a gun), began an auto chase into the central Negro district at high speed.

On NW First Court, the offenders bailed out of their truck and fled between down a narrow alley adjacent to a large residential tenement building. The author stopped, drew his weapon, and fired once, aiming low to avoid striking the occupied homes. The offenders kept running, but one was caught on the other side of the block by responding backup cars. The burglar's name was George Washington and he had been hit in the ankle by the bullet.

I am sure that not many officers can say they shot George Washington on Christmas morning, especially one with no beard and not wearing a red suit.

One sidelight of the case was that a resident living three buildings north was sitting in a rocking chair on the third-floor porch when the spent bullet landed at his feet. I advised him to keep the bullet as a souvenir.

This is yet another reason it is so difficult to police a densely populated area, a fact that our GIs are currently enduring in the Middle East as they attempt to root out insurgents who are mixed in with ordinary citizens in very close quarters.

WHO SHOT MANNING?

Officer Gil Zamora and the author apprehended a dangerous nighttime cat burglar who nearly killed a homeowner in 1963. After a confrontation, Phil and Gil emptied their guns at Manning who was fleeing from S Miami Avenue Road and Thirteenth Street. The suspect was shot three times but still eluded capture until spotted by a citizen lying under a bush next to the chief of police Walter Headley's apartment on Brickell Avenue.

Detective Bob Gow arrived and began to question Manning before the arrival of the ambulance. The suspect inquired as to the name of the officer who shot him and Gow asked why he wanted to know. His reply, "I want to sue him." Gow immediately ordered Officer Frank Baker to remove the police blanket covering the suspect and said, "If that is the case, you are not going to use our blanket." Detective Gow also deflected a nearby resident's complaint of a bullet hole in his vehicle by instructing the owner to put a little putty in the hole and cover it up with shoe polish.

Later, Officer Zamora, a former Marine who was a sharpshooter, and the author had a lively discussion of who actually hit the suspect, each trying to claim the crowing rights. We headed for Jackson Hospital and asked if the doctor could remove the bullets in Manning for ballistic tests. The doctor inquired as to the reason, as it seemed unnecessary, and was told that the officers were very interested in which of them was really the sharpshooter. The angry doctor threatened to call the duty captain if the officers did not leave immediately. Zamora and the author never did determine which of them had the sharp eye and hand.

Manning, after recovering, was bonded out by his wealthy out-of-town family, staying at a beach hotel while attending trial. Before the completion of the trial, he robbed his own family and fled the state.

By this time, his prints were finally processed by the FBI and it was determined he was also a prison escapee from a Midwest prison. He was later recaptured and spent a stretch in the clink.

A MOTORMAN'S DILEMMA

By Motor Officer (Name withheld)

While patrolling the south end on an evening shift, I stopped a driver for a noisy exhaust. The driver, a woman, explained that she had just had a new exhaust system installed and perhaps there was something wrong with the installation. Having inherent faith in the honesty of an individual, I bent down to look under the vehicle to determine the problem. It was in fact a new system that had been improperly installed.

In the process of bending down, my tailor-made riding britches split at the seam from knee to knee!

After sending the driver on her way, I began the process to determine who from the motor squad lived in the south end that would have a pair of britches that I could wear for the remainder of the shift. I recalled that a fellow motorman who was assigned in a far north end zone resided with his wife in my area. I proceeded to their residence at an apartment complex and parked my motor adjacent to the apartments, out of sight from the street, to ensure that the duty supervisor would not think that this "unnamed motorman" was out of his assigned zone!

I knocked at the door of the apartment and his wife responded in a bathrobe. I explained my plight and she directed me to their bedroom and provided me with a pair of her husband's uniform britches. She then explained that she was preparing to bathe as she had a pressing appointment and that I could let myself out after changing. While in the process of donning my fellow officer's britches, he arrived home! I made a hurried explanation and departed. My fellow motorman made no statement at the time and has made none since.

SEVENTH AVENUE MASSACRE

Citizens leaving the Miami baseball stadium every Friday and Saturday evening in 1964 were being mugged by gangs from Overtown as they made their way home. Chief Headley ordered the uniform task force to handle the situation.

Officers Joe Catell and Louie Cruz, dressed like women, encamped on bus benches (armed with iron rebars) with twenty or so other task force guys (including the author) hiding in a nearby rental truck, as the robbery attempts went down.

Our lieutenant Ken Parker advised us not to arrest anyone, just chase them into the apartment area adjoining Seventh Avenue. "Take no prisoners," he said. Several punks did show later at Jackson Hospital with Billy club welts on their legs and arms.

The following weeks were peaceful for the ball game attendees, as no robberies were reported in that area for the following months and the chief was happy.

PLAINCLOTHES POLICEWOMEN

By Lieutenant Mikele Carter, MPD Ret.

In the '60s, when I was a plainclothes policewoman working on street detail, Sophie Bevilaqua, Dorothy Gramling, and I were working downtown on Flagler Street and NE Third Avenue at the bus stop. We were standing around, watching for pickpockets at the bus stop.

While watching, Sophie "chatted up" one of the men in the crowd. The next thing I knew, Sophie walked over to me and Dorothy and said that her new friend wanted to "hire" the three of us (whom he had seen hanging out at the bus stop on numerous occasions and assumed we were hookers).

When Sophie gathered the three of us, all of us working in street detail, the John explained that he had something new that he wanted us to do. He then explained that he wanted all three of us to perform, with him as an observer, with bananas. Sophie, without missing a beat, said, "Why, that's not new! You're the third person to suggest this!" After we had set the price and arrested him for solicitation of prostitution, he cursed us out, saying, "Of all the dames on Flagler Street, I had to proposition three female fuzz."

STAR OF INDIA JEWEL ROBBERY

During the mid-1960s, Miami and surrounding cities were plagued with high-end jewel robberies. The many wealthy bejeweled folks enjoying the winter sun and fun attracted hordes of jewel thieves to the area. Miami PD, the sheriff's office, and Miami Beach police were overloaded with cases of large-value thefts. Of course, a jewel thief had to have a market for his goods that provided employment for a number of "fences" who profited handsomely from the thug's efforts.

One of the highlights of this era was the burglary and theft of the famous skillion-dollar Star of India, a 563-carat diamond, and the DeLong Star Ruby, as well as nineteen other precious jewels. The theft actually occurred in New York City's American Museum of National Histroy, but all the planning and planned fencing of the world-famous diamond was strictly Miami. Alan Kuhn and Jack (Murph the Surf) Murphy, rocket stars of the jewel thief crowd, were living in a high-rise along Brickell

Avenue near SW Twenty-fifth Road. Miami PD's burglary unit and intelligence squad worked feverishly to reign in these punks but had only marginal luck until Sergeants Everett Kay and Mike McCracken got onto their tail.

A snitch had provided the information that Murphy was living up on one of the higher floors of a condo complex with a view of Biscayne Bay. It seems that Kay and McCracken then made some type of stealth entry to Murf's pad while he was out enjoying the nightlife and installed a listening device in the mantle of the fireplace.

Not long after, their new pal (the machine) picked up parts of a plan being drawn up for a big "hit" in New York, but never heard the exact target location discussed.

The detectives alerted the local FBI, and agents boarded the same New York-bound flight as the burglars. The tail was lost in the big city, and it wasn't until a radio news flash reported the huge robbery that the agents knew what the robbery target was.

Agents then accompanied all outgoing flights to Miami the following day and came up a known fence. The Star of India and many of the other gems were recovered from a Miami bus locker and the burglars were jailed. They were later sentenced to three years in prison.

While bonded out, the two became involved in the Whiskey Creek murders of two young ladies who had got involved with them. Both Kuhn and Murphy were convicted of murder and sent to prison for long terms.

Murph the Surf, by then a somewhat media darling, was able to convince the parole board that he had found God, learned computers, and wanted to preach to convicts about changing their life. (How many times have we all heard that?) He was released and since has made a living traveling around at government and do-gooder's expense selling his story. Some say he really changed! Maybe he has, but so what? The two murdered girls from the Whiskey Creek case are still dead.

What a great country?

BOLITA KING—RED RAINWATER

Before Power Bowl, there was bolita, although the latter was illegal. The Miami area bolita kingpin was Red Rainwater during the 1950s and '60s. Red had plenty of connections in the upper hierarchy of several local police departments and in the court system, which allowed him to prosper.

In 1963, Sergeant Jay Golden and I were assigned to a super secret surveillance of Rainwater by then Assistant Chief Glen Baron, on orders from the new city manager. No one else in the department was aware that we were shadowing him. We only had an unmarked car, binoculars, and a notepad and worked separate shifts. It is very difficult to follow another vehicle with one car without being detected or have the ability to keep up while driving through traffic. For sixty days, I woke this guy up, went on his rounds with him, recording all his contacts, and discovered the identity of his girlfriend, a black hooker who lived off NW Thirty-sixth Street and took him home at the end of the day. It was a most valuable experience for me as it opened my eyes to what was *really* going on and I learned who all the big vice guys were in Miami.

The only flaw during this assignment was getting involved in the only vehicle crash of my career, when an armored car changed lanes on NE Fifth Street and opened up the side of my car (actually, the city manager's car) with the precision of a can opener. Only my feelings were hurt as Rainwater lost his tail that day.

When the assignment was completed, I was offered a slot on the elite motor squad, which I declined, to the amazement of Chief Baron who thought it was every officer's dream to be a motor man. I opted instead for the crime task force and ended up loving every minute of it.

A couple of years later, both Baron and Golden got caught up in a wrecker company scandal and both were run off the department. I often wondered if there was any connection to the vice ring they were trying to penetrate or what was the real reason they were focusing on it.

Red Rainwater died of a drug overdose injection by his above-mentioned girlfriend a couple of years later.

CHIEF VS. MAYOR

During the period of 1958 into the mid-1960s, Miami's mayor was Robert King High, a diminutive attorney whose passion appeared to be criticizing the chief of police, Walter Headley. High was often quoted in the local papers as implying that the police were getting payoffs from local bolita operators. It made good press and probably helped High get reelected several times. Chief Headley rebuffed these allegations each time, and the feud continued for a decade.

At one point, High established a bolita squad outside the police department's chain of command to eliminate bolita in the city. He selected Captain Robert Knight as the commander of this squad, and Knight in turn selected the author (then a sergeant) and several others officers, including Jimmy Tombley, Al Donatelli, black officers Bob Ingram and Otis Davis, and a couple of others, operating out of offices at the Miami baseball stadium on NW Tenth Avenue.

Mayor High's passion was to narrow in on the alleged corruption that was supposed to be rampant due to the open bolita operations.

The squad instead narrowed their focus to the actual illegal operations themselves with any corruption uncovered to be handled by the special Dade County grand jury, headed by Joe Manners. Many arrests were made and search warrants served with the special prosecutors following up on the leads uncovered in the overall countywide operations. The special squad of officers joined up with a Dade County squad, both under the mantle of the grand jury, and proved to be quite effective.

The project ended when Mayor High suffered a fatal heart attack. The group was immediately reassigned back to MPD regular duties.

One sidelight of this effort was the production of a booklet that contained complete dossiers on all (over one hundred) of the high-level bolita and other gambling operators within the county. Many of these listed also had organized crime connections. When Mayor High died, the booklets had been completed and five hundred copies were in storage in the MPD property unit awaiting distribution to each of the field officers of patrol section and the detective units. The purpose of the booklet was to inform the "street" officers of these high-level vice criminals so that all methods of enforcement could be directed toward them.

A couple of days after the mayor's death, the author was advised by property unit employees that Captain Knight had ordered that the completed booklets were not to be distributed, but were to be taken to the city incinerator and burned. The author grabbed a box of fifty booklets and set about to mail (at his own expense) a copy of the booklet to each and every one of the twenty-six Dade County police agencies and every federal law enforcement agency listed in the Miami telephone book.

At least some lasting good came out of the effort.

WHITE BULLETPROOF VESTS

By Officer (Name withheld)

Too many to count. Long, long, time ago, the city issued several white bulletproof vests designed by the military. A few of us got them to test and report. I've got mine on and it's very uncomfortable. I've got it on during a tour of duty on the midnight shift. A possible Twenty-sixth (burglary) goes out to an old structure that sat north of the Four Ambassadors Hotel at Brickell and Eighth. As a supervisor, I went ahead and took the backup and was the first to arrive. To my knowledge, I thought this place was uninhabited. It's about 0300 and I start making a cursory look as one of my units arrive. I'm at the back and it's pitch-dark. As I'm looking through a dirty window, the building caretaker is in the inside looking out through the same window. Our faces come together at the exact same time separated only by the window pane. Talk about fright, he yelled, I yelled and ran back. Well, I have my vest on and start to hyperventilate. I rip my shirt and vest off 'cause I couldn't breathe. There I was with only a T-shirt and pants on and my shirt and vest on the ground. Guys that see me think I've been in a knockdown fight. I stop them before they start setting up a perimeter. You had to be there. Well, I didn't wear the vest again.

I'LL GO BY AND HELP

Sergeant Bob Ellsworth, the supervisor of the Taxicab Detail, was riding in the downtown area when he heard a radio call that alerted patrol units to a holdup alarm at Sidney Smith's coin shop on Biscayne Boulevard. Bob proceeded to the address with the thought of assisting the patrol units, but he arrived at the building first and went into the store.

Within seconds, he became aware of a very dangerous situation. Ellsworth observed two persons bound hand and foot on the floor and observed two gunmen looting the coin store. The next thirty seconds were harrowing as Bob shot two of the gunmen, one between the eyes, and cornered a third one at great risk to himself. Fortunately, the desperado's bullets went wild and Bob only suffered minor wounds.

Sergeant Ellsworth was awarded the gold medal for heroism and was selected the department's Officer of the Year award. After the incident, Bob asked for a transfer to the patrol division and became an outstanding sector sergeant handling the roughest area of the city during the following years. He has since retired to the quiet hills of South Carolina.

11 POLICE HORSES DIE IN FIRE

On March 8, 1967, eleven MPD police horses died in a fire at the city's stables, temporarily ending Miami's popular police patrol. Chief Headley, a strong proponent of mounted policing, led a drive that restored the unit through contributions by citizens near and far. The fire was determined to be arson, a person of interest identified, but insufficient evidence was available to make an arrest.

MPD's original mounted patrol unit was formed in 1946 under the direction of Walter Headley, who had served in the U.S. Cavalry and would later become chief of police. Headley convinced Joe Widener, father of Hialeah Park, to donate the proceeds of one race to start the unit. On New Year's Eve of 1946, Officer Karl Leib rode Buddy, a horse donated by businessman John Mobley, in the Orange Bowl parade. This event prompted other businessmen to sponsor horses and soon Miami had a mounted patrol. By 1949, the squad grew to twelve men and fourteen horses—all donated. The city paid for the maintaining and feeding of the horses.

The mounted patrol directed traffic, issued parking tickets, patrolled neighborhoods, controlled crowds, and performed in parade and ceremonies. They attracted residents and tourists alike who stopped to pet the horses and have their picture taken with them.

Sadly, tragedy struck the popular unit in March 1967. A fire broke out at the stables, and within thirty minutes, flames engulfed the entire structure—killing eleven horses. No group was more devastated than the mounted officers. At a special burial ceremony, a stunned patrol stood unashamed as tears streamed down their cheeks.

After the fire, Chief Headley vowed that the mounted units would ride once again. Miamians loved the patrol and, in true community spirit, pitched in to help with the rebuilding. Businessmen donated funds, private riding academies staged benefit shows, and even young children contributed their lunch money to the Miami Mounted Patrol Fund.

The unit was built back up to eleven officers and fourteen horses. A marker at the city stable honors the horses that perished in the 1967 fire. After the tragedy, the mounted patrol unit was never the same.

JOHN COOK BOMBINGS

For many years in the 1960s and 1970s, considerable MPD police efforts was directed toward the many organized crime figures that lived or played in the northeast section of Miami. One particular fellow, a nationally renowned jewel thief, John Clarence Cook, was the focus of much surveillance and other activity on both our part and the local FBI jewel theft squad. Cook lived with his family on a cul-de-sac just north of NE Seventy-ninth Street, the street dead-ending at Biscayne Bay. One of our officers, Bob Weiss, had picked up Cook's teenage son for some minor violation that required a trip down to the juvenile detail. Cook was none too happy as he made the charge that the officer was picking on his kid to get to him.

A short time later, another officer who rode that zone, living out in the Westchester area of Miami, was the victim of a bombing. Someone threw an explosive dynamite stick onto the lawn of Officer Jerry Saslaw's home, splashing glass onto his baby child's crib, as well as causing considerable damage to the home. The baby was not seriously hurt, but suspicion pointed to Cook as the perpetrator or the contractor for that criminal job. The police activity around the Cook home and surrounding area immediately increased fourfold. The word on the street was that the "big guys" of crime, many of them originally from the northeast part of the country, were quite upset about Cook causing this unwanted heat.

On the night of August 24, 1967, there was a large dynamite explosion caused by two time bombs at the Cook home, which destroyed his autos and the carport of his home. None of Cook's family was hurt, but Cook was furious. He screamed to the on-scene press that the Miami police were the offenders in this explosion and that the FBI, who habitually surveilled Cook's home, was witnesses to the act. The FBI denied being in the area that night.

The author was temporarily assigned to the grand jury as an investigator at the time. After checking with the station, I responded to Cook's home. Cook was ranting and raving and stated, "They blew up everything I own except my boat."

Two nights later, Cook's twenty-four-foot cruiser docked at a drainage canal at the rear of the house and valued at $12,000 was also blown up by an explosive device that was placed under the boat. Another boat and an auto were also wrecked.

Officer Saslaw soon took a transfer to the fire department. The case remains open although the bombing suspect was well-known to the police. He was later killed in a bar altercation.

MURDER OF GABLES OFFICER WALT STATHERS

Officer Stathers's murder is still unsolved. At about 4:15 AM, December 19, 1967, he requested a dog car without giving his exact location. Officer Jim Harley, later Gables police chief, guessed that Stathers would be in the vicinity of Anthony Abraham's home on South Alhambra Circle.

Abraham, a local car dealer, would decorate his home during Christmas season with Stathers keeping an eye out for the display when his night grew quiet. Officer Harley found Stathers's patrol car across the street from Abraham's home, engine running and still in gear. It had crossed the lawn and crashed into the patio at the back of 700 S Alhambra. Stathers, then forty-fice, was facedown on the lawn, shot in the back of the head. The homeowner heard the noise and saw the blue lights of the squad car. His maid observed a tall, thin black man wearing black pants and a white shirt pedal away on a twenty-eight-inch English-model bicycle with a chrome fender. Stathers's weapon, a .357 Colt Trooper, was missing. Stathers also had a bruised arm twisted back.

Miami police, many of whom knew Stathers personally, responded to assist and flooded the Gables residential area with uniform squad cars and K-9 units, and Dade County homicide detectives commenced their investigation. The tips flooded in the next day, but each one fizzled despite a large reward being offered that was contributed by the residents of the area that twenty-one-year veteran Stathers patrolled.

One known criminal, a teen, was found in Alabama and returned to Dade for questioning but was released for lack of evidence. An informant advised John Heywood, an MPD detective, that a nineteen-year-old street tough from Coconut Grove tried selling him the gun. The lead went nowhere. The weapon has never been recovered. A private investigator, David Bolton, continues to work on the case and still suspects the guy that Heywood led him to, but former Dade cold case investigators say the guy, who was still living in South Miami a couple of years ago, is not the right one. Dade cold case investigator Ed Carmody advised recently that the case is still considered an active investigation.

Despite a standing reward close to fifty thousand dollars, this vexing case is still only one of two Dade County police officer murders yet unsolved. The other is that of Miami officer Leroy LaFleur shot dead in 1951 (Wilbanks, *Forgotten Heroes*, 1996; and author's knowledge).

WHEN THE LOOTING STARTS

During the holiday season of 1967, Miami experienced a rash of violent crimes including numerous murders. Chief of Police Walter Headley, who headed up the department for nineteen years, called a press conference to announce what action he intended to take to combat this crime wave. A press story on the twenty-seventh of December spelled out Headley's statements quite well so we will relate it to you through their dispatch.

Police Chief Walter Headley says that the community relations programs in the city's Negro district have failed, so his officers are under orders to combat with shotguns and dogs "young hoodlums who have taken advantage of the civil rights campaign. Felons will learn that they cannot be bonded out of the morgue," Headley told reporters at a news conference.

Criticism from civil rights leaders was swift even as beefed-up patrols in the central Negro district began enforcing the "stop and frisk" law—searching persons on the street without arrest or warrant. A lieutenant said six three-man task force cars and five K-9 cars were in the district in addition to regular patrols Tuesday night.

"We don't mind being accused of police brutality," Headley said. "They haven't seen anything yet."

"Ninety percent of our Negro population is law-abiding and wants to eliminate our crime problem," Headley said. "But 10 percent are young hoodlums who have taken advantage of the civil rights campaign."

Headley, chief of the department for two decades, said he took his action after the Christmas holiday weekend in which there were fifty-eight violent crimes in the area, including three murders. "In only three, white criminals were involved; the rest were Negro men," Headley said.

"Community relations and all that sort of thing have failed," Headley said. "We have done everything we could, sending speakers out and meeting with Negro leaders. But it has amounted to nothing."

Headley's statement was in contrast to recent comments by Dade County Sheriff E. Wilson Purdy who has credited his department's community relations program and special training projects with successfully preventing civil disorders.

"We haven't had any serious problems with civil uprising and looting because I've let the word filter down that when the looting starts, the shooting starts," Chief Headley told newsmen. "These are my orders: Not three days after, but now."

"This is war," he said. "I meant it, every bit of it."

Headley, sixty-two, who joined the force as a patrolman in 1937, became chief August 11, 1948. He successfully fought moves to replace him in the past.

When a reporter asked him what reaction he expected, Headley said, "I don't care how anyone reacts. My job is to enforce the peace and I am going to do it to the best of my ability. I hope I have the support of the whole city, including the city leaders."

Mayor Stephen P. Clark, who was not present at the press conference, said later, "I am confident that Chief Headley and his police force will take the proper steps to combat crime on the streets. When you deal with murderers, you have to deal on common terms. Felons, especially people who take life in their own hands, will be treated in like kind."

Marvin Davis, of Tampa, state field director for the National Association of Colored People, said, "We will do all we can to get him [Headley] to resign. If necessary, we will get a lawsuit to keep him from enforcing this type of arbitrary action. I'll go before the city council trying to get him suspended until his attitude changes."

At the time, the author was a supervisor on Headley's task force. The forty-five-man group, supplemented by our crack K-9 officers, was led by Captain Bob Knight and Lieutenant Garland Watkins (later Chief of Police), and responded with gusto. Many raids of notorious bars and nightclubs were conducted, stopping and frisking the young hoodlums. When we entered a bar, one could hear the guns and knives being dropped onto the bar's floor. Field interrogation cards were prepared on the hoods hanging on the street corners and many were picked up on outstanding warrants. One of the task force officers would pick up the latest warrants from the Dade court clerk's office in the afternoon and issue copies to the teams at the evening roll call.

The response of Chief Headley drew national media attention, many of whom sent reporters to the city.

I recall one humorous incident when Herb Kaplow of NBC came down to ride with us. Of course, we knew we were under the spotlight and acted accordingly. One evening, with the newsman in the front seat of my unmarked car and two of his camera guys in the rear, we went to an area search where a robber had abandoned a stolen car and was being chased through the alleys by the task force guys. As I turned up one dark alley, I abruptly stopped and inquired if the reporters had NBC insurance coverage on themselves due to the danger. Kaplow responded haltingly that they had as the two in the backseat slid down below window level. You could cut the silence with a knife. The TV crew realized that this situation, dangerous as it appeared to them, was what the average American cop went through every shift in his career. The resulting story they posted was much more supportive than what their producers were hoping for. It seems that they expected "Bull Conner" actions from us rather than the professional approach we took.

I chucked silently (Author's knowledge, plus numerous local and national newspapers stories).

COURT SLEEPING

By Officer (Name withheld)

This has probably happened to more officers than will admit—going to court after a tour on the midnight shift. I check with the state attorney's office and they said, "Go sit in the police area of the courtroom." Next thing I know a bailiff is asking if I am all right. Well, I had fallen asleep and was drooling. I must have been dreaming because I was mumbling and moving. The courtroom had a nice laugh, but I was completely embarrassed. The judge gave me a piece of his mind after court, but did understand.

SHOULD WE TELL THE CHIEF?

Chief Paul Denham had the reputation of being *the* authority on anything to do with traffic and auto crashes in the entire state of Florida during his distinguished career. Most of his jobs during his tenure on the department were various assignments within the traffic section. I had the pleasure of working for this soft-spoken leader on special projects in the '60s and '70s and had a great admiration for his integrity and dedication.

He would often be assigned as acting chief of police when Chief Headley was out of town. Sometime around 1967, while I was a task force supervisor, a complaint was received from Denham's office relative to customers of the T&D Drive Inn on NE Seventy-ninth Street receiving an enormous number of chicken s—t tickets from task force officers as the customers exited the restaurant. The chief put a notation on the complaint tickler inquiring why the unmarked crime prevention team was concentrating on minor traffic violations instead of chasing burglars and robbers.

We had a dilemma. We did not want to embarrass the boss, but it was evident that he did not realize that the drive-in restaurant was owned by a known Mafia hoodlum from New York and that most of the "customers" were either big-time Mafia hoods themselves or scumbags coming in to purchase narcotics.

A pile of rap sheets was prepared and packaged up with a copy of the original complaint and "someone" shoved the entire wad under the boss's door at 3:00 AM. We never received another complaint from Chief Denham about our traffic enforcement efforts.

ANOTHER COURT SNOOZE

Midnight-shift guys had two hours to kill before city court opened. The author usually would ask Bailiffs Ben Girten or Tom Jervis to awaken me when the judge arrives so I could catch a couple of Zzzzs while waiting.

One morning, I forget to alert Tom and fell fast asleep in the last row. Tom woke me about ten o'clock after all the night-shift cases were completed. "What happened to my case?" I asked. Tom advised, "Your partner, Joe Catell, handled it for you and the bad guy got sixty days in the stockade. Joe testified very well, covering all bases, and your testimony was not needed."

The only problem is that I was riding alone on that arrest and Catell was several zones away and out of my sight for the entire night. (Thanks, Joe.)

MACKLE GIRL BURIED ALIVE

On December 17, 1968, Barbara Jane Mackle, twenty, daughter of Robert Mackle, wealthy Coral Gables-based Florida land developer, was kidnapped from an Atlanta area hotel room where she was recovering from the flu, attended by her mother. At 4:00AM, the suspects, Gary Steven Krist and Ruth Eisemann-Schier, tricked Mrs. Mackle into opening the motel door and took the daughter Barbara and buried her alive in a tubelike container in a wooded area near Duluth, Georgia.

The kidnappers contacted the father and instructed him to pay half-a-million-dollar ransom. The ransom drop was to be made at the small Fair Isle Bridge off South Bayshore Drive in Miami's Coconut Grove area. After the drop was made, kidnapper Krist and his cohort picked up the money and drove their stolen boat a short distance near to the entrance of the Rickenbacker Causeway, where their Volvo getaway car was parked.

The Miami police were unaware of this FBI-led ransom dropoff. Officer Bill Sweeney, riding Miami PD unit 923, was accustomed to meeting a Dade County officer who patrolled Key Biscayne, an adjoining area. The two officers would chat and drink coffee in the pull-off area adjacent to the causeway entrance during the quiet early morning hours.

Sweeney observed the suspect walking through the adjacent brush and called out to him. Krist answered by firing one round in Sweeney's direction, then fled on foot. A search by Miami zone cars alerted by Sweeney was unable to locate the suspects. The duffel bag filled with $500,000 was recovered, as well as the weapon and the Volvo, which contained items that identified the kidnappers. The money was picked up and driven to the Miami station by Lieutenant Jimmy Knight. Knight had to drag the bag across the roll-call room down to the property cage as it was so heavy with cash.

It was unknown by MPD at that time, due to FBI secrecy, that Sweeney had interrupted the ransom drop.

Krist and his girlfriend were later arrested, and the brave Mackle girl was found alive by FBI agents in an underground coffin in Georgia (MPD records).

WILLIE JOE IS THE MAN

In Miami's Orange Bowl, January 12, 1969, the underdog New York Jets faced off against a great 13-1 Baltimore Colts team. The Colts were heavily favored against the AFL champion Jets. Anita Bryant led off the day by singing the national anthem to a sold-out crowd and Bob Hope was the lead star in the pregame ceremony honoring *Apollo 8* astronauts. In the large crowd were numerous national celebrities.

After guaranteeing a victory prior to the game, Jets quarterback Willie Joe Namath completed 17 out of 28 passes for 206 yards and the Jets upset the Colts, 16-7. It was one of the greatest upsets in sports history.

The author had a ringside seat that historic day as he was assigned to guard Vice President Agnew and Bob Hope, who were sitting down near the east 30-yard line. Adjacent to these special guests were the Kennedy family, led by father Joe Kennedy, who had recently suffered a stroke. With old Joe were several of the sisters and nieces of President Kennedy as well as Senator Ted Kennedy. The crowd did not bother the vice president and Hope as several Secret Service agents surrounded them, but the Kennedy family was besieged with autograph seekers. Two additional officers had to be assigned to prevent the pestering of the Kennedy family.

During the halftime show featuring the famous Florida A&M band and Bob Hope, the author became Hope's bodyguard. Duties during the game consisted of shuttling back and forth between the two celebrity groups. A few informal moments revealed that Agnew was quite sociable but that Hope gave the impression that he was a big deal by curtly brushing off anyone who approached him. The Kennedy family was courteous with our officers and truly appreciated the security provided them as they were quite anxious about the father's health. We even received a thank-you letter from Teddy the following week.

Neither the Colt's Earl Morrall nor Johnny Unitas, later in the game, were very effective, as Namath was the star, despite not throwing a touchdown pass the entire game. That was the day that Willie Joe became a national sports hero. I had to escort him through the crowd to the locker room and he, in the author's opinion, appeared to be a super nice guy as well as a star on the field.

During the next few years, our night patrol guys got to know Joe quite well. He would zoom north Biscayne Boulevard in an open convertible heading for a private club at Sixty-ninth Street and the Bay. Several times he was stopped for slightly excessive speed but got off with only a warning as he was so apologetic and friendly. On at least one occasion, one of our guys had to drive his car, as there were doubts about his ability to keep the wheels straight. But he was such a happy and funny person, none of our guys had the heart to write him. This behavior was in stark contrast with the rude actions and sour demeanor of many of the celebrities and sports stars we would encounter on the early morning streets of Miami.

JIM MORRISON PINCHED AT DINNER KEY

A raucous and raunchy gig at Miami's Dinner Key auditorium on March 1, 1969, resulted in famous rock star Jim Morrison getting arrested for indecency by MPD Officer Ted Seaman and Sergeant Jim Cox. Morrison was convicted, but died before the sentence was carried out.

In late 2010, outgoing Governor Charlie Crist, who was bidding to become a Florida senator, and a huge fan of the rock group, voted to pardon Morrison.

Crist was defeated in his election attempt.

THE TIDE TURNS

As a task force supervisor in the late 1960s, incidents would occur that would create occasional friction between the "old guard" and the young "Turks" on the department.

One afternoon, St Patrick's Day 1969, is memorable. Two of our officers in an unmarked car were staked out in the area of NE Thirty-ninth Street and Second Avenue looking for muggers. They were parked in front of a nondescript two-story office building. A man approached the building, glanced at the two young officers, and entered a stairwell to the second floor. A few minutes later, another guy emerged from the stairwell and dropped two twenty-dollar bills into the lap of the officers. I responded to the scene upon their request and we tried to figure out the guy's motives. Just then, a little old man emerged and was questioned by the officers. It turned out that an illegal card game was in progress in a second-floor office involving over twenty people.

Officer Willie Chippas, and another officer, scaled onto the roof of an adjoining building and accessed a vantage point at the opaque-type window where the card game was in progress.

They observed money and cards being exchanged for several moments. I then went to a call box (no cell phones in those days) and called the duty city judge in an attempt to get a warrant, but he was not available.

We accosted another man heading for the stairwell and conned him into ringing the buzzer, which would unlock the upper entrance door to the hallway. A group of us then went to the door where the game was in progress and knocked loudly without a response.

The entrance door upstairs to the card room had been replaced by a much-heavier door, but the replaced door was still propped against the wall of the corridor.

Using the old door as a battering ram, I rammed the door and down it came (to this day, my shoulder still feels a little pain on rainy days).

We arrested seventeen of the players for a misdemeanor and the manager of the game, a guy named Robert Malone, for operating a gambling house. His brother was Luther Malone, an icon of the Miami gambling scene, operating out of the pool hall on West Flagler Street and Second Avenue. At city court the next day, the judge threw out all the cases after a vice detective (still living) testified that one cannot view through that type of glass, therefore being impossible to verify that a felony gambling crime was in progress.

The following day, I filed a felony case against Malone at the state attorney's office. Defense Attorney Taylor filed a motion to dismiss with Judge Stedman, who wore very thick glasses. With the same detective testifying for the defense, the judge could not decide if we indeed had probable cause. The prosecutor (and later judge), the great Ellen Morphonies, suggested the court take a look themselves. The following Friday evening, a Miami fire truck hoisted Ellen, Judge Stedman, myself, and one of the original officers up onto the roof while other cops reenacted a card game in the same room. The judge looked through the opaque window for a few minutes and said, "I can see. Motion denied."

The case was set for the following week in Judge Sepe's court. On the day before the trial, a small fire occurred in the property bureau (then headed by Captain Griffin of Ali Baba fame), and guess what burned up? My evidence was a pile of ashes.

Some of the older guys in the property unit who knew and liked my dad, a city jailor, helped me to assemble a similar box of chips, cash, cards, and ledgers. When the case was called, the smirking vice detective was seated with the defense attorney awaiting me to say I had no evidence. But when they seen me haul in the carton and place it on the table in front of the bench, their faces turned white. Defense Attorney Taylor asked Judge Sepe for a thirty-minute recess. After resumption of the trial, they changed Malone's plea to guilty. Judge Sepe gave him a small fine and probation and asked me in open court, "Sergeant, don't you have better things to do than to harass some old folks having a friendly game?"

I advised him that we had proceeded due to the taint of possible corruption as the ledger I confiscated contained entries showing money being paid out to detectives who worked out of the chief's office over the years.

As I walked out, the clerk shouted, "You forgot your evidence." I replied that the box was only junk and had nothing to do with the case, which drew looks of disbelief from Malone, the vice detective, the defense attorney, and the judge.

The next day, the vice detective filed an Internal Security complaint against me. Fortunately for me, Assistant Chief Denham was the acting chief while the big boss was on vacation. After Denham heard the whole story, he transferred the vice detective to the burglary unit. When Chief Headley returned from vacation, he reinstated the detective and ordered Major Malcolm Gracey, longtime vice chief, to perform a special investigation *on me*.

I immediately called my friend, Mayor Steve Clark, and advised him that if this went any further, I would ensure that the ledger would end up on the desk of the *Miami Herald*'s editor the next day. This seemed to work, as the following day, the case was dropped and detective took an immediate pension. (The ledger somehow showed up later in the mailbox of the local internal revenue office.)

The chief's office had a cake for the vice detective the next day, his last on the job. He still had to finish his afternoon shift before calling it quits. Later in the evening, I was sitting in my unmarked car near the property bureau, going through routine worksheets, when I noticed the detective driving around the back courtyard and parked—what I thought—for the purpose of unloading his gear into his personal car. He drove away, just as I noticed that the tire of my personal car, a '67 Cougar, was flat as a pancake with an ice pick hole in the sidewall. I radioed a BOLO for him, but the task force guys were unable to locate him.

The following day, he noticed that his mailbox in front of his Grove house was flattened as he headed for the Coconut Grove bank to empty out his safety deposit boxes. On duty in the bank parking lot was an off-duty task force officer, Ed Hanek, working an extra job in the bank parking lot. When the vice detective emerged from the bank he discovered that each one of his four tires on his personal car had large ice pick holes in each. Officer Hanek had not done his crime prevention job—or did he?

The culture change in the department was by now pretty near complete, and the good guys came out on top. (Judge Sepe later was indicted for corruption.)

CARBERRY WOUNDED

A fierce gun battle erupted at NW Twelfth Avenue and Second Street during the evening of May 29, 1969, leaving Officer Ed Carberry, twenty-four, wounded and two gunmen dead. Luis Serrano and Israel Licor, both Miami area residents in their twenties, were stopped by Carberry as their vehicle fit the description of one used in an armed robbery of the Grand Union supermarket on Coral Way and Sixty-seventh Avenue. One of the bandits fired at Carberry, a second-year MPD patrolman, wounding the young officer in the shoulder, foot and hand. Two other marked police cars arrived, one occupied by Sergeant Bill Charnin, and immediately returned the gunmen's volleys. Both suspects were shot dead in their car.

Carberry heard a pickup call for a green Pontiac believed used in the Grand Union robbery and spotted the car at SW Third Street and Twelfth Avenue. He followed the Pontiac to NW Second Street and pulled the car over as two other police cars arrived. As Carberry approached the car, the suspects began shooting, unaware that assistance had arrived. Carberry yelled, "I'm Hit," as fellow officers Sam Streiner, Ed Hunt, Raymond Flores, and Sergeant Bill Charnin closed in. Charnin went straight to the rear window of the Pontiac and blasted away across the backseat. Two dozen shots were fired in less than two minutes. Bandits Serrano and Licor both tumbled out the driver's door fatally shot.

In the suspect's car were two grenades, a sub-machine gun, and automatic pistols in addition to a paper bag containing $400 in cash that was taken in the Grand Union robbery. This capture also solved the case of the murder of two Columbian visitors who were gunned down in the rear parking lot of the Trojan Bar, SW Eighth Street and Eighth Avenue, earlier by .45-caliber machine gun shots.

Officer Carberry recovered and continued on his career, finishing it as a commanding officer in the detective bureau. He is presently an investigating supervisor in an anti-corruption state unit (Interview with Ed Carberry and author's knowledge).

Former MPD Officer Kenneth Kubik, twenty-six, was killed in action in Vietnam while serving with the U.S. Marines. Kenny graduated with Miami Academy class No. 58. A year later, Ken volunteered to return to the Marines to help his buddies out and was killed in action. He was awarded the Silver Star posthumously (*Miami News*, 10/22/1969).

BONDSMEN RULE

Like most city jails around the country, the local bondsmen hang around, especially on weekends, to pick up business by bonding out misdemeanor arrestees. It was common knowledge that some of the booking sergeants in the jail were overly friendly with certain bondsmen, for obvious reasons.

We had one company, Slatko Bonding, which seemed to spend more time in our jail booking area than our employees despite an ordinance that prohibited this practice (and a grand jury rebuke). Although this was prior to folks having cell phones, it seemed that Slatko's men, especially Sam Siegal, would arrive just after (or before) the incoming paddy wagon arrived at the station with a load of petty thieves and prostitutes.

When the author got promoted to lieutenant, I was assigned as a patrol shift duty lieutenant. Being a rookie commander, I oftentimes ended up holding down the duty captain's chair while the captain was out of the office. It just happened that my dad, Joe Doherty, was a city jailor who had the same shift as I. Dad would use the jail phone in the back to alert me that Slatko's men were loitering up in the jail awaiting the incoming wagon. I would saunter up to the jail and order them out while at the same time chewing out the booking sergeant for allowing this unlawful practice to exist.

I am sure they both knew who was tipping the rookie lieutenant off, but the culture was changing and they no longer had any one to complain to.

RIOT ERUPTS IN LIBERTY CITY

August 1968 in Miami was the scene of the Democratic political convention during a time of tense race relations in America. Although the venue for the convention was actually in Miami Beach, many of the national politicians and news media converged on Liberty City to focus attention on the plight of black Americans in our country. The media announced appearances by Reverend Ralph Abernathy and other black leaders, including sports stars, at various locations in Miami's black districts.

At the time, Miami PD's task force, a complement of about fifty police officers, was assigned to keep the peace at a critical location in Liberty City, the intersection of NW Seventeenth Avenue and Sixty-second Street, just east of the city's border with unincorporated Dade County. Lieutenant Garland Watkins (later the chief of police) assigned three squads to that area, positing one squad each on both sides of Sixty-second Street, including the rooftops, and the third squad in the intersection itself. For several hours, the force was able to minimize criminal activities of the area youth, despite the fact that a raucous meeting was being held nearby in a storefront meeting hall. Rumors (not true) of a planned appearance of a black basketball star drew large numbers of excitable youths.

Back at police headquarters, Acting Chief Denham dispatched Captain Jack Maddox to Manor Park, a mile from the tense area, to set up a police command post. Numerous radio and telephone calls were exchanged between Lieutenant Watkins and superiors at the command post and headquarters regarding the situation, with commanders urging the retreat of the task force to the park's command center. Lieutenant Watkins kept advising that the situation was in hand and further predicted that a withdrawal of the uniform officers would set the stage for chaos. Watkins further urged that the county be instructed to halt eastbound vehicular traffic and for MPD to halt northbound NW Seventeenth Avenue and westbound Sixty-second Street. Not one of the department's command officers ever personally came to the explosive area to size up the situation and, in the author's opinion, lost a chance to prevent the riot by keeping uniforms in the hot area.

Late in the afternoon, Watkins was ordered to retreat to the command center a mile away. As the task force left in four-man cars, the author and others observed rock-throwing and innocent vehicle operators being stopped a couple of blocks east, with one car being set afire. The riot was on.

The vehicle assigned to the author and fellow supervisor Sergeant Harry Mills had disappeared, either being taken by departing officers or by someone in the crowd. As youths, observing the police departing, surged toward the intersection and the author was surrounded, the swift action of black officer Tommy Marshall saved the day (and the author's butt) as he approached the crowd with drawn weapon. Tom and the two sergeants then caught a ride out of the area with a roving accident prevention car.

During the following sixteen-hour days, the entire Miami PD force scrambled in an attempt to control the rioters, not only in Liberty City but in Overtown and Coconut Grove as well. Several innocent citizens and a few rioters were killed and many officers were injured. Millions of dollars in damage resulted from the fires and vandalism until National Guard troops finally calmed the situation down on the third night.

The three days were certainly hectic, with rocks and bullets flying, especially from the Liberty Square housing area fronting on Sixty-second Street. The author, and the other supervisors of the task force, Sergeant Harold Whitaker, Ed Lejeune, and Harry Mills, were provided two officers, equipped with long guns, to offer protection during these dangerous hours so we could safely supervise. Our lieutenant (Watkins), a very intelligent and courageous leader, was himself injured during the riot but refused medical care until after the riot was over later in the week. In times like this, some men (including many commanders and supervisors) disappeared and a few others grew to ten foot tall.

Many incidents are still fresh in my mind but space prevents relating them in this publication. One particular event that stuck in my mind was coming upon twenty-five or thirty newly graduated officers standing in the street at NW Fourteenth Avenue and Sixty-eighth Street, with only their sidearms as equipment. No tear gas, no riot batons, no water, or any other necessity and apparently no supervision or mission.

I commandeered Officer Carl Olsen, an old-timer who was riding one of the paddy wagons. Carl was an affable fellow who probably hadn't done much real police work in years. I put him in charge of these green troops, one of whom was my brother-in-law. Carl organized and positioned them, went to the property bureau, and checked out long guns, riot batons, first aid supplies, etc., and equipped all these young guys. He mothered them through until we later found a supervisor to relieve Carl. In the years since that night, as I progressed through the ranks, I did have occasion more than once to "pay back" Carl by downgrading or eliminating discipline actions against him for minor departmental violations. He was there when we needed him, which is more than I can say about some of our high-ranking supervisors and commanders who never got the first rock thrown at them or had the experience of being reeked by tear gas.

Having experienced working this riot was a career changer for this author as it no doubt affected my perceptions of many of my colleagues in the later years. Those who stood out in this trying time would, in my opinion, be the guys who could handle the future difficult assignments and the others would best be suited for some of the other "soft" positions within the department.

THIS DIET IS KILLING ME

On June 4, 1969, Sergeant Charlie Crocker collapsed in the canteen at 5:00 AM just after leaving a burglary scene on Bayshore Drive. Sergeant Lucious Burnett was with him at the police canteen. "I swear this diet's about to kill me," said Crocker, who was sweating and feeling dizzy. As soon as Charlie finished breakfast, he keeled over dead. Charlie had stopped smoking six weeks ago and was dieting to lose some of his 200 lbs. A popular officer, who came to Miami from Anderson, South Carolina, joined the MPD in 1956 and was known as a "great kidder" who took everything in stride. He was survived by his wife and two children.

We lost a good guy that day.

PLANE CRASH ON THIRTY-SIXTH STREET

By Wally Clerke, MPD Ret.

In June 1969, a DC-4 aircraft belonging to Dominica Air Lines, with an engine afire, crashed onto busy NW Thirty-sixth Street as it was trying to circle back to Miami International Airport, where it had just taken off from. The four crew members were killed as well as seven persons on the ground when the four-engine airplane plowed through four business blocks of Thirty-sixth Street, coming to a stop at Thirty-third Avenue. At least a dozen others on the ground were seriously injured.

Four of the dead were in an auto body shop, with two of the victims being the sons of the owner. The plane first hit a three-story building then skipped along the tops of several other buildings before coming to rest in front of a used car lot. Numerous power and telephone lines and poles were knocked down and gasoline spilled out of fractured pumps at service stations.

The airline said that the pilot had advised that an engine was afire and he was trying to ditch the plane, loaded with autos, into the nearby Miami River.

Numerous Miami fire and police units responded to the scene, set up a command post, cordoned off traffic, and dug through the wreckage for victims. Thousands of onlookers surged into the area, causing further chaos. The wreckage was everywhere along four blocks of Thirty-sixth Street, the main route to the airport. Most of the buildings in the plane's path were damaged or destroyed as well as numerous automobiles (*Miami News*, 6/24/1969).

One on-scene officer tells of the story of how his squad car was rammed by an arriving fire unit. As Officer Clerke and his partner were evacuating tenants of a nearby apartment, the fire truck came roaring up too fast, could not brake in time, and smashed into the police unit. The incident, because of the chaos at the scene, was written off as a hit-and-run by an unknown red vehicle.

"Why get the fire guy in trouble when he was desperate to save citizens from harm?" Clerke said.

Retired Detective George (Deeby) Foss, seventy-two, died today. Foss joined the force in 1934 after a leg injury forced him to give up a major league baseball career. Foss was a third baseman with the Washington Senators (*Miami News*, 11/12/1969).

IN OUR LIFETIME

THE INSPECTOR'S LAST CAPER

Inspector Francis Napier, a thirty-one-year MPD veteran, was an old-school detective who had been one of the detective district captains for many years. He was now practically powerless, nearing the end of career, and was apparently attempting to squirrel away some cash for his retirement. On his last week of work, he arranged for a large marijuana purchase. One of his cohorts snitched on him and the U.S. Customs and our Internal Security squad caught wind of his plan. Napier was nabbed by MPD and federal agents with a truckload of grass, which was confiscated. Napier was sentenced to seven years in federal prison for conspiracy to import and sell 225,000 lbs of marijuana in a Jamaica to New York crime connection. Napier ended up doing time instead of playing golf with the rest of the MPD retirees (MPD records).

CLASH OF CULTURES

In late December 1969, Poet Alan Ginsburg had a poetry gig at the Marine Stadium on Miami's Rickenbacker Causeway. Shortly into his poetry presentation to a small crowd, a Miami City official, Mannie Costa, upset with the profanity-laced offerings of Ginsburg, cut the power to the microphone. Ginsburg continued without the mic, but Costa ordered that music be blasted over the loudspeakers. The tune was "Casey would walk with the Strawberry Blond," which drowned out the rest of Ginsburg's poems.

A few minor arrests of the attendees for various minor violations were made according to Lieutenant Jimmy Knight, but Ginsburg went on his way to spout another day.

MOTOR OFFICER GUNNED DOWN

Officer Ron McLeod, thirty, had just left the police canteen where he had a coffee break on the afternoon of May 7, 1969. His assignment was traffic duty on his motorcycle in the downtown area, but he would often respond voluntarily to criminal calls anywhere near his area. This eight-year veteran heard a robbery call dispatched, along with a description of the offender. McLeod drove into the area of NE Miami Court where citizens had advised that the robber had fled, stuffing the money into his waist. McLeod rounded the corner on his motor and observed Jessie James Gavin, twenty-one, a recent prison escapee, hiding behind a tree. While McLeod was stopping his motorcycle, Gavin ran out toward the officer and fired at close range. McLeod was mortally wounded and died hours later at Jackson Memorial Hospital without regaining consciousness. He was killed from a bullet to the head by a cheap "Saturday night special."

Five hours after the killing, MPD ID artist Walter Depp drew a composite from the robbery victims, and the sketch was recognized by Lieutenant Charlie Shepard, who had returned Gavin from Tampa earlier on a different murder charge (that was dropped when the witnesses disappeared).

Gavin fled Miami en route to Memphis, Tennessee, before he was identified as the suspect. Ten days later, he was wounded in a shootout with two Memphis detectives where one of the Memphis officers was slightly wounded by Gavin.

Gavin was extradited to Miami with two Dade sheriff's officers transporting him. During the transport, Gavin reached through the safety screen and obtained one of the officer's revolvers. That began a fifty-mile chase in the Oxford, Alabama, area where the transporting car finally crashed and Gavin was arrested.

Gavin pled guilty to first-degree murder and was sentenced to two life terms, consecutively. His release date is in 2047, at which time he will be one hundred years old.

McLeod left a wife, Donna, and three small children. Ron is buried in Vista Memorial Gardens in Hialeah (Wilbanks, *Forgotten Heroes*, 1996; and author's knowledge).

Author's Note: I had spoken with McLeod just before he left the police canteen the day he was murdered. Ron, an Edison High School graduate and an air force veteran, had been a member of Academy Class No. 45, just months after I graduated from no. 44. He was an all-around nice guy and good cop, who I often think about.

BULLETS FLY INTO NIXON'S YACHT

The hours of the old task force were often from 6:00 PM to 2:00 AM. Due to the late hour, most bars were closed (except for the expensive clubs) after work, so the nineteenth hole was the parking lot behind the old police academy on NW Twelfth Avenue. By 2:15 AM, there would be a dozen or so cops quenching their thirst and exchanging stories on the evening's work. I would make a stop once in a while, but being a newlywed, a new sergeant, and one without many funds, I headed home most nights—and was glad I did in this particular occasion.

I received a call early the next morning after only a few hours' sleep from Major Newell Horne, the patrol commander, who ordered me to the station *right now*. I was met by Sergeant Kay of the intelligence squad and the local head of the U.S. Secret Service in Miami. After determining that I was not present at the previous evening's choir practice, they wanted me to question, without fanfare, that evening's task force roll call to determine if any of the guys fired a rifle in the parking lot the previous evening, and if so, was it accidental. I inquired why and was told that a rifle slug fired during the night hit the side of President Nixon's yacht, which was in dry dock across the street at Merrill Stevens boatyard. The Secret Service agent, and Kay, stated that no action would be taken at all *if* the shot was an accident.

At roll call, with no visitors allowed that night, one of the guys fessed up that he was displaying his new rifle when a round went off about 3:00 AM.

I relayed the info to Kay, and true to their word, we never heard another peep about it from the Secret Service or the chief. We did ban any further weapon displays, and our lieutenant (Garland Watkins) ordered the guys to move down under the Twelfth Avenue bridge for their nightcaps.

TELEPHONE CALL

By Anonymous MPD Officer

One day I received a telephone call from a citizen. He told me that he saw this police car pull a car over and the skinniest policeman he ever saw got out just as the driver of the other car got out and ran at the officer with his fists clenched. When he got close enough, the skinniest policeman met him with a straight right that knocked him unconscious. The policeman looked at him for a moment and then got into the police car and drove away. A couple of minutes later, the other driver woke up and left the scene. I called the desk sergeant and asked if Officer Christiano was working in the zone and left word for him to call me when I was advised he was. Christiano verified the account of what happened and said he didn't know what to do with him as he had only stopped the car to tell the driver his stoplight was not working.

ROOKIE KILLED ON NW EIGHTH STREET

A twenty-one-year-old rookie officer had planned to take his young girlfriend to a prom that evening, May 23, 1970, but was shot and killed at 3:00 AM in the alley behind the sleazy Imperial Hotel on NW Eighth, just off Miami Avenue. Rolland Lane II, a rookie with only four months on the job, along with partner, twenty-three-year-old Fred Harris, had stopped three men for questioning in front of the Imperial Hotel on NW Eighth Street. One of the suspects fled with the officers in pursuit. Lane ran back through the hotel in an attempt to intercept him. A gunman, who was not one of the three suspects, shot Lane in the back of the head as the officer was searching the hotel corridors. The shooter, Willie Garrett, a known black militant, opened fire as Lane exited the rear door shooting the rookie in the back, knocking him to the ground, then fired three more times as Lane was lying on the ground. Officer Harris was warned by a room clerk that Garrett was also waiting to ambush him, helping the second officer to escape death. Harris ran to the street where Lane was sprawled and radioed for medical assistance and backup. Lane died before they arrived.

Garrett had been living at the Imperial Hotel. His neighbor across the hall was the local Black Panther leader, Al Featherstone.

Willie Garrett, twenty-six, an ex-con with a long record linked to the Black Panther Party, was taken off an airplane several hours later in Orlando as he headed for New York, still in possession of the gun used to kill the officer. He had firebombed Smiley's Bar in Miami early the same evening he shot Lane. Garrett was committed to a mental hospital as insane but later attempted to gain his freedom by claiming he was cured. After years of legal arguing over Garrett's mental capacity, he was finally sentenced to life imprisonment plus ten years by Judge Ellen Morphonios. That conviction was later overturned by the federal district court due to Garrett being held for an unreasonable period prior to trial. Judge Morphonios devoted five pages of her autobiography, *The Life and Times of America's Toughest Judge*, on this case.

After Garrett's release and return to Texas, he was charged with the attempted murder of his mother and was sentenced to ten years in prison.

Officer Lane, a Hialeah High School graduate, was completing his college work at Miami-Dade when he was killed. While attending the police academy, MPD Class No. 70, Lane was the cadet commander.

Lane left a fiancée, his parents, and a brother. Officer Lane was buried in Vista Memorial Gardens (Wilbanks, *Forgotten Heroes*, 1996; and MPD records).

SULLY SHOT ON ST. PAT'S DAY

By Sergeant Bob Sullivan, MPD Ret.

On St. Patrick's Day, March 17, 1971, plainclothes officers Bobby Sullivan, Bert Naylor, and George Silva were posing as delivery men in order to apprehend robber's intent on hijacking delivery trucks. Here is Sullivan's account of the incident.

"Bert Naylor was driving; George Silva and I were in the back of the truck. George had a shotgun and his revolver. Burt had his weapon in his belt under his shirt and I also had a shotgun and revolver. At the Motor Pool, we had drilled small holes in the back doors and sides of the truck for peepholes. Burt wanted to get us something to drink as it was very hot that day. He parked the truck on the west side of the RR tracks at NW Fourteenth Street across the street from the little store on the corner and walked over to the store. I was watching him through the peephole in the rear door. Silvia was sitting down reading a newspaper. I saw a small group of locals standing around the back door of the store and I saw Bobby Lee who was wearing a blue shirt take an automatic pistol from under his shirt. I said to George, "Holy shit, they are going to rob Bert!" Lee then pointed the pistol at the truck and began firing at us. Rounds were coming through the back doors. George was moving toward the truck's front door and I had been hit in the right hand. I later found that I also had a graze across my chest. Silvia got out of the truck and fired his shotgun at Lee. I think he shot high. I found my portable radio and advised central of the situation and asked for help.

Naylor later told me that Lee tried to shoot him as he came out of the store but the gun failed to fire. Naylor fired at the offender and missed. The chase was on and the MPD cavalry was coming to the rescue!

VT Campbell was the first uniform car to arrive. I got in his car and he drove me to the JMH/ER. A young orthopedic surgeon came into the ER and told me he had just returned from Vietnam and that his specialty was hand surgery. He worked on my hand in the ER. His name is Dr. Charles Virgin, the son of Dr. Herbert Virgin, the team doctor for the Miami Dolphins football team, who is still in practice in Miami.

While in the ER, I heard that Lee had been captured and was in custody. After my wound was treated, I was transferred from the ER to a small hospital room in the main hospital. When Sergeant Pappy Quinn saw the tiny room, he called an Eastern ambulance to the room and had me transferred to a big room with a bayview at Mercy Hospital. As the Eastern crew was wheeling me down the hall at JMH with Pappy as my escort, the nurse kept saying, "You can't do that. You can't do that."

Meanwhile back on the scene, thirty-plus Miami police units flooded the area, sealing off a several block section between NW Fourteenth and Sixteenth Street. A half hour later, Officer Vincent Smith entered a narrow walkway between buildings when his K-9 dog alerted and started to bark. Smith looked under the building and pulled the offender out with the assistance of several other officers. He was identified as Bobby Lee, a twenty-five-year-old forklift operator who was already out on bond on felony drug and weapons charges.

The following day, Justice of the Peace Charles Snowden released Lee on only $1,000 bond for three counts of assault to commit first-degree murder of a police officer. Snowden never checked Lee's record nor asked the bailiff for the background report. Judge Snowden later sent me a letter at the hospital apologizing for the error. I thought that was an honorable thing to do.

Lee testified at his trial that he had no idea that anyone was in the truck and was only using the truck for target practice. He also said that he never had the means to go to a shooting range because of his poverty. The jury convicted him but he only got ten years. I don't remember what he was convicted of, but I think it was for firing into an occupied vehicle.

Years later, I met a lady who was on the jury and she told me that of the six jurors, one was a lady who refused to believe that a nice boy like Lee would do what he was accused of, and a man who said that he just wanted to get out of there and he would vote guilty or not guilty to make it unanimous. (A 2010 check shows no Bobby Lee, still incarcerated.)

MISSING CANDY STRIPER

Debra Rehfus, thirteen, was abducted July 6, 1971, while walking to her home at 354 Flagami Boulevard from Westchester Hospital where she was a hospital volunteer candy striper. It was reported by Mrs. Anderson, the wife of retired MPD Inspector Alfred Anderson, who lived on the route Debra was walking, that Debra entered a small white van.

A person of interest, a relative of Debra, was questioned as he had a similar van and was in the vicinity at the time Debra disappeared. Several fields were searched in the days following her disappearance with the assistance of police recruits and police dogs but her body was not located until bone fragments of Debra was unearthed by an animal in a South Dade field in February 1973. Because the body was found outside of Miami City limits, the case was turned over to the Dade County sheriff's department.

Miami detectives Mike Gonzalez and Louise Vasquez worked hard on this case but were unable to file charges. The detectives even took the person of interest out to eat on the anniversary of her disappearance each year, hoping to gain an admission from him.

The author, who was on temporary assignment as homicide unit commander at the time of the abduction, recently (2011) reached out to retired investigator, eighty-two-year-old Gonzalez, with the hope that new DNA technology would lead to an arrest after all these years. Contact was made with ninety-year-old Dr. Joe Davis, the renowned Dade County medical examiner, who still had a copy of the file. As a result, retired detective Gonzalez turned over any of the information to the Dade County sheriff's department cold case squad.

However, further checking showed that the suspect passed away several years ago in Citrus County, Florida. The case remains unsolved.

THE POLES

By Unidentified Officer

Early in 1970, the officers patrolling 10 sector on the midnight shift would periodically congregate at a location we called "the poles." It was an FP&L lot located north of Seventy-first Street, behind the warehouses, adjacent to the railroad tracks. There was a paved drive-through, with light poles stacked high on either side. We would pull all the zone cars in and have an informal meeting well protected from public view. Participants included JD Barker, Pete Skumanich, Gene Cummings, Phil McDorman, Paul White, George Griffin, Ron Walters, C. W. Reynolds, Hiram Turner, and several others that I cannot recall at this time. This type of congregating was frowned upon by the command: Captain Frank Morrow, Lieutenant A. W. Smiley, and Sergeant Robert Boyd. We had all been caught congregating one time or another at Jumbo's or Lum's, and threatened with demerits. We felt certain our sergeant had no idea where we were, so an occult whisper of "poles" into an open mic was our call to meet. This went on for months.

One cold and dull night, someone keyed on and said, "Poles!" JD Barker and myself zipped down NW Seventh Avenue to Seventy-first Street, west a couple of blocks, north to the tracks, and into one end of the drive-through. The three other sector cars arrived at the same time, all from different directions. In the middle of the drive-through, we boxed in a young thief trying to remove the license tag from a new Cadillac, freshly stolen and as yet unreported. I think we were as surprised as he was. We all drew down on him simultaneously and he gave up immediately. Naturally everyone on channel 1 listened as the case developed, and it was not long before Sergeant Boyd showed up. The offender kept demanding to know how we found out he had stolen the car and who told us where he had gone to change the tag. It did not take Sergeant Boyd long to figure out the relationship between the location of the stolen car and the meaning of the mysterious radio transmission "poles," and he let us know it. We were all praised for making a good catch, and we all knew no merits would be forthcoming. Such was the end of a great on-duty meeting place.

ASSASSINATION OF VIC BUTLER

The times were scary in the late '60s and early '70s with officers being targeted all over the country. You tried not to think about it and I am sure it was not on the mind of forty-three-year-old Officer Victor Butler, on the evening of February 20, 1971. Butler and his junior partner, Otis Pitts Jr., twenty-eight, son of a longtime MPD officer by the same name, were dispatched at 10:27 PM on their last call for that day, a domestic argument at 1336 NW Forty-sixth Street, just south of Allapattah Junior High School. The officers split up the quarreling couple, with Butler taking one out in front of the duplex in an attempt to settle the problem. As Butler was silhouetted in the lighted doorway, two snipers across the street took aim and fatally shot him by rounds from two different .30-caliber rifles.

Butler had no warning and was hit by gunmen who most likely had no idea who he was. They just wanted to kill a police officer, white or black. Butler was a twenty-year veteran black officer of the MPD and a hardworking father of three who had patrolled the Liberty City area for many years.

Despite a massive manhunt, no suspects were apprehended that night, and a long investigation indicated known black militants were the offenders.

Homicide detectives focused on a small group of black militants who belonged to the Black Afro Militant Movement (BAMM), led by Al Featherstone. The most likely of suspects were John Lane, eighteen, and John Murray Johnson, nineteen, but there was insufficient evidence to indict or convict them.

Seven years later, Detective Bruce Roberson obtained a confession from a Jan Thurston who claimed that he was the driver of the getaway car that dropped off and picked up Lane and Johnson at the murder scene. Lane and Johnson were indicted in October 1978. The case collapsed when Thurston disappeared. He was found a year later in Minnesota but "recanted" his confession. Thurston was then charged with the crime, but a judge threw out the confession. The case is classified as "cleared" by the MPD despite none of the three suspects doing jail time for the random assassination of a fine officer (Wilbanks, *Forgotten Heroes*, 1996; MPD records; and numerous local news stories).

Officer Butler was in the author's patrol squad years earlier. He was an aggressive but fair officer who did his job day in and day out. On the evening of the killing, the author, then CO of the intelligence squad, responded to the scene and then staked out the northwest Miami "church" that BAMM members called their headquarters. The effort was to no avail as none of the group showed up.

Butler's wife, Juanita, passed away a short time after Butler's killing, leaving three children as orphans. His partner, Otis Pitts Jr., quit the department soon after and has worked in various social service roles in the community since.

THE MARKET CONNECTION

It was fairly common knowledge among law enforcement officers that more judicial cases were settled at Frank Martin's gas station than in the courts of Dade County and the City of Miami. Newly appointed Chief Bernard Garmire was determined to halt this practice as one of the results of this corruption was that good arrests made by his officers were continually being tossed out of the court system for little or no legitimate reasons. Chief Garmire assigned Major Bob Knight's special investigation section to the task, the team being headed up by then Captain Garland Watkins (later Chief of Police).

Wiretapping of Frank Martin's gas station in the curb market area of Miami on NW Twelfth Avenue began on September 1971 by agents of the SIU Unit of MPD together with Dade sheriff's OCB unit. Surveillance was set up by renting a room across from the gas station with teams of MPD and Metro watching the action at Frank Martin's gas station.

After a period of surveillance, MPD joined with the Federal Strike Force under Doug McMillian and others and obtained indictments against several Dade judges and others for corruption.

Frank Martin himself was given immunity but refused to testify and later was jailed in 1976 for not cooperating with the grand jury. All of the "Market Connection" cases were eventually dismissed by the courts, but the effect of the probes chilled the blatant court corruption. Later cases developed by the "Court Broom" (court investigations) project ended with convictions of several of the judges from the circuit and city courts (*Miami News*, 4/4/1973 and 3/27/75).

ROBBERY VS. HOMICIDE AT PIER 17

Detective Wally Clerke and Sergeant Dennis Fitzgerald, both highly decorated MPD cops, were assigned in 1972 to the robbery tactical team. One particular late night after a difficult shift, they stopped in at a local watering hole frequented by off-duty officers and Jackson Hospital nurses. Three other men were also in the hangout that neither Wally nor Dennis recognized. One of the men made a crude remark to a nurse that offended Wallly. Words led into fisticuffs and a minor brawl was on, ending up on the Seventeenth Avenue sidewalk. One of the other guys was huge, but Wally held his own, finally deciding to arrest the guy. As the fight grew in intensity, both MPD guys pulled out their revolvers. In the struggle, a shot rang out, plugging a neon light on the other side of the street. Fortunately for all involved, sirens of coming on-duty officers cooled things off quickly, with one of the other group taking leave rapidly on foot.

When the on-duty officers arrived, it was determined that the other three guys were Dade County sheriff's officers assigned to their homicide squad, including a lieutenant and a sergeant (the big guy). Lord knows who the third guy was.

All of the combatants were taken to the MPD station per orders of Captain Minix, night commander of MPD patrol. The staff duty officer, Major Bob Knight, was called in from home. While Knight was conducting the inquiry, he stashed Wally and Fitz in the Xerox room. They found a phone there and made a quick call to the author at home, who was their robbery lieutenant during that period. I responded to the station and conferred with Major Knight and the proceedings were closed for the evening, with Wally and Fitz heading home to rest after their ordeal.

The final result was that Clerke and Fitzgerald were cleared of initiating the fight and were returned to regular duty status. The fate of the Metro detectives was turned over to the sheriff's department and no known discipline was meted out to them either. I did instruct both guys to stay out of that joint in the future.

Fortunately for our public relations, this early morning skirmish did not come to the attention of the news media until weeks later, when ace crime reporter Edna Buchanan of the *Miami Herald* posted an article. By then it was old news and did not create too many waves.

Both of the MPD guys have moved on. Wally is a business executive and Dennis, who went on to the DEA, and then later into the practice of law, and has authored legal textbooks on informants that is used throughout the world by judges, lawyers, and professors of law (Interview with Officer Clerke and Detective Fitzgerald, plus personal knowledge of author).

GABLES OFFICER BILL DeKORTE MURDER

Coral Gables officer Bill DeKorte, a forty-nine-year-old veteran of nineteen years on the force, was assigned alone to Zone 203, for house-check duty in the affluent residential area of the city on January 21, 1972. The often-honored DeKorte heard a holdup alarm call radioed to another unit at about noon and headed his marked cruiser to the Happiness Boys' liquor store at 238 South Dixie Highway, adjacent to a low-rent black housing complex. DeKorte arrived within one minute and was shot by two armed robbers he struggled with in the store's doorway as Officers Charles Richards and James Butler arrived. Richards pursued Raymond Bradley, seventeen, in one direction while Butler chased Walter Sanders, twenty-one. At this time, these two officers were unaware that DeKorte had been wounded.

Suspect Sanders, now armed with Officer DeKorte's weapon, fired four shots at Officer Butler who retuned fire and killed Sanders in the driveway of 137 Florida Avenue. Bradley disappeared in a large apartment complex one block from the crime scene. A force of over one hundred Miami, Gables, and Metro units blanketed the west Coconut Grove area. At about 6:00 PM, a tip was received that Bradley, dressed as a woman, was hiding out in an apartment at 107 South Dixie Highway. Four Miami officers responded quickly, apprehended Bradley, and charged him with the murder of Officer DeKorte.

DeKorte, although weaponless, began to chase the offenders from the liquor store but soon returned to his squad car and headed for the hospital. Citizens then reported that DeKorte's car had jumped the curb and hit a palm tree at Ponce and Granada Boulevard. DeKorte was dead, a shot through the lungs and other gunshot wounds to the arms.

The Ridgewood, New Jersey, native, whose wife, Ruth, worked the drive-in teller window at the nearby Miracle Mile branch of Florida National Bank, had been a highly decorated member of the Coral Gables police department. Shortly after the killing, longtime Gables Chief Bill

Kimbrough arrived at the bank and informed Ruth of the death of her husband. The chief escorted her to the DeKorte home in South Miami to break the sad news to their three children, ages nine to seventeen. DeKorte had been by the bank an hour before the shooting to chat with his wife and to plan an upcoming vacation. DeKorte's daily off-duty job at the Greyhound bus station had enabled him to afford to take the long-awaited trip with his family.

On the day of the crime, suspect Sanders was free on a $1,500 bond for a recent burglary that he was due in court for trial the following Monday. Sanders was on a fifteen-year probation for a string of burglaries he had been convicted of in 1968. He was sentenced to five years in prison for these crimes but had been released on probation in August 1971.

DeKorte had been the Coral Gables Outstanding Officer of the Year for 1966 for his excellent work that included apprehending two offenders in the act of holding up a local savings and loan bank. Chief Kimbrough, head of the 140-man department for over thirty years, had often preached his officers not to physically tussle with armed offenders, saying, "Two fellows, named Smith and Wesson, evened those physical odds long ago." Sergeant Lou Mertz advised that DeKorte was invariably at the scene when something happened. "He was the kind of guy you couldn't make mad, I never seen him angry." DeKorte was later buried in Miami Memorial Park (Wilbanks, *Forgotten Heroes*, 1996).

SEAPLANE SKYJACKING

On March 7, 1972, two black males hijacked a Chalk's Flying Service Grumman 73 from the MacArthur Causeway dock adjacent to Chalk's terminal. During the hijacking, a gunfight erupted between arriving police units and the criminals, wounding the pilot, mechanic, and one passenger. The plane was still able to take off over the waters of Biscayne Bay and headed for Cuba. Officer Ted Seaman was one of the first arriving officers, with Art Epperson and Felix Eades sliding up shortly after.

Miami's large airport is outside the city's jurisdiction, so we never gave a thought to prepare for a skyjacking, let alone one at the docks.

Both Epperson and Eades got into some hot water over their use of firepower but not too seriously, as the MPD did not have guidelines for skyjacking situations (Interview with Epperson and Eades).

COPS ATTEMPT JAI-ALI ROBBERY

Officer Dale Deskins and former officer David Collier were caught by off-duty security officer Lieutenant Gil Zamora in the parking lot of Jai-Ali, armed, and dressed and made up like blacks in what appeared to be a robbery attempt. As Zamora confronted Deskins, the later pleaded, "Gil, it's me, Dale Deskins."

Both were charged for loitering with the charge later dismissed by the judge who disagreed with the constitutionality of the ordinance. Collier later served time for other offenses, and Deskins was fired and was last heard from out in Texas (*Miami News*, 3/31/73).

TALES FROM A DAILY WORKSHEET

By Officer Brian Glaccum, MPD Ret.

It was either rip-roaring busy or decidedly dead. Long, quiet hours on patrol sometimes, and other times, it was totally frantic. Some "calls" were predictable; you knew many of the people involved in a 34 (disturbance) before you got there. Or which 25s (alarms) were good calls and which way they would run. Then, there were people like David Lee Cromey. Cromey had shot several men while in an angry rage during a bar brawl over a couple years. His victims never came to court, and Cromey skated. The last time he did it, I waited for him to come home after the bolo was put out. When he did, he calmly handed over the gun and climbed into my car without complaint. But this time, his victim died, and James Lee served time, at last! On a 38, April 7, 1974, at 230 NE Forty-fifth Street, late one night, Charley Love encountered two women who answered the door completely nude and laughing! When Charley asked about the reason for their call to MPD, they replied that their puppy dog in the backyard had been barking. We left. Charley swears this was a setup by IA! Cruising down the boulevard one night when I was first riding solo, I heard a loud crash and then the place went dark. There were brilliant staccato arcing flashes of light, and residents in bathrobes and slippers began milling around in their yards. The ground was wet from earlier rain. Finally the breaker bus bar popped and it went totally dark, but I found the cause: a 35 (DWI) had knocked over a pole. I got FPL, MFD, and a tow truck on the scene. By the time I got everything done and the DUI's blood drawn at Ward D, it was nearly 06 time. I think that was my first 3-17 (accident investigation) that I handled while riding solo four months out of the academy. Does anyone else remember taking an 09, 04, at the old station, beginning C shift, to zip up Twelfth Avenue to the Motor Pool and nearly running out of gas on the way because day shift left it on empty? Did that old shoe shine machine in the back of the old roll-call room ever work? Remember slapping the portable radio securely into the dashboard ashtray? Didn't it seem like at least once a week we got a flat tire? Do you remember what "Fence It" means? Steve Smigelski and I responded to the airplane crash the early morning of December 16, 1973. A load of Christmas trees had shifted in the cargo hold, bringing down the plane, which landed in a residential area. I can still remember the smell of burnt rubber and aviation fuel. In the madness of it all, we tried to keep motorists from driving over fire hoses and we were looking out for looters. Sometimes Sergeant Lanier, who was the roll-call sergeant at that time, put me on the front desk. Got strange phone calls at the front desk. There was one lady in Texas who called every night to ask me if I found her runaway son. She must have been tormented by her loss. You could hear it in her voice. Sometimes I wonder how many cups of hot coffee I brought to George Green when he worked off duty at the guardhouse off Biscayne and Fiftieth Street. It's a wonder we didn't all get poisoned from the smoke at the old range. Mr. John Keller was the gunsmith there and he must have reloaded a million rounds. We had to qualify every month, so it kept him busy. There were two times when the chief was my backup—once on a "possibly armed" prowler call when I was a one-man unit, east of the boulevard around Thirty-second Street, when Kenneth Harms swung by. Glad for the 15 (backup)! Thanks, Chief! Another time I was on a 25 near the top floor of 211 NE Second Avenue, an office building, and who should step off the elevator but Herbert Breslow! Seems I had left my car on the street out front unlocked. He was nice enough to bring me my eight point!

TANGLEWOOD TRIPLE HOMICIDE

Two pretty Louisiana sisters, both professional models and beauty contestants, were found murdered in Apartment 108 of the Tanglewood Apartment complex on NW Thirteenth Street and Twenty-seventh Avenue, Miami, on October 19, 1972. Denise, twenty, and Diane Heathum, eighteen, were killed as was the boyfriend of one of the sisters, Jack

Smith, thirty-one, a known drug trafficker. The bodies were discovered by U.S. Customs Agent Jim Welch, who had intended to track Smith in the hope that he would lead Welch to locate wanted fugitive Charles Bennett, who was connected to a recent Hollywood drug raid involving members of the Dixie Mafia gang. Smith was savagely beaten before being shot, and it was theorized that the girls were killed because they witnessed Smith's killing. All three victims had marks indicating that wire coat hangers were wrapped around their necks in addition to being shot with a .22-caliber gun. The motive was most likely over finding the location of 1,000 lbs of marijuana that the gang lost, with Smith being beaten to a pulp before his death in an attempt to extract from him the information.

An extensive investigation resulted concentrating on Dixie Mafia thugs Ricky Cravero, Norman Christian, Charles Bennett, and John Elbert Ransom, all known hit men associated with the Dixie Mafia gang, led by Kirksey Nix Jr., son of an appeals court judge out west. Nix, sentenced to a life term for murder earlier in 1972, was reputedly still running the gang, which specialized in large-scale marijuana importation and sale, while in prison.

Stanly Morris, the director of the U.S. Marshals Service, was quoted as saying that Cravero and the others were believed responsible for at least thirty-five drug murders during the past few years.

The MPD's response was rapid upon being notified of the killings. Detectives Mike Gonzalez, Louis Vasquez, and Joe Ramirez were the lead investigators, aided by Detective Gene McCracken and other homicide unit detectives. Within thirty minutes of the being notified by Welch of the killings, the author, then a robbery tactical CO, and Sergeant Frank Huntley of the robbery squad responded with all on-duty robbery and robbery tactical officers who conducted a room-by-room interview of the occupants of adjoining apartments in this large complex.

The all-out investigation continued for weeks at full speed, with robbery detectives assisting the homicide squad officers. The investigation spread out to neighboring Broward County communities, and eventually, detectives from these cities as well as Broward and Dade County sheriff's department began rounding up many members of this gang on a variety of charges with the aim of solving the triple homicide. MPD Detective Keith Hardin was able to gather (I won't tell you how he did it) telephone records of calls between Dade and Broward locations (a toll call at that time), and a minute-by-minute record was compiled showing the interrelationship of these thugs. The information was then computerized along with other leads, by Chris Quakenbush, homicide steno, and the author, that provided daily leads to the lead detectives. This was perhaps the first-ever computerization of a criminal investigation by a state or local law enforcement agency. The MPD was able to accomplish this as we had Eric Wilson, a computer expert in the SIS section who coincidently was working on the development of just such a process. It is now commonplace to set such a process in motion in large criminal conspiracies.

Many arrests were made and gang members went to jail, but the Tanglewood case remains unsolved today. The most prevalent theory by investigators was that Cravero and/or John Ransom were the most likely to have committed the crime. Cravero was later a suspect in the killing of Judge Skerry in Alabama and was convicted of killing fellow gang member Stanley Harris in Dade County in 1974. Cravero, sentenced to life imprisonment, later was able to escape and was on the loose for five months until apprehended by Kevin Dougherty of the Dade sheriff's office, working with a squad of officers under U.S. Marshal Danny Horgan with multi-jurisdiction investigators. A gang member and a hit man himself, Gary Bowdach once stated, "Cravero's acute paranoia resulted in numerous homicides of Cravero's lieutenants and others."

Ransom died in Georgia in 2006, his many years of being a "hit man" finally over (MPD records and personal knowledge of author).

A TEST OF CHARACTER

This short tale is about individual character and appearances. Sometime in 1973, I was close to the top of the list for promotion to captain. I was just waiting for an opening that would be created by one of the sixteen current captains to retire. The list only lasts two years so one had to be fairly close to the top in order to receive the promotion and nice pay raise that went with the next step.

One noon, I was leaving the police café; two of the then current captains were having a cup of coffee at an outside table, neither of whom I had worked under for any long period of time. One guy was a very sharp dresser, spoke very precisely with an excellent vocabulary, and had the overall demeanor of a successful police executive. The other captain was an amateur race car driver and mechanic on his off-duty time and had ground-in grease on his rough hands, uniform sleeves rolled up at the cuff, shirt pockets unbuttoned, was plain spoken, and gave the general impression of one who was slightly unkempt, especially in his position.

The pretty one inquired about my chances for promotion and, after some small talk, advised that he was thinking about retirement and would most probably accept $5,000 from me to ensure his papers were dated prior to the expiration of the promotional list. I was sort of amazed as this offer was totally improper and most likely illegal or at least in violation of our department's ethics. I politely declined.

An hour or so later, the other captain (the unkempt one) called me into his office, shut the door, and stated to me, "I have been thinking about retirement myself, and if, near the end of the life of the list, you have not got promoted yet, I will make sure I leave so you can get my bars—and you don't have to give me a damn cent."

I learned a good lesson that day. Appearances do not make the man, it's the character. I thanked Captain Jack Maddox for his intentions and will never forget his lesson, even though I did make the promotion on an unrelated guy's retirement.

BATMAN AND ROBIN SHOT

Two decorated robbery tactical squad officers were seriously wounded during a gun battle on NE First Avenue the evening of June 1, 1973. The story by reporter Philip Hamersmith was published the following day in the *Miami News*:

> Miami police killed one man in a blazing midnight street gun duel in which two officers were wounded. A wide search was on today for a second man who fled the battle scene.
>
> A civilian who tried to catch the fleeing suspect was nicked by a ricocheting shot.
>
> Miami's 1972 Officer of the year, Gerald Green, 25, and his robbery squad partner, Walter Clerke, 25, both was reported in good condition at Mercy Hospital. Green was shot through the hand by a slug which also wounded him superficially in the chest. Clerke was shot in the left leg.
>
> Left dead in the street, face up and torn by shotgun blasts, was Hershey Williams, 25, no known address.
>
> The scene was in front of the Dolphin Hotel, 937 NE 1st Avenue, where Williams allegedly started firing at the officers

when they investigated a taxi driver's complaint about the two fares who acted suspiciously.

The man still sought was described by witnesses as a black man about 5 foot, 11 inches tall, weighing 190 pounds, braided hair and wearing a brown flowered shirt, dark pants and elevator shoes. He was the subject of a massive manhunt in which a helicopter and searchlights were used to scour the downtown area.

Slightly wounded in the shootout was a passerby Willie James Scott, 23, an employee of the Royal Biscayne Hotel on Key Biscayne.

According to reports by Scott and the two wounded officers, Williams and his unidentified companion attempted to flag down a taxicab in front of the Dolphin's tavern at about 11:45 PM.

Suspicious, the cab driver asked the two men to raise their shirts so he could check for guns, before letting them in his cab.

An argument followed and Scott, outside the bar, intervened, telling the two men not to make trouble.

At that moment, according to police sources, the officers in a new unmarked brown Chevrolet stopped by.

Leaving their unit, the officers attempted to question the two men and according to the wounded officer, Williams "drew down on them and fired hitting Green in the hand."

Near Williams' hand, police found a white handled pistol. Spent shotgun and pistol cartridges littered the street in front of the hotel.

The second suspect, who was unidentified, fled down the street as Scott; himself nicked by a bullet in his right leg, chased him and scuffled with him.

Unable to hold the man, Scott then used the police car radio to call for help for him and the two wounded officers.

Police units made intensive street searches and stopped dozens of persons in the hunt for the fugitive, who apparently was not hit in the gunfire.

Clerke and Green are both five-year veterans of the force.

We're Lucky to Have Survived, Officers Admit after
Shoot-Out

Edna Buchanan, the *Miami Herald*'s Pulitzer Prize reporter, followed up with a June 3 story in the *Miami Herald*. (Edna often referred to Clerke and Green as Batman and Robin in her news stories.)

Admitting that luck kept them alive, Miami's top award-winning police team moved into the same hospital room Saturday after both were shot by an ex-convict they finally killed on a downtown street Friday night.

Hershey Williams, 25, died after being hit by several hand gun and shotgun blasts.

Officer Gerald Green, 25, and Walter Clerke, the partner with whom he split a $1,000 Outstanding US Officers' award two months ago were listed in fair condition at Mercy Hospital.

A bullet bounced off a bone and was still lodged in Clerke's left thigh. Green slowed a bullet with his left hand, probably saving his life, doctors said. The slug went through the hand into his chest directly over his heart.

"It's one of these things that are happening across the country," Green said. "People would rather shoot it out with police than submit to a routine arrest."

"We have restrictions on our use of firearms. We were 90 percent sure he had a gun. But we have to be 100% sure. You can't start shooting when somebody reaches under his shirt. They could be hiding narcotics. We didn't want to shoot him. Our hesitation got us shot. When we were finally sure he had a gun and was going to shoot us—we were already shot."

Police said Williams, who came here several weeks ago from New Orleans, called a cab and left his room at the Dolphin Hotel, 927 NE First Ave, about 11:45 PM. Diamond Cab driver Arthur Lawrence Katz, 22, edgy about recent robberies, became suspicious and refused to allow Williams and an unidentified male companion in his cab unless they would lift their shirts to show they were not carrying guns.

Williams, who wanted to go to the Castaways, angrily refused. Willie Scott, 33, a hotel worker, stepped in and tried to quell the argument. The frightened cab driver drove off, according to Sgt Mike Gonzalez, as Williams pulled a gun, waved it and shouted to witnesses that he should have shot the cabbie.

From their unmarked patrol car a block away, Green spotted the disturbance as the cab left. "I said, 'Wally, it looks like that guy in the black hat has a gun out on the street.'" Clerke drove toward Williams who saw their car stuck the gun in his belt and pulled his multi-colored dashaki over it. The officers got out, guns drawn and ordered the two men to put their hands on the car. The companion complied. Williams did not, witnesses said. The officers said they ordered: "Don't reach. Put your hands up." "He tried to go for the gun and we got in a fistfight," said Clerke.

"I don't care if you're cops or not. You're going to have to kill me. Come on! Let's shoot it out right now. Kill me! Kill me!" witnesses quoted Williams. When Williams drew his gun, Green, busy with the second suspect, ran over, grabbed the gun and all three grappled. Green and Williams fell to the ground. As they struggled Williams fired, wounding Green in the hand and chest.

"I knew I was shot. I was bleeding all over the place. I could feel the chest injury and didn't know how bad it was. I started shooting at him." Clerke, three or four feet away, also opened fire. "I wasn't sure if he had shot Gerry. I started shooting. He turned and fired two shots at me. He hit me once in the left thigh. It felt like a sharp kick. My leg buckled. There was no place to hide out in the middle of the street. I was thinking that it was him or me—and I hoped it would be him," said Clerke. "I saw him shoot back and get Wally," said Green. "We both started looking for cover." Williams ran to the other side of the police car.

"I shot at him again. He ran down the street and he shot at us again. I started shooting as fast as I could pull the trigger. None of the bullets stopped him," said Green. Clerke emptied his gun and ducked behind a post to reload. "We stopped shooting when he went down behind a truck tire about 50 yards away," said Green. "We thought it was all over. Then he started shooting again. I saw him point the gun right at me. He fired about four more times.

"Wally was out of bullets; he grabbed the shotgun out of the car. We both opened up on him. Wally with the shotgun, me with a handgun. Finally, he stopped shooting.

"He rolled over on his face. My gun was empty. Wally's gun was empty and we were out of ammunition." More than 25 shots had been fired.

The dead man's gun, lying next to him, was also empty. Police said they found a dozen rounds of ammunition in his pocket and a box of bullets under the mattress in his hotel room. At the scene of the hand-to-hand struggle police said Williams dropped a plastic bag containing several hundred pills.

In his room, police said, they also found 95 grams of marijuana and 200 to 300 additional pills, "uppers and downers," Gonzalez said.

During the gun battle Williams' unidentified companion fled. Scott, the would-be peacemaker, picked up Clerke's police radio and chased him to a nearby alley but was hit by a ricocheting bullet fragment that caught him in the leg. He was treated and released from Jackson Memorial Hospital. Police said the man who fled did nothing wrong, would not be charged and they asked him to come forward.

Police said Williams' New Orleans record included charges of rape, armed robbery, burglary, narcotics violations and theft of a mail truck. He served one two-year prison term, according to Sgt Gonzalez. A half brother in New Orleans reacted "indifferently" to news of Williams' death and a grandmother "said he was a bad fellow that she wouldn't permit in her home," said Gonzalez.

Neither officer says the experience has soured him on police work. "This has been happening across the country," said Green. "You can't be afraid. I felt he wanted to take on some policeman. I'm glad he took on two who could handle him." "It's part of the job. You have to expect it," said Clerke, "and hope that you're luckier than the next guy. Keep you and your partner alive, that's the important thing."

The first uniform patrol car that responded to the citizen's call for help was Officer Ron Quackenbush, along with a rookie. Quackenbush had previously worked with Green and Clerke on the task force. The author recently visited Ron out in Oklahoma and Ron's recollection of that evening was as vivid as if it occurred the night before. Quackenbush's recollection:

On June 1, 1973, around midnight, I was working the 40 sector (downtown) with a rookie whose name I cannot remember. We were at Biscayne Boulevard and NE Tenth Street and could hear gunfire. Being an old task force guy, the hair stood up on the back of my neck and I started looking for the action. That is when the world as I knew it started falling apart. Things went real bad when the voice on the radio started yelling for help at the Dolphin Hotel. At that point, I was one hundred yards away from the call.

As I turned the corner and stopped the car, I saw four things that have stayed with me for all these years. I'm unsure why, but the rookie that was with me jumped out of the car, pulled his weapon, and started running south down NE Second Avenue. As he ran, I looked south and saw Jerry Green leaning up against a vehicle; I truly believed he was dead. I heard someone yelling and I looked over my left shoulder and saw Wally Clerke lying on the ground. The blood was overwhelming. As I ran to Wally I saw the bad guy lying on the sidewalk. I never did see his injuries (bullet holes) but was told later that he was DOATG (dead on arival to ground). I then knelt down to pick Wally up. When he was in my arms, another unit pulled up. I ran with Wally to the unit and got into the backseat, yelling for the officer to "GO!" I cannot tell you who was driving the unit but he was one of the "old-timers." As we pulled away from the scene, an ambulance was pulling up for Jerry. I looked down the street, Jerry was still standing there and I still felt he was dead. I do not remember the ride to Jackson Memorial, but when we arrived, there were several medical personnel standing at the door waiting to take Wally into the hospital. When

I got out, it looked like every officer in Dade County had ascended on the parking lot. As they took Wally back, another set of lights pulled up to the doors and again the medical staff surrounded the unit and brought Jerry in. That was one of the most heartwarming things I have ever experienced. Jerry, a friend and fellow officer, was not dead and stood a chance to make it. This experience turned out to be something that has, to this date, been engrained in my mind and keeps me very grateful to God for what happened and how he saved my friends and brothers.

Two years earlier, Green and Clerke were among a group of young patrol officers who had been selected by the author to form a robbery control team that was integrated into the robbery investigation unit. These officers did not investigate the cases but, instead, went aggressively after known robbers, one of the facets of the prevention program that also included target hardening, bait packs, flash recognition training, and other innovative methods, including the use of rental cars, the purpose of which in this tourist town was to give the robbers the fear that the every tourist rental car on our streets could very well be occupied by a police officer. The team dressed in sport coats and ties and this helped Green survive the shooting. In his breast pocket was a sheath of mug shots, which the bullet hit after penetrating his hand. The shot was then deflected by the slick-sided photos and struck the area of Green's sternum. By then, the bullet had lost most of its velocity and did not penetrate the chest cavity. The bullet fell out of Green's clothing at Jackson Hospital ER and is now in Green's home display case to this day.

Both officers, a few months prior to the shooting, had been selected as *Parade Magazine*'s Officers of the Year for the entire United States. They also had been selected or nominated several times for MPD's Officer of the Month along with other members of this robbery tactical team.

The author transferred off this team a month or so earlier upon promotion to captain, but I still felt that these were "my guys" and was quite relieved when hearing that they would survive.

After the completion of the robbery project, both Green and Clerke went on to be homicide detectives. A few years later, Clerke resigned to enter private business. Green stayed with MPD for over thirty years and was involved in numerous interesting cases and events that the department encountered over the years. He was again wounded during a Haitian riot in the early '90s but was not seriously injured. He is now retired and is the current president of Miami's PBA. Their "partnership" continues to this day (Interview with retired lieutenant Jerry Green, Officers Wally Clerke, and Ron Quackenbush).

THE BOBBY YEE SHOOTING

It was just the regular 7:00 AM ritual in patrol's Platoon A, reading the roll call and overseeing the switching of patrol cars from the off-going nightshift.

The calling of the rolls and then a few words about the Green-Clerke shootout over the past weekend were said at the briefing. Then, the fresh officers headed out from the station toward their zones for a day of work in the Miami streets this Monday morning, June 4, 1973. It was not unusual to receive several alarm calls first thing in the morning as store owners arriving for work would discover their bells ringing. Bobby Yee, a young twenty-year-old patrol officer, received one of these calls at the Burger King, West Flagler Street and Eighth Avenue, not far from the station.

Bobby promptly arrived at the address, closely followed by his backup unit. He encountered two men in the parking lot, one of whom raised a pistol and fired at the officer. Yee immediately returned the fire and hit one of the suspects. Bob, however, was himself shot in the foot as the injured suspect fired shots from under a car where he had fallen. The injured suspect limped across SW First Street, attempting to hide in a building under construction but was soon apprehended by a flood of arriving officers, responding to Yee's call for help. The offender was hospitalized for bullet wounds in the stomach and shoulder.

Yee was rushed to Jackson Hospital where his wound was judged not to be life-threatening and a large manhunt began for the second suspect. I was then Platoon A's captain (Bob's commanding officer) and sped to the scene. The four bridges leading across the Miami River were ordered to be raised to prevent the fleeing black male from retreating into the maze of Overtown where he could easily melt into the morning rush of folks heading for work. Thousands of commuters heading for downtown office buildings from the west residential areas sat for close to ninety minutes in their cars as scores of Miami PD officers flooded the area in one of the largest daytime dragnets seen in the city. Practically every patrol, detective, and motorcycle units on duty, as well as some now off-duty night-shift guys, responded to the Little Havana streets. Finally, one of the motor units grabbed the offender as he worked his way toward the Seventh Avenue bridge toward Overtown.

The impetus for Yee to become a police officer grew out of an incident in New York City five years prior when an NYPD officer saved the life of Bob's oldest child, Diana. A well-liked Cuban American of Spanish and Chinese parentage, Yee was an enthusiastic cop who was impeccable in his appearance, especially his police shoes that always had that mirror-like shine. Upon his return to work several weeks later, he was warmly greeted by his fellow officers. After his first roll call, he came into my office with his equipment replacement paperwork, which would provide him compensation for the damaged shoes. As a joke, we scratched out the amount for replacement of the shoes and halved the amount, stating that there was nothing wrong with the other shoe, leaving no reason to replace a perfectly appearing article. I still can remember the look of disbelief in his face. Naturally, we were merely trying to loosen him up.

When the shooting occurred, units were dispatched to the Yee residence to transport his wife and mother to Bob's bedside at Jackson. This was normal departmental procedure, but the Yee family greatly appreciated the gesture as well as follow-up visits, including the babysitting of his kids to allow mom to make hospital visits. When the following New Year's Eve arrived, Yee invited my wife and me to his home for a traditional dinner. Ordinarily, I would spend that night with my parents as it was their wedding anniversary but Bob would not take no for an answer. When we arrived at his south Dade home, four tables, seating at least forty relatives, were arranged in his side yard adjacent where a pig was being roasted. Yee had me sit at the head of these tables, a gesture of genuine gratitude by his family. Bob and I remained friends for the many years since, but he would always ask me why he could not buy both shoes, not just the one with the bullet hole.

Sadly, just this past year, retired captain Bob Yee, working as a security and crime prevention officer at a Miami River boatyard in his retirement years, was gunned down in an assassination by a hired hit man and killed. The killer had shot Bob at close range with a silencer-attached handgun secreted in a bag. After the murder, the hired thug dropped the bag and the silencer slid out of its slot and was recovered by investigating authorities. This evidence, fingerprints and DNA, led to the identity of the killer, who was by that time incarcerated in a New Jersey jail on other charges. He was recently indicted and extradited to Dade County to face a first-degree murder charge for killing Bob Yee—a good man and a good cop (MPD records and personal knowledge of author).

WATCH OUT FOR SHORTCUTS

By Unidentified Officer

We were working midnight shift in 20 sector in the midseventies, I was riding a one-man unit and so was one of the other guys in my sector on this night. It was the middle of the week and we were getting no calls at all; it was boring as hell. We were in the area of Bisc/Thirty-eighth Street when about 4:00 AM we get a 26 in progress (burglary). So we start driving to the call, we begin to race down the boulevard to see who gets there first. I'm headed northbound on the boulevard and the other unit is behind me, I can see him in the rearview mirror turning into an empty lot between Bisc and NE Fourth Court, so I slow down. He is stopped in the field when I come back around. As I am pulling up, I see him putting the vehicle in reverse a couple of times. I realize that he is stuck on a rock or something. He finally stops after several attempts to drive over the rock or back up off of it. Finally he is able to back up off the rock. We both get out of our vehicles to see if there was any damage. As we walked to the front of his vehicle, we discover that it was not a rock at all but a wino who fell asleep in the field, he had ran over him several times. The wino got up, yelled at us for breaking his bottle, and walked away as if nothing had happened.

Moral of this story: watch out for shortcuts.

THE GANS KIDNAPPING AND MURDER

A 1975 FBI Screwup

Thomas Knight, twenty-four, kidnapped local industrialist Stanley Gans and his wife, Lillian, forcing them to withdraw funds from their downtown bank on NW Fifth Street. Suspect Knight stayed in car with Lillian. The FBI agents ordered our guys to back off while FBI and MPD units followed the vehicle to a south Dade sandpit. Knight killed them both before the FBI moved in. Lieutenant Mahoney and Sergeant Ahearn of our narcotics squad, part of the surveillance team, had a clear-shot opportunity in front of the bank, but was instructed by FBI to just watch and not to take Knight out.

The author, on duty as staff duty officer that day, monitored the radio frequencies and was dismayed at the amateur performance of the FBI that day, which was overseen by the agent in charge of the Miami office (who happened to be a personal friend of mine).

Knight was found concealed by K-9 units at the sandpit and later was convicted of two counts of murder, receiving a sentence of death in the electric chair.

Six years later, Knight killed a prison guard, Richard Burke, and was again sentenced to die in the chair. As of this writing (2010), Knight is still sitting on death row, the second longest prisoner in Florida's prison death row (Interview with Lieutenant Ernie Vivian, Ret., and personal knowledge of author).

In 1976, the Miami police installed mobile digital terminals in all of the uniform patrol zone cars. These computers provided real-time information to police officers on persons and vehicles. Later enhancements were added to show active calls for service in the neighborhood. Prior to the procurement, several commanders (including the author) visited Kansas City, Seattle, San Jose, Huntington Beach, and Los Angeles County to view the state of the art.

The funds for the MDTs were provided by Miami bond issues and supplemented by federal grants. This was one of advanced innovations that kept Miami on the pace as a very advanced agency in modern law enforcement. Many of these efforts were brought about by Chief Bernard Garmire, who instituted the Modern Miami Police Department project while he was boss during the early 1970s.

O. J. GOES BALLISTIC

Super Bowl X between the Steelers and the Cowboys was played on a cold day in Miami's Orange Bowl on January 19, 1976. Pittsburg beat Dallas, 21-17. on Terry Bradshaw's long touchdown pass to Lynn Swann, a memorable play.

However, I have a more vivid remembrance of an event that played out pregame inside the stadium. At the time, I was MPD's patrol major and assigned game commander for Super Bowl X. The game was hyped as a celebration of the U.S. centennial. Adding to the excitement was the filming of the movie *Black Sunday* that day.

The National Football League Corporation had rented the press box area that day for a pregame party for invited high rollers. I was called to the area to meet Jack Danahy, NFL security chief, a retired NY FBI boss and his assistant Jackson. Both men were attempting to eject Buffalo Bills star O. J. Simpson and another NFL star from the Vikings (name withheld) from the party area, as they were not on the invitation list.

O. J. Simpson was screaming and cursing, his eyes flashing and face contorted. His loud verbal venom was being directed toward NFL Commissioner Pete Rozelle, seated nearby. Simpson screamed, "I made this league, and should be allowed to stay." O. J. ignored Danahy's command to leave the area. The other player, also not invited, was a gentleman and was urging O. J. to leave.

Knowing trouble was ahead (an understatement), I had to be reassured that Rozelle would prosecute if we had to use force to remove Simpson, which of course, would lead to an arrest. Rozelle replied affirmatively, so I firmly advised Simpson and the other guy to leave immediately. Simpson, appearing to be in top physical shape, loudly erupted with abusive language directed at Rozelle. Simpson's face was scrunched up and contorted and his body was shaking. I was amazed that this was the same "nice guy" we would see on TV during football season.

I quickly reviewed my roster of 110 officers and called on the radio for five selected motorcycle officers and my brother-in-law, 6'4" officer Steve Vinson. They soon arrived (to my relief) and I restated the demand for Simpson and his companion to leave the area by entering the down elevator or he would be bodily carried out by these officers and tossed into the paddy wagon. Still screaming, cursing, and frothing at the mouth, he headed for the elevator with his buddy pulling on his shirt to hurry him out. As big and strong as he was, I had no doubt that our MPD hulks (I think Travis and Guanci were in my group) could handle him.

Was I surprised when he was charged with murder of his ex and friend in 1994 out in California? *No way.* The actions and demeanor of Simpson that day at the Super Bowl is etched into my memory. Simpson, cleared of the murders, was later convicted of robbery and is now serving thirty-three years in Lovelock Correctional Center in Nevada.

On a side note, my stomach went through another churning episode just prior to kickoff. The *Black Sunday* movie hype had stirred up the pregame media, supplemented by our SWAT practicing anti-terror drills at the Orange Bowl all week. The NFL called a midfield meeting before the coin toss to discuss possible crowd (80,000 plus) evacuation in case of chaos (bombs, etc) in the stands during the game. I stood next to Referee Norm Schacter, NFL Security, Miami Fire, a National Guard rep, and the team captains discussing who would make the enormous decision to evacuate the teams and crowds while millions of fans worldwide watch on TV. Guess who they all pointed to? Me. Wow. I was a bit nervous during the first half thinking about worst-case scenarios. By the second half, I had calmed down and sat in Steeler owner Rooney's box for the remainder of the game. Exciting day.

MIDNIGHTS IN HOMICIDE

By Unidentified Homicide Sergeant

It was a dark, cold, winter night. I was working the midnight shift in the homicide unit. My partner was Sergeant Art Scheeren. The night was extremely quiet; the radio barely made a sound, only the occasional blare of the dispatcher giving the hourly time checks and the descriptive "Miami KID 381." As 2:00 AM approached, we drove along NW Fifth Street toward Biscayne Boulevard, crossing the railroad tracks east of where the current Miami police station is located. It was so quiet that even as I was driving, I began to have difficulty staying awake. Scheeren was inadvertently assisting me in my wake-up effort by firing up his stinky ass pipe from time to time, causing me to roll down the window and gasp the chilly night air for breath. Passing over the railroad tracks on Fifth Street, Scheeren suddenly sat straight up in the seat and, peering past me from his position on the passenger side of the car, began following with his eyes a black male who was walking rapidly in a westerly direction against the cold wind blowing through the street. Speaking quietly, as though someone might overhear him, Art whispered, "Turn around, partner. I've got an outstanding murder warrant on that guy." I quickly whipped the car into a U-turn and speeded past the suspect, swinging the unmarked unit up onto the sidewalk and into the path of the black male. Slamming on the brakes, I threw the car into "park" and reached under the seat for my gun and handcuffs. It was not a well-kept secret that most homicide detectives, unless at a scene, would keep their equipment under the front seat in order to avoid wrinkling or putting bulges in the suit. Art, in the meantime, had leaped from the car, right into the face of the suspect, shouting as he threw the door open, "Freeze, you son of a bitch. Put your hands against the fence and don't move or I'll blow your ass into kingdom come." I had grabbed my handcuffs and slipped them into my jacket pocket as I scrambled from the car. My weapon still lay on the floorboard as I ran around the back of the vehicle to where the prisoner was standing. I recognized the suspect as someone from the Overtown area with a lengthy arrest record, primarily for aggravated assault. He was quick to use a knife on anyone who got in his face, and most smart folks along NW Second Avenue stayed out of his way. However, during the past week some fool, full of liquor courage, had paid the ultimate price for questioning our man's integrity during a crap game. Art was telling him that he was under arrest for murder and to stand still while I patted him down and cuffed him. All the while, the arrestee never took his eyes off of Scheeren, staring at him with an unusual intensity. As a member of the task force, I had been on arrest scenes with this guy before, so as I patted him down, I reached under his sweater and retrieved a carpet knife stuck down in the small of his back. Then there was the knife slipped into his sock and finally the razor blade secured in the matchbook cover. Now I was ready to put the cuffs on him. Scheeren barked the order for him to "put your left hand behind your back." I placed the cuff on that wrist. "Now, put your right hand behind your back. Do it slowly. Don't get any smart ideas or you'll leave here in a body bag." Throughout it all, the pat down and the handcuffing, the prisoner's eyes had never left Art Scheeren. Now cuffed I took the suspect by the arm and began to open the rear door to place him in the car.' For the first time, he pulled back while he continued his fixed gaze on Art. "What *is* dat?" he asked, as I followed his look toward Sheeren's right hand pointed directly into the midsection of the arrestee. HOLY SHIT! While I was handcuffing this violent, knife-slashing, murderous son of a bitch, my goddammed partner had been holding him at bay with the point of his *stinky ass pipe*.

EMILIO MILIAN BOMBING

For one who is not familiar with Miami's turbulent background during the 1970s, it may be difficult to comprehend why a popular Cuban exile radio commentator would be so hated that someone would put a bomb under his auto. In the spring of 1976, Emilio Milian was probably Miami's leading exile radio host, whose programs at WQBA drew high ratings and was a voice of moderation. However, he did speak out loudly against the ongoing terrorism in Miami that had resulted in numerous bombings in the South Florida area. One morning, Milian exited his office in broad daylight just off West Flagler Street and Fourteenth Avenue and his car blew up as he turned on the ignition. The explosion blew off both his legs and left him maimed for the remainder of his life.

His crime, evidently, was that he had opened up his show to some of the more liberal members of the community who were opting for a more open policy toward Cuba, although Milian himself was regarded as a staunch anti-Castroite. First to reach him after the bombing was Commissioner J. L. Plummer, who applied emergency first aid until the Fire Rescue guys took over.

Sometime later, Milian returned to work but was assigned a less prominent role at the station than previously held. Several months after returning to work, he was terminated by the station's owners, who then moved to a much more strident format than Milian had preached.

The Miami police were requested to station a uniformed officer around the clock at the Milian residence out in the west end for many months after the terror bombing. The bombing certainly chilled free expression on the subject of Cuba as evidenced by the change in tenor of the local politicians who now became much more vocal in addressing the issues of Cuba and what the U.S. foreign policy should be regarding Cuba. In fact, the Miami City Commission actually articulated a foreign policy platform that was completely irrelevant to running the City of Miami. This incident exacerbated the job of the Miami police for years to come.

Well-known bomber and part-time police informant Ricardo (Monkey) Morales was called before a federal grand jury and it soon developed to what they now call a person of interest in the case, Gaspar Jimenez, a strident exile who was a suspect in many of the Cuban exile bombings. The case dragged on for years by the MPD, the Dade sheriff's department, and the FBI.

By the time Milian died in 2001, the case still had not been closed officially.

SWAT TRAINING

The chief got concerned about a couple of injuries to officers at SWAT training, so he directed the author (then commander of patrol) to investigate. I thought the best way to do so would be to participate in *some* of the training. I spent parts of several days with the group of about thirty officers being put through their paces by Sergeant Bob Sullivan. On repelling day, each guy had to repel off the top floor of the five-story Fire College tower. Sully offered me a chance to try it, but I begged off as I have a fear of heights. He said, "Just try it from the second floor." No problem, I said, thinking this would get me off the hook, as I strapped the gear on and jumped out from floor no. 2, pleased as punch. Sully then said, in a very loud voice, in front of all my officers, "Major, if you can do it from floor no. 2, you can do it from the top, as it is the same procedure."

Well, I could either worm out of it with embarrassing shame, or I could kill myself in honor, so I did jump from the top a couple of times without a problem. However, I did leave Sully with one thought: "SULLY, I <u>WILL</u> GET EVEN."

WHO TOOK THE MARIJUANA?

In the early 1960s, a big marijuana catch usually resulted in confiscating a "brick" of marijuana, which probably weighed about two pounds. By the mid-'70s, we were grabbing it by the truckload. We moved into our nice new headquarters on NW Second Avenue in 1977 and had a large property room. Dope from cases would be stored there until the court hearing, and then taken to the incinerator with an order signed by the judge for burning.

One particular case stirred up all of us. A bale of marijuana was placed in the evidence locker at the storeroom, weighing in at seventy-six pounds. A week or two later, the investigators retrieved the bale, weighing it in order to testify about the precise amount of the evidence. The bale was put on the scale and it came out five or six pounds short.

A major internal investigation was commenced and all the property clerks questioned. Just prior to running polygraphs on all of the clerks, the investigators finally figured out the problem. The new storeroom was air-conditioned, unlike the room at the old station. Being stored for ten days or so had dried out the grass as five pounds of moisture had evaporated. A truck was soon rented to store the smelly grass confiscations outside in the station parking lot.

Case closed.

JUST LIKE OLD TIMES

One of my favorite people on the job was Harold Whitaker. This West Virginia native was one of the most intelligent, friendly, and humorous guys I have ever met. Harold had been a motor officer, patrolman, and a K-9 trainer and now a patrol lieutenant. He had also served several months as my aide when I was the patrol division commander. His last assignment was as a shift patrol lieutenant. I enjoyed stopping in to his shift's roll call when he was readying the troops for the night's work. I often would ask if he could give us all a few lines of Shakespeare or Kipling to calm us all down before facing the street. He would then, from memory, recite entire verses of these artists. He surely had to possess a photographic memory.

I attended his last roll and waited around after so I could buy him a coffee and piece of Key Lime pie at Jumbo's and relive a few quick old memories as he faded off to civilian life. We left the station in his uniform lieutenant's car with me driving. Near downtown, I reminded him of the quiet nights from our task force days when we would run up behind a car that was driving normal and activate the emergency lights and siren, which would prompt an occasional criminal in a stolen car to begin to flee from us, thinking we knew the car was stolen or that he was wanted for some crime.

As we pulled away from the light at NE First Street with a vehicle in front of us, I reached over and turned the switch for the lights and siren. The car ahead of us immediately accelerated and ran the next two lights and the chase was on. We boxed the suspect's car in near Lindsley Hopkins School and pulled him out. He was indeed driving a stolen car, was wanted, and was a DUI. Both Whitaker and I could hardly keep a straight face while completing the arrest. We were in stitches.

We called one of the zone cars by and Harold signed the arrest affidavit. I intended to mail him a copy after he reached Richmond but it slipped my mind—but my memory of him and that event remains stuck in my memory bank.

Lieutenant Whitaker passed away shortly after the 1999 task force reunion, which was the last time I saw him. He remains near the top of my personal list.

DEL VALLE MURDER

Elaido Del Valle, a person of interest in the assassination of President Kennedy, was murdered in February 1967. Del Valle's body was found in the trunk of a car in the Central Shopping Plaza on NW Thirty-seventh Avenue. Detective Andy Giordano of Miami homicide was the lead investigator. After several weeks of handling the case and producing a large amount of reports, Andy went on his annual vacation. Upon returning to work, he found that the case file only contained the original police report. Agents of the FBI had combed the file as well as the CIA and the Dade sheriff's department. The case is still unsolved and whereabouts of the file is unknown.

Many assassination scholars believe Del Valle was possibly the second shooter in Dallas, and the author agrees with them (Interview with Sergeant Giordano, Ret., and personal knowledge of author).

A CITIZEN POSSE

On New Year's Eve of 1976, as the patrol commander, I was heading down to check out the Orange Bowl parade when I came upon a commotion that caused me to inwardly chuckle. Two teenage punks had snatched a purse from Rose Vernell, fifty, of Miami Beach, who was also headed for the parade. Although she was knocked to the ground, her lungs were fine as she started screaming as she got up and began chasing the thieves.

"They grabbed her purse and took off running," said Thomas Hill, a department store salesman who started the chase, which was quickly joined by fellow employee Jack Carr. Rudolph Shoucair was across the street. He, too, started running and screaming. By now, Mrs. Vernell was also after the thieves, all the time hollering and yelling at them.

The chase went by a rooming house where about thirty residents were relaxing on the porch. One elderly man jumped up, shouting that the fleeing teenagers were the same ones that robbed him earlier. He and the others on the porch joined in on the pursuit, which ended abruptly when the fleeing suspects ran up a dead-end street.

Hill grabbed one of them and the old man wrapped a chain around his neck. They sat on him and I went and grabbed the other suspect.

"The robbers were glad to see me," said Major Phil Doherty after he "rescued" Johnnie Battle, nineteen, and a fourteen-year-old boy whose name was not released. "It was heartwarming to see the citizen response," added Doherty. "Young, old, black, white, everyone in the neighborhood joined in. In this case, they overwhelmed them with numbers."

The bad guys didn't even have the courtesy of sending in a thank-you letter, but we know they were happy to escape the posse (*Albuquerque Journal* and personal knowledge of author).

RODNEY—CLEAN UP DOWNTOWN

Every Christmas season, the downtown merchants would plead with the city commissioners and the police chief to "clean" up downtown so their holiday sales would not be impeded. The word would filter down to the patrol office and various schemes would be implemented to sweep the streets of vagrants, panhandlers, winos, and the like. A favorite strategy would be to send down a group of officers who would not have to handle radio calls but simply enforce every possible municipal violation.

Another gimmick that worked well was assigning the public service aides to drive every spare uniform car to selected locations in the downtown area and park the squad car, moving it to another location every couple of hours, as a deterrent. In the meantime, these young people, in a training-type police uniform, would walk with the assigned beat officers.

One particular season, then Sergeant Rodney Sayre was dispatched with a squad of VIN officers to "enforce all ordinances." Rodney, who was really up on the laws, noticed that the huge wooden newsstand on Flagler Street and First Avenue was on the public sidewalk. This stand had been in the same place since about the time Henry Flagler came down with his train back at the turn of the century.

Rodney commandeered a city trash truck and, after dismantling the thirty-foot stand, instructed his troops to toss all the stand materials into the back of the truck and head for the dump.

You can guess what happened next. The chief's ears got singed by so many big shots calling to complain that their *New York Times* or *Wall Street Journal* was no longer handy. Then the politicians started calling. Poor Rodney did not realize that, regardless of what laws are on the book, politics rule in the end.

The city workshop designed and constructed a brand-new larger stand for the operator, paid for by the taxpayers, and set the illegal stand back up—on the same sidewalk—where it most likely is to this day.

The only thing that saved Rodney was that he was nominated for the Officer of Month (no way did he get it) for doing an otherwise fabulous job in suppressing crime in that area during the holiday season. He was soon transferred to an inside administrative job and many commanders later would wish him back attacking newsstands downtown as he exerted the same zeal toward each and every project he engaged in—to the dismay of some of our non-energetic bosses (Interview with Captain Rodney Sayre, Ret., and personal knowledge of author).

GREEN SLIME OF LOW TIDE

By Officer Wisner's Best Buddy

It was in the late '70s, exactly when escapes me now. It was a typical Friday afternoon that was slowly turning into evening. I was assigned to SPU, but that night I was working off-duty at the Everglades Hotel. Officer Mark Wisner, probably my best friend in the world, had come by the Everglades Hotel to see me. After about a half-hour BS session, he left and, for reasons that I have lost to memory, headed for the area of the Japanese Gardens off MacArthur Causeway. In the meantime, I went about my business of rejecting Rickets, hookers, whores, and other city politicians from the hotel lobby.

A short time had passed when I heard something strange over the radio. It was Mark's voice. There was something different about it. It seemed strained, under pressure. Mark was requesting his sergeant to respond to the boat ramp at the Japanese Gardens. His sergeant was another pillar of Miami law enforcement, Sergeant John Chapek—a man whose legend is so intense that a convention room at the Homer's Restaurant in Sebring was named after him (the Manatee Room). Anyway, after responding to Mark, Mark requested John he QSY to 4 (change channels so a one-on-one conversation could take place). I'm sure that every officer working channel 2 that night changed channels with John. Because of Mark's voice, it had become an established fact that "something" was up!

I turned to channel 4 and became even more confused. I heard Mark request John to come to the boat ramp at the Japanese Gardens. John responded in a puzzled manner requesting to know what happened. Once again, Mark requested he respond. "OK, Mark, I'm on the way, but what happened?" Mark then said that immortal sentence that will follow him the rest of his life. "Sergeant, I'd rather not say it over the air, could you please just come over here now!" In my attempt here to make a long story short, I'll cut through parts of the story I consider "less interesting" and pick it up at Sergeant Chapek's arrival at the boat ramp.

I remember questioning Sergeant Chapek later as to what happened on his arrival, and if he had ever decided to change professions, the descriptive storytelling is one he should have considered.

The following is a memory excerpt. Sergeant John Chapek said, "I pulled up to the boat ramp and immediately saw Mark standing there, alone. I asked what was wrong, he didn't say anything, and he just kept looking out at the water. I again asked him, 'What's wrong, Mark?' He continued to stare blankly at the water. I looked where he was looking and there was nothing there but open water. No boats, no people, nothing, just blank, open water. About that same time I noticed that there were several people standing around laughing. They were looking at Mark and me and were laughing. I then realized that his three-wheeler was nowhere in sight. So I asked him where it was. He turned and looked at me, then turned back to the water, and pointed. He still had said nothing. As I looked out there once again, I had the sudden realization of what happened. At that exact moment, a huge bubble broke the surface of the water followed by Mark's briefcase."

Mark had apparently fallen victim to what can only be described as "the Green Slime of Low Tide." Unaware of what physics and the law of gravity can accomplish when working together, Mark had driven his three-wheeler too close to the water's edge. The rest is simply a matter of Miami police history. And a damn funny one.

SERGEANT DUFFY, DO ME A FAVOR

How does that saying go? "Be careful about what you ask for"?

The chief of police called me (then commander of patrol) one day to advice that the *Miami Herald* was complaining about the bums residing in a homemade plywood hut in Bicentennial Park near downtown Miami. The park was in view from the *Herald*'s executive offices off

NE Fourteenth Street. The chief asked me to arrange to clear out the homeless as they were an eyesore to the *Herald* executives.

I met Sergeant Duffy, a uniformed supervisor (a real character), in the hall and asked him to take on the task as his assigned sector was in the area of the park.

I thought no more about it until the following Monday morning when an irate chief called me and demanded an explanation.

It seemed that Duffy went to the park, commandeered a small bulldozer and the driver, had the worker dig a large hole and buried the entire plywood hut, and then covered the hole with dirt. I could hardly restrain a laugh but the boss was not happy.

The expectation the *Herald* guys had was that the police would seek alternative shelter for the bums (I mean homeless), dismantle the shack, and move it away from view of the executive suite.

It was (and still remains) my view that I gave "Garcia" a message to handle and he did so.

Sergeant Duffy recently passed away after enjoying the mountain life of north Georgia during his retirement.

SNAKE STORIES

By Officer Curtis Reeves, MPD Ret.

SNAKE AT FLORIDA POWER & LIGHT

What a lot of people don't realize about Miami is that exotic animals *thrive* in the Miami weather. Everybody has heard about the alligators in the swamps in the Glades, but they don't hear about the boas, pythons, iguanas, and other large lizards that people turn loose, and *really* love the place, and get a *lot* bigger. A number of officers on the department have already run into them. Like Jerry Jewett. The Florida Power & Light station on SW Second Avenue, on the Miami River, is a pretty large place, and it has a good-sized hedge decorating the front. This part of the story I heard later, after I arrived. During the night, they had two security guards patrolling the plant due to a labor situation. One of the guards was a former MPD officer, Matty Horan.

Horan was checking the front gate, and a *very* large python came out of the hedge, went partially across his feet, and went back into the hedge. Matty was so scared that he just couldn't move until the snake went back into the hedge. He *swears* that the front of his pants got wet when he brushed up against some wet equipment. He was hysterical when he ran to his coworker, screaming about a twenty-foot snake in the bushes. His partner said, "I don't know what you've been drinking, or what you've been smoking, but there's *no* twenty-foot snake in those bushes!" The guy was so upset that his partner decided to call the police anyway. The complaint sergeant knew Horan but sent a patrol car anyway. Officer Jerry Jewett got the call.

When Jerry arrived at the scene, we went to the front gate and were talking to the guards. After hearing the story, he started laughing and told the Matty that he didn't know what he was ingesting or inhaling, but reassured him there was *no* twenty-foot snake in those bushes!

Out came the snake, and Jerry and the guards were *gone*! I was at the station, and I had just put some property in as evidence. At that time, we had the old radios, with only four channels. Three channels were for the three different districts, and one channel was for radio checks and car to car. The property unit was listening to channel 4, the car-to-car channel, and I could hear Jerry talking to the complaint sergeant. He said, "Sarge, there's a big snake in these bushes, and I don't know what *you're* going to do about it, but *I'm* not going in there after it!" That was about the time that I got on the radio and asked the sergeant if he wanted me to go there to see what I could do.

When I got on the scene, I saw that Jerry's car was parked by the front gate, but Jerry was about a block east of there on foot! I got him on the radio and asked what was going on, and he said, "That snake is in those bushes, and when you get rid of it, I'll come back and get my car!" That's when I found out that he didn't like snakes. (As a matter of fact, he threatened to shoot me one time if I came *near* him with a snake.) The security guards were *well* inside the Florida P&L compound, and they yelled to me that the snake was in the bushes. I got a big bag out of the trunk of my car, and some other units were just arriving. I asked the guys to shine their lights onto the bushes as I climbed inside to look for it. Once I got behind the hedge, it surprised me how long it took to find it, but finally I did. I was happy to see that it wasn't twenty feet long. It was only about fifteen feet. When it turned its head away from me, I grabbed it behind the head and tried dragging it out. It was wrapped around the bushes, and with

the help of the other officers, we were able to drag it out and get it into the bag. Jerry had disappeared. We had to raise him on the radio to let him know that the snake was secure, but he still wouldn't come back until I was gone with it. The snake turned out to be a reticulated (retic) python.

At the time, only the K-9 guys could take their car home. However, when asked if I could transport the car home (with snake in the trunk), I got a rapid OK.

I took the snake home to my wife, Marcia. I've got a weird wife. How many guys do you know who can bring a snake home to their wife, and they *love* it?

SNAKE ON THIRTY-FOURTH STREET

By Officer Curtis Reeves, MPD Ret.

I was riding 30 sector one night when the dispatcher asked me to go to channel 3 to answer a snake call. When I changed channels, the dispatcher asked me to go to an address on NW Thirty-fourth Street, between Third and Fifth Avenue. She said an elderly lady was complaining about a snake in her yard. When I arrived, this little old lady met me at the front of her house, on the sidewalk, holding her dog. I got out, and she came running up to me, saying, "There's a big snake in those bushes over there, and it was trying to eat my dog!" I said, "Sure, lady. Don't worry. I'll take care of it if I can find it." I went to the trunk of my car, where I keep pillowcases for my snake calls, and out a pillowcase, quietly laughing to myself. I *knew* it was only going to be a red rat snake, and they only get to about three to four feet long. I had my pillowcase in one hand and the flashlight in the other as I went for the bushes. The next thing, I'm in full reverse, backpedaling away from those bushes. That sucker could have eaten *three* of her dogs at once! It was fifteen-footer. I looked at the snake, then the old lady, and then the pillowcase. I just threw that case up in the air and said, "That's sure not going to do me any good!" I got back on the radio and raised the dispatcher. When she answered, I said, "Could you have another unit come by to help me with this snake? This is a *big* one!" John O'Neal, a.k.a. Radar, was the first unit to arrive.

I asked John to shine his flashlight in the snake's eyes and to rattle the bushes near him, and I would grab him behind the head. The plan worked sort of great! When he turned his head, I grabbed him, and he went *whacko*! That sucker started bouncing all over the place and was trying to wrap around me! I looked up, and John was beating feet for the road! I was going, "Dang! I gotta do something now!" Once my feet were clear, I got a running start and dragged him out to the road as fast as I could. By this time, every unit on that channel was arriving. It took four of us to wrestle him into the trunk of John's car. We were soooooo happy to close that trunk! But then, we had more, but different problems getting him out!

We had the station call a company named Pesky Critters and asked if they could come and get the snake, but they said that they couldn't show up until after daylight. We needed to "store" the snake someplace until they could show up. We got to the station and got one of those large wire mesh garbage cans that were out in the parking lot, and piece of plywood for the top, and an old tire to use as an anchor point to hold the top on with flex-cuffs. We didn't know what was going to happen when we opened the trunk. We *did* know that the snake was *not* in a good mood, so everybody was ready for action when we popped that trunk open. We had problems. That snake had wedged his head between the wheel well, and the outer fender of the car, and we could *not* get it out. I ended up stripping down to my T-shirt and pants and had to climb into the trunk with the snake. Four guys held onto the length of the snake as I tried to work it loose. Every time we tried to pull the snake out, it would puff itself up, and wedge itself, so we couldn't get it out! I held on to it as close to the wheel well as I could, and when it would relax, I would be able to pull it out about half an inch until it puffed up again. It was hot, muggy, the snake stunk, and John Scanlon had gas. It was *miserable*, and it took us an *hour* to get it out!

Once we got it out, it was no problem to get it into the garbage can. It was just as tired as we were! We got it in, and it filled up the can. We got the top strapped down and decided to put it in the shade, by where the motormen park their bikes, in the transfer line. I hung a sign on it that said, "Please pet me. I'm hungry." I *had* to wait around and see what happened when day shift came in. When people read the sign, they would start looking through the mesh, and it looked like it was full of garbage.

When they realized that it wasn't garbage filling the can, you could see a *lot* of fast movement, and it was always *away* from the garbage can. The motormen were really the good ones to watch though. You know these guys that when they have a flat on their bike, they tuck it underneath their arms and walk with it to the side of the road? These guys were going backward so fast they were falling on their backsides, ripping their holsters off because they forgot to unstrap their guns, knocking each other down, and *all sorts of good stuff*!

PAINT THE TOWN GREEN

The South Florida Emerald Society put on a parade of 101 units on St. Patrick's Day, March 17, 1979. It was their first (and almost the last) big green parade, marching proudly down Miami's Flagler Street's green line to the delight of the crowd, consisting primarily of viewers born in Cuba.

The author, together with MPD Lieutenant Ed McDermott, was on the Emerald Society's executive board and parade committee. The MPD and the city manager's office was noncooperative during the planning of the event, forcing the Emeralds to pay much of the expenses, unlike the costs associated with the annual Orange Bowl parades and other special events that the city always covered.

City Manager Joe Grassie ordered the Public Works not to use their labor and material for painting the street green, and Chief Harms ordered me not to spend any on-duty time performing parade planning. The day (and the green line) was saved by Steve Clark, then the Dade County mayor and an Emerald member. He instructed the county road guys to paint the line, providing that the committee furnished the material.

The paint was ordered from the Stein Paint Co., a Miami retailer who himself, although of Jewish extraction, was raised by an Irish family in New York. Stein would change his name each March 17 to O'Stein. The store gave us a discount on the washable paint and the work was done at midnight, under the supervision of MPD (off-duty) member Mike McDermott, to the delight of the committee who watched the handiwork from in front of the courthouse with ample libations in hand.

A few days after the successful parade, City Manager Grassie called my office (then assistant police chief) and asked when the green paint would be washed off the street. I advised Marie, my secretary, to tell the manager that the fire department would perform that task on Sunday evening, while traffic was light.

I went on to my lunch engagement with Fire Chief Herman Brice (great guy). During the luncheon, Brice got a call from Grassie forbidding him to use Miami fire units to perform that task. After a couple of phone calls, the Miami Beach Fire Department agreed to do the job (their chief was of Irish heritage).

The shocker came later when we found that our good friend Mr. O'Stein had provided us not with cheap washable paint but with the best oil-based paint that lasted for months.

The Emeralds, I, and many others grinned each time we passed it by, even though I took considerable heat from my bosses.

HARRY'S DINNER BREAKS

Every department has one, a loveable old sergeant that is not tough on the troops like most other supervisors tend to be (or at least the guys think so). Throw in the fact that he was a union (FOP) representative who has the opportunity to address the daily roll calls. You are talking about *our* Sergeant Harry Lenchner.

Harry was on the afternoon patrol shift in the mid-1970s, which gave him an audience of one hundred or so cops to preach to daily. When it was Harry's turn to say something, he never passed and would stretch a valid discussion into some union complaint. The author was the patrol major at the time and I would gently nudge the shift captain, Paul Shepard, to shut Harry up so these guys and gals could check into service and start handling the calls for service. We are like the airlines in some way, as one measurement stick is how quick we can get a uniform car to the front door of the citizen who makes the request. Well, you can't respond to a call when you are on the receiving end of Harry's latest speech.

Finally, we came up with a resolution to Harry's loquacious roll-call behavior. One of the dozen or so sergeants on each shift would come in to work an hour late so he or she could be available to approve the reports at the end of the tour of duty for the troops that had late reports to turn in (without adding to our perpetual overtime problem). The captain switched Harry to that assignment and our arrival time was greatly improved.

But I had to get sort of even with Harry. It was not a difficult job as Harry had the habit of drifting out of his assigned sector during his shift for one reason or the other. His favorite routine was to meet two administrative sergeants and the three-wheel sergeant at the cafeteria on Biscayne Boulevard and NE Nineteenth Street several times a week to catch up on the news he missed at roll call. (And to get a meal that was provided free to the regular zone car officer and the area sergeants.)

Both of the administrative sergeants (Bob Angelone and Al Cinilia) had broken me in as a rookie and we had been friends ever since. With their main duties behind them by five-thirty in the afternoon, they would leave the station to head for the cafeteria. My office adjoined theirs and they would give me a "heads-up" when leaving. I would then wait about eight minutes to give Harry (who was way out of his assigned south-end sector where he should have been) time enough to put the food on his tray and begin to eat. I would then call the dispatcher on the south-end channel (from my office) with my mobile and request an immediate meeting with unit 250 (Harry), way out at the far end of his assigned sector, West Flagler Street and Seventy-second Avenue, miles from the dining spot. Harry would finally answer and advise he was on the way. I then would wait another four or five minutes and then notify the dispatcher to cancel my request, which by that time Harry was back in his car, stuffing the last of his meal down. This went on for a couple of days a week during a two-year period and Harry never caught on and I never said a word.

His buddies would tell me what Harry's expression was when he would get my call to meet me. "That sonofabitch." This routine was known by many of Harry's troops, but none ever gave it away.

Years later, both Angleone and Cinilia passed on. (I miss these great guys.) It was at this point, with both Harry and I retired, that I told him the story. You should have heard him. Now, when we exchange visits and telephone calls, he never fails to bring it up, to *my delight*.

Harry is past eighty-eight years now and still acts like the Energizer bunny. He was a World War II navy hero and an MPD icon. We all love him as do many other officers around the state who know him from his longtime FOP involvement.

McDUFFIE KILLING

In the early morning hours of December 17, 1979, uniform officers from Miami-Dade sheriff's department began chasing a speeding motorcyclist in Liberty City. The chase continued for several minutes, ending at NW Second Avenue and Thirty-eighth Street, in the City of Miami. Numerous Metro units converged and it was alleged that McDuffie was beaten by sticks and fists while handcuffed. Other deputies apparently damaged McDuffie's motorcycle to make it appear that he had been injured by his motor crashing.

Miami officers Dick Gotowala, John Gerant, and Sergeant Wayne English arrived at the scene and observed portions of the beating and damaging of the motor. The Miami guys had no part in the beating of the suspect and were not charged with any law or departmental violations and all fully cooperated with the investigation. The Fire Rescue crew from Miami transported McDuffie to Jackson Hospital where he later died of his injuries.

After an investigation by Metro detectives, four of the Metro deputies were arrested for manslaughter and four others were relieved of duty.

The trial of the officers was moved to Tampa several months later and the result will be the subject of a later story in this publication (Numerous publications, both local and national).

DEATH OF A FRIEND

Edward (Ed) McDermott, forty-eight, died May 18, 1980, in the middle of the McDuffie riot. Ed was escorting National Guard troops north on South Dixie Highway at 12:30 PM. At SW Seventeenth Avenue, Ed had a heart attack while driving, causing the police car to jump the curb, hit a fence, and finally stopping. Officer Jerry Kaline, riding with Ed, called immediately for the Fire Rescue squad who provided emergency first aid and transported him to nearby Mercy Hospital, where he was pronounced dead.

McDermott, a twenty-one-year veteran of MPD, had been working for seven straight stressful days with little sleep (and without going home at all). Authorities determined that this situation led to his death. The death was later ruled to be a line-of-duty death, enabling his family to be eligible for compensation.

McDermott, a dear friend of the author's, had been a patrol and accident investigation officer and later a homicide detective. He was a very quiet and an extremely intelligent guy who displayed bulldog tenacity in his investigations. Ed was a New York native, attending NYU, and joined the MPD in 1959 with Academy Class No. 42.

Edna Buchanan, the Pulitzer Prize-winning crime reporter for the *Miami Herald*, described Ed in one of her books as "a quiet Irishman and a strong, old-fashioned sort of cop. He was very private and sort of sad, a man you could call a friend but never really know."

The author *did* know Ed well and spent many hours with him, both on the job and while we were both on the executive board of the South Florida Emerald Society. Ed thoroughly enjoyed being one of the members who produced the Emerald Society parade in downtown Miami in 1979 and other Irish activities in the area. He was an extremely cerebral police officer who worked diligently in the planning and building of the new police headquarters on NW Second Avenue in 1975-76, where he was assigned as coordinator under Major A. J. McLaughlin. The author was also assigned to the project with responsibilities for the communication and data management of the modern MPD, spending much time with McDermott. I came to regard him as one of the hardest-working public servants that ever served in the MPD. I still miss his company.

His family took his remains back to Long Island, New York, for burial (Wilbanks, *Forgotten Heroes*, 1996; and personal knowledge of the author).

I NEED SOME GOLD PLUMBING

Johnny Jones had worked himself up to be appointed the first black superintendent of schools for Dade County, holding that job from 1977 to 1979. Johnny was doing so well he purchased land in Naples, Florida, and began building a second home. One of his employees and a longtime friend and business associate Solomon Stinson was promoted to a high administrative post in the school system by Jones. Stinson was in charge of a vocational project that gave him the authority to purchase equipment for the work his students were performing.

Stinson would often purchase supplies at the Bond Plumbing Company in Coral Gables. Everything seemed to be on up and up until Stinson began purchasing gold plumbing fixtures, allegedly for the student projects. One of Bond's employees tipped off the *Miami Herald* and reporters began to follow both men. It turned out that the gold fixtures were for Jones's vacation home in Naples.

Jones was arrested and convicted of diverting public money to pay for the gold fixtures and later was also arrested for witness-tampering on an unrelated bribery case. The gold fixture case was later overturned but the other charge stuck. Jones became a short-order cook after his release from jail and died a few years later.

Stinson, however, landed on his feet. He was busted back to area superintendent at the time but worked himself back into good graces.

He became an associate superintendent and later was in the running for the big job several times, but always denied. Stinson was described as an extremely intelligent, competent tough administrator. His past with Jones as well as having the reputation of being extremely vindictive seemed to be the reason he never made it to the top (Numerous stories from local TV and newspapers).

TWO WEEKS—TWO SHOOTINGS

By Curtis Reeves, MPD Ret.

While riding 30 sector one night, I was up around NW Thirty-fourth Street, between Twenty-second and Twenty-seventh Avenue, checking out a house where a wanted subject was supposed to be hanging out. A call went out about a silent burglar alarm at a pawnshop in a mini strip mall on the east side of NW Twenty-seventh and about Twenty-third Street.

The call was given to a two-man unit, but since I was near, I headed for it too. I got to the scene first and drove by the front door. Seeing the door appeared secure, I didn't stop and went to the rear of the business, driving down the alley. The back of the business had a high fence around it, but it appeared secure, so I stopped the car and looked for a place where I could get up on the roof. About two businesses south of the pawnshop, I found a spot where I could get up. Once I got on the roof, I drew my gun and started working my way north. I watched as a guy popped out of a hole in the roof of the pawnshop and yelled for him stop. Instead of complying, like a good law-abiding citizen, he produced a Tel-22, a .22-caliber semiautomatic with a firty-round magazine, pointed it at me, and started running east on the roof. That's when I went full auto with my Glock, and the race was on. I wasn't leading him enough, and those rounds were going "POP! POP! POP!" hitting the wall *just* behind him, as he hauled buggy toward the edge of the roof. Units were just arriving, and they were on the air, yelling, "Shots fired!" He hit the edge of the roof and kept right on going without even slowing down. I could hear the "splat" when he hit the ground. One of his next problems was that he landed right in front of a K-9 unit, which had just arrived. I understand that it came as a sort of surprise to the unit seeing this person flying through the air and landing in front of his car, and even more so when he just hopped and kept right on running. They caught up with him on the next block. I couldn't see them, but I could hear the dog having lunch.

Since I didn't know if there was anybody else inside of the pawnshop, I stayed on the roof, covering the hole. After questioning, the offender said that there was somebody else there inside, and since there were more guns inside, SWAT was called in. A SWAT officer came up on the roof with me, and when the owner arrived, SWAT put in tear gas and entered the building. Well, not only was our subject a crook, he was a liar. The business was empty.

Next came Internal Security and ID. They got the fire department there to put up a ladder so they could get on the roof where I was. Since this was all taking some time, I was considering myself lucky, since I had a pocketful of cigars. I would have been *highly* upset if I had run out. After all the measuring, they decided that I was shooting at the offender at a distance of 95', in the semidark, with him running. I didn't feel too bad about missing. The IS investigator was Sergeant Jessie Kelly. He had just transferred to IS, and I was his first case, with another sergeant as his trainer. I spent the rest of the night doing paperwork and giving statements.

TWO WEEKS LATER

The department goofed up again and put an observer with me. The guy's name? Lawrence Elmhorst. I understand that he was never the same after riding with me that night. It had been raining off and on all night long, and he kept rolling up his window, and I had to keep reminding to roll it back down after the rain stopped. I liked having the windows down so that I could hear alarms, screams, shots, etc.

I was riding 30 sector again, but I got a call to assist K-9 in searching for an armed robbery subject in the north end. Since I was on NW Thirty-sixth Street, I was heading to get onto SR 112 at about Fifteenth Avenue. When I got to about Fifteenth Avenue and Thirty-sixth Street, I could hear shots being fired just south of me. Looking south, I could see a guy standing beside a Mustang, firing off rounds with a .45 automatic. I started heading toward him, and he jumped into his car and took off, heading right for me, northbound, in the southbound lane, which I was in. You could see his silhouette as he sped toward me, and you could see that he had his arm up, with the gun pointed toward his passenger window, which would be the side I would have to pass him on if I tried to avoid hitting him head-on. If his round hit our passenger side, and came through the window, it would hit one of us. Not good. I thought about being in a shooting two weeks before, and the department's going to shit a brick if I get into another shooting. Not good. My passenger window was up, and I'm going to have to shoot through it. Not good. I have a passenger between me and the window. *Oh well!* (It's amazing about some of the things you think about in such a short time.)

I yelled at Elmhorst, "Lean back! Lean back!" and threw my arm across his chest to keep him from leaning forward. I jerked the car to the left and fired off a round. That window just *exploded*! Glass went flying all over the place, the spent round bounced off of Elmhorst's nose and landed between his legs, the driver of the other car ducked (he didn't get his round off), and our two cars went whizzing past each other! Now, I've got a gun in one hand, a radio in the other, and I'm trying to make a U-turn. I dropped my gun in Elmhorst's lap, yelling to him, "Here! Hold my gun!" I made a quick "uey," yelled at my partner, "Give me my gun back!" and off we went! The guy only went about three blocks before he wrecked his car and bailed out on foot. A perimeter was set up, but a unit picked the guy up as he was trying to flag down a car on the SR 112 Expressway. It turned out the car was stolen from an Orlando cop during the police olympics. I don't think he was happy with the bullet hole in the car, or the dents from the wreck.

Back to the paperwork, the statements, and the IS investigation. The investigator was Sergeant Jessie Kelly. *Now* I was his first case that he was doing on his *own*! I told him that I hoped that I was breaking him in right! I was sitting outside of IS, and Elmhorst was sitting across from me. He looked up at me and said, "You know . . . I saw that car coming right at us, and there was no doubt in my mind that he was going to ram us. When you yelled for me to lean back and threw your arm across my chest, I thought that you were bracing me for the accident. I DIDN'T EVEN KNOW YOU HAD YOUR GUN OUT!" I was already laughing when he thought that I was bracing him for the accident, but that last *really* broke me up! When I gave my statement, I mentioned what Elmhorst said to me, and the investigators broke up, saying he had told them the same thing!

Funny thing though, I never had an observer riding with me again all the way to my retirement.

WHERE IS NORM?

Norm Evans was my recruit classmate in 1960. We rode together daily to attend the academy classes and I became close friends with him and his nice family over the years. Norm was assigned to patrol unit duty for many years and did his thing until late in his career when his wife gave him the boot for some extracurricular activities. Norm soon took up with a young one who was employed in a massage parlor downtown and who liked to sniff white powder, which, they say, is an expensive habit. One evening she and Norm (who was not known to the gal's boss) decided that Norm would grab the owner's bag of cash receipts while he was en route to the bank with a deposit. The haul would certainly provide enough cash to finance her habit for a stretch. You would have thought Norm would have learned something about criminal activities over the years—but he obviously did not—as he utilized his own auto, with his current license tag attached, as his getaway vehicle during the snatch-and-run crime.

A brief investigation resulted in strong-arm robbery charges against Norm, less than a year prior to his retirement. He then was faced with the standard fight-or-flight decision. If he took off prior to the trial and hid for a spell, the prosecutors might not be able to locate the massage parlor owner to identify and prosecute Norm, but there goes the seven-and-one-half percent of his pay he deposited into the pension system during all the years of sweating in the zone cars. His other choice was to take his chance in court. He lost.

The pension money had to be pledged to his attorney (even the losing ones get paid) for handling the case, so now Norm was both convicted and broke.

To duck an obvious stretch in the can, joining some of the thugs he put there, Norm flew the coop. That was thirty years ago. We did hear he was pinched for DUI at some point during his second life but bonded out before the prints came back and he is now on his third life with a third identity. I bet he has wished a thousand times that he had worked a few extra jobs directing traffic at the bank instead of looking over his shoulder the rest of his life, for unlawful flight-type charges have no statute of limitations.

A twenty-one-year-old security guard sleeping in his car on his first night on the job was rousted by two MPD officers and accidentally killed when he bumped a police shotgun and took the full brunt in his head.

Rosendo Saavedra, Nicaraguan refugee, was asleep in his auto at NW First Avenue and Twenty-first Street at 4:30 AM when Officers John Sprague and Armando Guzman approached. He was ordered out of the car when officers spotted a gun on the car seat. The guard was wearing a jacket that covered his guard uniform. Saavedra was told to put his hands on the car and, in doing so, bumped his head against Sprague's shotgun barrel and the gun discharged, killing the guard.

Later, the immigrant guard's family claimed that the guard failed to understand the officer's commands due to a language problem. This was debunked by the fact that one of the officers was completely bilingual.

Lieutenant Bob Murphy of Homicide, lead homicide investigator Joe Fleites, and internal affairs investigated. No charges were placed on Sprague, a two-year officer. The case was ruled an excusable homicide (MPD records).

A FISHY STORY

By Howard Johnston, MPD Ret.

I was heading for afternoon shift roll call after running a five—or six-man funeral escort on a rainy afternoon. We were eastbound on 836 by the airport just west of Fifty-seventh Avenue and it started raining so hard you could just barely open your eyes. We were going along about forty or so and cars and trucks started sliding around bashing into each other. We managed to get over to the safety lane and stop without going down and could see a little better. The rain was pouring down and hitting the pavement and splashing up, but the pavement was covered about two inches deep with little shiny silver fish about two inches long, which were jumping and flipping up in the air. Seems like I'd read somewhere about it raining fish, or maybe dreamed it, but I thought I'd finally seen it. Well, the rain slacked off some, and as it turned out, one of the trucks was pulling a boat trailer with a big fiberglass tank on it. The driver said he had $3,000 worth of live wild Georgia shiners to sell at bait and tackle shows in the tank. One of the cars took the whole side out of the tank and the shiners hit the road. FHP got there and we were on to roll call. We squished into roll call and our always cheery sergeant said,

"How come you guys are late?" We told him it was raining fish on 836 and dropped a couple on the desk for proof.

MURDER OF OFFICER NAT BROOM

"It is impossible for me to forget September 2, 1981."
By Dick Witt, MPD Ret.

Every patrol shift starts with a load of paper on the captain's desk. Mine was no different, so it generally was close to noon before I moved from my desk. At that time I would leave the station for lunch. That had been my routine for more than a year. Edna, our shift secretary, placed another stack of paperwork on my desk. I stood, put on my gun belt, and started toward the lobby. Edna seemed surprised by this change in my routine and asked me where I was going. I didn't know, so I answered, "Out." Pulling out of the parking lot, I began driving slowly north on Third Avenue. The dispatcher put out a call and I realized that it wasn't even 10:00 AM. I stopped at the traffic light at Eighth Street and I thought about going west, but when the light changed, I continued north. Just south of Eleventh Street, a gray-haired man ran in front of my car waving frantically. Jamming on the brakes, I rolled down the window with every intention of verbalizing some very unpleasant invectives (?). Shouting at me, he yelled a police officer was shot. He was pointing toward the apartment stairwell. My radio was quiet and I realized that I was on channel 1 (north). Switching over, I started down the passageway, radio in my left hand and my right hand on my weapon. I saw nothing. Officer Burnard Fowler was climbing over the fence to my right. Fowler began running and then I saw the downed police officer. Other police officers came over the fence. Fowler had rolled the downed officer onto his back trying to administer first aid. Blood was everywhere. Officer Robert Anderson was now assisting Officer Fowler. The downed officer was Nathaniel Broom who was an FTO (field training officer) despite being weeks away from completing his probationary year. He had a rookie partner, but where was he?

Wednesday, September 9

After the funeral services, I went back to my office, closed the door, and sat. Two hours later, I pulled up once again in front of the little house. The lawn still had a scattering of neighbors and friends sitting quietly while trying to balance paper plates of food and cups of cold drinks. Inside the house, Lillian and John Broom sat across from one another at the kitchen table. The kitchen behind them had food piled everywhere and several women serving huge portions to the remaining mourners who stuck their heads in through the open back door.

Accepting a large plastic glass of sweetened iced tea, I sat with Nathaniel's parents. No one said a word until Mrs. Broom said, "You remember." It was a statement, not a question. I nodded, afraid that if I spoke, I'd cry. She smiled and continued speaking. Her eyes had a distant look as she remembered a brief moment in time many years earlier. "At first I wasn't sure," she said, "but Friday past, I was. It's the voice. I remembered your voice." Lillian Broom reached across the table and touched her husband's arm. He looked puzzled. "In all the years we lived in this house, we have only had the police come once. Do you remember now, John?" While John Broom's memory was taking him back, so was mine. It was a day twenty years earlier when I received a call reference to cars drag racing in the neighborhood. Entering the home, I stepped around a little boy playing with his tiny cars on the floor. Following the couple in, I saw at their kitchen table and took the information that they provided. Just as I closed my notepad, the little boy, barely more than a toddler, put his chubby little hand on my knee. His eyes were deep brown and very large. He was looking at me with the look that only children have. You know the look, when they are so full of trust. He looked at my holster and weapon, the uniform and badge on my chest with eyes that were full of awe and innocence. Quietly, he said, "I'm going to be a policeman."

I left the home of John and Lillian Broom, then, much as I had twenty years before. This time filled with a sense of Lillian and John Broom's loss of their only son for the little boy who had wanted to be a policeman. The little boy who had achieved his dream and became the young man we had said farewell to today and was buried in his police uniform.

Author's Note: Captain Witt retired as an MPD colonel and went on to be chief of police at Hollywood, Florida, for ten years, then two other Florida departments. Dick was the author's partner in patrol, the task force, and later in Robbery. He passed away in 2008. We still greatly miss him, his deep voice and his keen mind.

DISAPPEARING CLOTHES

By Unnamed Detective

Back in the early '80s, myself and three other homicide detectives set out to follow the wife of a murder suspect to see if she was going to meet up with her husband who was on the run. We followed her '68 dark blue Mustang all over the western portion of the county and into Hialeah, where she stopped in front of a small strip mall. We watched as she exited the vehicle and brought out of the trunk a large dark green garbage bag. The bag looked full. She carried it over to another car where a male was waiting. We moved in. The male was her husband and our suspect in the murder. "Let's go to the office," I told them. Thinking there may be some evidence in the bag, I took possession of it and brought it up to the Big "H" (slang for Homicide). We brought the suspect and the wife to the office. We needed a confession to solve our case. The bag of clothes was for the suspect who was on his way to Newark, New Jersey. "I was going on vacation," he told us. I looked through the bag and found nothing but smelly, old, raggedy clothes that were probably bought at your local Salvation Army. I found no evidence from the murder.

Meanwhile, the girlfriend of Detective XXX

(I think her name was ZZZ) brought a bag of clothes belonging to XXX from her house and into the homicide office. "It's over," she told XXX. She set the bag of clothes next to his desk, which was five feet away from my desk.

We finished the interview of the suspect and I told him that we were letting him go for now until we could gather more evidence and information on the case. I brought over the bag of clothes and told him he could go. Well, that night I received a call from a very angry Detective XXX. "Where are my clothes, my suits, my Guayaberas?" he asked. I didn't know what he was talking about. Then it hit me, the young Mariel murder suspect was now probably wearing one of John's best suits at a welcoming party in Newark. I never solved the murder.

John got his clothes back but that is another story.

THE 3:00 AM PHONE CALL

Actually it was 2:47 AM when the phone rang at the Chief Harms's household. It was his boss, City Manager Howard Gary. "You are fired," Gary stated. That began the Night of the Long Knives, as it was called.

Harms and Gary had been at odds for some time due to Gary's attempt to place some of his non-law enforcement friends into middle management and higher positions within the police department. There were also later news reports that Chief Harms was investigating Gary for allegedly illegal actions down at city hall.

Gary wanted the contents of the chief's safe, so he pulled the trigger on the firing in the middle of the night. Gary summoned Assistant Chief Breslow in the wee hours, anointing him as acting chief and ordering him to activate the SWAT team to secure the police station, especially the chief's office.

Harms had been chief since early in 1978, having been appointed by a different administration. The years were rocky under Harms's watch, especially the fallout from the McDuffie riot in 1980 as well as the invasion from Cuba the same year and the Cocaine Cowboys gangs that terrorized the area.

Gary, Miami's first black manager, using the ruse of an outside consultant's report, was inserting his non-law enforcement buddies into the Miami police system, with the assistance of a couple of Harms's aides, albeit without the knowledge of the chief.

After being notified of his firing that early morning, Harms drove by the manager's home and observed police vehicles assigned to a couple of his top executives.

Harms retained his civil service rank of captain and was assigned to the records unit by Gary. After a period of legal wrangling, the chief was allowed to retire as chief of police with both he and the manager being prohibited from publicly airing any details on the dispute.

Harms has remained in the Miami area as a law enforcement consultant, but Gary was subsequently arrested and became a government witness (snitch) in corruption cases involving the issuance of city bonds under his watch. Gary died several years later (MPD records and numerous local news stories).

HERE SHE COMES

By Point Control Officer (Name withheld)

It was 8:40 AM when I walked out of Walgreen's at East Flagler Street and Second Avenue. I could see a number of men standing along the sidewalk with their cups of coffee and looks of anticipation. And here she comes! The morning sun brings out a glint into her hair and shows just an outline of her body through her tight skirt and thin blouse as she bounced along in high heels.

This morning I saw a man speak to her and she angled across the avenue to where I was standing. "Officer," she says, "that man said, 'Honey, you have the finest set of coconuts I have ever seen on a woman.'"

"Do you want me to arrest him?" I asked.

"Heavens no, I just thought you might want to know."

"OK, I will see that he does not speak to you again."

I stepped out into the intersection and stopped all traffic so she could cross the street and watched as she walked down the block acknowledging each half-raised coffee cup with a brilliant smile. A tap of a horn reminded me that I had not restarted traffic while I was watching her admirers dispose of their coffee cups to start another dreary day.

DeLEON KILLED IN HIGH-SPEED CHASE

A twenty-six-year-old MPD officer, who had only been assigned to the motor squad two weeks ago, was killed on December 21, 1984, while chasing a speeder on SW Eleventh Street at 9:00 AM on a Friday. Jose DeLeon, a two-year officer, was in training for Motors with partner William Williams (who was himself killed in a traffic crash in 2000), when a motorist made a left turn just as DeLeon was passing in pursuit of the speeder, causing DeLeon's motor to roll over and crash, fracturing the officer's skull. DeLeon was pronounced dead at Jackson Hospital within the hour.

Cuban-born DeLeon had come to the U.S. in 1972 as a fourteen-year-old youth and graduated from Miami High School in 1976. He graduated from the police academy in July 1982 and was assigned to the patrol section.

He was survived by his wife, Blanca; a son, Jose, two; and a stepson, Alex, five. Officer DeLeon was buried in Miami Memorial Park in southwest Miami.

The driver of the auto that struck DeLeon was cited for failing to yield the right of way to an emergency vehicle (Wilbanks, *Forgotten Heroes*, 1996; and MPD records).

MIAMI RIVER COPS

Crime in Miami exploded in the early 1980s, highlighted by an increasing murder rate and the activities of the Cocaine Cowboys. The Miami department responded by hiring several hundred new officers in a hurry, resulting in a lowering of the hiring standards. One particularly unsettling crime was the robbery rip-offs of drug dealers by other criminals in police uniforms.

In the early morning hours of July 28, 1985, six men were off-loading 350 kilos of cocaine on the boat, the *Mary C.*, at the Jones Boatyard on the Miami River, within the jurisdiction of the Dade sheriff's department. Twelve uniformed men stormed the boat, advising the boatyard guard that they were the police. The men were in fact wearing police uniforms. When the raiding party boarded the boat, they were yelling, "Kill them." The six men loading the dope all jumped into the river to swim for their life. Three of them drowned. The raiders loaded the huge amount of cocaine into a stolen van and escaped. A small story in the *Miami News* two days later mentioned the deaths on the back pages.

An FBI informant passed on information to Metro Dade detectives that the offenders were in fact Miami police officers. These officers, all bilingual Latin officers, were normally assigned to south-end zones, which ran adjacent to the Miami River. Most had been hired in the employment rush in the early '80s.

Detective Al Alvarez, the lead Metro Dade investigator, began a long investigation that resulted in the arrest of many of the twelve raiders and was able to turn a few into testifying against the gang leaders. The case mushroomed into a widespread criminal enterprise case that involved over thirty officers. Newly appointed Miami chief Clarence Dickson, assisted by corruption squad leader Captain Rodney Sayre, with help from federal and county detectives, jailed many of the gang, some of whom eventually served time in federal prison. Dickson formed the special squad, led by Captain Sayre, to investigate this wave of police-related crimes, which resulted in numerous arrests, dismissals, and retirement of many of the bad apples. Dickson took the high road in dealing with the sad situation with the goal of eliminating the corruption cancer that had evolved from the south-end police bandits and some higher-ups in the department.

A look back to the possible causes of this crime spree pointed the finger at the rushed employment of so many new officers under the previous administration, with many claiming that the lower standards set the stage for the later crimes. Other factors included the assignment of non-Spanish speaking field supervisors over the bilingual squads.

Although many of the offenders were fired and jailed, the criminal acts of the uniformed officers smeared the reputation of the vast majority of honest, hardworking officers who went out their job with dedication to the law and their oath (Captain Sayre, MPD Ret., and numerous local news stories).

CARBON MONOXIDE KILLS YOUNG OFFICER

David Herring, a four-year MPD officer working solo on late-night shift in a marked patrol car, died from carbon monoxide poisoning from a defective muffler on his police car. Herring had contact at 6:00 AM with another officer and had radio contact at 6:05 AM, but did not respond when he was given his 06 signal (end of shift). No follow-up was made by the radio dispatchers, and Herring sat in the car unresponsive with the motor running until citizens attempted to rouse him at 8:25 AM without success. Headquarters and Fire Rescue was finally notified, but Herring was dead when help finally arrived.

Herring was a twenty-five-year-old Miami native who graduated from Miami Lakes High School in 1979. He joined the MPD in 1982 and spent most of the next few years on the night shift in patrol until his death on September 3, 1986. His sergeant Frankie Maye had submitted Herring's name for Officer of the Month a few months prior to his death for outstanding work. Herring was also a member of the MPD Honor Guard squad.

The death vehicle, a 1981 Plymouth with sixty-seven thousand miles on the odometer, was due to be replaced at seventy thousand miles. An inspection of the car revealed that the muffler was defective and that fumes were leading into the vehicle. The car had been turned in to the city Motor Pool on two previous occasions but still had problems with fumes. A grand jury investigation pointed out that the city Motor Pool had system-wide problems in maintaining the police fleet as well as management problems. No one was charged with malfeasance but the city paid up a large sum to settle a civil suit on the officer's death. The city also installed carbon monoxide alarms in each police unit after this death and rotate the patrol cars out of service at between forty and fifty thousand miles rather than the current seventy thousand.

The police department also changed their dispatch systems that began to require an automatic contact with each unit hourly.

At the present time (2011), officers have a take-home police vehicle that is used by them exclusively. One result of this take-home policy is that the vehicle maintenance and appearance has greatly improved over the 1986 period experience.

Herring was single and was survived by his parents and other relatives. He was buried at Dade Memorial Park in Opa Locka, Florida (MPD records and Wilbanks, *Forgotten Heroes*, 1996).

THE POPE IS IN TOWN

In 1987, Pope John Paul II made a historic visit to the United States, first stopping in Miami. Preparations had to be made at four different venues that the pope would appear. Archbishop McCarthy, head of Miami area Catholics, hired a private construction firm, the Gerrits Corporation, to complete the altars, stages, etc., who in turn hired the author (then retired) as the company's papal project director.

The police departments of Miami and of the Dade County government, as well as other departments, undertook significant responsibilities for the security of the September project. Major Dean DeJong handled the project within the City of Miami at St. Mary's Church and the downtown Cultural Center, doing an outstanding job. The Tamiami Park huge altar and mass and the airport venue (where the pope and President Reagan appeared together) was set up by my employer, the Gerrits Corp., the church, and the Secret Service. The preparations beginning in February for the fall visit was a very complicated affair, but the U.S. Secret Service and the local departments worked hand in glove with the church to make it a successful and safe event.

The author had previously commanded Super Bowls, Orange Bowl parades, and other large events, but the planning and coordination for this papal visit far exceeded the scope of anything experienced during his career. The author had also labored with many federal agencies during his law enforcement career and must say that the United States Secret Service was head and shoulders over any of them, including the FBI.

On a personal note, being present with the two leaders of the free world, President Reagan and the pope, who brought about the end of the Soviet Union (along with Margaret Thatcher), and having a personal discussion with the pope will remain at or near the top of the author's career experiences.

VIC ESTEFAN GUNNED DOWN

A well-known police accident investigator, forty-nine-year-old Vic Estefan lived, worked, and had attended school in the Little Havana section of Miami. For twenty-one years, he had patrolled his own neighborhood and became known to thousands of citizens as well as being highly respected by his fellow officers. Victor, an army veteran born in Cuba, spoke four languages and had joined the Miami force in 1966, receiving hundreds of awards and commendations over the years.

On the evening of March 30, 1988, Estefan had just completed a traffic stop when he spotted a vehicle driving without lights in the area of SW Thirty-sixth Court and Ninth Street. He chased the vehicle only a few blocks to the 3300 block of SW Ninth Terrace, where it came to a stop. Victor exited his marked squad car to address a minor "driving without lights" violation. The passenger stepped out of the right side and pumped three bullets into Estefan with a .357 pistol. Estefan, not wearing his bulletproof vest, pulled out his Glock but was unable to fire at the fleeing auto.

Officer Estefan was rushed to the hospital, accompanied by J. L. Plummer, a local city commissioner. Estefan, still conscious, was able to describe his assailants and their auto. Surgeons worked on him throughout the night but the bullets had caused extensive damage and he died the following morning.

Over 1,500 law enforcement officer attended the funeral of Officer Estefan, who was buried with full honors by his colleagues. His wake and burial location were within blocks of where he lived, worked, and was slain.

A citywide manhunt of more than two hundred officers failed to locate the offenders or their auto that evening. The Mazda getaway stolen car was located abandoned the following day and incriminating prints were obtained. A month later, a California highway patrol officer made a traffic stop in Paso Robles, California. Again, as in the Estefan murder, the passenger exited the vehicle and fired at the officer but his gun misfired. Three male occupants of the vehicle were arrested. Two of them, brothers Douglas and Dennis Escobar, were identified as the slayers of Estefan by the rear seat passenger. Detective Morin of MPD interviewed the Escobars in California and obtained an admission of guilt and the prints found in the killer car matched.

The brothers, illegal alien felons from Nicaragua, were convicted in California of attempted murder of a law officer and sentenced to life imprisonment. They both were then extradited to Florida, tried and convicted of murder, and were sentenced to death in 1991. The verdict was overturned in 1997 due to the brothers being tried together and testimony of one was used against the other. The shooter, Dennis Escobar, was due for retrial in October 2011. The other brother remains in custody but may not be tried due to his mental condition (MPD records and Wilbanks, *Forgotten Heroes*, 1996).

BLACK CHIEFS OF POLICE

Clarence Dickson made history once again when he was appointed the first black chief of police. Chief Dickson was used to making history. In 1960, he was the first black officer admitted to the Miami Police Academy and the second black to attain the rank of major. He retired in July 1988, after three and a half years as chief of police.

Perry Anderson Jr. was appointed as the second black police chief and the sixth chief in nineteen years. He worked tirelessly to change this department's image and improve morale. He tackled crime by stressing professionalism and teamwork and increased the number of crime prevention programs for adults as well as youth. One way was through the police-sponsored program "Do the Right Thing," which rewards students who were doing just that. This highly successful program became a national corporation and produced training materials to help kick off new chapters all over the country. Chief Anderson left the department in 1991 to become the police commissioner in Cambridge, Massachusetts.

Calvin Ross was appointed the new chief in March 1991. Chief Ross, the third black police chief, grew up in Overtown and Liberty City and was well-known for his honesty and integrity. One popular change during his administration was the creation of the Neighborhood Enhancement Team (NET) program. This program divided the city into eleven neighborhoods and has now grown to thirteen and the cornerstone of the city's efforts to make each neighborhood cleaner and safer area in which to live, work, and play. He left the department in July 1994 to serve as the Florida secretary of juvenile justice. His latest assignment is the chief of police position at Florida A & M (MPD records and personal knowledge of author).

DOUBLE HEROES II

Shortly after World War II ended, the Miami Police Department hired numerous military veterans. They went about the business of being police officers and did not dwell on their military service. At an annual reunion a few years ago, three older MPD vets were huddled in the lobby talking quietly about their D-Day experience. Four MPD guys landed in France that day in 1944, three by parachute and one by glider. They were Ken Parker, Jack Sandstrom, Ross Cefalu, and Robert (Hoot) Gibson. This caught the interest of this writer, and I checked around and found that we had many "double heroes" on the department. Detective Norm Coplin was one of the few survivors of the USS *Arizona* at Pearl Harbor. Chief Klimkowski was across the bay that day at Hickam airfield. Al Gurdak, Chad Kaye, Carl Carter, Lou Rousch, Ed Carberry, and many others spent the war in the South Pacific, fighting their way to Japan. Others were pilots in both theaters of the war and yet others walked to Germany (under fire) like Captain Frank Morrow, assigned to a unit that was trapped earlier in the Battle of the Bulge but fought their way out. Some rode with Gen Patton's tanks en route to save the day at Bastone. The list goes on and on.

Guy Howard, an MPD detective, was killed in action in the Pacific while serving in the Marines as a master sergeant. He was the only MPD fatality during this war.

Many others served in Korea. Leo Welch and Art Voss were among the warriors that fought their way to and from the Chosin Reservoir, while Frankie Kessel flew combat jets above.

The trend continued into Vietnam, which funneled many guys into the MPD. The list is quite long, so I am fearful of missing some, but will note that Paul Zabriske, winner of the Silver Star for heroism, is typical of our young double heroes. Each has his story. The story of one, the beloved Harry Lenchner, now eighty-eight, was published in the MPD vets newsletter recently and is presented in its entirety (MPD records and personal knowledge of author).

USS *ARIZONA* SURVIVOR

Detective Norman Coplin, born in Nebraska on November 25, 1919, served in the U.S. Navy prior to and during World War II. He was stationed on the USS *Arizona* in Hawaii's Pearl Harbor on December 7, 1941, during Japan's strike against America. Coplin was one of the 113 men who survived the sinking that cost the lives of 1,177 U.S. Navy sailors. The decorated Coplin was not seriously wounded and helped those who were. He was then transferred to the USS *Lexington* on December 12, serving in the South Pacific until his discharge.

After his military service, Coplin joined the MPD and served many years, most of which as a detective in the burglary unit. Sergeant Coplin died on August 2, 1996 in Broward County, Florida.

Coplin was one of the many MPD officers who served in the military during the war. All of these men are regarded as double heroes (MPD records).

HARRY LENCHNER HONORED

On June 17, 2010, at the opening ceremonies of the Fraternal Order of Police June Conference, a special honor was given to one of its members. The conference was opened by and dedicated to Harry Lenchner. The following bio was read to honor this man.

Harry Lenchner was born in Bronx, New York, on December 6, 1923. He was one of four sons born to immigrant parents. His father was born in a small town in Poland and sailed to the United States by himself at the age of seven. His mother came from Hungary.

Harry spent his youth and his early life growing up in New York City. Then, with the outbreak of World War II, he, like scores of others from the greatest generation, joined the armed forces of the United States after the attack on Pearl Harbor on December 7, 1941.

He was shipped out to boot camp in September 1942 and was assigned to the Norfolk, Virginia, naval base after his graduation in early 1943. He was immediately assigned to a ship and set sail to Casablanca with a naval task force and returned to Norfolk a short time later. His ship was then retrofitted, restocked, and they set sail again traveling through the Panama Canal to Pearl Harbor, Hawaii.

From there, he spent the rest of World War II in the Pacific theater of war where his ship was involved in almost every major naval conflict:

Gilbert and Marshall Islands campaign, 1943-44
Battle of Tarawa, November 20, 1943
Battle of Kwajalein, February 1, 1944
Battle of Eniwetok, February 17, 1944
Mariana and Palau Islands campaign, 1944
Battle of Saipan, June 15, 1944
Battle of the Philippine Sea, June 19-21, 1944
Battle of Guam, July 21, 1944
Battle of Tinian, July 24, 1944
Battle of Peleliu, September 15, 1944
Battle of Angaur, September 17, 1944
Battle of Iwo Jima, February 19, 1945
Battle of Okinawa, April 1, 1945

His ship was also preparing to invade Japan until the Japanese surrendered after the dropping of the atomic bomb in August 1945.

Harry found a home in the navy where he stayed until 1948 traveling the seven seas, sailing into many foreign ports as a Goodwill Ambassador for the United States. With the downsizing of the navy and its personnel, Harry resigned from the navy and joined the ranks of civilian life. He worked for his uncle in the tomato business. Harry continued to travel up and down the East Coast of the United States until the outbreak of the Korean War.

Harry reenlisted in the navy in 1950, serving his county in Korea until 1952.

Upon returning to the U.S., he took it easy for a while then decided it was time to do something else with his life. He decided to take the civil service exams for the fire department, the post office, and the police department. The police department was the first to call him and he joined the MPD in September 29, 1953.

While on the job, Harry was a beat patrolman, since there were no cars or radios for policemen yet. He was promoted to the rank of sergeant in 1962. Once Harry was promoted, he served as a road patrol sergeant and as the radio complaint sergeant. During his tenure with the MPD, he experienced lack of benefits, low wages, and eight-hour/ six-day work weeks with no overtime! All of this for a grand total of $200 dollars a month—before taxes! These are some of the things that prompted Harry and several other members of the MPD to join a group called the Fraternal Order of Police in May 1954. Harry is one of the original charter members of Miami Lodge 20. This lodge and its leaders led the fight to change many of these poor working conditions that existed across the state. During those tough times with no time pools, no funds, and much opposition from the city and others inside the police department, they pressed on. Harry and the others used their own money and vacation time to continue the battle at home and in Tallahassee to help all policemen throughout the state of Florida. Many of the rewards they reaped back then are still being enjoyed today. Harry continued to serve the City of Miami until 1977, when he retired with the rank of lieutenant.

He has been an active member of Miami Lodge 20 and its executive board for over forty years in multiple elected roles. Even after his retirement, Harry stayed on the executive board and served as a trustee and was the lodge's first retiree liaison under Al Cotera. As retiree liaison, Harry kept the retirees informed by phone and by traveling around Florida and elsewhere checking up on all the older retirees and their widows. Harry has always given of himself and could be counted on in every way to assist the brotherhood he helped form so many years ago. He was back then and still is one of the FOP's biggest and most vocal supporters and is a walking history book of the Fraternal Order of Police and the Miami Lodge. He always has time to talk and explain things to the new members and reminds the older ones of the reasons the FOP was formed and the importance of its continuance today. His often colorful and fiery speeches add sparks to any conversation but show what a passion he has for the FOP. The only thing Harry puts above the FOP he says is his love for this, the greatest country ever may she always stand strong, and the dear loved ones and friends he has lost over the years. He regrets that they never got to enjoy the benefits and the way of life that he has because of the FOP and its service to its members.

When State FOP President Jim Preston completed reading this to the members, Harry was greeted with a standing ovation. Once he composed himself, he gave an emotional and humble thank you to the crowd. I can only say I wish everyone that knows him could have been there;

you would have had a tear in your eye like everyone else. We love you, Harry, and God bless (Miami Lodge 20, Fraternal Order of Police).

STORY FROM TOM PAINE

By Officer Tom Paine, MPD Ret.

After graduating with a Spanish degree in 1968 in my hometown of Nashville, I looked for a law enforcement job. An FBI friend told me that the MPD was very progressive and was developing one of the first videotaped mug shot protocols in the country. I also remember reading Chief Walter E. Headley's well-publicized comment on street riots in Miami: "When the looting starts, the shooting starts." OK, I thought, this is for me—strong chief, progressive technology, Spanish-speaking population, and lots of action.

Waiting for the police academy to start, I spent the first couple of months working in a brown cadet uniform, directing drivers in Spanish through a city auto inspection station. This was my first revelation that the foreign language spoken in Miami was not the same Spanish I had learned in school. I also spent several weeks working for Walter Depp in the modus operandi office.

I graduated from the police academy in 1968 with a great group of guys and instructors (too many to name).

Some of my training officers were Gaddy Rawls, Bruce Zipper, and Carl (Tom) Payne. My experiences with Bruce particularly stand out. We would drive down NW Second Avenue and Bruce had me get out, frisk men loitering on the sidewalk, and then put them in the back caged seat. After we had far more than the backseat would hold, we would have them pass their IDs to me over the cage and I would run want checks. We always had hits!

Then there was the time we spotted two robbery suspects who were on foot. They ran into the projects, and next thing I know, Bruce turns the car into a yard after the fleeing suspects. They looked back in disbelief as we gained on them driving between the buildings. Suddenly I realized that Bruce was no longer in the driver's seat but had jumped out of the moving car and caught them both! (The best I could do was to reach over and stop our moving car.)

I loved being on the street as a rookie, but I dreaded the occasional call from the patrol office to come in because the interpreter-clerk was off. I did the rosters and then had to go up to complaint room and act as the Spanish interpreter for incoming calls. I was actually the only interpreter on duty in the city, and I could hardly understand the Cuban Spanish, let alone when they were excited, which was always the case. I don't think I lost too many, however.

After a year in patrol, I was assigned to the newly formed SIU intelligence unit, part of new Chief Bernard Garmire's campaign to make a break with the past. My recollection of the supervisors and members of that new unit: Garland Watkins, Phil Doherty, John Czerenda, Ed LeJeune, Everett Kay, Eugene McCracken, Don Miller, Rafael Aguirre, Dan Bailey, Ted Hirsch, George Kemp, and Paul Tucker.

We updated the old Intelligence files, which consisted of news clippings from around the country of Mafiosi with nicknames wearing fedoras. Ted Hirsch discharged a round next to my foot while "clearing" his 9 mm in our second-floor office at 1145 NW Eleventh Street. Paul Tucker was a goldmine of organized crime information, contacts, and developed many successful cases on which I was privileged to work. Paul taught me how to use the old handi-talkie (with the long antenna and red light when keyed) as a lie detector with suspects (if you don't know, you don't want to know!).

Dade County SO Officer Jacque DeRemer and I worked surveillance of the market gas station watching Frank Martin in action greasing the wheels with judges and defendants. A highlight was personally arresting and reading rights to Mayor David Kennedy.

During the brutal riots, I remember being given a 16 mm camera to film troublemakers. We took rocks and firebombs to our car, and I proudly turned the camera in to ID the next day only to learn that they forgot to put film in it.

After a bomb went off in the second-floor hallway outside the homicide office of the old headquarters building, Phil Doherty rigged up a bogus, but realistic, security screening device with a metal plate and a coaxial cable (that was tucked under the counter) at the front desk. Visitors would place their hands on the plate for what they thought was fingerprint verification! Phil was ahead of his time.

Rafael Aguirre and I worked Cuban organized crime and terrorist groups who were blowing up the city and each other. Rafael was an outstanding intelligence officer and investigator and I was basically his driver/cover. He went on to DEA, working in Colombia, eventually retiring as a supervisor. I remember Rafael got a lead on an Alpha 66 guerilla training camp in the Everglades, and we went out there with Tom Brodie, the Dade County bomb tech. I was leaning over what appeared to be some kind of IED (but wasn't) when Brodie slapped his ham-sized hands together right behind my ears, followed by his low guttural laughter at my reaction to what I thought was an explosion.

I did a stint in training working with Jack Speakman, Mike Buff, and Pat Anderson, and then was assigned as the MPD strategic planner working for Keith Bergstrom keeping track of the MMPD (Miami Modern PD) bond funds and setting up planning systems.

As the lieutenant in planning and inspections, I worked with a "dream team," consisting of Captain George Green, Colleen Westmoreland, Wilhemina Porter, Ray Anderson, Bill Berger, Dean Dejong, Ray Kulzick, Ted Leamons, Bill O'Brien, Maria Pedrajo, Doug Rice, and Bobby Williams. If I've omitted anyone, it's the advancing years!

I haven't done justice to these and the many other people at the MPD for whom I had the highest regard, but you know who you are.

In 1982, I took a position in Colorado Springs as the police department's civilian planning manager, retiring in 2004. Over the years, I kept up with the trials and tribulations of the MPD. However, I wouldn't trade my MPD experiences for the world. I cherish those wonderful relationships, camaraderie, adventures, and accomplishments, and they are forever embedded in my mind.

Author's Note: Tom Paine, who contributed this article, was plucked from patrol early in his career due to him being extremely intelligent and proficient in both speaking and reading Spanish, and placed into our intelligence squad. His invaluable work will long be remembered. Officers such as Tom will keep our department in the top ranks of law enforcement.

DUI KILLS BILL CRAIG

Thirty-seven-year-old Bill Craig, a fourteen-year veteran Miami police motorcycle officer, was struck by a drunk driver on South Dixie in early morning rush-hour traffic on March 19, 1988, as he was heading for work on his motor and critically injured. Craig, married with two children, lingered at the hospital in critical condition for three months before expiring.

The driver had a record of two other DUIs and was operating on a suspended license that morning. Sean Ward, twenty-eight, pled no contest to the manslaughter and drunken driving charges and was sentenced to twelve years. He was released after three years' imprisonment.

Craig grew up in Tampa but came to Miami in 1974 to join the Miami force. He was a highly decorated officer who also was assigned as a SWAT team officer (no. 13).

I was the shift captain on Platoon A when Bill graduated from the academy and was assigned to Platoon A. I found him to be a very good officer who was serious about being a top officer, a goal he achieved as his career progressed. His wife, Debbie, and children are now living in a Phoenix suburb (MPD records).

CRASH KILLS CANALEJO

Twenty-eight-year-old MPD officer Osvaldo Canalejo was killed at dawn on October 13, 1992, in a traffic accident when his police vehicle was broadsided by an elderly man who ran a red light. Canalejo, a five-year veteran of the Miami force, died of internal injuries an hour later. He became the thirty-third Miami officer killed in the line of duty.

The sixty-two-year-old man who was driving the car that struck Canalejo had run the red light at Coral Way and Twenty-second Avenue and was charged with the accident and fined $575 and had his driver's license revoked for one year.

Canalejo, a Miami High School graduate, joined the MPD in 1987 and was assigned to the south station in Little Havana. Osvaldo was survived by his parent and buried at Woodlawn Park Cemetery with full police honors (Wilbanks, *Forgotten Heroes*, 1996; and MPD records).

FREAK ACCIDENT KILLS SANTIAGO

Around 10:00 PM on May 30, 1995, Officer Carlos Santiago, forty-seven, a thirteen-year veteran of MPD, and his partner Jose Paz were working the night shift when they spotted a man breaking into a car at North River Drive and First Street, a block from the Flagler Street bridge. Bystanders advised the officers that the vehicle may belong to the bridge tender. The officers drove to the bridge and Santiago exited his car to walk to the tender's booth. The bridge was being repaired and was in an "up" position. The side where Santiago approached was dark as thieves had stolen the copper wiring that provided the lighting to the sidewalk. Suddenly, Santiago fell through a three-foot opening in the span and fell fifty feet to a concrete platform. The fall killed him immediately as efforts to revive him by Fire Rescue was futile.

Santiago was a Jackson High School graduate and an army veteran. He joined the MPD in 1982 and, over the next thirteen years, received numerous commendations while working the night shift in patrol.

Carlos was survived by his wife and two children as well as his brother, Octavio Santiago, who was also a Miami police officer when Carlos was killed. Octavio has now retired.

Carlos was buried at Woodlawn Cemetery in Miami (MPD records and Wilbanks, *Forgotten Heroes*, 1996).

BLUE GLUE

Thirty years after politically correct police administrators disbanded the highly effective MPD crime prevention squad, the task force survivors, sixty strong, gathered in Ormond Beach, Florida, in 1999 for a onetime reunion. Assembling the group was facilitated by a simple website prepared by the spouse of one of the members, Lynn Appleget. This website enabled the committee to coordinate the event and search nationwide for the living members. The effort was spurred by Ron Eisaman and Tom Jurkowski, who recruited Paul Tucker, Dick Witt, me, and several other members.

At the conclusion of the 1999 reunion, member George Green inquired as to when the next gathering would be held. The author informed him that this was a onetime effort but that we would use this model to bring all retired members of the department together using the mode of the Internet, supplemented by quarterly newsletters. An organization was formed in January 2000 and it is running strong with over eight hundred members twelve years later. The succeeding website, also designed by Lynn, has both a public area and a member-only portion that has been visited almost one million times by the members (www.mpdvets.org).

The combined newsletters, 48 ten-page quarterlies, would fill a book with close to five hundred pages and will serve as historical basis of our MPD history in the twenty-first century.

This organization has truly been the "blue glue" that has kept us together.

Several years ago, our vice president Harvey Bach proposed awarding funds toward college scholarships for the children and grandchildren of our Miami Police Veterans Association members. To date, over 140 awards have been presented to a group of great young people. The funds were received from the association members only and no public solicitation was done.

Any net proceeds from this book will be donated to the MPVA scholarship fund. Purchasers of this publication will not only enjoy our history but will be contributing to the further education of some of our great youth.

The original 1960s task force accomplishments cannot be scribed in this overall history of the department due to space limitations. The surviving veterans who served in this unit and attended our emotional reunion can always be quite proud of their association with this unit. The task force officers were the best of the best—a true band of brothers (Personal knowledge of the author).

FAST RISE—FAST FALL

They seemed to come out of nowhere. Bob and Don Warshaw both joined the MPD in the early 1970s, shortly after their arrival in Miami from northern climes. After a decade of service at the police officer rank, both were vaulted to high staff positions within the department by Chief Ken Harms and Chief Herb Breslow in the early 1980s. Both brothers were smart, articulate, savvy, and politically nimble.

Brother Bob, with the rank of police officer, became Harms's aide-de-camp. Two years later, Bob was appointed to the rank of assistant chief of police. Don was an officer in the Public Service Aide program prior to jumping over several ranks to be appointed a major's position by Chief Breslow. The brothers attained these high ranks without serving at any of the intervening civil service ranks. A previous longstanding departmental rule of selecting majors from the ranks of lieutenant or above and selecting assistant chiefs from the rank of captain or above was either changed or circumvented quietly.

Chief Harms's firing in 1984 had no effect on either of the Warshaw's employment status, although brother Bob left the department when Harms's replacement, Chief Breslow, retired a year later. Bob went on to serve as chief of police in two other out-of-state cities and then served as deputy drug czar under President Clinton. He is now a law enforcement consultant.

Don was promoted to assistant chief in 1993 and appointed as chief of police in 1995, replacing Calvin Ross. Don was well liked in the community and the department as well and appeared to be a competent administrator. By virtue of his position as chief, he was placed on the board of directors of a youth crime prevention program called "Do the Right Thing," which were well funded.

In 1999, the city commission appointed Don Warshaw as the city manager with the heavy backing of Mayor Corollo. Events soon changed that backing. When the Cuban youth Elian Gonzalez found drifting on a raft while accompanying his mother in an escape from Cuba and was removed from a relative's home in Little Havana with the assistance of Miami officers, the mayor demanded that Warshaw fire the chief of police Bill O'Brien. When Warshaw refused, he in turn was fired.

An investigation then revealed that Warshaw and an accountant friend, Ron Sterns, had been taking significant amounts of funds from the charity fund for their own personal use. Don Warshaw was arrested on four federal counts of fraud and one of conspiracy. Stern committed suicide and left an incriminating note. Don was convicted and served ten months at a federal prison. The pension board then took away his police pension.

Don still is in the Miami area as a private consultant.

POST-TRAUMATIC STRESS

DÉJÀ VU (ALL OVER AGAIN)

Yogi Berra was right. You may recall the earlier story in the late 1930s about Chief Rowland confiscating the illegal slot machines around town and arresting the owners. The corrupt elected commissioners (not all) led by Mayor Williams fired Chief Rowland. It was discovered that the owners of these slots contributed heavily to Williams's election campaign. Later, Williams himself was arrested and tossed out of office for corruption charges.

As I was completing this book, Chief Mike Exposito, a thirty-seven-year MPD veteran (and a true professional), was confiscating illegal video poker machines and arresting the owners. The mayor subsequently fired Chief Exposito. It was later revealed that the owners of these machines contributed heavily to Mayor Reglado's election campaign.

As we close out, word has it that the federal authorities are investigating the current city leaders.

This pattern of controlling the police department's standard in enforcing laws in order to facilitate shady and unlawful actions by politicians is replicated in numerous American cities now, as well as in the past.

The author was fortunate to have toiled with many honest, intelligent, and professional officers. The list is many, including Chiefs Garmire, Denham, Klimkowski, Dickson, and Watkins; staff officers Ken Fox, Gene Gunn, Bill Harries, Newell Horne, and Charlie Price; commanders John Ross, Raul Martinez, Jack Farr, Dick Witt, Emory Putman, Paul Shepard, Don March, George Green, Paul Oboz, Kelly England, Jim Reese, Mary Stair, Harvey Bach, Carolyn Smith, Bill Starks, Harold

Whitaker, Joe Green, Leroy Smith; and many, many others. A host of these leaders moved on to head other agencies, including Dick Witt being chief of Hollywood PD and two others, Emory Putman heading up Mt. Dora PD. John Ross, Dave Rivero, Billy Riggs, Larry Boemler, Gwen Boyd, Nancy Olon, Vince Landis were just a few that went to head other various law enforcement agencies. Bill Berger is currently the U.S. marshal for Florida, and Ray Martinez is the chief of Miami Beach PD.

These and numerous others attended the FBI Academy, Southern Police Institute, Northwestern Traffic Institute, and other leading venues of higher education for police leaders with many attaining degrees from local universities. These officers were a credit to the Miami PD and to the City of Miami. I am proud of them all. These officers may not be Miami household names as they were not the subject of stories that the news media loves—corruption and gossip. These men and women came to work daily and did an outstanding job day in and day out during their twenty-five or more years of service.

The job was not all peaches and cream. Lieutenant Curry, back in the late 1910s, stepped in for the chief of police for several months while the boss was ill. Curry did an outstanding job according to press reports at that time. The first week of Chief Dillon's return to work, he fired Lieutenant Curry—for no reason.

Chief Guy Reeve took over a soiled department following the arrest of Chief Quigg and others back in 1928. Reeve started classroom training for the officers, enforced the rules and regulations strictly, and introduced many new procedures into the department. After the appointment of the Miami Klan leader Sam McCreary as public safety director in 1930, Reeve was put on the hot seat and finally resigned to go on to be the chief of detectives at Dade County and later to be the U.S. marshal for Florida.

Chief Headley's reputation was constantly besmirched by Mayor High, but big Walter prevailed.

Ken Harms was fired at three o'clock in the morning by the city manager because Ken resisted the manager's improper and illegal moves to have the department a dumping ground for the manager's unqualified, non-law enforcement buddies.

These are just a few antidotes to highlight the political interference of politicians that can be observed in most police departments nationwide.

Lastly, how does the job of policing affect the men and women who perform their tasks day in and day out? We hear much these days of PTSD in the military and how the battles affect the soldiers for years after they end their service. The average police officer sees horrible things daily—year after year—that the ordinary citizen most likely will not encounter in a lifetime.

The following story is how one call—yes, just one call—affected one officer for decades after his service. We are fortunate that the intelligent officer went on to become a medical doctor and is able to describe the case from both the viewpoint of a police officer and a medical expert.

It will cause you to think about the policeman's lot for many years to come.

KISSING A DEAD GIRL

By Dr. Vince Skilling, MPD Vet

It was a hot, sunny day in August in the Florida Keys. The seas were almost calm and a slight southeasterly breeze cooled the skin under the T-top of my boat. We were returning to land with a day's limit of lobsters collected earlier. Once inside the "No Wake" zone of Tavernier Creek, it seemed like we were quietly inching our way toward bayside. On board were my wife, Nan; one friend of almost sixty years; and another friend, now retired, from MPD. We talked about growing up and policing in Miami. The city had morphed from small southern city to international megalopolis earlier in our lives. All of us were now living in other cities both close and far away from Miami.

My childhood friend and I were recounting adventures we had along the bay front in our neighborhood known as the Brickell Area. Then I had a flashback to an incident, a tragic one that happened in 1970 while I was a police officer on patrol in the old neighborhood. I briefly recounted the story, which had lain, without attention, in my memory for many, many years.

It was of the death of a girl at Vizcaya, a local tourist attraction. I told of the impact it had on me personally. It was a very unpleasant life experience. My police friend commented, "We didn't have counseling back then." I thought to myself, "Yeah, back then the only cops that went for counseling were ordered there by divorce courts. Any other reason for counseling would bring the label 'sissy' or 'psycho' by the other cops."

I had a personal demon that was born of that incident way back when. That night it came back and interrupted my sleep. It rewound the tape in my mind and played it back over and over again. It hung around and would not go away, even after we returned home to Georgia.

From my studies in psychiatry and psychology, I knew how to start dealing with this type of disturbance. By writing about it, I could bring all of it out in the open. Only then could I begin to understand the issues and start resolving the problem. So I sat down at my word processor and started to write. I barely got into the story when I become emotionally overwhelmed. Tears started running down my cheeks. The tape was now being played as an IMAX-sized image in my mind. I pushed forth writing in slow motion until my emotional energy ran out. Nan saw what was happening to me and tried to assuage my emotions with sympathy. When that didn't work, she said, "Maybe you need to see a counselor. You know that Jim would be happy to talk to you about this." I agreed.

Jim is a licensed, professional counselor with a wealth of life experiences. A military vet, he had worked in many fields from EMT to business sales and management. He was now an ordained Lutheran minister who did counseling as a vocation. We had known each other for several years and had mutual respect for our professions. I called him and he said, "How about this afternoon?"

After a few pleasantries, we sat down in his office and I started telling the story. The words flowed with ease, and surprisingly, there was little emotional overlay—only a couple of tears. Jim recounted to me what I just told him to make sure he understood what had been said. I agreed; his accuracy was close to 100%.

"How did you cope with this when it happened?"

"I drank heavily for a couple of days."

"Are you drinking now?"

"No, I'm not. I know that didn't work before. Besides, I know that to solve this problem, I have to write about it. I started to do that, and it has become very painful. That's why I came to see you."

He said that he was pretty sure he knew what was going on with me. However, it would do me no good for him to tell me. He said that I needed to go back and slug it out with the word processor, finish the story.

"This isn't about the girl. It's all about *you*. You got beaten up pretty bad by this and it's not going away until *you* do something about it. When you finish writing, put it down for a couple of days, then go back and reread it. Things will be much clearer to you. Then come back and see me."

Summer 1970

My first assignment after I graduated from the Miami Police Academy was a two-man unit in 10 sector—Liberty City. From January through May, my knowledge base and experience in police work had been on a steep growth curve. I answered calls for service ranging from the frequent and most dangerous domestic disturbances to homicides and every imaginable type of assault and robbery. I wrote traffic accident reports (tedious, time consuming) and traffic tickets. There were court appearances that resulted from arrests I made, shifts with young and aggressive officers or old-timers who were just biding their time until retirement. The work schedule was one of swing shifts: four weeks midnights; four weeks afternoons; four weeks days.

May was a tragic month as one of my classmates, Rolland Lane, was murdered by a black shooter. I noticed that some classmates on my shift had started riding by themselves in one-man units, usually starting in the less-stressful sectors—20, 30, and 60. Those assignments involved lots of report writing and not many active felony crimes. Like most rookies, I could not wait to be able to work alone. I reasoned this as the final step in becoming a fully trained, self-sufficient, and well-rounded police officer. The next recruit class was due to graduate and I wanted to be riding alone when they hit the street. I spoke with the shift commander, Captain Frank Morrow, and he agreed with my request to ride alone starting at the next shift change.

Shift change on swing shifts was trying on everyone's biorhythm. Midnight shift transferred at 7:00 AM, and then turned around to work again at 3 PM as the afternoon shift. Sleep was fragmented and then abruptly cut short by having to report back to work less than eight hours later. The roll-call room was full of grumbling officers from the lowest to the highest ranking. I had not slept very much in anticipation of my new status and felt energized just thinking about it. I was wired.

As the administrative sergeant read out the assignments and car numbers, I bounced up and down on my tiptoes. When I heard my name called, I could not believe the sector and zone: 961—the Brickell neighborhood—where I grew up and still lived. This was a dream come true. I was going to police *my* neighborhood. I would be the Man.

With my equipment loaded in the cruiser, I picked up the microphone and checked into service.

I headed east on NW Eleventh Street, south on Seventh Avenue, then straight into North River Drive. At SW Second Avenue, I turned right and entered the territory of 961. Crossing the Miami River, I was elated at seeing the familiar buildings and streets that I had known for all of my life. At SW Eighth Street, I headed east and noted the decreasing numbers of the cross avenues until I reached South Miami Avenue. Brickell Avenue was next, and as I drove toward the end of Eighth Street, a new bridge reached out to the undeveloped Burlingame Island. This ten-acre parcel grew from a spoil bank when the channels for the Miami River were dredged years before.

To my left stood the home of William and Mary Brickell who cofounded the City of Miami. Their original two-thousand-acre property started at the bay and coursed west and then south to Coconut Grove. It was bisected by U.S. Highway 1 (Brickell Avenue) and South Miami Avenue. A diagonal section was called the "Roads." To my right were the Four Ambassadors. These towering buildings did not exist in my childhood. Along with my buds, we used to walk along the bay front from SE Eighth Street all the way to Vizcaya. We owned it. It was the source of entertainment and adventure all year long.

Turning onto the newly created South Bayshore Drive, the asphalt cut across the original estates that lined the bay all the way to SE Eleventh Street. The Ocean Ranch Hotel, where I learned to swim, was a pile of rubble surrounded by a chain-link fence. Like many other bay-front properties, it was slated for "development," which meant another high-rise building.

At SE Fourteenth Street, a left turn took me into Pointe Vue's bayside drive. A new wide seawall lined the shore where I had spent hours fishing. In the winter, I had gigged buckets of mullet as they migrated across the bay. During the spring tides, I netted shrimp at night by the light of a Coleman lantern.

The first two condominium apartments built on the legendary millionaire's estates of Pointe Vue faced the bay. On either side the old McMansions were in various stages of demolition as they fell to the plans of the developers. The Academy of the Assumption was still open.

This religious boarding school for girls was slowly being squeezed by other high-rise buildings.

Driving south on Brickell Avenue, more of the original bay-front estates were being replaced with bizarre-looking high-rises, some painted in colors that did not please the eye. These monstrosities blocked the prevailing easterly breezes from where I lived on South Miami Avenue. The nighttime sky was punctuated with flashing red lights on top of the buildings.

At SW Twenty-sixth Road, a giant twirling shark marked the entrance to Rickenbacker Causeway and, more important to me, the start of the Brickell Avenue Extension. These bay-front estates were isolated from the heavy traffic of U.S. 1 as it coursed north into Brickell Avenue. This seven-block stretch of shaded road held about ten bay-front homes that I could only dream of owning. Ahead at SW Thirty-second Road was the forbiddingly high wall that surrounded Vizcaya, the estate of one of the original captains of industry—James Deering.

The wall ended at the bay, and at low tide, we simply walked around its end and into fifty acres of native hardwood forest and an unspoiled stretch of the original bay front. A series of tidewater pools extended into the woods and provided a target rich environment for gigging. Farther down the coastline stood the magnificent Italian-style mansion and gardens that had been left to Dade County and was now operated as a tourist attraction.

Sneaking around the property, we learned the layout of the woods, house, and gardens. Often our visits were interrupted by the security guards who ran us off. Once, on a dare, I jumped off a ledge and into the mansion's swimming pool. Upon surfacing, I found myself abandoned by my friends and the center of attention to a gathering group of tourists. I ran into the woods and hid from the guards until the coast was clear.

Approaching South Miami Avenue, I saw a speeding car cross in front of me and almost become airborne as it hit the big hump in the middle of the intersection. I pursued the car at speeds up to 60 mph and pulled it over close to SW Seventeenth Avenue. The driver, a male in expensive clothing, bragged that he knew all the judges and would beat the ticket. "Sure," I said, "Say 'Hi' to them for me."

"Typical asshole," I thought to myself as I handed him the hard copy.

Now I had something to enter on my worksheet as I had not been given a call in almost three hours. Heading back north, I passed the northbound entrance to I-95, which was still under construction. Some jerk was moving the sawhorses apart to gain access from SW Twenty-fifth Road. "What are you doing?" I said into the loudspeaker. He quickly moved the sawhorses back and drove off. "Another asshole," I mused.

Radio chatter had been light. The two Coconut Grove units, 964 and 965, were busy with the usual activity in that area: hippies panhandling along Main Highway, domestic arguments in the low-income housing around Grand and Douglas, an accident at Twenty-seventh Avenue and South Dixie Highway, daytime burglaries discovered when people came home after work, drunks at the Dinner Key Marina. Units 963 and 962 had a couple of calls. I still had none. My drive down the memory lane of my youth continued uninterrupted by any calls for police service.

A request for dinner was approved without hesitation by the complaint sergeant. I wanted Cuban food from a small one-counter café. I ordered a Bistec de Palomilla sandwich, congris, maduros, and flan. I relished my most favorite Cuban meal.

Back in service with time to spare, I headed toward Simpson Park on South Miami Avenue. Farther south on the avenue was the block-long estate of former Cuban president Carlos Prio. Across from the Holiday Inn at Brickell and Twenty-fifth Road was the tropical forest we called Buzzard Woods—home to seasonal buzzards that decorated the green tree leaves with their white droppings.

The droning sound of the car's air conditioner was abruptly punctuated with a loud, piercing beep from the radio. Long, silent seconds passed before the emergency call was broadcast:

"962, a 332 [emergency—aggravated assault], 961 and 963, a 315 [emergency backup]. The garden at Vizcaya—woman down."

I turned on my blue light and siren as I pulled onto Brickell Avenue and sped off toward Vizcaya—less than one mile away. Entering at the main gate, I sped down the narrow driveway toward the house and gardens. Unit 963 was already there, looking around for which way to go from the parking lot.

"Follow me," I shouted as I ran past him, "I know exactly where to go." We both ran down the footpath that led to the gardens. The sun had set and twilight was erasing the shadows. Ahead a group of people were standing in a semicircle around someone lying on the ground. They were all looking down. Some were holding on to each other, some crying, nobody moving. Getting closer, I saw that they were looking at a girl lying on her back. She was looking up at the sky.

"How many times have I seen this scenario?" I thought to myself. "Someone injured and everyone standing around DOING NOTHING, ABSOLUTELY NOTHING!" Fire Rescue Captain George Bilberry's class on CPR kicked in as I dropped to my knees at her side and shook her shoulders.

"Hey, hey, hey, you all right?" Now she was looking at me, I thought. I did not notice that her gaze was vacant.

Jaw thrust, pinch nose, two quick rescue breaths. After the first breath, my mouth filled with fluid. A salty, metallic taste spread across my tongue. I spit it out and began chest compressions.

Something was not right. Her chest did not rebound. As I pushed down, it felt like hard, lumpy mush. I heard a crackling, grinding, sloshing sound with each compression. Looking back at her face, I saw dark blood pouring out of her nose and mouth. She was looking back up at the sky. I felt a hand grab one of my shoulders.

"She's dead, Officer," I heard a distant voice say. The voice got closer and louder.

"She's dead, Officer, you can't help her. I am a doctor, she's dead."

Then I heard nothing, only pure silence.

The hand pulled me back away from the girl. I stood up and looked around, everything was in slow motion. Everyone was staring at me. I looked at the girl; she was still staring at the sky. Only now her mouth open and dark blood was running down her chin and cheeks.

Someone was pointing at me. I wiped my mouth and looked down to see blood on my hand, on my white uniform shirt. I was horrified. The silence got louder. Now it was roaring in my ears. People's mouths were moving but I could hear nothing.

I backed into a big coral rock planter that was lying on its side. I sat down, swung my legs to the other side, stood up, and started to run.

"Run away!" The stares of the crowd were following me.

"Run faster. Got to get to my car, now!" The path is dark.

"There it is, door open, engine still running."

I get in, slam the door, and grab the microphone.

"Nine Twelve O-Nine."

"Nine Twelve QSY to channel 1," the dispatcher corrected me.

"I mean Nine Sixty-One, Nine-Six-One. O-Nine."

"QSL Nine-Six-One, O-Nine, Twenty Fifty."

I left the scene and drove around aimlessly. From time to time I looked in the rearview mirror at her blood around my mouth. I wiped my mouth on my sleeve. The steering wheel was sticky from her blood on my hand.

"I've got to clean up. Where can I go? Got to go to the fire station, it has a clean bathroom."

"Nine-Six-One, gimme a Ten—SW Twelfth Avenue and Thirteenth Street."

"QSL Nine Sixty-One, a Ten. Twenty-one Thirteen Hours."

I parked on the side of the fire station and walked past a couple of firefighters who were sitting on folding chairs in the driveway.

"Hey, buddy, you have to clean somebody's clock?" said one.

"Or did someone clean yours for you?" chimed in the other.

I washed my hands and face several times. I could not stop looking in the mirror at my eyes. My eyes became her eyes and I saw her face looking at me with that same vacant stare. Time was suspended. I was now standing in my own bathroom looking in the mirror and seeing her. I don't remember how I got home.

She was still there looking at me. I was looking at her. The images alternated back and forth between the plain one, the bloody one, and my own face. It was a horror movie playing just for me.

I cleaned her blood off my badge and name tag. I put on a clean, starched uniform shirt and got back into my car. I started driving but don't remember where. I was in the Twilight Zone. Then I heard my call sign come over the radio.

"Nine Sixty—One."

"Sixty-One, K?"

"Are you clear your Ten?"

"QSL."

"QSL Nine Sixty—One, O-Nine, O-Six. Twenty-two Fifty-five. City of Miami Department of Communications, K-I-D Three Eighty-One."

At the transfer point, I turned the car over to an oncoming officer.

"Tank's almost empty," he said. "You musta had a busy shift."

As I walked into the roll-call room, I felt that everyone was looking at me.

"Hey, Doc." It was one of the guys from the Vizcaya call.

"What's it like to kiss a dead girl? Hahahahaha." He was sitting on the countertop with his legs swinging back and forth. Heads turned, other officers were staring at me.

"Fuckyouinthefaceyoulittleimmigrantasswipe," I thought to myself. "Why don't you go back to your banana republic and shove a big plantain up your ass."

"Skilling, HEY, SKILLING! Where's your worksheet?" It was my sector sergeant.

"Come on, hurry up, I want to go home."

"What was your ending mileage?"

"I dunno."

"All you did for eight hours was one backup and write one ticket. And this 10 signal, what were you doing for two hours, playing pocket pool?"

"I . . . I don't want to talk about it."

"Well, if you want to make probation, this kind of worksheet won't win you any points. Better shape up!"

In the dark parking lot, I threw my gear in the backseat of my car and changed into a T-shirt.

I drove to my regular watering hole. It was cool inside and had the familiar smell of tobacco smoke and booze. I went straight to the bar, sat down, took out my Marlboros, and leaned on my elbows. I ordered a double: scotch-rocks.

"Bar or Call?" asked the barmaid.

"JW Black, please. And line me up another."

I slugged down the first and started on the second. I was oblivious to everything, everyone who was in the bar, the music, everything.

"What's the matter, honey?" she asked. "You look like you have just lost your best friend. Didja get jilted by some girl?"

"No, I don't want to talk about it. I'll take another." And pushed the glass toward her.

"Just leave me alone," I said to myself.

I lit up a cigarette and just sat, smoked, and stared off into space. The events of the evening were running through my mind at warp speed. They jumped back and forth, in sequence, out of sequence, snapshots in still life, fast-forward and reverse, total confusion. Nothing seemed to make sense.

More scotch, another cigarette, tears running down my cheeks. No sobs, another double, and another, and another. I don't remember how many I drank.

"What are you crying about?" interrupted the barmaid. She put her face close to mine, eyebrows turned inward.

"I haven't seen this much water on my bar since hurricane Donna. Tell me, honey, what's bothering you? I know you're hurting."

"Just bring me another."

"No, baby, you have had way too much. You need to go home now."

"Please, just a couple more. Please?"

"No, no more! You are getting drunk. Go home!" She was getting angry. "I don't know what your problem is, but if you don't leave, I'll call the duty captain."

I took all the bills out of my wallet, slammed them on the bar. I stood up, took a deep breath, and headed for the door, which now was a moving target. As I was groping for the door pull, the barmaid grabbed my hand and put some of the bills in it.

Looking at me face-to-face, she said, "Here's your change. You want me to call you a cab?"

I couldn't look at her, "Naw, just leave me alone."

I don't remember much else after that. I did drive home and pass out in my bed. Back to work the next day, I rode alone in another zone. That night I drank at home, alone. I kept this routine up for a couple of days.

Then, without warning, a "civil disturbance" broke out in Liberty City. I was put back up there in a two-man unit. Everyone worked double shifts for roughly a week—sixteen hours on, eight hours off. No leave time was allowed. The contrast was mind-boggling. The area I had worked in, the one that I remembered as an everyday neighborhood, was now like a war zone. Business buildings were on fire, gunshots punctuating the day and night, looting was rampant. Fire and fire rescue vehicles were getting vandalized and trashed. Here and there mobs of angry people would form and disperse in the blink of an eye. Rocks and bottles were the order of the day. I would go home, drink, and go back to work the next day. The riot ended as quickly as it started.

After working about ten consecutive days, I finally got three days off. A friend from high school was home from the army. We got together and commiserated over our experiences. We comforted each other then drank away our demons. Mine came from the girl at Vizcaya. Hers came from rehabilitating wounded warriors from the Vietnam War. My person was dead. Hers were living, maimed with traumatic brain injuries, amputations, shrapnel, burns, and other disfiguring wounds.

Going back to work, I started to forget the Vizcaya incident. I believed that I had coped with the problem. It was now ancient history. I tired of all the drinking.

A few years passed and I entered medical school. In my senior year, I did a clinical clerkship at the Dade County Medical Examiner's Office. I was considering a residency in forensic pathology.

While at DCME, I read the autopsy report and viewed the photos of the girl. Her chest and abdomen had been crushed. The great vessels and organs of those cavities were described as being "dissected, avulsed, fractured, macerated, torn, lacerated, etc."

She was killed outright when a massive coral rock planter fell on her. The picture of her face was exactly as I remembered her. It was all very "clinical" and did not bother me at all. I had no "flashbacks," no sleep disturbances, or other signs and symptoms of post-traumatic stress. After all, the demon was gone forever. Or so I thought.

Miami—1916

To create his winter residence, James Deering brought over one thousand craftsmen and laborers to Miami from around the world. At the time, it was estimated that this workforce represented 10 percent of the of the city's 1916 population. The main material for this Italian Renaissance mansion, gardens, and village was Cuban limestone and coral rock mined locally in South Florida.

Coral rock is limestone. A mineral (calcium carbonate) laced with inorganic grains. They come from the skeletal fragments of marine organisms such as coral and foraminifera. Coral rock will effervesce and weaken when exposed to salt or acidic air pollutants. Wind and rain enhance the process by washing away the effervescent powdery residue. This exposes more rock to the natural destructive forces and further weakens its structure.

Miami—1970

Debbie Pushkin was a student at Shenandoah Junior High in Miami. She and a group of her friends had gone on a summer outing to Vizcaya. They were probably not very interested in Vizcaya's history, architecture, paintings, tapestries, furniture, or plants. In the gardens, they were horsing around the massive coral rock planters that were shaped like giant vases on narrow stems. Fifty some odd years of exposure to salt air and the elements, along with a number of hurricanes, had taken a toll on the coral rock from which the vases had been carved. One of Debbie's friends jokingly pushed a planter toward her. It snapped at the stem and fell fully on her torso before rolling to a stop.

Most likely the police complaint room was given little information other than a woman was hurt and she was lying on the ground. That phone call set into motion a series of events in which I became involved. Those events would culminate in me personally being confronted for the first time with the vultures of human misery that feed on the ego. I was not prepared for that massive emotional assault.

My actions that evening brought me in contact with Debbie's humanity, the witness of which was on my tongue, face, hands, and white uniform shirt. Everyone present saw what I tried to do. My ego was bombarded with feelings of failure and embarrassment. I was humiliated in front of my peers by comments made about what I did. Following that, there was the unintentional indifference of what was said to me about my work product. Nobody knew the storm that was brewing in my mind.

With limited life experience, I could not comprehend the entirety of the situation. My ego was traumatized. I was angry but did not know at what. I had done what I was trained to do. I had not done anything wrong. In order to deal with the overload of negative emotions, I drank heavily. It was the only way I knew to cope with the situation, to ease the pain. My ego was the demon I drowned out of my memory. The repression was powerful. It interrupted the cycle of grief for forty years. I still had unfinished business to attend to.

The energetic imprint of that night lay in my brain until I recalled it that August day in 2010. Talking about it triggered its release. The "flashback" was a powerful discharge of stored emotional energies, like a taser, to my brain and body. It was a signal that the confusing and frightening circumstances of that event still needed to be resolved.

Resolution of traumatic events and circumstances only comes through grieving. Grief, and all other reactions to emotional trauma, is uniquely individual. It is an emotional "fingerprint" of singularly particular circumstances and how they affect us. The grief cycle is normal; it is a useful perspective for understanding our own and other people's reaction to personal trauma and change, irrespective of cause.

Kissing a Dead Girl
Epilogue

While writing the story, I was able to examine my wealth of life experiences and relate them to what happened to me. Through these experiences, I learned how to understand and cope with my emotions. By recognizing them for what they are, and admitting them, I could bring them out in the open and deal with them. Trying to hide or drown them would only delay the inevitable.

As a physician, death was a frequent visitor to the hospital. Be it a "code" in a patient's room, a stillborn in Labor and Delivery, a trauma in the emergency room, or a desperate surgical operation that went south. My personal involvement was clinical; I could understand what was going on from a medical standpoint and not be bothered by it. The exceptions were the pediatric and adolescent patients. Then I was bothered, but not driven to drink.

When I finished writing the story, it was free from the denial that hid it from my conscious mind. I now understand what happened to me that night and I can deal with it. My friend Jim was correct in what he said—it was all about me.

ONCE BLUE, ALWAYS BLUE

Miami Police Worksheet

by Chief Phil Doherty (Ret.)

Assistant Chief of Police, Miami, Florida

Founder and President (2000-2010), Miami Police Veterans Association

P.O. Box 291121
Port Orange, FL 32129
August 2012

Proceeds derived from this book will be contributed to the Scholarship Fund of the Miami Police Veterans Association (MPVA)

President: Harvey Bach
Vice President: Lyriss Underwood
Secretary: Anne Atchison
Treasurer: Charles W. Reynolds
Director: Dr. Vince Skilling
Past President and Director: Phil Doherty

ACKNOWLEDGMENTS

Many MPD stories are exchanged at our various retiree functions each year. And of course, the crowd numbers dwindle yearly as the grim reaper calls more often. Retired Lieutenant Harvey Bach, the current president of the Miami Police Veterans Association, has been urging me to document some of these rich stories before they are lost in time. Two years ago, he talked me into doing the book (actually he conned me into it) by suggesting we publish the book in an attempt to obtain additional college scholarship funds for our organization. His encouragement has been the juice that kept the project going. Harvey will also be designing the cover and will manage the sales and marketing of our product.

The stories of our slain MPD officers are dear to our hearts naturally. Many thanks to Dr. William Wilbanks for giving us permission to use excepts from his excellent and detailed book *Forgotten Heroes* (1996), which contain stories about slain officers who toiled for departments within Dade County. We are grateful to him.

Thanks also to Tammy Larkin for use of her grandfather Forest Nelson's photo on the cover.

A thanks also to Major Joe Longueria, Ret. (another history buff), for his assistance in this endeavor.

The Internet (home of a thousand libraries) sources have been invaluable, particularly the *Metropolis/Miami News* online archives via the University of Florida. Hundreds of hours were spent reading nationwide newspapers, police reports, and other material that helped us fill in the blanks of history.

To MPD folks who provided a story, thanks. The stories direct from you far exceeds our version, I am sure. No doubt there are countless more stories out there. Why not share them?

ABOUT THE AUTHOR

Phil Doherty, a New England native, joined the Miami Police Department in 1960 at age twenty-one after completing a four-year stint in the air force. He rose through the ranks, attaining promotions every three years: PFC in 1963, sergeant in 1966, lieutenant in 1969, captain in 1972, major in 1975, and assistant chief in 1978.

Phil attended Miami-Dade, University of Miami, Florida International University, and took short courses at the University of California, Michigan State, University of Georgia, St. Pete Jr. College, Nova University, the FBI Academy, U.S. Secret Service, and completed the commanding officer course at the University of Louisville's Southern Police Institute, where he topped the class.

During his years at MPD, he excelled in a variety of positions, including patrol and task force officer and supervisor, accident investigator and anti-corruption vice squads, patrol lieutenant and captain, robbery tactical CO, inspections CO, SIU (Intelligence) CO, and commander of the vast patrol section for three years.

His last assignment was as assistant chief, where he headed up both the operations division and the administrative division.

Over the years, he has been active in Miami's police organizations, including fifty-plus years as a member of the FOP and PBA (serving periods on the executive boards of each). He founded and was president of the Miami Retired Fire and Police Association and was the founder and ten-year president of the Miami Police Veterans Association, implementing websites, newsletters, and scholarship programs.

In retirement, Phil entered into private businesses, including operating a private investigation agency, construction management, and was an investigator for the Broward County court system. In 1987, he spent nine months on the planning for the pope's visit to Miami.

Phil is now retired, living in The Villages, Florida, with wife, Doris, of fifty years, practicing grandparenting.

87836796R00188

Made in the USA
Columbia, SC
20 January 2018